TERMINATION SHOCK

by

GILLIAN ANDREWS

Interstellar Enforcement Agency
(Book One)

ISBN: 978-84-09-16377-9

DEPÓSITO LEGAL: DL PM 1486-2019

COPYRIGHT AUTOR Y EDITOR @ GILLIAN ANDREWS 2019

PRIMERA IMPRESION 2019

2..0

Illustration @Tom Edwards

TomEdwardsDesign.com

1

Sammy was glowering and Mel was looking down at the decking. Neither of them thought I knew how to lead a squad. They were right, but I wasn't about to tell them so.

Sammy cleared his throat with a sort of huffing sound. "They'll send someone else, Rye," he told me, trying to seem helpful and not denigrating, something he could use some practice at.

I gestured with my M596 long barrel, making a huge effort not to sigh. "Just aim at the Avaraks, Sammy. Let's get the job done." I didn't have to say the same to Bull Cunningham. He was in his element, eyes shining, carelessly notching up accurate shots at the enemy. Despite being a Terran Flatlander, he was one of those souls born to be a marine. He hadn't got there yet, but I was pretty sure it wouldn't take him too long. If I hadn't had two weeks seniority on him he would have been leading this team now. He would probably have done it better.

For a moment I considered handing the job over to him, but the small Tyzaran girl clutching at my uniform made me focus. She hadn't been in our remit, but having found her huddled shaking in a doorway, I knew I had to try to save her. There was no way she should have been here. All the visiting Tyzaran dignitaries had been hastily evacuated twelve hours earlier. She had just leapfrogged to my top priority.

The sounds of inter-vessel torpedoes hammering old *Commorancy* continued. The ancient hull plating was shivering with transformed kinetic energy, making it hard to concentrate.

I kicked Wolseley's legs out of the way. No man left behind, I thought fiercely. Yeah. Like that had worked out well. Our intrepid leader wouldn't be going anywhere anytime soon. He was missing most of his torso. I couldn't have taken the remaining bits of him with us, even if I had wanted to.

Major Wolseley hadn't thought much of my insistent suggestion to fall back and regroup. He was old school. Gung-ho and give your all for the ship; what do you think we train you for, and so on. Rewards in heaven, I supposed. I'm a Spacelander too, but I didn't believe in all that claptrap. He should be proving or disproving it pretty soon, I calculated. He must be hammering at the pearly gates about now. I hoped he found his misplaced stubborn heroism worth it.

Unfortunately his rigid sticking to the rules had now left those of us remaining in combat with little choice. We could die or we could fight. Half the Avarak intruders had taken advantage of the delay to advance from the port side, trapping us in the corridor between the main engine room and the EM core, and we sure as fitz weren't going to be retreating anywhere now.

As for Captain Tevis ... I didn't think we would be seeing him anytime soon in this corridor. Not that I knew him. I knew *of* him. He'd been responsible for the death of one of my uncles. His specialty was keeping his own head down and persuading others not to. The captain would have more pressing work somewhere else on the ship. Somewhere more protected, my subconscious snarked. I tried not to think about it. Like it or not, I was now the de facto head of this decimated squad. I had better things to do than wonder where *Commorancy's* just-give-me-my-decoration captain had got to.

Mel's eyes were sidling towards Sammy. She was wondering whether to mutiny or not.

I cocked the firing mechanism and pointed my gun at her. She rolled her eyes, but at least that brought them back in my direction. She pushed the barrel of her own M487 XRS against her shoulder and squinted down the corridor at the invaders. The sound of her firing was just one more boom amongst the juddering metal which screeched its demise. If we didn't clear this position soon we were lost. Tears were streaking down her cheeks. I wasn't sure if they were of rage or fright. It didn't matter. All she had to do was keep firing. If she didn't I might shoot her myself.

I turned to cover our rear. Poor old *Commorancy* was groaning like a collapsing whale. This ship wasn't going to last much longer.

A computer voice suddenly crackled into life over the ship's loudspeaker system. "Abandon ship. Abandon ship. This is not a drill. Proceed to your nearest exit port and board the shuttles in an orderly fashion."

Thanks a lot. Would if we could. I guess the announcement was one step better than 'we are about to abandon ship leaving the rest of you to die in this old bucket', which is what our esteemed captain really meant.

Mel wavered. My back was jammed up against hers. I could feel her gun go quiet as she processed the information. A bullet hit Sammy, who collapsed on the floor.

I snarled backwards at her. "Keep firing, damn it! Don't you even think about taking your finger off that trigger!"

I felt, rather than heard, the gasp of outrage, but my words were effective. She started to return fire again. I squashed the Tyzaran girl between me and Bull. She was half our size. At least we could act as human shields for her. She was cringing at the sounds and the flashes of gunfire, her crest sticking out rigidly from her scalp in panic.

I tugged at Sammy's shoulder lapels, dragging and pushing him slightly to one side, where a small doorway gave him a little better cover. I couldn't spare the time to look at him. I just kept returning their fire. The shuttles in the stern cargo hold might as well have been ten kilometers away. We were not going to get there in time. I was pretty sure our part in this newly born war was just about over. I was pretty sure our part in *life* was just about over.

Still. There were a couple of things worth trying first. I unpinned my last two dunker grenades with my teeth without stopping firing and threw both of them together at the Avaraks blocking our retreat. I was careful to count to three first, to cook the grenade. Didn't particularly want to give the Avaraks time to toss them back at us. Better to be too close to the flashpoint than on top of it. That had been drilled into us earlier in this three-week space defense course. Dunker grenades were about all the live ammunition we had been allowed to play with, and I was lucky to have a couple still hanging off my belt. They created a combination of a dazzling flash, electronic whiteout and heavy smoke. We had thought we would never need to use any of it. The Avaraks had decided differently just as we were about to take our final day exam.

"... Four ... Five." I grabbed Mel's head and pushed it downwards. Bull protected the little girl's eyes.

There was a small explosion down the corridor, followed by a tremendous flash. Smoke billowed down towards our position. I grabbed Sammy again and tugged at Mel's arm. Bull picked up the Tyzaran child and followed us.

The very first thing a true Spacelander does on a new ship is explore the network of crawl tubing hidden behind the bulkheads. That's where you see what sort of a ship you're on. Now I was glad I had. I knew that there was a service hatch about ten feet towards the blast center. It was certainly our only chance of escape.

We galloped along in tandem like a lame pantomime horse, Sammy's legs bouncing on the decking as Mel and I manhandled him along between us. There was just this small window of opportunity before the smoke cleared and the Avaraks got us back in their sights. Thankfully they were not dumb enough to shoot through smoke when their own units were on the other side of the supposed enemy position.

I tore the hatch open. Mel jumped through and dragged Sammy inside. I stood aside as Bull and the girl dove through. As they did I ducked and slipped behind them, pulling the hatch shut behind me. I locked it fast, knowing that the feeble lock wouldn't hold the Avaraks for long if they wanted to follow. I was pretty sure they wouldn't be able to. Avaraks are substantially larger than us. I didn't think they would fit in the narrow passageways. Female Avaraks would, but I hadn't seen any on *Commorancy*.

It wasn't much, but it was a chance. Bull and I now slung Sammy between us and ran for it, Mel racing ahead of us, pushing the girl before her.

I was trying to recall the schematics of this end of the ship. If I was correct we could turn into the right main service tunnel and then slip down through the emergency lift bypass – a drop shaft that would finally lead into the secondary shuttle bay, in the bows of the ship. That was all of twenty decks down. But who was counting? We would either make it or die. Good motivation.

We went down those ladders like the very devil was after us. Sammy was gasping with pain and trying to hang on to our necks as we half fell, half shimmied down the iron rungs. Mel was still crying. I wondered where she had all that liquid. I was about as dehydrated as a man can get and still function, but then, she was a woman.

I shouldn't have had that thought. Fate must have been listening. I snagged my arm on one of the rungs. That skewed my fall, throwing me roughly against the other side of the ladder and crashing me sideways into one of the jutting supports. My shoulder blade slammed into the metal and cracked. I felt the fracture. I found I did have some liquid behind my eyes. Who knew? I couldn't help a tense smile at the irony. 'Never ask for whom the bell tolls', and so on. Two bawling Spacelander recruits. Maybe it was lucky Captain Tevis was somewhere else. I'd rather die than have this witnessed. I turned my head away so that Bull wouldn't notice. Fine leader I was.

It was even harder with only one arm to climb down the ladder. The liquid behind my eyes dried up but the pain sure stayed. It wasn't only the shoulder blade: the whole of that side of my torso was burning. I was cursing the lot of them by then. All the brilliant Avarak strategists who had somehow put old *Commorancy*, a teaching ship, at the epicenter of a battle. Even though I had no idea what this Avarak incursion was all about it was odds on to a tadpole that somebody further up the line of command would. And somebody on board had just put a neat red line through *Commorancy's* name as an acceptable loss. I started my imprecations at Major Wolseley and worked my way up past Captain Tevis.

I had run out of people to cuss by the time we had traveled past twelve decks. Sweat was proving again just how much water a body holds even when you think it is dry.

"Rye?" I caught a hint of Mel's sympathy. I hated it.

"Shut the hell up! I'm fine!"

For once, she did as she was told. I turned my attention back to the Tyzaran girl, who, because of her size, was struggling with the spaces between rungs. She was barely managing, her crest perpendicular to her scalp and her face tight with concentration.

I had time as we dropped through deck after deck. Decks are numbered up from the lowest to the highest. From zero to twenty-five on the *Commorancy*, stacked one on top of the other. The cargo bay, where we were going, took up three deck heights, so the numbers skipped from zero to four.

"We need a shuttle," I snapped to Mel. "When we get down, clear any opposition and secure the nearest and biggest thing that flies."

She nodded. "Do my best. Err ... are you fit to pilot?"

I gave her what I hoped was a supercilious look. "Naturally. And even if I weren't, Bull here could. He was fast-tracked." I didn't tell her that, not being a Spacelander, the sum total of his experience was twenty hours on a simulator. She hadn't been in the same group and she didn't need to know. The first thing they teach you on this course is need to know. It helps to ensure people follow orders everybody else knows will kill them. Good policy, if you want to avoid being shot by your subordinates.

Bull grinned. He just didn't care. He had been waiting all his short life for this. I could almost feel lines of worry popping out on my forehead, but his face was shining with exhilaration. The Tyzaran girl was staring at him with mistrust. Tyzarans are highly intelligent beings who are fascinated by progress and technology. They resort to violence if necessary but don't relish it. All her instincts were telling her to run, but her intellect knew there was nowhere to run to.

We finally clattered into the cargo bay, our boots sounding like castanets on the deck plating. Subtle we were not. We dropped Sammy onto the decking, none too gently, and brought our weapons up.

"No Avaraks!" Mel reported after a moment.

Bull was checking our six. "Clear!"

I pursed my lips. They were right, but there *were* people here. They were hiding from us, but they were here. I could sense them. Spacelanders spend so much time alone that we can tell when we are surrounded by living, breathing organisms.

Well, if they were hiding they weren't Avaraks. Avaraks had no artifice. Their huge body mass and dominance had taught them to walk straight up and confront you. They weren't ones to shiver behind cover. Not subtle at all.

I took a step forward. "All right. Come out! We won't hurt you!"

Mel gave me a surprised look. Her finger tightened on her gun. I reached across with my good hand and pushed the barrel down. She frowned.

A rustle told me they were obeying me. At first one, then five, and then more children appeared.

I dropped my rifle butt and blew out air. The powers that be hadn't even evacuated this school class. From what I could see, there must be a couple of dozen kids filing out from amongst the oil drums.

"Why haven't you abandoned the ship?" I demanded, singling out a young Terran male instructor who was stepping in front of his charges with no attempt at a welcoming smile. This group must be one of the sub-teen Terran familiarity groups that visited the training ship every few days. It was an attempt to introduce future spacefaring rookies to their destiny. Or vice versa. No one was sure.

"Abandon ship? Why would we do that?" His nose was up and his tone was supercilious despite his obvious fear. It made my own hackles rise. The Tyzaran girl looked over to me, picking up on the man's antagonism and my involuntary response to it.

I stared. "Are you deaf? They have been broadcasting the order for the last half-hour."

"Not down here. I was told to bring all the children down here and wait for instructions. The sound system must be down." The man breathed in and out a couple of times. Self-preservation must be telling him not to alienate people he would normally class as backward illiterates, telling him that he might have found some fool to get his nuggets out of the soup pot. His eyes flickered to Bull and lingered on the Flatlander's rifle. He made some attempt to smile, to appear likeable. I could have told him it wasn't working. So could the Tyzaran child. She was growing on me.

I nodded to Mel, who slipped away in the direction of the parked shuttles at the far end of the bay.

The false smile slipped. "You have to do something. Don't just stand around! Help us!" The instructor had straightened his shoulders and assumed an air of bravado in order to attempt to boss me about. I had never seen him before, but *Commorancy* was very compartmentalized, and I hadn't been on board that long. I was used to my own ship, *Faraday*. I had never taken these three-week courses seriously. They had always been more about meeting others like me, rather than actual, useful training. Bull and Sammy and I had dedicated most of our down time on this one thinking up how to meet some of the girls and how to obtain at least a decent measure of alcohol.

"How many of you are there?" We all ducked automatically as a particularly huge tremor tore at the ship's metal sheathing.

He waited until the sound abated slightly before answering. "Thirty children. Thirty-one altogether, including myself. You can't just leave us here. It is your duty to help us."

"We'll see." He wasn't a Spacelander. I should make allowances. There is a reason we know them as Flatlanders. They live in a really limited environment. I tried to make my voice gentle but the adrenalin was still pumping through my body, my arm was killing me and he wasn't my idea of a hapless civilian. "I'll do my best." I looked around the shuttle bay. The noise of failing metal was strident. "This old lady won't last much longer."

He gave a frown. "You have to get us out of here, Cadet!"

"I don't 'have to' do anything, Instructor, and there are no ranks on training courses. We are all merely temporary recruits. However, I will attempt to evacuate all of you. Now, please stop talking, gather the children together, and follow me. We are trying to secure shuttles."

He looked as if he were about to say something more, then thought better of it. As I walked towards the rear of the hold, I could hear his voice raised behind me, organizing his charges, stewarding them into two neat files that followed us. Bull brought up the rear, pushing the Tyzaran girl child in front of him and checking continually that the Avaraks still hadn't discovered our whereabouts. It seemed they were busy elsewhere. I hoped our good luck would continue.

Mel was down at the end of the bay, in front of the largest shuttle, her two feet set well apart to keep her balance on the shuddering deck. She must be terrified but so far she was still functioning. She was doing good.

There was the lanky figure of an Enif near her. I looked around for its partner – its *faliif*. They always came in pairs. But this one seemed to be alone.

Mel introduced us by poking her rifle towards the figure. "Engineer," she informed me succinctly. "Trapped working down here. Name of Didjal."

At last, some decent news. "What ships are ready?" I asked it.

It was a thin alien, graying at its black temples, with a grizzled look around its mandible. It gave me an offended look, its multi-faceted eyes glittering. "All of them. But you won't get all that lot on just one shuttle. These are personal shuttles, meant for private, short-hop use. They will only have life support autonomy for a few days, at best. The biggest, the Henson-Avinger IIIs, can take seven at a pinch plus pilot, but there are only two of those. The Berlinger Vs would be overweight with four each plus pilot. You'll have to take four of the Berlingers as well as the two Avingers if you want to evacuate all those children." Its voice grated; Enif talk between themselves by tactile communication. Vocal communication comes to them with great difficulty, thanks to a cylindrical touchpad translator strapped to one of their forearms. The translation has an unfortunate tinny quality.

"Can you pilot a shuttle?"

There was a silence, accentuated by the dull explosions going off tens of decks above us. The creature looked even greyer. "I never have. I could try." It seemed to be scanning the hold. "But I must find my *faliif* first. I will not leave without Eshaan."

I compressed my lips. "All right. You have five minutes." The Enif disappeared, using its elongated tarsal bones to help propel it across to the far side of the hanger at high speed, making it look almost robotic.

Piloting was going to be a problem. Sammy didn't look to be in a fit state to fly anything. Mel didn't know how. She had been diagnosed as being claustronetic at an early age. She detested traveling by spacecraft, being hypersensitive about the thin metal canisters we worked and often lived in. It was no longer called claustrophobia, because many Spacelanders claimed that there was nothing irrational about the condition, and it could therefore not be classed as a phobia. Such people argued that to be scared of spaceships was rational and indeed logical.

Claustronetics normally stay on one of the Spacelander planets for virtually all their lives. Mel had too, but even claustronetics are required to undergo basic ship training every five years. They can't remain Spacelanders unless they do. So there are invariably a few trainees who shiver their way around the ship, staring anxiously out into open space. You can always spot them; they have a desperation about them which is hard to miss as they linger around the airlocks.

Her father, a member of the space-founding Estamain family, had been so disappointed in her that he had refused to train her for anything at all when she was little. He loved to belittle her in front of the rest of her family, ensuring she never developed any self-esteem. Apart from that, his fierce regimen of disapproval had made her obsessive about not breaking even the silliest of rules.

That left Bull and I and an elderly alien engineer who looked as if it was close to the Enif end-of-life 'state of enlightenment'. Three of us, and we were going to need five pilots. Not the best scenario.

I turned to the instructor. Worry made my voice sharp; he almost winced at my tone. I moderated it. Even to myself I sounded a bit too authoritative. "Allocate your pupils: ten to this shuttle, eight to that, six to the other two. We can only take four ships. We don't have six pilots."

I treated Mel with a challenging look, knowing that her need to follow regulations was going to make her protest the increase in passengers on board each ship. She grimaced, and then gave me a short nod. She could see there was no choice. She was looking even paler now she knew we were moving from a big ship to a small shuttle.

The instructor did the math too. His eyes flickered to the first shuttle, one of the Hensons, and he took a small step toward it. I shook my head, and nodded sideways at the second of the Berlingers. He met my gaze. We exchanged a long look before he dropped his eyes. He began to organize the egress, his lips so thinned that they looked glued together.

"Mel, get Sammy on board that one." I pointed at the other smaller vessel. "He knows how to fly her. You can pilot; he can tell you what to do."

Mel froze. "You've got to be kidding."

"There isn't anyone else."

"No, but ..." Her voice trailed off. She stared around at the children, still on deck, their eyes huge. Like hers.

The instructor counted off the first ten from the line. The small alien girl was still standing next to me to one side of that line. I drew her apart, signaling that she would be going with me.

We followed him as he ushered his charges towards the first Avinger

III. "Come on then, those of you I have picked ... quietly and quickly onto this ship."

They straggled up the ramp. I put the Tyzaran girl on the copilot's seat, and wedged her in with a larger kid on either side. There seemed to be nowhere for the rest to perch, so the instructor told them to sit squeezed onto the deck just behind the two command stations. Then we started to fill up the other three shuttles.

We left space for the Enif and his *faliif* on the second of the larger Avingers, though there was no sign of them yet. I put one of the kids on the copilot's seat of the Engineer's shuttle and the remaining seven on the floor.

Mel settled Sammy into the copilot's station. He was still conscious, but grey around his eyes and mouth. He managed a weak nod to me. He was grateful we hadn't left him behind. He would manage. So would Mel. At twenty-six, she was two years younger than me, but she'd got through the last half an hour. She wouldn't stop now.

Finally Bull pushed the instructor into the copilot's seat of the shuttle he would be taking, instructing him curtly to strap himself in. Then he signed the last kids to squeeze into the remaining space behind the station before executing an agile jump into the pilot's chair.

I made my way back to the first Henson Avinger and clambered up to the cockpit, just as Didjal clattered back around the corner with another Enif lagging behind it. At least, I assumed it was Didjal leading. I couldn't tell them apart.

As it buckled itself into the pilot's seat and its life partner settled in the copilot's seat, I was able to talk with it through the comlink. I asked the engineer its age.

It vibrated. That was probably something quite rude in its own language. I had to grin.

"Young enough to want to live," it told me severely.

"Good. Now, how much help are you going to need?"

It vibrated again. "I suppose I can manage. I have a few hours sim practice. But I don't know anything about navigation."

That was some relief, at least. "Just follow me. No need to do anything else. Try not to hit anything."

I still couldn't figure out why these Earth kids hadn't been evacuated on the *Seyfert* twelve hours ago, when this attack could only have been a remote possibility in some leader's head. Avaraks were not prone to attacking without reason. They were miners. Tough survivors who knew better than to lob bombs at other cultures. Somebody had to know what was going on. Somebody had messed up. A familiar wave of frustration crept upwards from my stomach, flooding through me. I tried to stifle it, though some of the ways the Space Trust worked were almost incomprehensible to me. Back on *Faraday* we had organization beaten into a cocked hat. We had to. Out on the edge of the Rift you could lose your life too easily if you didn't.

Why the Space Trust wasn't as efficient was beyond me. After all, they were responsible for teaching half a million young Spacelanders basic military and defense strategies each year. You'd think they would have at least *considered* what to do in a real attack by one of the other species sharing this galaxy with us. Especially since there have been sporadic wars between all of us in the past. Nobody likes sharing deep space. There is always the fear of expansionist dreams on the part of armed aliens. It never goes away.

All four shuttles were powered up. I opened a private channel to the engineer. "Can you open the shuttle bay doors, Didjal?"

Its voice, dimmed by some static, came back immediately. "I can. I have the remote codes."

"We need to go." The voice that broke in was unknown to me. It was almost liquid, yet quite pleasant. "The *Commorancy* is about to break up."

My eyes slid to my right. Sure enough, the Tyzaran kid had slipped on the copilot's headset. She caught my look. "I can feel the ship's distress," she told me.

"Thanks, kid."

Her widely spaced eyes gave a dangerous flash. "My name is

Zenzara."

"Nice name. So ... you think we ought to get out of here?"

She inclined her long neck and the ridge running over her head and down toward her back slowly settled back to her scalp as her distress faded. She trusted me, for some reason. "I deem it immediately advisable, yes."

"Didjal?"

"Inputting the codes now."

I heard faint tapping in the background. Enif have quite long, almost metallic-like digits. I checked around at the other shuttles. Their pilots responded with thumbs up.

The huge shuttle bay doors began to screech open. There had clearly been some damage, because they were objecting to every centimeter we made them separate. We were lucky they hadn't been a primary target. This was only the small VIP shuttle bay. The rest of the crew would have evacuated from the main shuttle bay, fifteen decks up and aft of us. They would have made more of a target. We were coming out of the bows of the ship, rather than the stern.

As soon as the doors were half open, I lifted the shuttle off the deck, wincing at the pain in my arm, and let her slide towards the opening. She would just about fit through. It would have been better to wait for another five minutes, but I took the kid's comment very seriously. Tyzarans are known for their fabulous ability to sense stuff the rest of us can't. Young or not, she could just be right. I tilted the wings of the Henson-Avinger and slipped through. The engineer followed, rather more slowly. He was followed by Mel and then Bull, the latter flashily tilting completely sideways to scurry through. I felt sorry for his passengers. If you aren't used to it, that can really turn your breakfast to acid.

I didn't have to do any navigation. I have been doing stuff like this since I was three. My mother used to make us take a shuttle three times round the shipstation every day when we were just toddlers. I simply pointed the nose away from the Avarak ships and pushed the throttles as far as they would go. Although I had heard Avaraks were scrupulous about not shooting down escape pods, I didn't want to risk looking in the least dangerous or aggressive. Even though shuttles weren't normally armed, they could still carry weapons. I wasn't about to hang around to see what the Avaraks would do. I planned on getting as far away from the danger, as fast as I could.

We shot out of the dying ship like corks out of champagne bottles, a tiny string of life trying to escape what was about to become an inferno. Didjal was clamped so close to my tail that I would have had to think twice about throttling back. Its shuttle was weaving from side to side, and for one moment I seriously thought the Enif might have its eyes shut.

I took the group fifteen minutes away from the fray, then brought us carefully around in a large circle, until the others could see that we were simply marking time. When they had all checked in and were ready to slow our speed in unison, I began to pull back on the two main throttles.

Soon we were bobbing in space, side by side, facing our old ship.

So we were watching as *Commorancy* blew herself to hell.

Ludicrously, it was quite pretty. The different structural metals contained colorful elements. It was like watching a firework display magnified a few thousand times. Except it incinerated people I had known. Quite a lot of them, probably. Even the kids couldn't rake up any enthusiasm for the show.

We sat waiting as the fires died down, soon extinguished by the lack of air in outer space. We watched the three Avarak vessels tire of their vigil. They turned, and within ten minutes all three had gone FTL.

It was three hours before *Seyfert* arrived. They contacted us on a tight-beam, which is a ship-to-ship communication system of audio only.

"Shuttle group of four, what is your status?"

"One Spacelander trainee, status bullet wound in leg, unconscious. One ... err ... Spacelander trainee, broken scapula. One Tyzaran female child, status unharmed. Thirty Terran children, status unharmed. Two Enif ... engineer and partner, status unharmed. One further Spacelander trainee, female, status unharmed. One Terran trainee, status unharmed. One Terran instructor, male, status unharmed." I felt like adding that he was hostile, but thought better of it.

There was a short pause. Then: "You have been designated low priority. Please wait where you are for further instructions."

"Copy." I looked at Zenzara. "They don't seem in a hurry to get you back."

She rolled her eyes. The Tyzarans have big eyes. There was a lot to roll. I am surprised she didn't make herself dizzy. With all the extra skin she sported in folds around that small face of hers it looked really strange. "Their decision is quite correct. I am unharmed, which makes me of secondary importance."

I grinned to myself. I could hear the chagrin in her voice. She was unused to being made to wait, if determined not to let it show.

"Never mind, Zenzie. I care."

Her eyes flashed. "My name is not Zenzie."

That's what she thought. "'Tis now. How old are you, anyway?"

She put her chin up and out. "Eight. Why?"

A sudden buzz told us that we were wrong. She had been missed, after all. Turns out, so had I.

"Zenzara, are you there?" The voice was harmonious if stern.

The girl jumped. "Y-Yes, X-X-Xynia, I am."

"Spokesdesignate Xynia, if you please. Perhaps you could explain to me what circumstances caused you to miss the evacuation, thus causing great dismay to the Ambassador and the whole diplomatic mission?"

I saw the girl wriggle uncomfortably in her seat. "I regret I was not paying attention, Spokesdesignate Xynia."

"We were forced to assume that you were deceased."

"I ... I am alive."

"This is seen, Zenzara Zylarian. You have caused much distress."

"I am sorry, Spokesdesignate. I was in the area of the engines when fighting broke out."

"Is it your opinion that you would have died if left alone?"

Zenzie suddenly looked sick. "I ... that is ... errr ... yes, I suppose that is true." She gave a swallow and I saw her look quickly in my direction.

"And were you assisted by the whole group, or one individual?"

Now she was green. "I was accepted into the group at the request of one individual, Spokesdesignate."

"Then you do realize that the Savior Protocols will now apply?"

"Yes, Spokesdesignate."

The Tyzaran fell silent, but someone else came on the line.

"Tevis here. Who is in charge there?" a rather fastidious voice demanded.

I started, forgetting my injury. Pain shot through my arm again. "Captain Tevis? It's Mallivan, Sir, from the training program. Ryler Mallivan Bell." The Captain, then, was safe. He must have been one of the first to abandon poor old *Commorancy*. What a surprise.

"What are you doing there? Who is your team leader?"

"Major Wolseley, Sir. He didn't make it."

His voice sounded puzzled. "Didn't make it? Then how did you get out?"

His level of confidence in his own trainees spoke volumes.

"We used our own initiative, Sir."

"Initiative?" He actually sounded disapproving. Were we expected to have gone down with the ship? "You mean you fought the Avaraks on your own?"

Should we just have laid down our arms and waited to be shot? "That is correct, Sir."

"Then I really don't see how you all survived." He seemed quite put out. I heard the voice of one of the Tyzarans in the background.

There was a pause as Tevis seemed to listen, and then he came back on line. "Unfortunately you have Terrans with you. They are responsible for this aggression and we cannot at present compromise our own situation by taking them on board. As a Spacelander ship inside the Local Shell, our status is currently non-combatant."

What a surprise. Tevis was going to take the route that provided most safety for his sorry body.

He hadn't finished. "You will be rescued as and when we are able to do so. Our current situation is complex."

"Yes, Sir." I just bet it was.

I looked at Zenzie. She was staring at me, a wary look on her face, her crest looking strangely droopy. I gave her a grin. "What, kid? You in trouble or something?"

She looked down quickly. "No, no, nothing like that. I ... err ... I will tell you about it later." She began to fiddle with the fit of her headset, which was far too big for such a small skull.

I looked sideways at her. So, Tyzarans could lie too. I was glad to find that out. They had always seemed an irritatingly perfect race to me. Not that I had ever been this close up to one of them before. My knowledge of most of the alien races had been theoretical till now.

I turned to the rest of the kids on my shuttle. "Breathe slowly and don't move about. We don't know how long we are going to have to stay out here. We need to conserve air."

They all nodded hastily, but the whites of their eyes were showing. They weren't too happy with their new situation. None of them had been in a war before, and they weren't liking it much. I sympathized; I wasn't either. One thing I was sure of: it was one step better than being aboard *Commorancy* when it had exploded.

We waited for a full day before I realized that I had to do something more. We would all die of asphyxiation if I didn't. The oxygen circuitry had been running on overload for five hours now, and I was beginning to get light-headed.

When I looked over at Zenzara I was surprised to see that she was staring back at me, her eyes troubled. She blinked, and for a short moment I saw the second eyelid the Tyzarans had, just visible underneath the outer one. Tyzaran eyes are normally purple, but hers were a cross between sapphire and gold. I found myself wondering whether they would gradually lose that wonderful shade as she grew older.

I was staring. I blinked deliberately, aware that my brain was sliding away from the topics I really needed to be concentrating on. My whole head was heavy. I knew there was something I needed to do, but it floated away when I tried to focus on it.

Zenzara had unstrapped from the copilot's seat, and she was dragging one of the two heavy spacesuits over to me. She shook it in front of me and gestured.

I nodded, submitting as the girl tussled with the heavy suit to help my broken shoulder and sore torso into it. It even seemed slightly funny, I remember. The suit was bigger than she was.

As soon as the helmet was snapped into place and the new supply of oxygen hit my brain the humor of the situation evaporated. There was nothing remotely amusing about any of this. Nearly all of the Terran kids were unconscious.

I grabbed for the communicator.

"*Seyfert*, come in please."

There was silence from the air around us. I tried again. "*Seyfert*, our situation is an emergency. ICD 10. ICD 10. ICD 10." This was the interstellar code for respiratory failure on board a starship. "Please come in. Our life support is now compromised. We need emergency evacuation." I signed to Zenzara to try to get the pilots of the other shuttles into suits. She nodded and began to call each ship, as I activated the automatic distress beacon.

Five minutes later there was a crackle on the tight-beam. I leapt for the scanner. But it wasn't the *Seyfert*. It was an Avarak ship, identifying itself as the *Raktor*. She came up on screen as a small cruiser, with only minimum armament. Perhaps they were in the area mopping up any Avarak casualties of their own. As a cruiser, she would be armed, but not with the heavy weapons which had hit *Commorancy*. All the same, it surprised me that they would show interest in rescuing us.

There was a short wait after they established that I didn't speak Avarak. At least, not more than a few words. Finally a male voice came on that was reasonably fluent in Universal. "Spacelander shuttles, please advise us of your passengers."

I sighed, but I had no choice. We were light years from the nearest planet; we weren't going anywhere. *Seyfert* had either disappeared or was running quiet. I could see no other option. Zenzie inclined her head at me, confirming my own reading of our situation. But her crest was up and her forehead crinkled with folds of skin; she liked it as little as I did.

There was a longish wait after I had informed of our situation. Then the Avarak voice put us on hold while some discussion took place. The cold tone came back on air after perhaps a minute.

"You will be taken aboard this Avarak ship, but all Terrans must be sequestered immediately. The other races are not currently regarded as our enemies, despite your ship having taken arms against us." There was a rather ominous crackle. "That status may change as we become aware of details of further battles."

I stiffened. "I am required by Space Trust law to demand fair treatment for all those under my protection."

"Acknowledged. Casualties will be given medical treatment. All Terrans will be considered hostile and taken to our homeworld for internment, but they will not be harmed. The rest of you will be carried to the nearest star system and dropped off, unless specific charges are brought."

I thought. If I didn't accept we would all be dead pretty quickly, except maybe for the two Enif, who could probably survive on very little air.

I pushed the button. "Are we still in the Local Shell?"

"No. We crossed the border into the Bifold Shell several hours ago."

"I accept your conditions."

"Await our arrival."

The other pilots were now suited up, except the Enif, who had indicated that they didn't need more oxygen. I explained what was happening.

The Flatlander instructor went a sort of blotchy red under his space suit, which he had grabbed when he saw the pilot suiting up. "You cannot do this! How dare you take such a decision upon yourself! You are condemning the Terrans among us to being prisoners. Unacceptable! We have done nothing wrong."

I wasn't so sure about that. "There must be some reason that the Avaraks have decided to wage war on you."

His eyes flashed and he looked suddenly more dangerous. I found myself thinking that he might know far more than he was telling me.

"We have done nothing wrong," he repeated, with rather less conviction.

"I am very sorry. *Seyfert* has left us behind. We have no other options."

"I refuse to accept this! We should fight or run from the Avaraks!"

"We can do neither. Your pupils would die within the hour, either way."

He looked quickly around at his charges, a momentary flash of anger and frustration showing behind the visor of the suit. Then his shoulders slumped. He knew that I wouldn't condemn them to death just to save him. In any case, he had nowhere to go.

Zenzie breathed again. Her ridge had stiffened more and more as she listened to the Terran's comments. She began to relax, and her eyes met mine. I nodded. I really didn't need her empathy to tell me what a faulty specimen he was. I was beginning to wish we had left him on old *Commorancy*.

Thankfully, he then sat down, accepting his fate. I decided that, as long as he kept his mouth shut, I could cope with him.

There was a welcome hail from the tight-beam. The *Raktor* had arrived. It was only just in time. Most of the children were already unconscious. Even though we had been fighting the Avaraks a day earlier, I was glad to see them now.

I followed the instructions given to us and led my sorry convoy into the aft hold of the cruiser that appeared in front of us. For the time being, our resistance to the Avaraks was over. We would just have to wait and see what fate had in store for us next. We powered down the engines and opened the shuttle doors. I was no longer in charge. In a sense, it was a bit of a relief.

2

I came to in the Avarak infirmary some hours later. Their doctor had decided to put me out while setting the bone in my shoulder. Now it was aching, but I was much more comfortable. I was lying in a Zeroth triage chamber to aid regeneration. But I was not alone. The Tyzaran child was sitting placidly next to me.

"W-What are you doing here?" My mouth was dry; an enlarged tongue made sticky noises against my palate.

"Waiting for you to wake up."

"What has happened since I was under?"

She seemed placid. Her ridge was flat. "They took the Terrans away and put the rest of us into quarters at the back of the ship. We are under observation, but free to move about, so long as we keep away from active areas of the ship."

"Like ...?"

"Like the bridge, the engine rooms, the armory. That sort of thing."

I nodded.

She held up a drink with a straw and I gratefully began to sip at it. "Thanks. That's better."

"We have to decide what to do."

"We?"

There was a quick nod. "We. You and I are now bonded."

I frowned. I had no idea what that meant. "Bonded?"

She looked away. "Our race call them the "Savior Protocols"

My head was still thudding, but I thought I could remember the spokesperson from her group mentioning those words. "Look, kid, just spit it out, will you? I'm not feeling so good."

She pulled a face. "In our society, if somebody saves your life, you are indebted forever."

"Forever?" I croaked. I wasn't liking anything about this.

"Yes. Your life is renewed but the previous lifeline is considered to be broken. You may no longer follow the path you would have taken. A bond is formed between you and your savior, and you stay with them for the rest of their, or your, lives. You are required to hold yourself ready to repay the debt if the chance arises."

She was an eight-year-old alien. "S-Stay with them?" I hoped she couldn't pick up my thoughts now. I was horrified. There was no way I wanted a child alien dogging my steps for the rest of my life.

Her mouth curved down. She could sense my doubts. The ridge rippled. Her expression wobbled.

"Not that you are not a nice person," I said hastily. "And I appreciate your efforts."

The ridge settled down.

I breathed again. "But is there ... anything we can do to change that? Surely your ... your parents must want you back?"

She shook her head. "No. They will understand. The Savior Protocols are stronger than any other social obligations. They will not expect me back."

"I see. And, err ... just how close are you supposed to stay to me?"

She began to giggle. "I don't have to go to the bathroom with you, if that is what you are worried about. But I will accompany you wherever you go from now on." She thought about it, her delicate head tipped slightly to one side. "Like I am now your ... your shadow."

"What about your school work?"

She gave a shrug. That was clearly not a topic she cared much about. "I will be sent the tasks from Tyzar. They will grade me at a distance. That is not a problem."

I gave a sigh. How had I managed to complicate my life so much in such a short time? Only two weeks ago I had been a normal Spacelander with a normal life. Look at me now. I closed my eyes.

She got up, her eyes worried. "I have tired you. You need to sleep?" No. But I needed some space. I was wondering how to tell her when she sensed it anyway.

"I shall be outside. Rest. You must get your strength back." For sure. I wasn't going to be much of a leader like this. I needed to get out of the triage chamber and back on my feet. For the time being, I let my brain slip back into the comforting blackness waiting behind my eyes. I would think about all this later. A lot later.

I was in and out of full consciousness several times over the next few days. The triage machine seemed determined that I should stay still. Each time I awoke, Zenzie brought me up to date with the news. For a being of only eight years of age, she was pretty good at finding out information.

She explained the reasons the Avaraks had reacted against the Terrans. "The Ethnarch, head of the Terran Omnistate, has declared the entire Local Shell as belonging to Terra. They are claiming that whole area of space, together with everything inside it."

My jaw dropped. "That's a sphere of more than 300 light years in radius!"

She nodded. "Sol is almost at the centre of that sphere, and the Terrans claim that the walls of thicker gas surrounding the Local Shell give them a clear boundary to defend."

"They must be mad! It is completely arbitrary. What about the thousands of other star systems within that area?"

"Foolish, certainly. The Avaraks have mining facilities on many planets and asteroids within the Local Shell, especially over towards the Bifold Shell, where their homeworld is. They will not cede any territory without a fight."

"The Avaraks feel they are morally in the right."

"They do. They claim that such a border is territorially expansionist and quite unacceptable." There was a small pause. "And, err ... my people, the Tyzarans, are also against it. Even though Tyzar is also far away in the Bifold Shell, they do not agree on any one species claiming so much territory in space."

"Yeah, well, your people would, wouldn't they? I mean, The Tyzaran and Avarak homeworlds both lie within the Bifold Shell, so that could hardly belong to either of your races. Stands to reason they wouldn't like the Flatlanders claiming all the Local Shell. It might set an unfortunate precedent." I frowned. It had been a long time since the Spacelanders in the Landau Rift and their Terran ancestors had found much common ground, but even so, it was strange of the Flatlanders to take a stance that was bound to be controversial. There are several other advanced species that we know of in the Major Shells. Unilateral declarations hardly seemed wise. But then, what did I know? I was just some Spacelander trying to whittle out a living in the Rift. At least, I had been. I wasn't quite sure what I was now.

I asked after the others. Zenzara had been around the *Raktor* while I had been sleeping.

"That Bull Cunningham will get himself killed one of these days."

"What has he been doing?"

"He seems to spend most of his time with the Terran instructor. They get on like old friends."

"That is ... unfortunate. But then, they are both Flatlanders."

Her ridge rippled. "The Avaraks still think he is a Spacelander." She gnawed thoughtfully on her bottom lip. "Bull is a very active sort of person. He may decide to precipitate events rather than wait for them to unfold." She gave me a curious look. "Why did you not tell the Avaraks he was a Flatlander? He should have been sequestered with the rest of the Terrans."

Good question. Because he had begged me not to? I hoped I had been right to trust him. I blew out air. "Can you ask him to visit? And tell Mel to keep an eye on him."

She hesitated. "Mel may not ... be open to that. She is saying you threatened to shoot her."

I thought about it. I did have some sort of vague recollection of shoving the barrel of my gun in her face. There hadn't been time to stop and figure out the most politically correct way to give an order. I sighed again. I would clearly go far. "How is Sammy?"

"He is recovering well. He is in the next room, also in a Zeroth tank. They think he will be able to walk again, though it will take time. Your own prognosis is better. They will be letting you out of the tank later today."

Zenzie got up to go as a female Avarak aide scuttled into the medical bay I was in. The nursing aide avoided looking at me. Maybe I had offended her too. Still, she moved competently at the controls and within seconds proved herself to be a diligent carer.

I looked at her. Avarak females are half the size of the males, and have a self-effacing kind of blurriness about their features. The males are chiseled, muscular, dominating. The females are unremarkable, much smaller and thinner, hard to tell apart from each other and subservient. They could almost belong to two different races. The males take from five to twenty females to mate because the difference in size creates huge problems for the females when giving birth. Many do not survive. Certainly the lack of detail to their faces makes them appear almost irrelevant. I wondered if she would speak Universal. Unlikely; Female Avaraks would not have been taught it.

"What is your name?"

I could see from her face that she understood, but she looked away. "Are you not allowed to speak to me?"

No answer.

"What do you think about this war?"

A slight pause in her step told me that she was surprised by the question. It got a reply, though in Avarak.

"I am a loyal servant to the Avarak Republic." My understanding of their language is pretty basic, but even I could translate that simple sentence.

It fit in with the little I knew about the Avaraks. They are an obedient sort of people, with strict laws about following policy. I get the impression they are not encouraged to think on their own.

I fell silent as she began to drain the Zeroth tank. The things are filled with a gel in order to avoid pressure sores. She wasn't going to tell me anything. I would simply have to wait until I could get out and about again. A pity, because patience has never been my strongpoint.

She was helping me into a loose medical tunic when a shudder traveled the length and breadth of the ship. Somebody was lobbing missiles at us.

The Avarak nurse paused and then moved to a device set into the bulkhead. She spoke into it with the guttural speech of the Avaraks, then listened carefully to the sharp reply.

She stared over to me, before replying slowly in a labored Avarak, to make sure I was able to follow her meaning. "*Raktor* is under attack. That shot disabled our FTL drive. We are going nowhere. There is a Terran fleet around us and the Captain has been asked to surrender."

"Will he do that?"

"Never!" The Avarak word, '*Navikkx!*' sounded so much more definitive than Universal.

I hurried to tie the tunic around my waist, wishing I was dressed in my more familiar ship's fatigues. I felt vulnerable.

The aide motioned me to stay where I was and then hurried out of the medical bay, closing the door behind her. It didn't stay closed for long. A small arm appeared around it and Zenzie's lined and pixie face peered inside.

"We should go," she told me. "The *Raktor* is outgunned badly. I counted six ships approaching. If the Captain is determined to martyr himself and his crew, we need to get off this ship."

We were in the middle of a hostile environment. Again. Zero for two. This wasn't going well. I pulled a face. "We need to extricate ourselves. And that isn't going to be easy."

"I know."

Small arms fire came clearly from the other side of the wall. A bullet shattered the bulkhead just in front of me. I swore and ducked, grabbing Zenzie and jerking her hard, so that she fell to the ground. We froze until the fire moved away.

I swore. "Well, that wasn't the Terran fleet, for sure. They would hardly be firing pistols from their ship. It sounds to me as if there is a revolution on board *Raktor*."

"It does."

Right. It didn't take a genius to figure out Bull Cunningham would be somewhere in the thick of this. I had made another mistake. Clearly, I wasn't cut out for leadership. "So, let's make sure Sammy is all right, then try to find the others. We may have jumped from the frying pan into the fire. If this ship is going to be blown to smithereens like *Commorancy* was, we might need to think about getting off it."

"Do you think *Seyfert* told the Terrans about us? Does the attacking fleet know we are here? And would it make any difference to their attack if they did?" She looked at me earnestly. "I don't know much about the Terrans."

If I had had a ridge of my own it would have been perpendicular. My knowledge of the Flatlanders didn't give me any reason to think they would care one way or the other. "I think they will attack anyway; we are simply collateral damage to them."

Surprisingly, her own ridge stayed flat. "That's what I thought."

"Ready?"

She took a deep breath and then nodded. "Ready."

We ducked out of my medical bay and the Tyzaran girl pulled me into a room nearly next door. We found Sammy, still in a triage chamber. He was looking worried, though his brow cleared once he saw us. He had been struggling to disentangle himself from the tank. I realized at once that it couldn't be. His leg was still almost in shreds.

I closed my eyes momentarily. I didn't want to say this, but there was no way around it. "You have to stay here."

He wriggled a little more. "I can't! I won't!"

A figure we hadn't even noticed uncurled from her position propping up one of the walls and pointed to Sammy's leg with one long finger.

It was the Avarak female aide, the one who had been tending to me. She was so non-descript that she had faded into the background as if she had been camouflaged.

"*Navikkx! Nikkx!*" She burst into Avarak speech, making several clicking noises and fast guttural sounds I had no hope of understanding. Seeing our faces, she raised both hands and crossed them in front of her in a diagonal cross. I got the message. It would be fatal to him.

So had Sammy. "No! *No!* Rye, take me with you! Please!" The whites of his eyes showed.

I shook my head. "Can't be done. Sorry. Take care of yourself. We'll be back for you." I stared into the eyes of the female. Her face reminded me of one of those old statues, gradually made featureless by centuries of erosion.

"What is your name?" I racked my brains. "*Axrankk?*"

She shivered. Her answer was slow, but the first word was in universal. "Belong Solutor."

It seemed a strange way to introduce yourself. "Do you not have a name? A name you were born with?"

She inclined her head. "Belong father – Hegaton. Now belong Solutor." She slapped her chest. "*Axrankk* – Seyal." Then she slapped her bony chest again. "*Axrankk* – 'Seyal belong Solutor, from Hegaton'". So she did speak at least some words of universal. I wondered where she had picked them up. She patted her stomach proudly. It presented a small bulge. "Child belong Solutor, *Axrankk* - Segaton."

All this 'belonging', which she seemed quite unconcerned about, made me uncomfortable. Words like slavery were popping into my head. We Spacelanders are kind of against stuff like that. But such things shouldn't, couldn't concern me. This was not my race. Something I was glad about. "Congratulations on the baby. Well, thank you for your help. We appreciate it."

She gave a short bow.

I mimed firing. "Who is shooting inside *Raktor*? Err ... *Devekk*?"

"Avaraks *Nikkx*." She changed to her carefully slow Universal. "No Avaraks. Terrans."

My heart sank. The nasty feeling Bull Cunningham would be looking down the crosshairs of a gun just got stronger and more accusing. I *knew* this was going to turn out to be due to my own bad judgement.

The whole conversation had taken mere seconds. Then we were out of the medical bay area. I was following Zenzie down a long corridor which was bordered by high bulkheads on either side.

She led me nimbly along the length of the ship, away from the direction of the small arms fire. I felt numb. It was hard to leave Sammy behind and in danger. We'd known each other almost all our lives.

She sped the length of the ship, leaving me breathless in her wake. My arm was good, considering, but the whole recuperation process had taken it out of me. I struggled to keep up. She checked back on me to monitor my progress, her eyes worried.

"I can keep up. You concentrate on where we are going."

"I am taking you to the bridge."

I stumbled and nearly fell. "The bridge? I thought we would be making for one of the shuttles?" I may have glared at her.

Her ridge flared, but she stuck to her guns. "No. If they don't know about the Terran children on board they will assume we are the enemy and may well fire on any shuttles that leave. To escape the enemy fleet surrounding this ship we need FTL drive. And we need the bridge to find us something FTL capable."

Faultless logic. I just couldn't see how we were going to talk our way out of this one. I was beginning to see the problems of being led by an eight-year-old alien. She might have lots of wrinkles, but they didn't denote experience. I opened my mouth to counter her version with something more likely to succeed, but there was a huge explosion to one side of us and a large piece of metal, amongst other debris, punched across the corridor in front of us. This time she needed no prompting to throw herself on the floor. As we did, both Zenzie and I caught a glimpse of Bull Cunningham ducking away, recharging his weapon. I closed my eyes. So he *had* taken up arms against the Avaraks. And, apparently, us. That didn't make any sense. Great. Just terrific. I pursed my lips and looked up at the ceiling.

We were still huddling down on the floor when a group of heavily armed Avaraks surrounded us and threatened to shoot us. More good news.

Zenzara stood up and placed herself deliberately in front of me. She began to speak to them in their own language. I assumed from the gestures that she was demanding we be escorted to the bridge.

There was some general muttering of unwillingness and a long speech by the heaviest of the Avaraks.

She stared him right in the eye, her ridge perpendicular from her skull. She looked quite imperious, at contrast with her age. Her words took on a stronger tone, clearly in an attempt to convince.

The large Avaraks looked slightly bemused. They eyeballed each other in an attempt to agree a response. None of them wanted to shoot a Tyzaran; that much was clear. On the other hand, none of them looked particularly keen to obey her either. I can tell you one thing. They had never had a female speak to them like that before.

She looked crossly from one of them to the other. I swear she stamped her foot.

The Avaraks began to look uncomfortable. There was a clear hesitation, which Zenzara utilized to cajole them more. Finally, the largest of the Avaraks gave what seemed to be a small bow, and gestured for us to pass them by in the corridor.

The Tyzaran girl inclined her head and swept past, as if it were her right. I fell in behind her as quickly as I could. This alien child was hard to typify; one moment she was vulnerable, another as tough as steel. I was beginning to realize just why the Tyzarans were considered one of the most advanced civilizations in our galaxy. Few species are prepared to confront the Avaraks. Avaraks can be tricky. They don't much care for aliens and they certainly don't take orders from other species. But the Tyzarans have certain advantages. They are considered by many to be the most technologically advanced species of the Major Shells. If they had not shared their technology with the other races, it is doubtful any of us would have progressed as far as we have.

We were ushered along more corridors until we came to the bridge. There, the central figure, clearly the captain, was at least half as big again as the rest of the Avaraks. He regarded us with displeasure. He demanded something in Avarak, and then changed to Universal.

"Who are these aliens?"

Zenzara's head went up. "Who are you?"

He growled. "My name is Solutor."

"Oh yes; we met your wife down in the infirmary."

He glared down at the slight Tyzaran figure in front of him. Zenzara only came up to his hips. "You are fighting with the enemy. You will be interned."

"No such thing. We have come to stop all this unfortunate quibbling."

He stared at her, his lower jowl dropping. "Quibbling? There is a large fleet surrounding us."

"Exactly my point. You cannot win. You are clearly surpassed in size and fire power. You need to barter. You must offer to exchange the Terran prisoners on *Raktor* in exchange for your safe passage."

He puffed out. "Avaraks are not afraid to die!"

"I am sure they aren't, but it would be a worthless sacrifice. Tell the opposing fleet that you have Tyzarans on board. They won't attack."

Solutor's frown was slow and cumbersome. "There is only one Tyzaran on board."

"It will make no difference. I shall talk to them. You will see; they will withdraw rather than attack a ship with Tyzarans."

"This cannot be. I will not give up my prisoners. The Terrans started this war; they are responsible for everything."

"Surely the differences can be sorted out by mediation?"

"They have claimed the entire Local Shell as their own territory! It is quite monstrous! Completely unacceptable! You do not understand how we Avaraks think!"

I stepped in. "That may be true. But however much you undervalue your *own* death, that of an unborn son ..." I stressed the word unborn, "... is a heavy price to pay. And you would not wish to alienate the Tyzarans – or the Spacelanders, surely? Not more than they already are?"

Several muscles moved in his jaw. His eyes darted around him at his officers, and I wondered how many of them had understood what had been said. Their expressions had not moved one iota.

Zenzie stepped past me. "Please," she said urgently. "At least do not give your son's life away for nothing. It is senseless."

More movement in the jowls told me that the conclusion the Avarak was reaching was unpalatable. I saw from the small drop in his shoulders that he had decided to sacrifice himself and his ship.

The ridge on Zenzie's skull spiked completely. She looked stricken. I put my right hand on her shoulder.

There was a long silence. Then, at last, Captain Solutor pressed his lips together.

"Avaraks never run. However, I will allow your allies and the Terran children to evacuate before we attack. You will be allocated my personal shuttle; it is the only one which is FTL capable. In addition, there is an adequate medical bay which will enable your wounded comrade to be evacuated." His eyes met mine steadily before going on, "I will allow a skeleton Avarak crew to accompany you, since you are unused to our hardware. You will need a nurse, a doctor, and a navigator. There will not be room for more." His eyes had darkened. I saw him blink once as if in pain as he regarded the surrounding crew on the bridge. The members of his crew looked away. None of them wanted to be picked. Finally his eyes settled on a young Avarak who was standing some paces away, in the background.

"Orison, son of Tungor, you will accompany the aliens to the shuttle *Rastin* and evacuate them." Then he repeated the order in Avarak.

The young officer stepped forward, but he was shaking his massive head slowly. He made a long speech to Solutor and then stood waiting for an answer, his head low.

Solutor thought for a long moment, and then his heavy voice sounded again, in Universal.

"Your father was my best friend for many years. You are a young officer and I can spare you. Salute him from me. Tell him my debt is now paid in full. Obey your captain!"

Orison seemed to diminish in front of us. He nodded and turned towards the passageway.

"This way, if you please." Then he looked back at Solutor and the rest of his crewmates. He put one large fist across his heart and inclined his head.

"*Avarak Karax!*"

The entire crew copied his gesture and echoed his words. "*Avarak Karax! Avarak Karax!*"

Solutor gazed down at us. His decision made, he was anxious for us to leave. His face was wiped now of all emotion. As we were led out by Orison, I saw the Captain turn aside to push a button and talk gruffly into a comlink.

Zenzie had taken my hand. She was squeezing it tightly. "He is talking to one of the doctors," she explained, "telling him to get Sammy's Zeroth unit on board the *Rastin*, and he is telling him to find Sammy's aide, who is also to accompany us." She listened intently. "The doctor is protesting. He says his duty is to attend Avaraks, not aliens. But he has agreed to send the nursing aide and Sammy to the shuttle." She listened to Solutor's answer. "Solutor is telling him to do as he is bid."

We could hear no more after that as we made our way away from the bridge and back along the convoluted corridors. Solutor must have made further calls, for when we eventually moved into the huge hold which held the *Rastin*, we found we were not the only ones there.

Mel, Didjal and Eshaan were standing under guard near the door. They looked relieved as they saw us approach. Sammy's Zeroth was slowly being pushed along the bay towards the large shuttle, and, much to my surprise, Bull Cunningham was stretched out on the deck, by the entry ramp. He was hog-tied hands and feet, but still clearly conscious and quite furious. Three Avarak guards stood over him. He was protesting his innocence.

"Why have you tied me up? I'm a Spacelander!" His lie was fluid, his virtuous face convincing. If I hadn't seen him wielding a gun against the Avaraks with my own eyes I would have been convinced. That made me wonder whether I had been taken in from the start by him, as the Avaraks were now. Why *had* he been on that Spacelander course? Had he really won the trip as a Terran prize for coming top in his year, as he had told me, or had there been a more sinister reason from the start?

The pieces began to click together in my mind. That was why he was so good with a rifle. I felt a burning sensation of betrayal sweep through me. He had fooled me as easily as he was fooling the Avaraks. They were going to pay with their lives. Would I? Would the others under my protection? My face flushed with mortification. Out of the corner of my eye I noticed Zenzara staring at me with concern.

Bull hadn't finished playing to the gallery. "You saw I had no gun! It wasn't me! That Terran Instructor escaped. He was shooting at me! I am the victim here."

I felt like shooting him myself. With real bullets. "Bull! What have you done?"

"Nothing!"

"You might convince the Avaraks, but do you really expect me to believe that?"

He glowered towards me. His eyes shifted towards the Avaraks, as if asking me to vouch for him. They lowered as he realized I would not. "How would you understand? I am not lying. That Terran instructor did escape!" His voice rang with sincerity.

I rubbed my eyes. This was getting too complicated. I wasn't even sure who was fighting whom. And I definitely didn't know where my fellow Spacelanders stood on the issue. The lines were blurring; nothing seemed straightforward any longer. We had fought the Avaraks on *Commorancy*, for sure, but that had been mere survival. We were about to be blown out of the sky by the Terrans. Did that make the Flatlanders the new enemy? Was Bull Cunningham suddenly my adversary? I had been to numerous bars with him, had considered him a friend. We had spent hours together dissecting life and our fellow recruits. It was hard to regard him as a potential enemy. I found myself blinking, unsure as to my next move.

He was lucky that these Avarak guards seemed prepared to believe him. I looked in their direction, wondering what their intentions were, but that was soon made obvious. Two of them scooped Cunningham up and stomped up the ramp with him, tossing him into a corner with utter disregard to his well-being. Then a winding line of terrified Sol children was escorted up to the ramp and inside the shuttle.

I wondered what had happened to the instructor, but I didn't care enough to interrupt the evacuators to ask. I knew he had become responsible for his own fate as soon as he had taken arms against the Avaraks. I was amazed that they had not kept Cunningham as well. Surely we hadn't been the only ones to see him?

Finally Solutor's wife solemnly pushed Sammy's Zeroth tank up the ramp. She turned her featureless face in my direction as she passed and gave me a brief nod. I nodded back. She had tears streaking her cheeks. She knew what was happening, and why. Belonging or not, she cared for the imminent death of her husband. Or perhaps it was that of all these Avaraks she had traveled with.

There was no sign of the doctor. I turned to Orison.

"Is the shuttle full? Can you not take anyone else?"

He frowned. "This class of shuttle is built to take up to twenty-five Avaraks. We have two Adult Avaraks, the four of you, the Zeroth chamber, the bound Terran and thirty-five Terran children." He paused for a moment, heavy face crinkling as he calculated. "I suppose we could take a little more weight."

Zenzie walked up to him. "Then bring the children. The Avarak children."

He stared at her. "They will wish to stay. They will not abandon their parents."

I looked quickly over at Zenzara. "There are Avarak children on board?" I glared at Orison. "Then they should certainly be evacuated."

"T-That is impossible. I have orders to leave immediately, and their parents would need to give consent. Quite imp—"

His explanation was cut off by the sight of six small bulky figures being ushered across the vast hanger. Solutor had come to the same conclusion as Zenzie, it seemed. I doubted he had taken the time to get whatever consent was necessary. It was good to see that the Avaraks also had the desire to preserve their issue. It made them more ... no, not human, I know. More ... familiar.

We hurried them up the ramp and Orison busied himself at the controls as Seyal tried to settle all of the children in safe places. We were about to leave when a huge Avarak with an angry expression appeared on the ramp, peering up at us.

"Doctor Vebor," he announced, jowls high in the air, as an introduction. "I have been ordered to board." He clearly wasn't at all keen. Solutor must have been most insistent. The presence of two burly armed Avaraks on either side of him might have had something to do with it.

I stepped forward. "Welcome aboard."

He pushed past me, propelling me into the bulkhead. Not a friendly alien, then.

"Avarak Karax!" he declaimed, his small eyes showing exactly how much he despised all the other races in the Major Shells.

Right. Just what we needed. An Avarak who hadn't wanted to be saved. I gave a sigh. This was going to be a smooth flight. For sure. At least it wouldn't be long. Shuttles only usually had autonomy for some few tenths of light years. The *Rastin* wouldn't get us to any inhabited space. Not without help.

Even so, the Tyzaran girl might just have saved all of our lives. I gave her a glare. "Kindly remember who is in charge of this mission. It isn't you!"

She assumed an expression of saintly innocence. "Me? Of course not!"

I gave a grunt, surprising myself at how much like an Avarak I sounded.

She giggled.

3

Surrounded as the *Raktor* was, it was going to be nigh impossible to find a safe vector to distance us from the besieged ship. The shuttle needed to get at least ten kilometers away from the bigger ship in order to transition to FTL. We were prolonging our exposure to danger every second that we were still in system.

As we slowly drew away along our vector, we could see the beginnings of the end for the ship we had just left. The Terrans had decided that they weren't going to wait any longer. They were already taking advantage of the Avarak ship's lack of maneuverability; rail gun fire was pouring across open space. *Raktor's* point defenses were opening up to take out as many of the small but lethal projectiles as they could whilst still carefully avoiding our own vector. They weren't going to succeed. My mouth went dry as I watched.

Orison gave a shout of encouragement as the *Raktor* managed to fire off several bursts of heavy torpedoes at the fleet surrounding it and he glowed with pride as one of them caused a large Terran cruiser to shudder and then explode soundlessly into the surrounding space.

A few minutes later, his face fell. *Raktor* itself was now receiving punishing ultrapulses along a hull already splitting under the blasts which had cut clean through the point defense system. He dragged unwilling air into his huge lungs, holding it as he waited for the inevitable climax. Finally his head dropped as *Raktor* herself disintegrated in a huge blast. The fire had reached her main core.

Zenzie's eyes were wet. So Tyzarans cried, like the Earth-stem races.

It was strange that we had that trait in common, Tyzarans being so different to us.

Avaraks didn't. At least, Orison didn't. Our pilot's face showed no emotion, but his colour gave him away. The dark grey habitual color had faded to a pale white.

I turned to the other Avarak on the bridge, the doctor. He, too, was ashen as he stared at the screen. His lips were rigidly straight and his eyes were full of hatred.

Zenzie moved closer to Orison. "I am sorry that your ship has been destroyed," she told him, peering up at his face anxiously.

I was beginning to realize how much of a problem-solver she was, but this was one thing she couldn't make any better. I reached out and grabbed her arm, causing a small jump of surprise. Her ridge crested.

"We are very sorry for your loss," I told the Avaraks. "Come, Zenzara, we must check up on Sammy." I half-pulled her off the bridge. They needed to concentrate right now in any case. We had to go FTL or we would meet the same fate as the *Raktor*.

Zenzara stumbled along beside me, a bemused expression on her pixie face. "What did you do that for? I was trying to help."

"You can't."

Clearly, she didn't agree. "I can try. Living beings are special. They are obligated to try to help each other."

In principle, she was right. But since we had somehow managed to get ourselves fighting with the Terrans against the Avaraks on *Commorancy*, and with the Avaraks against the Terrans on *Raktor* it didn't seem like we had the moral high ground.

I tried to explain this to her. She pulled her small mouth into a moue of consideration. "Hmm. I see your point. Perhaps my help would not be appreciated right now."

"You should keep out of other people's problems, kid; realize that you can't solve the whole universe."

She was unconvinced. "I will take your comment under advisement."

I looked suspiciously at her. Her face was bland, but she was radiating stubbornness. It seemed to me she would keep on doing exactly what she felt like doing. I had to sigh. Mentoring the young Tyzaran girl wasn't going to be an easy job for anyone. I was determined it wouldn't be mine.

By this time we had made our way to the improvised medical bay. Sammy greeted us with a wave of his hand and a grin which turned into a grimace of pain. I grabbed his hand and we did a Spacelander handshake.

"Hey man! Are we safe yet?" He was a lot happier than he had been last time we had left him.

I nodded. "We are on our way. But ..." I looked quickly over at his Avarak nursing aide, "... *Raktor* has been destroyed."

Solutor's wife—widow—Seyal—was already very pale. This was not news to her. She turned away, busying herself with the preparation of some medicine or other. Zenzara took half a step towards Seyal and then looked sideways at me. I shook my head slightly. The Tyzaran girl hesitated, before deciding to move up to Sammy's Zeroth chamber.

"How are you feeling?"

Sammy smiled. "I'm good. Seyal thinks I can come out of the tank in another week or so."

Good news. Except I had no idea where we would be in another week. Or who we would be fighting. This whole thing made little sense to me. What had made the Avaraks attack *Commorancy*? Even if they were responding to the Terran expansionist ideas, it seemed out of character that they should attack a training ship. And why would the Terrans attack a relatively insignificant ship like *Raktor*? The top brass on *Seyfert* might know. But *Seyfert* was not communicating with us, which meant that we were on our own. My aim was to keep us out of any further trouble. That brought my train of thought to Bull Cunningham. He might know a bit more about what was happening.

I made my way to Bull, Zenzara and Didjal at my heels. He was in the same corner he had been left in, still tied hand and foot. I hesitated, then undid the ropes. He sat up, rubbing his ankles with both hands.

He wasn't happy.

"You could have come sooner! I have been lying here for hours!" He stared darkly at Didjal. "And why did you bring *him* with you?"

Didjal straightened up. "We Enif are proud to be hermaphroditic," it said with gravitas. "Please do not degrade us by using sexually biased pronouns. It is insulting." He walked slowly away.

Bull stared after it. "What did I do?"

"Surely you know Enif require neutral pronouns?"

"No! Why would they?"

I stared. "Because they think bisexual races are less efficient?"

He gave a snort. "Sure. Less efficient."

"Bisexual reproduction *does* use up more energy," I pointed out.

His eyes glittered as he watched the Enif leave. I got a sudden impression of intense dislike.

Bull must have caught the involuntary tightening of my shoulders, because he gave a rueful shrug. "They probably are more efficient," he said with a disarming smile. "How long have I been here?"

"Around two hours. You deserved it. Why the Shells did you attack the Avaraks?"

He looked away. "Oh. That."

"Yes, that. What were you thinking?"

"I'm Terran. David Simmonds – the instructor – said that the Avaraks attacked Earth first. And we *were* fighting them on *Commorancy*." He gave a shrug, his eyes sliding evasively away from mine. "It just seemed like the correct thing to do – protect the Terran children. He said we had to."

Why did I not believe him? He sounded truthful.

"On *Commorancy* we were just trying to survive. And you heard me broker a truce with the Avaraks."

"We-ell. I guess. But Simmonds said they were going to torture him."

"And you believed him?"

Bull's eyes opened wide. "Why shouldn't I? He's Terran, like me."

Then he amended that statement. "He *was* Terran."

"Did he tell you anything about why the fighting was happening specifically around *Raktor*? And around *Commorancy*?"

Bull shook his head. "He didn't tell me anything."

"I should tie you back up again. You can't be trusted."

Bull gazed up at me, eyes pleading. "I mean, I didn't know I wasn't supposed to fight the Avaraks. Come on, Mallivan! It's what we were doing on *Commorancy*, after all! You aren't going to hold a little thing like that against me, are you? The Avaraks let me go. You'll do the same, right?"

I didn't have to look at Zenzie to know her crest was signaling danger. I could feel it coursing through me. I already knew. I should tie him up.

I couldn't. I sighed, still looking down at him. "I think it's time we parted ways."

Bull's eyes almost popped out of his head. "You're kidding me, right? You only have two weeks seniority on me!" His façade of affability slipped again for a moment, making him seem suddenly menacing.

"I know. And who knows what will happen next? You can stay with the Terran children, protect them. Haven't you just said that was your aim? You just won't be coming with Zenzie and me."

"Zenzie and me or Zenzie and I?" The Tyzaran girl's face was tilted to one side inquiringly. She really wanted to know. Her English was stilted, but good enough for her to detect areas of flexible grammar.

"Whichever."

"Really? Because I thought that—"

Bull was pulling himself to his feet. He towered over Zenzie, who shrank back.

"Tell your pet Tyzaran to shut up," he snarled. "You don't seem so keen to dump *her*. Maybe you figure she'll be a good addition to your bed."

There was a rustle to one side of me, and then Bull was back on the metal floor plating again with a very angry Tyzaran pinning him to the deck. Zenzie was glaring down at him, her ridge completely vertical and her small claws splayed out at the tips of her fingers.

She hissed at him like a cat, her lips drawing back to show sharp white teeth. "Don't even s-s-suggest anything of the s-s-sort! Tyzarans hardly ever mate with outside species. And we never even mate at all until we are in our late twenties. I'm only eight. Euwww!!"

I had to grin. Bull was shrinking back, intimidated by her. "She makes a good addition to the *team*," I told him. "You don't."

His face was ugly. "I just made one little mistake."

My stomach felt like I'd just swallowed a cold brick. How could I ever have thought this man was a friend? "I'm sorry."

His lips tensed. "You should be."

He hobbled out of the bay and disappeared along the corridor, leaving a sensation of discomfort behind him.

Zenzara watched him go. "Will he fight the Avaraks again?"

"I don't know." I wasn't too pleased with myself. I hadn't handled the conversation very well and I was almost sure I was doing the wrong thing in letting him walk away. I sighed again. They were becoming regular, these sighs. At this rate I was going to be grey before I was thirty.

"Maybe you should take some exercise."

"What?"

"You appear to be huffing and puffing too much. You must be out of shape. I am suggesting that exercise will help you."

I pushed past her and made my way back to the bridge, deliberately leaving her behind. She was a spunky little thing. I even quite liked her, but I wasn't planning on spending the rest of my life with her any time soon. What a mess.

It took us four days to reach the nearest faintly suitable landfall and it certainly wasn't anything I would have called habitable. It was little more than a large round rock and had no atmosphere.

We set down and disembarked from our overcrowded conditions. We were all the worse for wear, and I don't think any of us would have got back into the shuttle for another four days in space, even if there had been fuel for that long. We waited with as much patience as we could muster as an inflatable emergency dome was set up over the shuttle, and then each group claimed its own patch of land.

The Avaraks took the southern side of the ship, with the Avarak children. The Terran children, together with an unapologetic Bull Cunningham, the northern. We set up camp by the shuttle. The three groups never mixed. They simply glowered at each other from a distance. I was glad Bull had no access to any arms. He looked as if he would have liked to use them. I was pretty sure now that his camaraderie on the course had been a cover. That he had been a part of this from the start.

The two Enif, together with Zenzie, Mel and myself, huddled close to the shuttle, near the Zeroth chamber Sammy was still having to lie in. Surprisingly, Seyal had stayed with us. Perhaps she considered her duties to Sammy had priority over her Avarak race. Perhaps she simply didn't want to go back. She was an individual of few words. She didn't explain her actions to us. But she stayed. The unwilling Dr. Vebor occasionally forced himself to cross the 50 yards separating us and give Sammy a desultory examination. A little more interest wouldn't have killed him.

We were hungry, thirsty and tired. The emergency provisions on *Rastin* were running out and we were severely rationed. There were few complaints from any of my group, though. Avarak food and drink made us gag; it was quite difficult to force it down even though we were desperate.

The two Enif lay side by side, chatting silently to each other through tactile communication wherever their skin touched. It was strange to watch. Their skin seemed to shiver and crenellate in waves.

Didjal was the practical one, Eshaan the artist. Enif always form life partners with complete opposites. They spent hours chatting to each other. I asked them what they found to talk about at such length.

Didjal gave the Enif equivalent of a laugh. "Eshaan is our artist. I am taking this time to discover all I can about our legacy to the Enif people."

I must have tilted my head on one side; he realized I was confused and hurried to explain.

"We believe that our souls will join upon our death. Everything we have achieved will become known as our joint work. Even our names will be conjoined – we will be known as Dishaan once we have passed into the sky. As I am the practical one, little that is lasting will live on after my death. Perhaps one engine running more smoothly than another. Perhaps I may have made a small insignificant addition to our total scientific knowledge as a people. But my *faliif* ... my *faliif* is a true artist. Eshaan's work will be appreciated for many centuries after we are both dead. Since it is to be mine too, I am merely catching up on all that we will be leaving after us."

Zenzie nodded. "Enif are the most artistic race in the Shells. My parents have a beautiful Enif mural."

Eshaan touched his translator band. "Who was the artist?"

Zenzie wrinkled her brow. "Errr ... oh yes, I remember! Someone called 'Bervalean'."

Their skin crimped in pleasure as the two Enif discussed such news excitedly.

"Berviil and Ashalean formed a great artist. Your parents are very lucky to be able to study their work on the walls of their house. What does the painting depict?"

"It is the inside of an EM core, transforming into some sort of live being."

More excited quivering. "We know the piece," said Didjal. "Your parents are most honored to have been allowed to purchase it."

"They think so. They have it for a hundred years, I believe."

"Yes. A place has been reserved for it in the Siinala Monument. The pattern is already deposited there." Its eyes went blank as it consulted an internal memory. "Slot 34-101-BB-756."

"Do you know where every piece of art will go?"

"Not all, no. But many. It is the purpose of our whole lives, after all. Places in the Siinala Monument, even though it is huge, are limited. Not all Enif can hope to exhibit there."

"Will *your* art have a place in the Siinala Monument?" The words were out of Zenzie's mouth before she caught my instinctive movement to stop her. She turned to give me with a '*what?*' sort of look. I rolled my eyes. She turned away again.

There was silence. Eshaan was looking at its feet.

Didjal shook its head. "No. We have not yet been chosen for such a great honor. But Eshaan's work is exceptional and our lifespan is not yet over. There is still time to achieve posterity. We strive for such immortality."

See what you have done? I stared hard at Zenzie's back. She didn't notice.

The Enif separated, Eshaan walking back into the shuttle. Didjal got up to examine the cables attached to Sammy's tank. Zenzie, unaware of having caused any pain whatsoever, was idly tracing a circle in the sand she was sitting on with one finger.

I frowned. The Tyzaran's unilateral Savior Protocol had failed to take one small detail into account. That the recipient might not actually want to be part of this protocol. I planned to set them straight on that point as soon as I could speak to one of their spokesdesignates. I couldn't help feeling Zenzara might not take it well.

The first ship to reach us was Terran, which was a disappointment. The second was Avarak, which was even more of one. That meant we had to make a choice, and I didn't like either of the possibilities. Whoever and whatever had started this war, it was either the Avaraks or the Terrans. I felt we needed a third option if we were to stay out of the fighting.

I needn't have bothered. As it turned out, we did need a third option. Neither the Avaraks nor the Terrans would agree to carry us anywhere.

When the Terrans arrived on a large shuttle, it was Bull who welcomed them. He had become the children's champion, and it was soon apparent that the incoming Flatlanders felt they owed him something. I narrowed my eyes as they arrived.

First, a detachment of marines surrounded the Avarak encampment, then another surrounded ours. My protests were ignored completely. I must say, I resented being on the wrong end of one of the Flatlander guns. As the Terran children were escorted onto the Earth shuttle, I saw Bull talking earnestly to one of the marines. None of the children bothered to say goodbye to us. If we had been expecting thanks for saving them, we were to be disappointed. They ran up the ramp thankfully, ignoring both us and the Avaraks present.

Then a Terran woman disembarked. She was wearing the bands of an Admiral of the Fleet. She was stocky and short, but held herself with dignity and great presence. She walked smartly over towards Bull and held out her hand.

Bull placed a small package in it and then looked over in my direction and smirked.

The woman vanished inside the shuttle doors to safety, allowing Bull to fall in and follow her. The Terran detachments saluted to the woman.

Perhaps we had our answer as to why both *Commorancy* and *Raktor* had been attacked. *Commorancy* must have been carrying some sort of intelligence. Something both the Avaraks and the Terrans had wanted. Something both races were prepared to kill for rather than let fall into the other's hands. And Instructor David Simmonds, who most definitely had been more than just an instructor of children, had been carrying it. He must have passed it to Bull when he realized that Bull might be allowed off the *Raktor*, but he wouldn't. And, like a fool,

I had facilitated that. A slow anger began to burn inside me. I had the distinct feeling that my short-sightedness would cost even more lives than had already been lost.

Bull vanished onto the Earth shuttle that had come down nearby, omitting to say goodbye to any of us. He focussed ahead with a stony expression, ignoring Zenzie, who had stuck her tongue out at him as he went past.

I gave her a nudge in her ribs, and a hard stare. She looked cross, but closed her mouth. "Well; he was rude."

"So were you."

"I wasn't rude! I just attacked him. He deserved it!"

"Attacking people *is* rude."

She shook her head. "Attacking people is a legitimate defense."

I opened my mouth to point out how much was wrong with that sentence, when I realized that the last of the Terrans were about to withdraw.

I ran up to the leader of the detachment. "Surely you aren't going to leave us here?"

He frowned. "I have no instructions to take you on board."

"There is an injured man. You must take us with you!"

He pressed his comlink and passed on my request. A few moments later we heard a muttered reply, but he shook his head. "Sorry, Sir. Admiral Ellison sends her regrets, but there is not enough space for you, and the Avaraks are in final approach. She suggests you ask them for passage."

The soldiers headed back to the shuttle at the double, leaving us staring after them. My mouth was open. So were my eyes, which is how I saw Bull's gesture from one corner of the ramp, before he disappeared for good inside his safe haven. It was a two-finger parody of a salute.

I had made an enemy.

So had he.

Zenzie grabbed at my arm and squeezed it to get my attention. She led me apart from the others. "Did you see that? Did you?"

"I did."

"They have stolen something. Something important."

"That would seem to be the logical conclusion."

She frowned, causing the wrinkles on her face to bunch up. "Not a conclusion. An inference."

I may have raised my eyes heavenwards, because she narrowed hers before continuing. "—And there is only one thing I can think of that would be worth all the trouble they are going to."

The light bulb in my brain flickered dimly. Then it came on. "The Tyzaran ZEPH drive."

She nodded. "Our new Zero Point Hyperspace drive – ZEPH drive, as you just called it – is a huge advance. And it is just what you would need to patrol your borders if you had unilaterally claimed ownership of the whole of one of the shells. No wonder the Human Omnistate wants the new drive. They could hardly patrol a sphere of 300 light years in diameter with EM drive. It wouldn't be practical. They had to have been pretty sure of getting our new technology before claiming the shell as their own."

"And the Avaraks would be determined to stop them getting it. Yes, that makes a lot of sense."

Zenzie's mouth was trembling. "I have to contact Tyzar. The authorities need to know about this." She gasped. "We could have stopped this!"

"We can't be sure that the ZEPH drive is what Bull was carrying. It could be some other intelligence." No, it couldn't. As I spoke I realized it was a stupid thing to say. Occam's razor told me it had to be the new drive. It was the only thing big enough to explain everything that had happened. She was right. We could have stopped this. We should have searched Bull. Incapacitated him in some way. "But how could they have got ZEPH technology? Who aboard the *Commorancy* would have access to it?"

Zenzie's eyes widened. "I wondered why there was a Tyzaran

delegation on the *Commorancy!* It was very strange." The wrinkles on her little face deepened as the implications of that sank in. "Nobody in our group could have anything to do with this, could they?" she asked in a small voice.

I felt sorry for her. "One of your friends or family is a traitor to the Tyzarans. The conclusion, sorry, the *inference*, is inescapable."

She went absolutely still for several seconds. Then her crest flared. She nodded, more to herself than to me. "There has to be a Tyzaran traitor somewhere." Her voice dropped to almost a whisper. "But that is impossible. No Tyzaran would betray their government. Not like that. Not to the Terrans! It is unthinkable!"

I couldn't share her faith in her own people. Seven out of the eight Major Shell founding races have independently developed justice and penal systems, implying the existence of criminality amongst them. The Macers are the only race that hasn't. I didn't think anyone would *accidentally* bring cutting-edge technology onto a training ship belonging to another race. I hoped we were wrong, but I could feel in my bones that we weren't. I pulled a face. "It explains why the Avaraks attacked *Commorancy*. It explains Bull Cunningham. It explains why Simmonds was acting as an instructor to those children. It gave him a perfect cover story."

She gasped. "Surely the Omnistate wouldn't utilize children that way? They could have been killed!"

Why did I have the distinct feeling that the Omnistate wouldn't have cared if they had? That they had simply been expendable? I found my distrust of the Flatlanders shifting to outright dislike.

Zenzie had reached the same conclusion. "They didn't care!"

"If we are right," I pointed out, "then it is in Omnistate interests that we don't get a chance to contact our respective governments. We may be lucky the Avaraks are coming. That Flatlander admiral can't shoot at us if she is too busy escaping with the intelligence she wanted. I guess." I thought about it. "... I hope."

I looked up towards the departing shuttle. The others followed my gaze. It sure would be all too easy for them to lob a couple of ultrapulse bombs on top of us. But Zenzie's crest remained down. Logic said that the Flatlander admiral wouldn't hurt us. We were not a priority to the woman. The intelligence she had just got hold of was.

Once the shuttle had disappeared into the dark we rejoined the rest. There was a burst of angry conversation. It was hard for the others to believe that the Flatlanders had left us behind.

"What is wrong with them?" demanded Mel, arms akimbo as she stared into the sky. "Don't they know we saved those children?"

Neither Zenzara nor I felt like replying. Sometimes you feel a very small part of a very big universe which doesn't seem to care very much. I suppose, to a cluster of galaxies, one life truly is ephemeral. Unimportant. I felt a shiver of unease. I had grown up with a certain balance to my small area of the cosmos. That was melting into something approaching chaos. I wish I knew what all this was leading to.

Eventually we all sat back down again. We all knew that movement and conversation simply put more of a drain on our meager resources.

A few hours later I was awoken by excited chatter in the Avarak camp. They had just been contacted by their heavy cruiser. It would be over our position in another hour.

Sammy looked worried. "I still need to regenerate in this Zeroth tank for another three days. Do you think they will take this shuttle? Who does the *Rastin* belong to? Will they leave us behind too?"

A slight rustling behind me made me react. I twisted around and reached out. It was only Seyal. She leapt back with a cry to avoid my lunge.

I held up both hands in an apology. "Sorry. I'm a bit jumpy. You always move about so quietly."

Zenzie muttered something unflattering about Spacelanders and their ability to hear.

Seyal stepped past me. "Me stay," she said, pointing firmly to herself. "Me stay you. *Rastin* stay you."

Now she had all our attention. "Will they let you keep the *Rastin?*" I asked.

She shrugged. "*Rastin* belong Solutor." Her forehead creased as a memory came to her. She walked to the shuttle and came back some minutes later with an envelope, which she had opened. Her eyes were surprised. She held up the paper. "Solutor give me."

I felt admiration for the burly Avarak who had foreseen this need. He had been about to die, but had made time to try to protect his unborn child. I didn't think he would have done it for his wife.

"It is your personal craft now? That is good news. Can you get us back to one of the Spacelander worlds?"

She inclined her head.

We all began to chatter at once. I held up one hand. "Wait!"

They looked at me.

"Do any of you want to travel back with the other Avarak ship? I mean, you don't *have* to come with us."

They eyeballed each other, but there were headshakes all round.

"We should at least have asked the Terrans for some food." I cursed myself for not thinking of that earlier. I didn't think they would have obliged us, but I should have asked.

"I don't think we would have been high on their priority list," pointed out Sammy. "All they were concerned about was getting away from here before that Avarak cruiser arrived."

"You have a point."

So we sat quietly to one side as the Avaraks brought down a couple of shuttles and fussed over Orison, Dr. Vebor and the Avarak minors.

Dr. Vebor went into a huddle with the new arrivals. He seemed very eloquent about us; they all kept looking over in our direction. I made signs to them, asking them to take us with them. Vebor's showed all his teeth as he leant forward to make sure he had my attention and then slowly and deliberately shook his massive head. It was the first time I had seen him happy.

One of the newly arrived Avarak officers marched himself across to our small group. He glared at Seyal and snapped out a question. She entered into a long conversation in Avarak with him. He didn't seem to like what she was saying. He examined the paper with a tight face. Whatever was written there didn't please him. He began a diatribe against her, overshadowing her with his larger body, using his superior size to intimidate her. She was forced to cringe back.

Seyal swayed at the stream of angry words coming from him, then Zenzie scrambled up and faced the large being. She lifted her chin and treated him to a long monologue in her fluent Avarak. His eyes got wider and wider.

She finished with a burst that sounded like it could have come from a machine gun, before grabbing Seyal's hand in solidarity.

The large Avarak spoke sharply into a hand-held communicator. There was silence for a moment and then an equally harsh answer was returned.

"So there!" crowed Zenzie.

I put my hand on her shoulder, in case she was tempted to stick her tongue out again, but she gave me half a smile. "They just checked the ownership. It did belong to Solutor, and the letter is valid, so they can't legally take it. At least, not right now." She turned back to the Avarak. "So there!" she repeated with glee.

I thrust her behind me. "Do you have any water to spare?" I asked, in my painfully bad Avarak. "Food suitable for aliens? Fuel?"

His face twisted; perhaps my accent was so atrocious it caused him pain. Or perhaps my very existence bothered him. He jabbered some more into the communicator. When the answer came back he almost managed a smile.

"*Nikkx*," he informed me, almost sweetly, letting his eyes slide meaningfully in Zenzie's direction. Then he turned and strode away.

I pushed Zenzie back behind me again. She seemed inclined to go after him. "It isn't worth it."

"But they don't want to help us! How can they leave us here like this? Sammy is sick! That is terrible! There should be an interstellar law obligating aid in such a situation!"

She wasn't wrong. "Maybe one day, there will be. But there are only six of us now. We should have enough to get to the Landau Rift. We will be careful with our rationing."

In the end, we didn't have to be. Orison came over, dragging behind him a large crate. The new ship had routinely sent down two pallets before they knew the true situation. "We shan't be needing them," he told us, after nodding in slight deference to Seyal's new widow status. "They will help you get to your destination. There is food, water and half a crate of fuel capsules." He looked down for a few moments, before meeting Seyal's eyes again. "Your husband died bravely. I would have wished for the honor of dying at his side. I hope that my future holds such an honor for me, too. *Avarak Karax!*"

Seyal inclined her head, tears running down her cheeks. "*Avarak Karax!*"

Orison smiled at us all, ignoring the angry looks he was getting from the rest of his group, particularly Dr. Vebor. "Safe journey!"

We wished him the same and then watched as he walked back to his group. The Avaraks then filed into the two shuttles and took off, leaving us to load up our meager supplies and blast back into space ourselves. Hopefully the limited stock of fuel capsules would be enough to get us somewhere better.

4

We managed half a day of EM drive before we were forced to stop. Fuel was not the only problem we would be facing, it seemed. The core had overheated, rather drastically. There was no way we could continue like this. We were in the middle of nowhere. Naturally. Jhaharada's Law. If you are going to break down, why let it be near a nice and safe space station? Much more fun for karma to make it light years away from any civilization.

Rastin hung in space, with the backdrop of the Peliss Nebula in the far distance. I had a bird's eye view of it, because Mel and I were outside, checking the hull-side cooling conduits. The shuttle's skin sparkled as the ship spun uselessly below our feet. It was magnificent, frustrating and terrifying, all at the same time. Our air supplies were good for a couple of weeks, and we could further ration our few remaining food supplies, but after that we had no chance of survival. Again. I looked across at Mel, who had volunteered for EVA because claustronetics generally prefer being on the outside of a ship rather than on the inside of one. Personally I can't see why. Space is continually dangerous. Whether you are inside or outside a ship is pretty irrelevant. In fact, you are probably safer inside. Still, she was the one who had volunteered, and I wasn't about to say anything about it.

She had one of the inspection hatches open and was engrossed in the loops of conduits exposed. She seemed to have found a certain calm after *Commorancy*. She no longer looked so scared all the time.

"This way of cooling is really risky," she told me as she peered more closely at one of the couplings. "Why don't the Avaraks protect these conduits more? It leaves their ships tremendously exposed to cosmic dust and debris." Then she gave a short gasp, and her legs disappeared altogether as she dragged herself further into the sub-skin. "Oh no!"

I scuttled hastily over to her position and pulled myself inside the hatch. "What?"

"We won't be going anywhere. Look!"

No kidding. There was a gaping hole about ten meters further in. All the tubes had been obliterated. She was right. This shuttle was dead in space.

I frowned. The edges of the casings were all facing outwards. This had been no casual collision with space flotsam. This was the result of an explosion. And I didn't think it was by chance.

My blood began to boil. "This is Vebor's work!"

"You can't know that!"

"Can't I?" I moved my head, letting the light from my helmet play over the whole area as I spoke. "It had to be after we spoke to the Captain of the Avarak cruiser, right? I mean, before that nobody knew if they would take the *Rastin* or not."

Her brow crinkled. "I guess …"

"And who is the only Avarak who went inside the shuttle after that?"

She turned her helmet to me. I saw the whites of her eyes through the plexiglass. "Shells! You are right. He went to pick up his medical instruments. It was either him or one of us. I *thought* he was in there a long time!"

"Yes. I think we have a small score to settle with Dr. Vebor. Though perhaps they don't have to swear to the Hippocratic Oath when they qualify on Rhyveka."

"Why," she wailed. "Why would he *do* that?"

I saw the old Mel for a moment. The shaky, petrified Mel. I didn't want her to slip back into that state of panic. I tried to keep my voice even. "We may not even have been the target. He may just have been expressing his anger at Seyal's keeping the *Rastin*. You know how the Avaraks feel about their womenfolk. I mean, let's face it, women's suffrage has a way to go on Rhyveka."

Mel's mouth formed a large O. I could practically see the cogs working. Eventually she just let all the air out through her teeth. "Then he deserves everything he gets!"

I couldn't help but agree. I myself was looking forward to seeing him again. A real deserving cause.

"Have you found anything?" Zenzie's clear voice interrupted our thoughts. She and the others were waiting for our update on the situation.

I explained. There was silence over the comlink for quite some seconds. Then Zenzie's voice came back over to us. "What about Sammy?"

"What about him?"

"His tank is redlining too. It must use the same cooling system."

"Then get him out of the tank. We have left him in there as long as we could. Tell Seyal to open it up."

There was a hurried conversation in Avarak on the other end of the line. "Seyal says that he may be left with a permanent limp if he doesn't go the whole time, even though he only needed a couple more days."

"But he will walk?"

"Yes."

"Tell Seyal she has done all she could. It will be enough. The Agazeds are renowned for their leathery hides." I could hear Sammy disputing that indignantly. I ignored him, hiding a smile. "Deploy the interstellar distress beacon, will you?" That was a lottery, too, but if we did nothing, we would all die.

Another quick conversation. "Didjal has gone to do that. Anything else?"

"Do we have any propulsion at all? Apart from the core drive?"

"No. All the engines use the same coolant system."

"Then there isn't much else we can do. Unless anyone has any ideas?"

This time the silence went on for much longer.

"Right. Mel and I will see if we can mend any of these pipes. We will be back in when we run out of oxygen."

"OK. I'll tell Didjal to rest. I will too. He and I can take over from you later."

"You are too young to go outside, Zenzara."

The comlink huffed. "I have been training in EVA since I was four."

"All right! Fine! Whatever!"

"You know, Rye, you should try to relax. You get really uptight really fast."

I cut the connexion. Like someone aged eight would know stuff like that.

Mel was grinning.

I frowned. "Maybe we could get on with this?"

"Maybe we could."

There was still a grin in her voice, but I let it pass. We pulled ourselves further in between the twin skins.

I was fast asleep, curled up in a fetal position, when Sammy's none-too-gentle hand shook me awake.

"Whaa-a-a?" I blinked. My mouth was dry and tasted metallic. My tongue felt furry. "Wha-what time is it?"

"You have only been asleep for two hours, Rye. Sorry, but something has happened to Zenzara."

My brain snapped awake. "The kid?" I scrambled up. "Where is she?"

He held my arm, to restrain me. "She is outside the hull. She and Didjal were continuing the work you and Mel started, but Didjal says they were in the middle of a conversation when she suddenly stopped talking to it. It says she is breathing all right, but that she appears to have gone into a trance. She has been like that for fifteen minutes. It is going to need help to get her back in. It suggested I wake you."

"Of course. I will put an EVA suit on. Is she completely catatonic?"

"Nearly. Didjal says she smiles at it, but she won't answer its questions. It is almost as if she has been drugged."

I flipped mentally through everything I knew that could cause that sort of a reaction. Lack of oxygen? I didn't think so. Carbon monoxide? Possibly, but where could a sufficient quantity have come from? Why the fitz had I let her persuade me to send her extravehicular? What had I been thinking?

I dragged the EVA suit over my legs, cursing to myself. The Tyzaran girl was more trouble than she was worth. Well, it would be the last time she was allowed to go anywhere except the bathroom on her own! And I was certainly going to contact the Tyzaran authorities. They could just take her back. There was no way I was going to be lumbered with a child to look after.

I stormed out of the hull hatch and into the icy confines of space. The change in temperature was noticeable through the suit, though not really uncomfortable.

I pulled myself hand over hand across the hull, using the welded steel clips put there for that purpose. Within a minute I was over the gaping hole in the hull.

I found a worried Didjal clutching Zenzara tightly. I nodded and took her out of its hold into my arms. She was as light as a feather.

"Zenzara? Kid! Are you all right?" She didn't reply, so I shook her, probably harder than I should have. "Answer me!"

She gave a frown, as if she was having a lovely dream interrupted. "Go away!"

"You have been drugged. I have to take you inside."

She smiled again, almost drowsily. "No. Not drugged. I have been chosen."

Like that made any sense.

"I am taking you inside. Right now!"

She clutched at me suddenly. "No! Not yet! Wait!"

I couldn't help shaking her again. "Wake up, will you!"

She gave a sigh. "Stop it, Ryler Mallivan Bell. You are disturbing the Chakran."

"Chakran? What Chakran?"

"The Chakran who has found me. I think I am becoming a Chyzar."

"I have no idea what you are talking about. Chakrans are a myth."

She looked pained. "Please let me concentrate. I will explain everything, but I need some more time out here."

I checked her breathing apparatus. "You only have half-an-hour's air left."

"That will have to be enough then. But don't disturb me." Her eyes opened and she found mine. I could see from their expression just how serious she was.

"Will you swear to me that you are not hurt? Not drugged?"

"I swear to you on my crest that I am in no danger."

Certainly her crest was flat against her skull. There appeared to be no reason for her sudden lethargy. I hesitated.

She gave me a nod. "Thank you." Then her eyes closed again and she lapsed back into something like sleep, a blissful expression on her face.

My eyes met those of Didjal. It shrugged. "Don't ask me. She's been like that for nearly an hour now."

"What do you know of the Chakrans?"

Its skin rippled along its glossy black appendages. The Enif didn't need EVA suits. They could survive for quite long periods in open space. However, I was in full EVA, which made it much harder for us to communicate. There was a delay in its answer as my software worked overtime. "Nonlocal entities. Many species assume them to be fictitious."

Exactly. Things that didn't really exist in real life.

It wasn't finished. "They extend over huge expanses of spacetime. Individual cells can be hundreds of light years apart. Yet they form some sort of a whole being, about which little to nothing is known. Because each cell exists so far apart from the next, inter-cell communication must be by quantum entanglement and possibly, elective quantum decoherence. So far they are only known to have communicated with Tyzarans, and then only very occasionally. The Tyzarans seem to be the only Major Shell species that is in any way compatible."

I looked down at the alien girl in my arms, wrinkles slightly smoothed in peace. Surely not?

Didjal's compound eyes whirled. "We Enif believe the Chakrans exist."

I pulled a face. "Spacelanders don't. I was taught that they were a myth."

I felt like taking Zenzara back inside, back to safety, yet something kept me outside, stationary under the starry black light. Her face was so calm, so beatific, that I couldn't bring myself to remove her from it. I felt she was begging me to let her stay just a little longer. And for some reason my inner self was listening. It was uncanny. It made me shiver slightly.

Didjal and I waited out there together like two sentinels, surrounded by the grey slate of space. I remember staring at the Peliss Nebula, wondering if I had gone slightly mad. I remember the comlink chattering to me as the others asked for updates. I reassured them as best I could and then everything went quiet as the minutes ticked by.

I wasn't the individual having this strange experience, and yet it was touching me too. I was aware of a certain aura of importance about this moment, of a solemnity. I could feel that something of great import was occurring; I just didn't know what. The Enif and I stood to attention, silent witnesses to something greater than both of us. Aware that we were privileged, but unsure why.

I doubt I could ever forget those moments.

I let her stay until the oxygen marker dipped into the red line. Then I nodded to Didjal. It tied all three of us safely together. We let her drift out from the hull as we pulled her back toward the hatch. She made no sign of noticing. We manhandled her back into the shuttle, where Seyal bustled up to take over from us.

As I removed her EVA helmet, her eyes flickered open. "Thank you," she breathed. "I think there was time." And she patted both Didjal's and my hands. Then she closed her eyes again and became still.

We let Seyal examine her.

After a few moments the Avarak aide turned to the rest of us. "She is sleeping. I can find nothing wrong with her. But I will take blood samples. I think we should monitor her, but leave her to sleep for as long as she needs."

If I had been on my own ship, *Faraday*, I could have researched the Chakrans. As it was, all that would simply have to wait. The *Rastin's* computer responded only to Avarak, and was really little more than a navigational tool in any case. It wouldn't have any answers about beings that might exist in the vacuum energy of spacetime. I shook my head to clear it. There was something extremely surreal about all this.

Zenzara hibernated for two whole days. By that time we were worried she would never wake up again. Seyal had her hooked up to an intravenous drip and was trying to keep her as stable as possible. The small girl looked like a waif as she lay on the cot in the tiny medical bay. Her crest was bedraggled and wilted. The wrinkles around her tiny face were dragging the skin outwards and downwards, so that the inside of her face was almost smooth but the outside surrounded by a ruff of skin folds.

The quality of life on board was hardly improving. If nobody answered our distress beacon soon, we would all be dead. We had enough food and water for a week, but the air supply was already degraded. I thought we would be lucky if it lasted another forty-eight hours. Zenzie might never wake up. She was probably the lucky one.

Eshaan was in charge of supplies. It was busy dishing out a ration of water when a small murmur from the medical cot made us all look that way. Sure enough, Zenzie was stretching. She was awake.

In an instant we were all surrounding her. She blinked up at us, relaxed but obviously confused. "What happened?"

"You don't remember?"

"Nothing. Why? What did I do?"

I smoothed her crest, which was quivering slightly. There was no point going any further with this if she truly remembered nothing. "You collapsed, is all. We don't really know why."

She frowned, the skin over her forehead crinkling with the effort. Then she gave a sigh of frustration. "No. No, I can't seem to ..."

"You don't remember anything about the Chakrans?" asked Didjal.

"The Chakrans? No! Should I?"

I gave her a few sips of water. It doesn't matter now. How are you feeling?"

She struggled to a seated position, propping herself up on her forearms. "Tired, for some reason. I can't think why I fainted. I ... I'm sorry."

"Never mind. You seem fine now."

"Did we manage to fix the tubing?"

Our silence gave her answer to that. Her face went blank. "I see. Then we are stuck here. Until ... until ..."

"Yes."

She stared around, before turning her eyes to me. "I have failed, failed in the Savior Protocols. I was meant to save your life, in exchange for mine. I apologize."

"Not your fault, kid. You can thank Dr. Vebor for that."

She looked slightly sick. "I still should have foreseen it."

"Don't beat yourself up. We may still get rescued. We are not out of time yet."

She stood up, shakily, and tried a few steps. Then she stopped. "I ... I feel different."

I moved towards her, just as she doubled over and vomited up a substantial amount of bile and water.

"Shells!" I leapt backwards, too late to prevent my clothes from being spattered.

Her mournful cat-like little face gazed up at me. "Sorry again."

I retreated more, fighting down my own nauseous reaction. "Not a problem. Why don't you lie back down?" I raised one eyebrow at Seyal. She nodded and gently pushed the Tyzaran girl until she was horizontal once more. "Time," Seyal told her severely. "You need time."

Zenzie's eyes were already closing again. "OK. Maybe I will rest a little longer ..." Moments later, she was fast asleep again.

I scrubbed at my shirt with a small amount of water still left in my ration cup. "Krikk! She could have aimed someplace else!"

Sammy was laughing. "Bit slow in your reaction there, Rye."

And suddenly it seemed the funniest thing that had ever happened. We were soon all hysterical. Lack of air, I guess. We laughed until it hurt, until the tears ran down our cheeks.

5

By the time help arrived we were past desperate. We had been sitting for a full week in a ship with increasingly stale air, getting hungrier and hungrier and more and more desperate. We were more than ready to be saved.

We had no way of knowing what sort of a ship it was that had answered our beacon. Our instruments had been affected by Vebor's sabotage, too. We were lucky the distress beacon had been on an independent circuit.

We heard metallic clunks as something coupled to the shuttle and the airlocks equalized to universal, then opened. We all stood as much to attention as we were then able.

A welcome smell of fresher air mingled with our stale atmosphere, unfortunately accompanied by three large Vaers. My spirits took an immediate dive. Jhaharada's law never disappointed.

Vaer Prime and Vaer Nova are large worlds on the North-Eastern side of the Great Shell. That's nearly five hundred light years away. There shouldn't have been a Vaer anywhere near our current position.

Vaers are of avian stock, though their beaks are foreshortened and curved downwards. The bottom part of the beak is more a mouth, which makes them appear almost more humanoid than avian. They are covered by patchy down along the face and neck, with feathers on the rest of their bodies. They walk on two feet. Rumor has it that they lost the ability to fly many centuries ago, though I wouldn't take a bet on that. They are bellicose, sly and dangerous. An adult male Vaer is twice the weight of a Spacelander.

Being natural predators, they are not your choice of aliens to meet out in space. It has been a long time since they needed to hunt other species for food outside the Vaer system. All the same, races like the Nepheal, who were decimated by the savage attacks of ancestors of the avians, do not forget how bloodthirsty they can be.

The first one drew out a tablet and pressed the record button. "We claim this ship as salvage," he said in a bored, business-as-usual voice. "Who is the captain of this shuttle?"

We looked around. Seyal met my gaze and gave me a small nod. I stepped forward. "I am."

"Do you wish to be rescued?"

"We do, yes."

"Are you fully aware that any rescue mission results in the rescuing ship being awarded full rights of all salvage?"

He meant that they would keep the *Rastin*. "I am not."

His sharp eyes flashed over his even-sharper beak. "Do you dispute this?"

"I do."

He grunted. "Then we are unable to help you."

I was restraining an impulse to lash out. He seemed to sense this, for he took a small step back before speaking again. "You have taken us out of our way for no good reason."

"Rescuing people is a good reason."

"We are merchants, working out of Vaer Nova. Our investors require profit."

That explained everything. These then came from the subgroup that had settled the outermost planet of Vaer. Vaer Nova had few natural resources. Over time, this had forced its inhabitants to find a different way of survival. They were practically pirates, from what I had heard, selling armament and weaponry to whoever came up with their price. I had heard many stories; none of them good. I wondered what nefarious business they could possibly be up to in this part of the Bifold Shell. It would be nothing altruistic. These guys were quite capable of putting a missile through *Rastin*, just to make sure nobody else got the bounty they thought they were entitled to. There was no way out of this.

I held up a hand. "No need to be so hasty, gentlemen. I am sure we can come to some agreement."

"Full salvage is agreed?"

I looked at Seyal. She gave a tiny shrug. She was leaving it up to me. I pressed my lips together. "It is."

The Vaer nodded. "Please give your full names and identifying codes."

We did. There was a moment while they consulted their off-site memory bank. The Vaer examined the screen closely. Then he wiped his beak a couple of times on his feathers. I was reminded of somebody sharpening a knife. "This is insufficient. Who is Mallivan Bell?"

I stepped forward again, my heart sinking.

His beak seemed almost to skewer me. "We will take your ship, the *Faraday*, as salvage too."

I was speechless. The Vaer turned to Eshaan and Didjal. "Your artwork is stored on Enifa. We will require the code for the vault, if you please."

Eshaan went so white I thought it was going to collapse. "Not the art," it stammered through its translator. "Please, not our art. It is our whole life!"

The Vaer regarded it down an imposing beak. "You are right. It is your artwork, or your life. We can leave you here floating in space if you prefer." The beak twitched slightly towards Eshaan's neck, one of the few parts of an Enif unprotected by the shiny tough carapace. Zenzie shivered and her crest spiked.

I took a step forwards, but Didjal was already standing alongside Eshaan, skin rippling in a soothing way as it tried to calm its partner. "Hush, Eshaan. We must do this. There is time to create further legacies."

Eshaan pushed it away. "There isn't. You know there isn't."

The Vaer was regarding the others with disgust. "Unfortunately the rest of you have nothing of interest to us. I am tempted to save only those who have paid their way." His acute avian sight examined Zenzie. "You are Tyzaran. That is unusual."

"I have nothing to give you."

The Vaer's eyes clouded as he consulted through his implanted chip. "Yes. You are no longer part of the Tyzaran census. Very strange. I am wondering whether to keep you. You may be worth money to us."

His eyes flickered back to me, catching my reaction. "You don't wish us to keep her? Or the other two Spacelanders? Very well. But I will require you to sign a binding document, giving us full ownership of both the *Faraday* and this shuttle." He indicated Seyal. "Can she write?"

Zenzie translated. Seyal nodded shyly.

"Good. She will sign the *Rastin* cession as well. I see it was deeded to her by her late husband, although there seems to be some doubt as to the validity of that document. Just in case. I like to have everything clear. Unequivocal, as you say." He gave a supercilious smirk. "Just to avoid future litigation. It has happened in the past."

The Vaer casually reached down with his beak to smooth down an errant feather, clearly very pleased with himself. "Good. You will now all accept my conditions and agree both verbally and in writing. This ship is heading for Triaris, in the Landau Rift. I trust that will be acceptable?"

There was nothing left to do but nod dimly. We had our lives, but it seemed we were to be left with little else.

The Vaer Ship took the crippled Avarak shuttle into their main hold. They left a skeleton crew, spare parts and enough tubing to effect emergency repairs on the *Rastin*, while we were escorted out onto the cruiser and led to a selection of cabins in the aft of the ship, all set off a wide corridor. Our corridor was separated from the rest of the ship by a heavy fire hatch. This hatch was closed and there was a Vaer posted on the other side in case we got through. Sammy was helped along by Seyal. He was limping badly due to the insufficient treatment. However, he was in good spirits.

"At least I am out of that triage chamber, Rye! I don't think I could have stood the itching for much longer anyway."

Zenzie, who had recovered from her ordeal, was looking worried. "I am sorry you have lost your family ship, Ryler Mallivan Bell."

I was still in shock. I had signed away my whole livelihood. *Faraday* was a family asset that was not strictly just mine. My mother had bankrolled the ship, and I still owed her a small fortune. It had been in my name because she trusted me to pay her back in full. My mind was trying to shy away from what had just happened. It was a huge problem.

I wasn't sure if she would expect me to return the money, under the circumstances. But even if I didn't, it would be taking money that by rights belonged to my sister Sibeal, too. And what about my children? My assets also partly belong to them, even though I rarely see them.

I suppose that bit about the children sounds strange. If you are a Flatlander you might find our system hard to understand. But Spacelanders have to be careful. There are not all that many of us, and we have high-risk jobs. At the start of our exodus into the Landau Rift, interbreeding was deemed to be a real problem. Nowadays, that problem has been solved. We all donate gametes when we reach eighteen. On our coming of age, we are required by the Space Trust to travel to the headquarters of the Genetic Institute on Zenubi. The donated material is used, after to a careful bloodline analysis, to engender artificially conceived future generations. In my generation we are still trying to consolidate the Rift, so each Spacelander is parent to six children.

I was no different, having spent a fortnight on Zenubi eight years ago. Of my six, three are being brought up in my family, under my mother's strict supervision, on the family shipstation *Bellaris*. The other three became the responsibility of the female donor and her family. I believe my co-parent is a girl from Sagrest, on the other side of the Landau Rift.

The loss of *Faraday* was making me feel shaky and unwell. The two Enif were also subdued. Their situation was probably even worse than mine. They had just lost their whole life's work.

We didn't trust the Vaer crew, either. They were clearly taking some kind of contraband to Triaris and it wouldn't have been completely out of character for them to throw us all out of the nearest airlock, despite promises given. So we maintained a low profile, keeping to our corridor and accepting their rather repulsive food and scant water with no complaints. We had little choice; the burly Vaer guard left outside the hatch was at least twice my bulk, and considerably taller than me. I would bounce off him like a tennis ball on a racquet.

Zenzie caught me staring through the plexiglass at him one day.

"Are you thinking of attacking?"

I shook my head. "Not worth it. I wouldn't win."

"I owe you a ship."

That did surprise me. "No you don't. Why would you?"

"You gave it up to stop them from keeping me here."

I turned away. "We don't yet know that they won't keep you anyway."

"They won't. I am more trouble than I am worth, I can assure you. They know that. I may not live on Tyzar anymore, but I am still Tyzaran. And we don't take lightly to our people being held captive." She frowned. "Why are you laughing?"

Mel slapped my arm. I jumped. I hadn't realized she was standing just behind us. "He agrees about you being more trouble than you are worth."

I gave her a slight warning push back. "Not at all."

"Sure, Rye. Whatever."

Zenzie was hurt. "Is that true?" she asked me in a little voice.

I shook my head as I walked away. There was no way I was going to answer that one. Zenzie was a lot of trouble, but she had also got us out of some scrapes. I was getting used to having her around. And I definitely wasn't planning on keeping her. She should be back in school, on Tyzar. Waiting for her flesh to grow into that wrinkled skin of hers. Giving unwanted advice to all her little schoolmates. Which she would.

I walked straight into Sammy, who nearly fell over, grabbing my shoulders to steady himself. He gave me a knowing look. "Problems?"

I pulled a face. "No-o-o."

"You don't sound convinced."

"It's just that I don't know what will happen to Zenzie if – when – I give her back. Will her parents simply accept her again? If so, then my duty is clear. But I can't send her back if she is going to suffer any kind of punishment."

He stroked his chin. "No. No, you are right. Tell you what, I have a Spacelander friend who works on the Spacelander Trade Center on Tyzar. How about I ask her to find out what Tyzaran law has to say on the matter?"

"Would you? Thanks. That would be a weight off my mind."

"Sure, Rye. No problem. I'll contact Neema." He gestured around him. "Course, it'll have to wait till we get back to some sort of civilization."

"How are you, Sammy? Does it still hurt?"

"Hardly at all." I could see how unsteady he still was. I suspected he was in a certain amount of pain, but every time I asked him he denied it bravely. "Getting better every day."

I doubted that too, but gave him a pleased smile and a quick shake of his shoulders.

"Rye?"

I turned back to him. His ears had gone pink. Now that was interesting. I tilted my head on one side. "What?"

"I, err... I don't know if you know, but ... well ... you know ..."

Zenzie popped up in front of him. "He is trying to tell you he has feelings for Mel." She crossed her arms in front of her bony chest and looked pleased with herself.

Both Sammy and I gaped. Sammy, redder than ever. Me, truly surprised. When we were kids he had been wont to refer to her as 'Smelly Melly'.

He cleared his throat. "You don't mind, do you?"

"Mind? Why should I?"

"Well, you are sort of the head of the group. Our ... our leader, I guess."

I thought about that. The two Enif were much older than I was, as was Seyal, but none of them seemed to have aspirations to take over as leader. That did put me firmly in charge of this mismatched group. Even so, it was a bit of a stretch for Sammy to think he needed any sort of permission from me to date Mel. They had both had their statutory six children, so there could be no objection to a short-term liaison. Such things are relatively normal among those Spacelanders who still retain a sexual drive. Shipboard flirtations don't usually last long. Space is so big that it tends to tear people apart. With no question of forming a family unit together, love tends to fizzle out after a while. We miss our children and all tend to drift back to our shipstations, literally worlds apart from each other. I also wondered how they would cope with Mel's claustronetia.

"No. That's fine, Sammy. I am glad for you both. Thank you for letting me know."

He shrugged, a little sheepishly. "Thought you should."

"Sure. I appreciate it. That's great." It wasn't. It was another complication that could cause problems. Sammy would now automatically try to protect Mel, and I wasn't sure that such concern wouldn't send her backwards instead of forwards. She had been improving, overcoming her shaking fears. I hoped she wouldn't duck behind Sammy now. That would be a pity.

I tried to give him a smile, but it felt a little empty. Zenzie gave me a strange look. She walked away with me.

"You are not pleased," she told me. "Why? Do you like Mel yourself?"

"No! Not like that, anyway. And stop following me around. It is none of your damn business!"

I could hear her chuntering as I walked away. Something about people getting too big for their space boots. *She* could talk!

I was two paces away from her when the relative peace shattered. There was a violent blow against the port side of the spaceship, and all hell broke loose.

I was thrown against the bulkhead and from there onto the floor.

Not again!

I was beginning to feel like a piece of flotsam. I felt around and found Zenzie's ankle with my hand. I grabbed it and held on. None of us had any clue what was happening. I was aware of smoke pouring into our corridor and of the hatch unsealing as the guard barreled in.

I shook my head, trying to clear the feeling of cloudiness. Something was hammering at the back of my skull, but I needed my brain to concentrate on survival and not a passing pain. I squinted along the few meters I could still make out.

Sammy and Seyal were within reach, both trying to pick themselves up off the steel-plated floor. Neither of them appeared wounded; at least, not more than they already had been. I nodded to them and then pulled myself back to the cabins. The two Enif had been flung across their space, but were also fine. Mel had not been so lucky. She was covering her face with one hand, and blood was freely flowing down her cheek. I peered more closely. Her eye seemed all right. It looked like a superficial wound across the top part of her cheek. I hoped it looked worse than it was. That was a lot of blood.

I motioned to her to join me out in the corridor, and as a group, we edged out of the quarters we had been given and into the corridor. The whole structure around us shuddered again. The guard, who was looking troubled, mumbled through his beak. I turned to Zenzie, raising one eyebrow. She had admitted to speaking some words of Vaer. She never ceased to amaze me.

"Terrans, he is saying," she interpreted. "Come to stop the weapons getting through to the Avaraks."

Weapons. Well, that explained what the Vaers were doing in this part of the Major Shells. They would be taking as much advantage as they could of this war. War, for them, was opportunity.

I bit my lip. We hadn't come this far just to be eliminated by some Flatlander vessel. Unfortunately, it wasn't immediately clear to me what we could do to improve our chances of survival.

Zenzie knew, though. She stepped up to the Vaer guard, her small head barely reaching up to his wing bar. "We are not safe here. You should evacuate us to the main cargo hold of the ship. We would be safer there, nearer the centre of the ship."

All Vaers who travel outside their territory speak Universal. This guard was no exception. The Avian raised his gun in a threatening sort of way, but he hesitated.

"After all," Zenzie pressed home her advantage. "You need us all alive. Otherwise you won't get our ships and our possessions. Will you?"

His head tilted ever so slightly. He was considering. I hoped she was right. I suspected those things had already been claimed by the Vaer Captain.

She held up her hands. "But it is your decision, of course. You will know best what action to take."

Another shudder told us that we were still under fire. There was a huge impact, somewhere near to us, and everything stopped for a long second. Then more chunks of the bulkhead detached and hurtled past us, only just missing the guard.

His eyes widened. Then he moved to one side and gestured with his machine pistol. We were to precede him along another, larger corridor. This seemed to take us away from the skin of the ship, down into the more sheltered centre area.

Zenzie threw me a triumphant stare. I rolled my eyes.

We were ushered into the main cargo bay, to the accompaniment of further jolts and bangs as the Vaer ship was hit again and again. An Omnistate cruiser could have finished us off by now, had they wanted to. They hadn't, which seemed to confirm that they wanted whatever the ship was carrying. It would have been rather pleasing to see the pirates attacked, if we hadn't been sharing their space.

Our guard knew his job. He never took his eyes or his gun off us. And he was far too big for us to take down. Not without being shot.

I eyed the cargo. Sure enough, there were crates and crates of missiles and even ultrapulses. No wonder the Terrans were here. Ultrapulses were very effective and highly expensive weapons made by the Omnistate.

Then I spotted something else. One of the smaller crates was marked as Tyzaran pulsers. Those would come in very useful, if only we could somehow neutralize our guard.

So I waited, hoping for an opportunity. Zenzara had done what she could. Now it was my turn.

Only it wasn't. I noticed that Didjal and Eshaan were chattering away to each other, because I could see their skin undulating. What I didn't notice was a certain determination come over both of them. Eshaan edged towards one of the large crates as Didjal seemed to expand into the space.

Seyal had been watching them. Now she stepped forwards. "Bathroom," she shouted in Universal. "Me need bathroom!"

The guard shifted his attention to her. A few seconds later Eshaan had leapt onto the second story of the crates of weapons and was using the Enif strength it possessed to topple the crate nearest to the Vaer guard over.

The guard started to turn back.

Seyal walked towards him, arms spread apart, pregnant belly very visible in relief in the semi-darkness of the hold.

The guard's attention snapped back to her and he brought up his gun until it was pointing directly at her stomach. Both Sammy and Mel, who were on either side of Seyal, stepped forwards into the danger. Mel's cheek was still bleeding sluggishly, the red blood shimmering against the shadows.

The guard's eyes hardened. I saw him pull the stock tighter to his body to minimize recoil. He was about to shoot.

"Stop!" I shouted. Not that it would have any effect, but it seemed like a good thing to do at the time.

Then there was a slithering, creaky sound as the case Eshaan was pushing careened across the top of the one underneath it, reached the edge, tumbled over, accompanied by one destabilized Enif, and crashed into the guard.

The guard went down without a sound, followed by Eshaan, who tumbled on top of the Vaer, grabbing the gun and then landing nimbly on the deck plating of the hold. Eshaan turned the gun quickly on the guard, but there was no need. The guard had been struck on one side of his head and shoulder by the crate. He was still breathing, but there was no way he would be any sort of danger to us for a very long time.

"Well done, all of you! Arm yourselves," I shouted, as further impacts juddered into the ship, close to our position. "There! The pulsers!"

We jimmied the top of the crate in question open and passed out two of the weapons for each of us. I grabbed a first aid kit off the cargo bay wall and motioned to Mel. "Here! Let me do something about that!"

She sidled up. I pasted about ten butterfly stitches across the cut, as fast but as best I could. It was hard to stop the blood long enough for them to stick, but at least it stemmed the worst of the seepage.

Mel grabbed two of the guns. Her teeth were chattering, but I could see that this time she was determined to react well. She studiously avoided looking at Sammy, and I was glad for her. She'd do.

Just as I was feeling a little more optimistic about surviving, Zenzie gave a strange moan.

I twisted round to her, just in time to see her eyes flick upwards into her head. I reached her side in two steps so that I could support her as she sagged, unconscious. A brief examination showed no visible signs of injury, so I picked her up in my arms and set off after Didjal, the others following on behind us. We needed to get somewhere safer. The cargo hold with all the ammunition felt anything but safe. I had a very bad feeling about it.

Didjal was the one who seemed to be infused with action. It surged ahead of us, its naturally elongated tarsus bones making it look rather like a Paralympic runner. It was dragging a rather battered Eshaan behind it, and its expression was a mixture of pride and disapproval. Eshaan was the artist; it wasn't supposed to risk its life as it just had done.

I glanced behind. Mel and Sammy were bringing up the rear, Mel glued to one side of Sammy to help compensate for his limp. It had been improving, but was still a factor for him.

We pounded along behind the two Enif. Zenzara jolted in my arms, but the mad race against time didn't wake her. I noticed a strange pulse in her brow. I hadn't seen it before.

Didjal led us unerringly straight to the bridge. I am not sure I would have gone directly for the Vaer command center, but I was too busy making sure Zenzara wasn't left behind to even think of what Didjal was planning.

We burst through the hatch. As we did Didjal opened fire on the leading Vaer. Its pulser beam traversed the Vaer's leg, who then collapsed with something between a shriek and a squawk.

I ducked to clear the way for Mel. Eshaan's shot had missed one of the other two Vaers on the bridge, but Mel was more accurate. Her target went down without a sound. She had gone for the kill rather than to incapacitate. Only a few loose feathers dislodged by the fall moved after he thudded to the ground. Mel stared at her pulser, suddenly unsure.

Seyal erupted into the room, brandishing a pistol in a confused sort of way. She finally managed to loose off a shot, one that narrowly missed my left ear. She dropped the gun and an expression of horror froze her face. By that time Sammy had covered the third Vaer. He raised his winged arms hastily with another squawk.

It didn't really matter if there were more Vaers aboard. I signed to Mel and Sammy to cover the one entry hatch to the bridge area. Then I pulled back the engines and left the cruiser dead in space.

"Terran ship, please respond."

"Who is this?"

I explained what had happened and requested rescue from the Vaer ship. I was hoping this particular Terran cruiser was unaware of who we actually were. We had a Tyzaran citizen with us. I was betting they wouldn't want to leave her behind.

The Flatlander captain, who was a fairly amiable sort, didn't take too long to decide. "We can have the armament?" he asked gruffly.

"Sure. It isn't anything to do with us."

"Acceptable. Please try to remain where you are while I send a team to clean up any Vaer pirates and secure the cruiser."

We breathed a sigh of relief. Nobody had been looking forward to mopping up Vaers. "Agreed."

All the same, I took possession of all the arms we could find on the bridge. We might still need them. Eshaan found a sort of duffel bag one of the Vaers had been using to stash money. He showed it to us. Around 35000 Universal credits. Enough to buy us a hotel room for a few weeks. No more. We sequestered that, too. Mel checked the rest of the bridge, but we found no more money. Pity.

The Vaer who had surrendered had a smile on his beak. "You are too late."

I glared. "For what?"

"Your ships have already been sold on. You lost title anyway."

"They were taken illegally."

"So sue us."

My black mood came back very suddenly. The Vaer was right. There was no truly interstellar court. No right of rebuttal. Nothing that all the species would abide by. A heavy feeling hit my stomach. My finger tightened on the trigger. I would very much have liked to shoot him.

Didjal pushed my gun barrel down. "And our artwork?"

The Vaer smirked. "That went first. It was taken out of the vault yesterday. We got the original patterns, too."

Eshaan touched Didj. Their skin rippled as they communicated. Finally Didj nodded. "Cards cannot be unshuffled. Entropy is part of the universe." It looked infinitely sad. "But it is a blow to our idea of self." The two Enif rippled a little more. "A great blow."

Their faces said it all. Mine must have reflected theirs.

A tall Terran appeared at the entrance to the hatch. Sammy and Mel ushered him onto the bridge.

He introduced himself as Commander Renfell, from the Sol cruiser *Sentinel*. "Thank you very much. We thought we would have to destroy this vessel completely. Recouping the stolen weapons is a bonus. We will gladly drop you off at the next stop we make."

"We need to go to Tyzar." I stepped forwards, Zenzara still in my arms. "There is something wrong with this girl and she needs medical attention from her own people. She must have treatment. Immediately."

He spread his hands. "Tyzar is a very long way away. But I'll do what I can. I will arrange for the Tyzarans to be contacted as soon as we are away from here. They may have a ship in the area."

"That would be great. Thank you. You have ansible communication, then?"

Rendell looked uncomfortable. Flatlanders did not have permission to purchase Tyzaran ansible technology, but with so many now being dispersed through the Major Shells it did not surprise me in the least that they had it. "We have. It is an older model, and takes up a good deal of room, but it does have subspace capabilities."

It had to have been stolen from either the Nepheals or the Tyzarans. I didn't think anybody else had it. The Nepheal ansible system was reserved for their own ships. The Nepheals did not generally trade technology and were zealous about security, so it was unlikely to be one of theirs. The Tyzarans did trade technology, usually when it had already become obsolete, but they never traded with either the Omnistate or the Vaers. The rest of the races were only just now buying ansible nodes, and the ones that were available were still quite bulky and extremely expensive. They took up a complete console and were a nightmare to fit. Not only that, but the Tyzarans had to approve your suitability to own one. The things had become a bit of a status symbol. My own family had only just been able to invest in one and my mother had rather preened herself when permission was granted.

I felt relieved. There had to be a Tyzaran ship somewhere in the quadrant, and Tyzaran ships would be bound to have Tyzaran doctors on board. I hoped. At least, there would be somebody who knew more than we did about Zenzie's state.

"That would be fine." I offered my hand. "What are you planning to do with this cruiser?"

He proffered his own hand and we shook. "We'll let them go. The Omnistate has signed a treaty with the Vaers. Even though this bunch are mere pirates, we don't want to give them any reason to pull out of that treaty. They have agreed to remain neutral in this dispute."

"The holdful of ultrapulses says something else."

"These are just pirates. Traders, they call it. If we stop one lot, another just pops up in their place. They go where the profit is. They take neutral to mean they can annex ships in distress and traffic with armament. It is their way of life." He nodded casually to the Vaer who had been captured, and the Captain, who was still huffing as he tried to stop the blood flowing from the wound in its leg. "No hard feelings?"

The Captain bared his beak. "Drop dead!"

"See? True allies!" He winked at me. "Enemy of my enemy and all that."

"Might still kill you."

"Oh, sure. I would have put an end to *them* if they hadn't given up the stolen ultrapulses. But it's nothing personal."

I was looking at the Captain. I could tell that the Avian was taking it very personally. I hoped we didn't have to deal with him again. It seemed to me that he wasn't taking this small reverse very well. I looked at the chair he had been sitting in. His name was set into the metalwork. Captain Frynee.

Frynee was glaring at all of us through dark slitty eyes of hatred. But there was a glint of triumph when they contemplated the Enif, Seyal and me. He knew that the money he had made on our possessions was assured. Until the law changed, the chances of our getting anything back hovered firmly around the zero mark.

Renfell took a step or two back and began to speak on his comlink. Another of the Flatlander officers stepped up to the navigation station and began to upload information from it. Frynee's expression went even blacker.

After around half-an-hour, a group of Terrans came up to the bridge, ushering several Vaers before them, the Vaers looking unhappy. They shuffled ignominiously inside the small area, trying to avoid the dagger-like gaze of their captain, who was still smoldering and giving the impression that they should have fought to the death. He reminded me of Captain Tevis. Do as I say and not as I do. Yet not all Captains, not all races, were like that. The Avarak Captain had been the first to sacrifice himself.

It had become very cramped inside the limited bridge area, so we were evacuated onto the *Sentinel* while the officers organized the transfer of the weapons cache.

Our new quarters were small but functional. Wonderfully, we had a shower between the seven of us. Mel took one look at it, dropped her gun where she stood, elbowed the rest of us aside and stepped into the cubicle. The door closed firmly behind her. Seyal moved closer to the door, subtly staking her claim. It seemed that the rest of us would simply have to wait.

Commander Renfell was soon back. "I have located a Tyzaran ship some light years away. They have given us a tentative rendezvous point in six hours." He frowned. "Though they were reluctant to give us their current position, and were not showing up on our scans, which is rather strange."

It would be, except I suspected that the Tyzaran ship would be equipped with the new ZEPH drive. If they were, they could be as far as 40 light years away, and still be able to meet that deadline. The ZEPH drive was able to propel ships at nearly 8 light years per hour, according to Zenzara. Personally, I was at a loss to visualize how it could be done. I just hoped that they would get here soon enough for Zenzie. That she would be all right.

She was still unconscious, but I had noticed that the small pulse on her forehead had calmed again. Still, there was little sign of her awakening any time soon. Seyal was now hovering over her. The Avarak woman seemed deeply worried by her charge's condition.

Renfell asked us to tell him about our encounter with the Vaer, and nodded grimly when he heard that we had been coerced into signing away assets to them. "This is not the first time they have done such a thing. Some of our own Terran forces have had their assets seized in a similar manner. The Omnistate say that none of them have ever been returned. They regard the Vaers from Nova as a serious problem to be dealt with in the future. However, they have been very clear that, as things stand right now, there is no possibility of recuperating assets signed away to them."

I sighed and, very reluctantly, asked for permission to hololink with the Landau Rift. This was granted. Minutes later, I was standing in the holo alcove, talking to my mother. I was sweating. Don't get me wrong; I love my mother. But she is the most rigid, controlling person I have ever met. When her older brother was still alive he could sometimes change her mind. Since his inopportune demise, she was about as malleable as a steel crowbar.

"Ryler! I have been concerned about you. We heard of the attack on *Commorancy*. I hope you are uninjured?"

"I am, now. Err ... I am afraid I have bad news, all the same."

Her eyebrows snapped together. "What have you done?"

I knew that tone. It was the one that had always made me feel around one foot high. It had been a while since I had heard it, though. I swallowed. "I ... I ...."

"What?" There was none of the pleasure showing in her face now. She looked about as frosty as a high mountain in an arctic gale.

"I have lost *Faraday*."

Her tension relaxed. "Of course you haven't. You left her here, remember? For a refit? She is almost ready. I was hoping to order space trials tomorrow..." Her confident voice trailed off as she spotted my expression.

"I was obliged to sign her away to the Vaers."

My mother's mouth opened and closed a couple of times, but no sound came out. She swayed and put a hand on the console beside her to steady herself.

"I'm sorry. I ... I had no choice."

Now she had flushed bright red. "I can't imagine what would possess you to do such a thing. Have you gone completely mad?"

I reached out a hand to touch her, but my holo image simply passed through her own apparent solidity. All the same, she flinched away. "Explain yourself!"

"I cannot. I signed the papers. We had no choice. I am not the only one to lose a substantial asset."

"A substantial asset! You talk as though we could afford to lose *Faraday*! We can't!"

"I am deeply sorry. But I repeat, Mother: I had no choice."

"I find that very hard to believe." She stiffened. "Well, you needn't think you can come home and find other ships at your disposal. There aren't any. You can find your own way from here on in."

That hurt. She didn't want to hear the circumstances. It was a devastating rejection. As if the fragile familial bond between us had evaporated altogether. I had hoped for some small measure of understanding, but it seemed I was not to be allowed to give an explanation of the situation. She had just assumed the worst of me.

A spark of defiance flared up deep inside me. It fanned a sudden intuition that I would never to go back to Mallivan. "Fine. I won't. However, you will please remove all my personal belongings from the ship as quickly as possible. The bailiffs will no doubt arrive very soon. They already went to Enifa."

"Enifa? Whatever have the Enif to do with this?"

"Mother, just do it. I have many private documents on board *Faraday*. Oh! And please ... can someone get Scout off the ship? I will pick him up as soon as I can."

"Now you want me to look after a pet Geiga? On top of everything else?"

"Scout will not cause any trouble. He is ship-trained, after all."

"It's a Geiga. How trained can a Geiga be?"

I wasn't about to get into a discussion about the finer points of keeping Geigas. She was never going to agree with me on that subject. She thought they were vermin. Their finer points had never impressed her, despite the loyalty they could show.

I had had Scout for nearly three years. There was no way I was going to let the Vaers take him. They would probably eat the poor thing. It was unthinkable. "Let me talk to Sibby, Mother. She will take care of him for me. After all, she has been feeding him every day since I've been away."

My sister must have been listening to the conversation from the other side of the room, because she broke in. Her eyes were moist, but there was no hesitation. "Of course I will, Mall. No problem. I will go clear the ship immediately. And don't worry about Scout. I will make sure he's okay."

I felt a glow of warmth. Sibby, at least, would know that something had happened to make me sign away *Faraday*. My sister and I had always been close.

I softened my tone. "Thank you, Sibby. I knew I could count on you. Take care of him for me, will you? And take care of yourself."

"I promise. You all right?"

"Sure. I can't talk more now."

"OK, Mall. Love you."

"Love you too."

As the hololink faded I saw my mother glowering at my sister. Not that Sibby would care about that. She would know what to do.

I passed the hololink on to the two Enif. Both were dejected. They weren't looking forward to giving explanations to their families on Enifa either. Seyal had passed on the possibility of contacting anyone on her home planet. She had sniffed and patted her bulging tummy. I don't think she felt any ties to Rhyveka anymore. She seemed happier with us. From what I knew of Avarak society, I couldn't blame her for that.

6

The Tyzaran ship was waiting as the *Sentinel* dropped out of space in front of her. We thanked Commander Renfell and made our way from one ship to the other as soon as the interspace docking link was secured.

I carried Zenzara through the serpentine tubing, Seyal trotting worriedly at my side. I hadn't seen the ship from the outside, but judging from the cavernous passageway, it was huge.

There were several crew members standing to attention, with three officers waiting in front of them. As soon as they caught sight of Zenzara in my arms, two of them stepped very smartly forwards.

"What happened to her?" The younger of the two glared at me.

"It wasn't my fault!" I let them take her from me. She was placed carefully on a gurney and as they rolled her away we all tried to follow.

The tallest of the officers stopped neatly in our path. "Please to follow me. Zenzara Zylarian is in good hands. It would be useful if you could tell us what happened to her." He made gestures to follow him. "We can do that while you eat and drink something. You will require refreshments after your journey."

No kidding. We had spent the last days on the edge of starvation. I had almost forgotten what it was like to truly enjoy food.

"Welcome to the research vessel *Aurynth*. I am very pleased to meet you." He looked around with interest. "My name is Denaraz. I am the spokesdesignate aboard."

The ship didn't look exactly like a research vessel, but I wasn't about to complain about that. I introduced him to my companions.

He nodded his greetings. "Tell me about Ty Zylarian."

I let Didjal explain to him what had happened to Zenzie on the outside hull of the shuttle. The Tyzaran asked me to tell him exactly what I had witnessed when I had joined them outside the ship.

I tried to repeat it verbatim. His face froze as I told him her words. "Chyzar?" He looked stunned. "Are you sure you heard that word?"

"That is what I understood, certainly."

"Please excuse me." He got up so quickly that he knocked over the chair he had been sitting in. "Err ... eat as much as you would like. I ... I will be back shortly."

He left the cafeteria at a run. We stared after him. Sammy immediately reached for one of the sugar-dusted delicacies. "What? Eat as much as you like, the man said. I'm just being a good guest."

He stuffed the whole cake in his mouth and chewed with obvious enjoyment. That was all it took. The scene deteriorated very quickly into the nearest thing to a food orgy I had ever seen. Even our resident Avarak female joined in. We were soon feeling full, and very content. Nothing like sugar to take the edge off your problems.

Tyzarans kept poking their heads around the door and staring at us. We had obviously leapt to semi-celebrity status on the *Aurynth*. We smiled at the visitors and waved them in. None of them joined us however. There was a buzz of excitement on the ship that we couldn't quite understand.

Around an hour later a young crew member actually got all the way through the door. "I have been asked to take you to your quarters," he told us. "—if you would like to follow me."

I stood up. "We would like to see Zenzara first, if that is possible. How is she?"

He looked scared. "She is still being treated. However, I believe that she is responding well. Spokesdesignate Denaraz will visit you in your rooms shortly. He is in attendance with Ty Zylarian at the current time."

We could hardly have forced our way into their sickbay, even if we had known where it was. We did the next best thing: follow placidly in the spaceman's wake and try to settle ourselves into what were very sumptuous quarters. I took advantage of their water showers, and dressed myself in the soft garments left out. My crusted old clothes went into the washing chute. I could get used to living like this.

We were all billeted in the same general area, with a small lounge common to all our rooms. That was where Spokesdesignate Denaraz found us.

He came in dressed in a captain's uniform, together with two other officers.

We stared at him, scared to ask how Zenzie was. His face seemed very solemn. The Tyzarans came to a halt in front of us and they bowed very slightly. It was not a subservient thing at all. In fact, I got the impression it was to reaffirm their own importance, their own consequence.

Mel was unaffected. "Are you going to stare at us all day?"

Denaraz coughed. "I apologize. She is well. In recovery."

"There will be no lasting effects?" I frowned, aware that he was holding something back.

"Oh, there will be lasting effects. She will never be the same again."

Seriously? He thought that was useful? I contemplated knocking his teeth down his throat.

Maybe I grunted; I don't know. The man looked at me. He knew exactly what I was thinking.

His nose twitched in dislike and he tutted slightly, which didn't help. "We believe that Ty Zylarian was visited by a Chakran."

"Yeah. That is what she said. But what does it mean?"

He gave me a pitying look. "You *do* know what Chakrans are?"

"Of course I know what ... well, I know about the legend of the ..." I sighed. "Why don't you tell me?" He would anyway. I could see it in his face.

He seemed to enlarge. He was going to talk for a long time. I glanced at Sammy. His eyes had glazed over too. I yawned a bit, turning it into a cough.

The Tyzaran didn't notice. He was still in the introductory stage. "… So, the Chakran entity or entities—nobody is sure which, although there has been much research on Tyzar about precisely that point, are pure quantum beings. They consist of individual cells, tiny cells, which although separated by hundreds or thousands of light years in spacetime, can communicate just like cells in our own bodies do. Of course, for centuries it was believed that they were not real. Indeed some species – the more backward ones," he looked meaningfully at Sammy, who stiffened, "still find it hard to credit their existence. We, the Tyzarans, are aware of them because on occasions they have been known to communicate with us. Naturally such communication is on a different level to what you, as Spacelanders, would have experienced. These are beings attuned to the vacuum energy, aware of life at the Planck-level scale. They are not about to discuss their favorite dish on the lunch menu." He paused and Mel managed a suitably toned laugh. He inclined his head in her direction before going on. "On very rare occasions Tyzarans have been affected by a Chakran cell. Some of these people have gone on to claim that the Chakrans can communicate with them. Historically this was not found to be credible. For many generations they were simply thought to be extremely eccentric, indeed, in many cases, deranged."

"What has this to do with Zenzara?"

"*Ty* Zylarian." He emphasized the honorific Ty, used generically for Tyzarans of any importance. He didn't like me using her given name, and he didn't like the interruption. "If you will allow me to finish …"

I felt another yawn coming on. "Please do."

"As I was saying, only in a handful of cases have the hosts honored in this way been able to understand what the Chakrans were trying to convey. The last to successfully do this lived over two hundred Sol years ago. Such Tyzarans who can communicate with Chakrans are known as Chyzars. They are addressed always by the honorific title

'Chy'. Chy Saphezzaraz was our last Chyzar."

"Zenzara is now a Chyzar?"

He gave me a patronizing look. "Zenzara has absorbed a Chakran atom. This indicates that she will probably become a Chyzar, although only around one individual every four hundred of your Sol standard years does so."

"Is she in any danger? How could one small atom or molecule have such an effect on her?"

"There is always a period of adaptation. The weakness occurs because the Chakrans are attempting to force compatibility. The atom must be isolated by the host, and neural interconnections woven around it. Such connections are tenuous and difficult to interpret. There is about a fifty percent success rate. In Chy Saphezzaraz's case, it took ten years before the Nexus was able to form in his mind and he was able to act as a conduit for the Chakran conscience."

I blinked. "Zenzara will be like this for ten years?"

He permitted himself a small smile. "No, no. She will be up and about within a few days. She is young, and we now know what measures work in such cases. It is only the initial shock which causes the organism to reset itself. She needed several massive doses of a specific type of kinase injection, and she will have to take such injections regularly for the rest of her life. But it may be many years before it is known whether she is going to become a Chyzar or not."

"So there are no other Tyzarans going through this same process at the moment?"

"There are not. Nor have there been for centuries. Ty Zylarian is ... special."

This would be the perfect excuse to stop her from following me all over the universe, at least. It seemed probable that the Tyzarans would want to keep her as close to them as possible. From his tone, it was obvious that the man in front of me considered these Chyzars as almost mystical beings. I felt better. Zenzara would be safe and well-cared for. I need have no misgivings. I grinned at Denaraz.

"Can we see her?"

He hesitated. "You may, I suppose. It is true that she has been asking after you. I hope I can rely on you not to overtax her."

"Of course."

He ushered us in front of him and we were escorted up a long straight corridor, finally entering a pristine medical bay.

Zenzara was stretched out on a grey hospital cot, attended by a large group of Tyzaran medical staff. She was awake, but clearly rather groggy.

I walked up to the bed and she reached out to touch my arm. I frowned down at her. It had felt like a warning. Sure enough, her eyes, almost lost in the worried folds of flesh surrounding them, were telegraphing something to me.

I perched on the side of the cot. "Zenzara. How are you?"

"I am fine, thank you, Ryler Mallivan Bell. I will soon be well enough to travel with you again."

"Yes. About that ..."

I was aware of another small movement of the girl on the cot, at the same time as the tallest of the Tyzarans present spoke out severely.

"Chy Zenzara will of course be staying with her people now. Things have changed."

There was an approving mutter from the doctors and nurses around the bed.

I opened my mouth. "Of course, I ... ouch!"

Zenzara, Chy or not, had kicked me. Her small voice sounded out clearly in the resultant hush. "Nothing has changed. The Savior Protocols may not be put aside just because I may or may not have become a Chyzar!"

The female Tyzaran who had spoken before stiffened. "Chyzars have always lived on Tyzar! Unthinkable that one wouldn't!"

"Well, this one won't ... can't."

"Can't?"

"My first obligation is to care for Mallivan Bell. The Protocols are more than clear on this."

I looked over at the tall Tyzaran woman. Her crest was almost perpendicular to her skull. She glared in my direction. "I shall take this to council!"

"Of course." Zenzie was prepared to be magnanimous. I could tell that she thought she had won.

Her opponent gave a small shake of her head. "Unthinkable!" she muttered under her breath. "A Chyzar out there in open space!" She gave an involuntary shiver of distaste.

Zenzie bristled. "Chyzars don't *have* to be restricted to their compounds forever, you know."

"It has always been that way." The thin lips compressed.

I was beginning to see where Zenzie was going with this. She was not the type to be shut up indoors to commune with the universe. Especially if she would be surrounded by Tyzarans like this one. No wonder she was prepared to fight to stay with me. She figured I would offer looser constraints.

I could have spoken out. Perhaps I should have. But I did feel a little sorry for her. She hadn't asked for any of this, and I really couldn't bear to see her shut away in some sort of gilded cage for the rest of her days. She might be a whole heap of trouble, but she certainly didn't deserve that.

So I kept my mouth firmly closed, earning a grateful smile and another small squeeze on my forearm from the patient.

I got up. There could be no candid conversation in front of this gaggle of Tyzaran staff. "Get well soon, Zenzara Zylarian."

"I intend to, Ryler Mallivan Bell. You will not be kept waiting here for long."

I must have frowned again, for the pleading expression came back into her eyes.

I sighed. "Very well."

"Thank you." Her eyes flickered around the rest of us. Everyone had wanted to see how she was. "Thank you all."

We shuffled out of the room, glad to escape. There was a silence between us as we made our way back to the area reserved for us. I think we were all feeling sorry for Zenzie. It couldn't be much fun to be surrounded by twenty or thirty people all your waking hours. Not something anyone would enjoy. No wonder she was railing against being confined on Tyzar for the rest of her life. It was hardly something to look forward to.

But we never made it back to our reserved area. Spokesdesignate Denaraz intercepted us. Mel, who was in the lead, stopped abruptly.

The Tyzaran man inclined his head, managing to look imposing. "I wish to speak to you, Mallivan Bell. About Zenzara Zylarian."

"Speak."

"Perhaps this would be better ... ah ... alone?"

"Perhaps not."

His crest twitched. But he smiled as though he weren't affected by my response, giving a slow nod. "As you wish."

"I am listening, Spokesdesignate. Please go on."

"I think there may have been some slight misunderstanding here. About what the Savior Protocols really entail."

"Really? A misunderstanding? In what way?"

"As you know, Tyzarans have some convoluted laws. In fact, many of them are not applicable to aliens such as yourself. We may have been ... hasty in telling Zenzara Zylarian that she would be bound by the Savior Protocols."

"I see." I could sense where this was going. Now she was a Chyzar, they were retrenching. She had suddenly become a valuable commodity. One they had practically given away to an alien. No wonder they were feeling ambivalent about their previously unbreakable Savior Protocols.

"You mustn't feel you are bound by our laws. How could that be? It would not be at all logical would it?" Denaraz saw my raised eyebrow, for he hurried on. "We would not wish you to be ... inconvenienced ... by our local rules and regulations." He stopped to take a deep breath. "I have been authorized to tell you that we do not consider you bound by the Protocols, and that you can safely leave Zenzara here with us. She will be well taken care of, I assure you."

This was exactly what I had been wanting to hear. But something had changed. It wasn't that I thought Zenzie would be more useful now she was a Chyzar. It was the pleading look she had thrown me in that hospital cot, surrounded by all those fellow-countrymen of hers. She had been scared, and I found that I couldn't leave her to a fate she clearly didn't want.

I pursed my lips. "You surprise me." I was looking over at Sammy as I spoke, wondering if he had spoken to the friend he had on Tyzar yet.

Sammy grimaced, but tilted his head slightly in Mel's direction. I looked at her. Mel stepped forwards. Rules and regulations. Of course. Her forte.

"Codex 452 of the Tyzar Authority Civil Legislation states that Savior Protocols, once instigated, cannot be withdrawn. Any attempt to so do would be in direct contravention of the Codex and punishable by imprisonment of up to twenty years on Tyzar."

I spread my hands apart. "You see? I'm afraid I am not willing to risk imprisonment. No, everything will simply have to stay as it is. Sorry."

Spokesdesignate Denaraz seemed discomfited. He tried another smile. "I don't think you understand. Perhaps I didn't explain well. Why don't we discuss this further?"

"No, no. It is kind of you to think of helping me. But I couldn't take the risk. And she really isn't so much of a bother. None at all, come to think of it. But I thank you for your concern."

We walked on, finally reaching the relative sanctuary of our rest area. Eshaan shut the door firmly behind him, leaving the Tyzaran man on the other side with an arrested look on his face.

Didjal was the first to speak. "They are not going to give up. They will want to keep Zenzara here."

Mel turned to me. "We can't let them do that, Rye. You saw how scared she was! They will put her in some sort of cage for the rest of her life. We must do something about it!"

"Well done with that Codex regulation, Mel. How come you know about Tyzar laws?"

She reddened. "Sammy told me you wanted him to contact his Spacelander friend on Tyzar, so I spent a little time researching their laws on Savior Protocols when we arrived here. I have a good memory for that sort of thing and I thought it might come in handy."

"It did." I turned to Sammy. "What about your friend? Would she be able to counsel us?"

He nodded briefly. "Neema? Maybe. She has a legal background. Except any calls we make may be monitored."

"That's true." I let my eyes flicker over the rest of the group. "What's the matter, Seyal?" She was looking dubious.

"I do not think these aliens will allow Zenzie to accompany us. I think they will stop us."

"By force?"

She inclined her head.

Didjal stepped forwards. "Then we must make a plan."

I grinned, which disconcerted the Enif.

"Did I say something funny?"

"No. I just realized that, somewhere on our journey, we became a unit."

Didjal communed for a moment with Eshaan. This appeared to be news to them, too. Finally their skin stopped vibrating. I waited for the result.

"Yes. It is true. The seven of us have become loyal to each other."

Loyal. An out-of-date word. But something certainly had bound us together. We might be a diverse batch of souls, but our destinies had become intertwined.

"So," Eshaan stretched out its dark digits and examined them.

"What are we going to do about Zenzara?"

"I don't know. But we can't let the Tyzarans shut her up for decades, for sure."

Mel stared at me. "You do realize we are 'guests' on a spaceship, don't you? I mean, we can hardly just walk out the back door."

"I know. I guess we'll have to wait until we reach wherever it is we seem to be going."

Seyal inclined her head. "Tyzar."

My face must have shown my surprise. "Their home world? Are you sure?"

The Avarak woman gave what was almost a grin. "I overheard two of the crew members talking. They think I cannot understand Universal. A compound near their main city is to be prepared for Zenzara."

Mel rubbed her eyes. She was tired. "Well, unless you can fly, Seyal, I don't see how we can stop the Tyzarans from taking her to Tyzar. After all, we are all on their ship. And she *is* one of them."

Seyal flushed. She was so self-effacing that she didn't even like us all to look at her at the same time.

I tried to divert attention away from her. "I don't think she is, not anymore." I lifted my chin in Mel's direction. "You said it yourself; Article 452 of the Savior Laws makes them unbreakable. I think we have to fight for Zenzie through the Tyzaran courts." I gave Mel a meaningful stare.

Mel looked slightly sick. Slow she was not. "You mean it depends on me? Why can't *you* trawl through all the Tyzaran laws? Why do you expect *me* to do it?"

She had a point, but I knew she would do the better job. Her obsessive attention to detail was just what we needed right now. I smiled at her in what I hoped was a winning manner. "Come on, Estamain. You know you are the only one for the job. And you have Sammy to help you."

She slid her eyes over to Sammy. "I ... I guess."

Sammy finally woke up to my urgent eyebrow signals. "What? Oh!

Yes, of course. I'll keep you on track. Sure. We can do this. Together."

Mel stared at him. Spacers are very much independent individuals. We don't *do* together. She slowly went pink. I was forced to turn a grin into a cough. She glared at me, clearly seeing through the attempt. "Shut up, Mallivan."

"Something in my throat." I coughed again. "I may be coming down with space flu."

"Sure, Rye. Space flu."

The two Enif had a private discussion along their arms. "We could concoct a palliative drink if you like."

Melody gave a wide smile. "I think you should, Didjal. I'm sure Rye needs a pick-me-up." She seemed to enjoy my glower. "Just what the doctor ordered."

Eshaan looked blank. "I think he has seen no doctor?"

"A way of speaking, Eshaan. Just a way of speaking. You two make up your concoction. I'm willing to bet Mallivan has no more coughing episodes."

I huffed. There wasn't much else I *could* do.

7

It soon became clear that the Tyzarans were indeed going to do their best to hold on to Zenzie. The following day I was served with a very long, convoluted document in Universal legalese by Spokesdesignate Denaraz. I understood around one word in three.

I handed it over to Sammy, to give to Mel. He rolled his eyes. "She isn't going to like it."

"No. Neither do I."

I know that's not what he meant, but I wasn't going to let him start telling me what to do. When he opened his mouth again I stared him down until he finally gave a half shrug and disappeared. I breathed again. I hate legalese. I hate administration. I hate paperwork. So I should have looked at it myself? Well, shoot me. Guilty.

It took Mel six minutes to get back to me. The expression on her face was not happy. She waved the document in my face. "What? You think I'm your secretary?"

"You're just so much better at this sort of thing than I am, Estamain. Come on, you know you are."

"It would be hard to be any worse!"

I spread my hands. "See? You agree with me."

"Yes, but ... wait a minute! I don't!"

"Too late now. You already said you did. And we need somebody sharp on all this legal stuff."

She was diverted. "Sharp? Do you really think I'm sharp?" She brushed the front of her tunic down. "Thank you."

"You're welcome."

"That doesn't mean I'm going to do all the work."

"Of course not, Mel. But I really need you to take a look at it. You will see straight through to the important bits, and you know I would get bogged down in trivia."

"I suppose paperwork isn't really your forte."

"No kidding. I learned to read two years after Sibby."

"Did you? Now why doesn't that surprise me?"

"Can I depend on you then?"

Her eyelids fluttered. "I suppose so. As long as you don't think I was put here to do all the work you don't like."

"Of course not. This isn't for me, in any case. It is for Zenzie."

"That's true. All right."

I smiled down at her. "Take all the time you need. As long as it's done by tomorrow."

She caught her breath. "Tomorrow?" Then she frowned at me. "And what will *you* be doing while Sammy and I are trying to make sense of this stupid document, if you don't mind my asking?"

"I'm glad you have. I shall be … err … making sure they don't force Zenzie into anything she isn't comfortable with."

Mel's mouth twitched, but she nodded some sort of agreement and disappeared. I was left with the two Enif and Seyal. They were looking at me expectantly.

Didjal was the one to speak. "What do you want us to do?"

I considered. "Seyal, you are the one we can use to spy best. They think you only speak Avarak. I want you to wander around the ship, on any pretext you can think up. Find out whatever you can."

She inclined her head. "Me washing. Washing clothes, I think. Good. I listen hard." She slipped away. One minute she was there, the next she wasn't. These Avarak women really could make themselves practically invisible.

Eshaan and Didjal were still regarding me.

"You two are going to stick out like a pair of sore thumbs amongst all these Tyzarans," I told them. "There is no way you can spy for us."

Didjal was regarding its own opposable digits. I frowned, until I realized it hadn't understood the simile. I held up a hand to pre-empt any comment. "Just a manner of speaking. I know your thumbs aren't sore."

It looked relieved. I was going to have to be more careful about how I spoke when I was around them.

"I think the best thing you two can do is sit with Zenzara. Your presence will help her and hopefully stop the Tyzarans from trying to intimidate her or force her to do anything she doesn't want to."

The Enif exchanged glances and then stood up in unison. "We agree," Eshaan told me. "I will use the time to begin a new painting. I must now catch up with a lifetime's work if we are to gain a place in the Siinala Monument."

"Good. I will come with you at first. I need to ask Zenzie if she informed Spokesdesignate Denaraz about the ZEPH drive, about what we suspect happened on board *Commorancy*."

We made our way sedately over to the medical bay. Zenzie was looking better this morning; her crest was relaxed and her color better. Her whole aspect brightened even more when she saw us.

I grinned down at her. Her face was smoother, but the extra skin had pooled around it on the pillow. It made her look very strange.

She wriggled. "What? Do I have a smut on my face?"

"Your skin looks weird."

She made an attempt to peer at her own cheeks, which made her look even weirder. "Does not!"

"Actually, it does. When are you going to fill out and use up all that extra skin?"

She reached up to try to pull some of the folds back up to the centre of her face. They piled up and then slid slowly off again under the force of gravity. I chuckled.

She raised her hand and punched me in the stomach. It felt like a tickle, but I duly complained and made a fuss. She knew she hadn't hurt me though. She gave a sigh. "On Tyzar, folds of skin are considered youthful beauty."

"I didn't comment on their aspect. I simply asked if you would grow out of them. Or into them."

Her crest twitched in irritation. "When I am thirty, they will begin to fill out." She finally said in a grudging sort of manner. "But our skin is only truly smooth when we pass a hundred years. It is seen as a sign of maturity."

"That's a long time in the future."

"I know that! Is there any news?" Her eyes pointedly went to the other Tyzarans present.

I nodded my understanding of the hidden warning. "Not so far. We are getting used to the idea of spending some time here."

"I see. Have you discussed your friend Bull yet?"

"No. You?"

"I haven't had the chance. One of us should bring that whole question up with the spokesdesignate. He is the only person who is ... qualified ... to err ... consider things like that."

"I will speak to him."

"Alone."

"Yes. Though he will want to corroborate it with you."

The crest twitched again. "I know."

"You are certain that he should be informed? This news might involve us in more ... delay?"

She bit her lip, considering. Then her whole rib cage shrank as she let out a huge breath of air. "I feel we must. Don't you?"

"I rather think they will already be aware of some of the circumstances."

"Even so ..."

I stood up. "Then I shall attempt to speak with him this morning. About something other than the Savior Protocols."

Zenzie's chin lifted. "Does he speak much about them?"

"Indeed. They seem to fascinate him. Particularly the legal aspect."

Now her crest was rigidly displayed on the pillow. Her eyes were hot. "Nothing has changed!"

"We are working on it, Ty Zylarian. You must remain patient." I indicated the two Enif beside me. "Didjal and Eshaan will remain here with you."

She thanked them both. They gave solemn nods. They would do their best to protect her.

As I left I saw Didjal settle itself to one side of the hospital cot and Eshaan to the other. The Tyzaran hospital staff were looking around with unease. Zenzara had already closed her eyes. Even our short conversation had worn her out. She needed more time to recover.

I found Denaraz after searching most of the top decks. He was in the gymnasium, practicing some sort of unarmed combat with a fellow-countryman. When he saw me, he bowed to his opponent and invited him to leave us alone.

"Would you like to practice with me?"

He had to be kidding. He was taller than me, probably weighed more and looked as though he dedicated eight hours every day to combat training. There were few things that appealed to me less. I held up one hand, as if that could ward off an attack. "No, thank you. I prefer jogging to stay in shape."

"Really? Good. We can do that too."

I would be trotting along beside him like a lapdog, but I assented. "May I talk to you in private first?"

He raised one eyebrow. "Certainly."

I gave him the long version of everything we knew and everything we had surmised. As I spoke, his face lengthened. "Much of this was suspected, little was known. I'm very much afraid that your inferences are correct."

I tilted my head to one side. "Really? Is there something you aren't telling me?"

His face smoothed as he prepared a diplomatic lie, but his crest betrayed his feeling. I looked pointedly at it.

He tapped his foot, then claudicated. "I can confirm there being further evidence that your interpretation is correct. I cannot tell you what that evidence is." He began to sweep out of the gymnasium. I bobbed along in his wake. We strode down the passageways and directly into the hospital wing. He stalked inside and asked all the other Tyzarans to leave with a gesture. They scurried to obey him. The two Enif turned to me for clarification and I tipped my head in the direction of the door. They acquiesced.

Denaraz subjected Zenzara to a searching interrogation, listening with acute interest to her answers. Finally, he got to his feet.

"I am sorry to say that our jog must be postponed temporarily," he told me. "I must pass this information on immediately."

I coughed. His attention snapped back to me. "Yes? Do you have something to add?"

"It occurs to me that ... depending on who you talk to ... you might be informing the traitor of our knowledge."

He blinked. I had the feeling he wasn't used to being spoken to as an equal, especially by a member of a species he considered inferior. "You have definite suspicions?"

I raised my chin. "It seems strange that Spokesdesignate Xynia should have been so uninterested in recovering survivors, don't you think? I'm certain I heard her voice in the background before we were left to our own devices on the *Commorancy* shuttles. Now, I hate to suggest this, but that could be because she knew that the ZEPH file was on board with us as soon as I listed the Terran instructor as being a survivor. It is strange that he made no attempt to evacuate the students long before this whole thing evolved into violence."

He thought about that. He didn't like to agree with me, but I noticed that both his crests were vertical to his scalp. There was a pause. Then: "I will ... consider ... your ... opinion."

"You may like to inform only the highest authorities on Tyzar."

His eyes flashed. "Do not presume to tell me what I should and should not do, Spacelander! You are speaking to a spokesdesignate of Tyzar!"

"Yes. The last one I spoke to left me ... and Zenzara ... to die. I suspect that if they had not been able to retrieve Bull Cunningham, Terran forces would have spared no expense in searching for him. And I would have been just one of the people in their way. You really can't expect me to take it all lying down."

"You should never have let this Bull Cunningham individual escape!"

I looked at the floor, feeling my face redden. I wasn't proud of that. Hindsight had proved me very wrong to have considered him a friend. The wave of chagrin that swept over me surprised me in its intensity.

The spokesdesignate moderated his tone. "But I thank you for informing me of the situation now. I shall take immediate steps to get this intelligence to my superiors. They will no doubt wish to speak to both of you, and your group."

Why did that not inspire me with confidence? "We are happy to co-operate." I gave a half bow, thankful I didn't sport a crest which would have given away my reservations.

He pushed past me, signaling to the waiting medical staff to return to the medical bay. I followed him out, passing the two Enif as they made their way back to Zenzie's cot, where they stationed themselves again on either side of her as sentinels. One of the medical staff was holding a large syringe with a long needle. I shivered, glad it wasn't about to go into my own skin. I hate injections. Judging from her face, so did Zenzara.

Later that day Sammy and Mel got back to me. Mel was clearly excited about something. Her face was glowing.

"I was right!" she said, thumping her own chest with her fist. "There is no way the Tyzaran authorities can overturn Codex 452 of the Tyzar Authority Civil Legislation. The Savior Protocols, once instigated, cannot be withdrawn!" She smiled at me. "They made it like that because so many of those bound by the Protocols wanted to go back to their own family, and there have been endless lawsuits brought by families reclaiming their children. There is no way of breaking a Savior Protocol. None!"

I frowned. "I think Spokesdesignate Denaraz's point is that I am an alien and therefore Tyzaran law is not applicable to me."

"He can claim away all he likes, but eighty-five years ago the Tyzarans won a court case against a Terran who had obtained Savior Protocols. Bilateral agreements were signed upholding several System laws. One of those referred to the Savior Protocols."

"Yes, but Terrans and Spacelanders are not the same thing."

She shook her head. "That is the great thing. In the judgement, the word 'Alien' was used instead of 'Terran'. The Tyzarans signed off on it and I think it would be impossible for them to retract that agreement now. It could threaten all the trade agreements in place between them and the other eight species."

"Good work, you two! How can we persuade them?"

Sammy pulled a face. "Unfortunately they might choose to oblige us to go through their courts, which will take a lot of money. We would have to retain attorneys and a defender. We would win the case, but it would still cost us time and money."

"Hmm. How much money?"

"Everything we have left. All the money we took from the Vaer ship."

Great. That would leave us with nothing for the future. I thought about it. "We will have to take a vote on that. That money belongs to all of us."

Sammy shook his head. "For my part, she can have it."

Mel nodded. "For mine too. Neither Sammy nor I lost anything to the Vaers. We were lucky. We would have given the money to the four of you who did anyway."

"Would you?" I was absurdly pleased by their loyalty. "Then I shall speak to Seyal and the Enif. I am pretty sure I know what Zenzara would say about it."

"But, Rye," Mel's expression had become suddenly serious. "We really need to get the right spokesdesignates on our team. We need to present a motion before the Tyzar Authority as fast as we can. It could take a month for the case to be heard."

I was already walking away. "I will get back to you within the hour. If I get the go ahead from the others, we can use Sammy's contact on Tyzar to set the whole thing up before we dock there."

"That might be a wise move. Otherwise Zenzara could simply be spirited off to some inaccessible facility and conveniently disappear. You know what governments are like."

True. The Tyzarans might decide to take things into their own hands. She was right. We would have to move fast.

I made my way to the small eating facility, where I found Seyal munching without much enthusiasm on a Tyzar ration. She raised her head as I approached.

"Anything new?" I kept my voice down, so as not to be overheard.

She looked away again. "*Navikkx.*"

I explained about the money. Her large eyes returned their focus to mine. "Seyal *nikkx*. Not want. You give Zenzara."

"Are you sure?"

She patted her maternity bump protectively. "I sure."

"Thank you, Seyal."

She shrugged. "Is not problem."

I wondered what this strange female would consider a problem. She had lost her home, her husband, her planet, her ship and now the only money she had probably ever seen. These Avarak women were more resilient than they appeared. I was coming to admire her fortitude.

I left her at the table. As I exited the space, I could hear the Tyzarans begin to talk amongst themselves again. They had fallen silent as I walked in, but Seyal was so self-effacing that they discounted her. I couldn't help thinking that was a big mistake. I decided then and there never to do that myself.

The two Enif were as convinced. I signaled to Didjal, who slipped out of the medical bay to talk to me. The decision was instantaneous.

"Use the money. We believe the group must stay together. The money is unimportant to us. Use it for Zenzara."

"You are not thinking of going back to Enifa?"

Didjal's whole body extended upwards and tightened. "We cannot go back. Eshaan needs time to try to produce more art. There is no place on Enifa for those who have no art."

"Do you not need to ask Eshaan?"

Didjal quivered as if laughing. "There is no point. I know what Eshaan thinks. I speak for both of us. In any case, I cannot disturb my *faliif* at this time."

I realized that Eshaan was in the process of creating art at that very moment. I had not looked closely before, as the Enif's body had been blocking my view. Now, I realized, I could see the edge of a large board that it was using as a canvas. Enif paint on any surface, because they can retain a pattern of every movement that is undertaken in the creation. This is then sent to Enifa, where it can be used to create an identical piece. Didjal had told me that the real 'painting' was considered to be the pattern. This is then licensed in one artwork at a time which may be sold for a period of seventy to a hundred years, after which that artwork must be destroyed and a new copy will be made on Enifa. Apparently the pattern includes every stroke, every nuance of pressure and of angle. Patterns for one painting can take up many Terabytes of storage. Such patterns are considered high priority for all Enif, and are transmitted regularly to the vaults on Enifa for evaluation. True experts are able to see the finished painting only from the data of its creation.

As I peered in I saw that several of Eshaan's long digits were extruding a sort of thread. The shapes and forms on the painting were emerging out of a frantic dancing of the Enif fingers. Eshaan itself seemed to be almost in a trance as it worked, the darting, dragging movements holding no doubt whatsoever. My mouth dropped open. "How is it possible to produce those colors?"

Didjal's voice could not express pride, but I could feel it in the stance and the posture. "It is innate. Those who are artists among us possess the ability, through chemical reactions within our bodies, to add three basic colors to the strands. So it is possible – after long training – to weave the other colors from those three."

I couldn't tear my gaze away. Eshaan was creating what appeared to be heavy links of golden rope and he was depositing them in swirls on the canvas. As I watched, a harsh Vaer face emerged. The Enif painter had captured the Vaer querulousness and greed perfectly. The avian could have stepped out of the painting and I would not have been in the least surprised.

"I ... I have never seen anything like it!" My voice was hushed.

Didjal shone. "My *faliif* is very ... very talented."

The golden thread had become a crimson so rich that you could not look away. Multi-faceted gems were appearing. The crimson became emerald, the emerald a flashing diamond.

I tore my attention away. I could see why Enif art was so highly valued. Zenzara had not even noticed my presence outside her cubicle. She was mesmerized by Eshaan's work too. Good. It would take her mind off her own situation.

I thanked Didjal and made my way back to the quarters we had been assigned. We needed to contact Tyzar ahead of docking there.

8

The *Aurynth* came in slowly to the docking port at the space station above Tyzar. I was standing towards the back of the bridge, together with Spokesdesignate Denaraz. He was looking worried. I asked him about it.

"It is nothing," he replied.

Sure, I felt like saying. And your crests are standing out at right angles because you're chilly. I toned down my answer. "Really?"

He gave me the Tyzaran equivalent of a smile. "It is hard to hide your feelings when you are Tyzaran."

"It is."

He gave a shrug. "Your news was worrisome. We have been aware for some time of a splinter group on Tyzar. They call themselves the Enclave. They are strong nationalists and believe that Tyzar should keep its technological advantage secret. They are very much against the sharing of new breakthroughs with the other Major Shell races."

"I see. And you believe they may be prepared to act against Zenzara? That doesn't seem to fit in with such aims, does it?"

He scratched one of the ridges across his forehead. "It shouldn't. However, recently the Enclave have become more and more active. They disapprove of all aliens. They would certainly disapprove of an alien recipient of the Savior Protocols."

"You think they may try something here?"

His crests rippled. "I sense danger, yes. But I cannot see exactly what that danger is."

"You are talking about Tyzarans fighting Tyzarans?"

The ripples became waves. "I am." His expression was grim. "I wish I weren't."

I raised one eyebrow. "We have arranged for a security detail for Zenzara."

"Yes. I am aware of that. However, I am unsure of the support the Enclave has garnered amongst my people. I think we should be prepared for any happenstance."

His quiet tone was chilling. I couldn't tell him that I was equally wary of his own actions against Zenzara, that I also thought his peers might want to secrete her away from prying eyes and put her somewhere where she conveniently couldn't be found. I just hoped we could protect her from both sets of opponents. I edged away back and left the bridge. If any attack was about to take place, I wanted our small group to be near Zenzara. She was the target; that is where we needed to be.

I found my friends by the medical bay. None of us had any armor to put on, and we had few weapons between us. However, we could form a barrier between Zenzie and any aggressors. It would be better than nothing. It would have to be.

Zenzara was lying on a wheeled trolley, surrounded still by the Tyzaran medical staff. She lifted a hand at me. I nodded to her as the cavalcade began to move out. We began the long trek towards the outer hatches as the *Aurynth* finished her mooring protocols.

There was a small group of *Aurynth's* officers waiting for us at the outer hull. There was also an armed guard of some twenty effectives. Ten of them fell in before us, ten to the rear. Denaraz was with them, his crests still at ninety degrees to his scalp. I noticed that Zenzara's one crest was also fully extended. She, too, was aware of some sort of danger.

It crossed my mind that we would present an easy target as we egressed through the airlock tubing. I made my way across to Denaraz.

"Do you think it wise for all of us to exit at the same time?" I questioned.

He considered my question, but then dismissed it. "I am under orders," he told me. "The Supreme Council have instructed me to bring the Chyzar to them immediately upon landing."

I signaled to the others to close ranks around Zenzie's trolley. I was not at all happy about this situation. It left us too exposed. Still, our own security detail could be seen waiting patiently on the other side of the station-side airlock. That would have to be enough. I just wished I didn't have this uneasy feeling that seemed to permeate my whole being.

We shuffled clumsily along the docking tube, though there was hardly room on either side for us to walk beside the gurney. However, as we finally exited the ship into the upper levels of a large hangar, it was easier to flank Zenzie.

I was about to introduce myself to the private security guard that our lawyers had contracted when there was a commotion. Just as the gurney was being quickly ushered towards the hangar bay lift on our right, shouting broke out far below us.

I ran towards the railing and peered over.

The bay was enormous – big enough to allow for three docking bays one on top of another. That meant the actual space must have been over a hundred stories high. It was like walking outside onto a planet, it was so immense. I leant over the rail and managed to focus on the activities below me. My stomach churned at the drop straight down.

From here the figures were tiny. There seemed to be many of them, however, and they were swarming up the steps alongside the lifts. That didn't bother me. Even though they were heading directly for us, it would take them far too long to climb so many stories. We could be long gone before they reached us.

"Turn back!" I shouted to those behind me. "Turn back. Back into the *Aurynth!*"

We all did a ninety degree swivel, just in time to catch the flash of explosives out in the accordion-like passageway which snaked from the ship to the airlock. There was a sharp tug on each of us as air raced past us, and then the failsafes on the airlock clicked in, and the hatch door swung firmly shut. The passage tubing writhed in open space, shaking those trapped within it free. I saw one or two *Aurynth* crew members float slowly off into the darkness. I was close enough to see the horrified expression on one. We all stared for a heart-stopping second, before Denaraz grabbed out at the gurney where Zenzara was lying. "We cannot get back to the *Aurynth*. We will descend a full level, to the next ship docked. I am authorized to requisition assistance from any Tyzaran vessel. Do as I say!"

I glared at him. His solution didn't seem a particularly safe option. I opened my mouth to express an opinion, but Zenzara struggled to her elbows and began to swing her legs off the gurney.

"Quiet, Mallivan Bell," she told me, ignoring the open mouth she had left me with. "There is no time. I sense something worse than—"

A flash permeated the hanger and we all ducked. Some few milliseconds afterwards there was a deep booming sound. I swear Denaraz's crests separated for a moment from his scalp.

I ran back to the railing. The bomb had gone off around a third of the way up the hanger. There was a frantic tearing sound and air began to whistle its way out of a hole in the triple skin somewhere. It couldn't have been very big, for I could detect no particular change in pressure.

Sammy and Mel, who were behind me, both gave a surprised grunt. The sound of guns being drawn out of holsters made me swivel around again. I was too late to prevent the shots.

Our waiting guard of honor was firing on us. Quite openly. Quite directly. Two of the Tyzaran crew went down. Didjal was caught by a pulser, but much of the energy must have reflected off the shiny black Enif carapace. It staggered at the impact, but continued to return fire.

Eshaan had thrown itself in front of Zenzara and was sheltering her from the attackers. Zenzie was muttering and unsuccessfully trying to push the Enif away from her, having already struggled fully to her feet. It was chaotic.

I reached Zenzara and pushed her down to the ground, ignoring her yelp of surprise. Eshaan went down with her and covered her with its black body. All I could see were a pair of weakly thrashing Tyzaran legs.

I turned to the honor guard. So. Now it was the Tyzarans who were attacking us. I wondered if it would be my fate to fight each and every one of the eight Major Shell races. I pressed my finger on the trigger of the pulser I had been carrying since the Vaer ship. It blazed obediently into action, mowing down my target in seconds. Pulsers are far more efficient than lasers. The beam spreads out in a much shorter distance, which can cause much more permanent damage to the target. Tyzarans, not being shiny and dark like the Enif, present good targets. The one I was aiming at simply crumpled into the decking as a huge hole the size of my head appeared in his chest with a rather sickening slurpy sound.

Mel and Sammy had already accounted for another two of the attackers, and Didjal was throwing itself at three others, seemingly oblivious of the returning fire. It must be nice to be so reflective. In the shiny sort of way, I mean.

I gulped for a moment, then precipitated myself at another group of three attackers, closing my eyes and wishing I had a shield in front of me. All I could do was prey that they would miss me. It seemed a pretty hopeless prayer.

I felt myself falter as I was hit. I didn't feel any pain at the time, so I was able to push my legs into recapturing the momentum I had lost. I was on top of my three within less than a second.

The pain flared just when I didn't want it to. The hand holding the pulser pistol refused to obey me. I tried again, but all the fitzing thing would do is hang helplessly at my side.

So I used myself as a human cannonball, propelling myself down and across so that my body would hit all three low and almost horizontally. They went down like skittles and we tumbled in a heap into the bulkhead. I snatched at my pistol with my good hand and tried to turn it against the traitors.

The only thing close to me was their legs. I shot at their feet and their ankles as best I could. There were cries from under me.

It was all I could do to shuffle slightly out from the bulkhead and train the pulser on the three of them. There was a pause as they considered their position and then all three dropped their weapons. All were bleeding profusely below the knee. They were not badly hurt, but at least I would be able to control them. I kicked their weapons out of the way, kept my pistol trained on them, and sat gasping. I was out of the fight.

It was hard for me to see what was still going on around me. I caught only flashes of the fighting.

Didjal had accounted for the three Tyzarans it had gone for. They were all lying unconscious in a heap. I made a mental reminder not to aim pulsers at aliens that come encased in glossy black exoskeletons. Didjal itself had moved on to another small group of attackers and was currently involved in bashing their heads together in the sort of scientific way you would expect of an engineer.

Denaraz was down. He had paled with the pain, though he was attempting to stand, and he still held his own Tyzaran ZR in his hand and was using it, though with slightly less than his usual lethal efficiency.

I blinked back the sweat from my eyes. Another huge explosion went off really close to our position. Denaraz caught my eye. He gestured towards the stairs down.

"Members of the Enclave! Must be trying to trap us on this level. They won't let you or Zenzara out alive. If they can't kill you directly they are capable of anything." His crests were rigid and white. "Anything. They are unpredictable."

I nodded. It didn't help me know what to do. The only thing I could think of was to nod to Eshaan and signal to him that we should try to close with each other. There might be more safety fighting back to back.

Eshaan sprung lightly to its feet and Zenzara blinked. I caught an extremely disgruntled face staring in my direction before the eyes widened as she realized I had been injured. Her face hardened. She began to unwind something I had always thought of as a necklace from around her slender throat. It unraveled to become a long piece of leather thong, with a heavy metallic arrowhead-like carving at either end.

In one fluid movement she held this up above her head and whirled it around. Then she bent swiftly and released both ends at the same time.

The length of thong hit one of our opponents just above the knee, wrapped itself around his legs several times, and brought him crashing down on the deck plating. I raised one eyebrow. He had been about to blow my head off with his ABlaser. Hmm.

Zenzie was not finished. Now she was ripping a brooch off her tunic. I saw that it was not merely a brooch. It had two long sharp prongs attached, but these had been invisible as they had been threaded through the tunic.

She stood there, a slim figure against the others, and her hand flashed. The brooch buried itself in the stomach of one of the guard of honor. He bent double, his eyes wide as his hands went automatically to his belly, covering the brooch. He stared at her for a few long moments before sinking to his knees and then keeling over.

Zenzara looked away. She was already reaching for her remaining brooch. This, too, buried itself deep in an opponent's flesh. Zenzara herself lifted her chin and stared at me with scorchingly angry eyes.

"I was taught the use of the nivala and the thoria when I was five," she snapped. "All Tyzaran girls are. We protect *ourselves*."

She gave poor old Eshaan a push and stormed past it towards the head of the stairwell, where I was. It looked at me. I shrugged. The Enif stared expressionlessly back and then trailed after Zenzara.

I gave a shout and a beckon to Sammy and Mel, who looked over and nodded their understanding. That left Seyal.

At first I couldn't see her, but then she appeared behind me. She was disheveled and had clearly not held back from the fighting. She caught my eye and pointed behind us, just as another bomb went off. This time it shook the supports of our walkway, bending one or two of them so that the whole platform tilted towards the decks below. We all scrabbled for a foot and handhold. Seyal didn't look away. She was staring insistently at me. I followed her arm, my eyes straining through the smoke to see whatever she was so sure of. There was another airlock, a smaller one used for water, waste and fuel pipes to be connected to a ship.

I shrugged. I couldn't see what she was saying.

Then another shattering explosion rocked our position. This time they breached the third skin and it was hard not to be moved by the explosion of outgoing air. I grabbed onto part of the bulkhead to keep from falling over the railing.

Seyal had touched Eshaan now. She was pointing again at the airlock. But it was tiny. We would hardly fit there.

Seyal made signs of an explosion with her hands. Then she made a shape of containment. Of course! Blast waves can't travel through space. Just putting a few meters of space between us and these blasts could save our lives. With no access to a ship there was only one way to do that. The portable safety airbag. My heart stuttered for a moment at the idea. Elderly spacers often state quite adamantly their preference to die rather than face a PSA airbag.

All station airlocks are required to have them. They are one of the safety measures obligatory on all space stations in the Major Shells. These days, even most large ships are equipped with them. Why hadn't I thought of that? Although my brain shied away from the possibility, I was coming to the conclusion that it was certainly an option.

Seyal was staring at me, an earnest expression on her face. She gave an encouraging nod.

I sighed. "All right." I grabbed Denaraz and began to pull him towards the smaller airlock. He frowned and wriggled slightly to express his disagreement. I ignored him totally and dragged him towards the hatch. Between my useless arm and his leg injury, we made slow time.

Zenzie was ahead of us. She had seen Seyal point to the PSA in the airlock and seemed to have realized what the new plan was. She had already ducked inside the airlock and was reaching for the small hammer that hung from our end of the long red cylinder that was stored high along the wall of the airlock. She took a deep breath then struck the red seal firmly with the hammer, breaking the seal.

She had to leap back as the PS airbag deployed, ballooning out of its bulkhead stowage and inflating to claim half of the airlock space. Zenzie was still weak and had to pummel at the growing space burlap to avoid being pinned between the material and the bulkhead. She managed to glare at me during this process. I could see that she blamed me for something.

She dragged the heavy duty zipper downwards. I knew that the gas cylinder would give a positive pressure outwards for twenty seconds, before the valve released the canister and the airbag could be deployed. The zipper needed to be closed by then. Twenty seconds is not a long time, but on some occasions it can seem an eternity.

Zenzara stretched out one hand to help me with Denaraz. I let her take some of the dead weight. Denaraz stared at me with a meaningful expression, and I knew exactly what he was trying to convey. The one thing we were in total agreement about was the need to protect Zenzie. And I could tell from the look she had treated us all to that she wasn't planning on quietly allowing herself to be evacuated.

I nodded back to the spokesdesignate.

He turned as if to say something to Zenzara. She bent slightly to be able to hear better over all the noise. He clamped a firm hand over her slender wrist and pulled her down and towards him so that she was inside the PSA.

There was silence for a long millisecond as she processed these events. When she realized what had happened, and why, she glanced furiously over to me.

I gave her an arms apart nothing-to-do-with-me shrug.

The deep creases on her face tensed so much that she got a porcupiney sort of look about her. I took an involuntary step back and held up my hands.

She was having none of it. She knew I had agreed to it. She stared down at Denaraz and I gasped, sure for a moment that she was going to lash out at him. Then she gave a sigh. The thin curvy bones across her shoulders slumped. She was unable to kick a downed man. Thank the Shells for that.

All this had happened in just a few seconds. Denaraz gave me another nod, to tell me he had control of her, and I grabbed back at Seyal and pushed her past me inside the airbag. Her body felt resistant for a moment, then acceded. She stumbled past me, almost on top of the other two. Fully deployed, these airbags only measured a little over a meter in all three directions. They were meant for two to three people. I looked around. We were going to cram seven inside.

Sammy and Mel had managed to get the attention of the two Enif and were helping them into the airbag. Didjal was trying to explain something to Sammy, but Sammy shook his head and firmly insisted that they got inside. Then he grinned at Mel and spoke, close to her ear. She looked up at him suddenly and her face fell.

I knew what Sammy had said to her. He had realized that somebody was going to have to activate the outer lock, something that couldn't be done once the airbag was vacuum zipped. He was volunteering, but I had reached the conclusion before him, and I knew who was going to do that small job.

I placed my foot squarely at his back and pushed. He tumbled inwards, taking Mel with him. They tangled with Eshaan and then Zenzara, who was still staring at me with something like anger.

I pulled the emergency closure cords and there was a metallic slithering as the vacuum zip began to seal. With so many bodies inside, it took longer than it should have to complete the operation. I could hear Mel scream as she began to hyperventilate in the tiny space. She would be absolutely terrified. I hoped Sammy would shut her up. She would use up all the air if she went on like that. Just as I had that thought, I seemed to hear a hard slap, and the high-pitched cry cut off abruptly. That wasn't going to be good for their relationship.

As soon as the light on top of the portable space airbag shone green, I stepped back out of the airlock. It was a second to press the inner lock button. The hatch rolled into place, finally shutting them off from the continuous fighting.

I nearly didn't make the second button. A large Tyzaran man slashed over at me with a knife. I only just managed to shrink back in time. I punched the final button, the red one, and the manual over-ride, just before I turned back to him. I heard, rather than saw, the outer hatch slide open.

I was surprised to find Denaraz's ABlaser in my good hand. He must have thrust it onto me before grabbing at Zenzie. The weapon, known to its users as the ZR, came up of its own will and fired.

The man in front of me dissolved.

I stared down at my hand.

Some gun. This was one technological advance that the Tyzarans hadn't shared with the rest of the races. Hmm. Interesting.

I had a moment to turn back to the airlock. The PSA had been pushed gently away from the ship by the small amount of air that escaped to the lower density. It was now floating slowly away from the hull. Only six meters or so at the moment, but I knew that would gradually increase. Six meters of space was enough to kill blast waves. They needed to be further than that to avoid shrapnel. That space burlap was strong, but it was only material. It was, quite literally, a sack. Pieces of metal would perforate it without even noticing. I was pleased to see that the emergency lights on both the bow and the stern were functioning. With seven of them stuffed inside the sack, they would have an extremely limited amount of air. Though the temperature of outer space would leave them like popsicles even before they could suffocate, I felt. I closed my eyes and wished them well. Then I turned back to the chaos around me. I was running out of time, too.

What was left of *Aurynth's* crew was still struggling with the men who had replaced the security detail. Worse, there were cries from the platform below ours, where the duty watch of the ship under ours were attempting to stop a large crowd from invading their platform.

I ran to the railing, trying to judge how long we had.

We didn't.

The main crowd was still at the lower platform level, but the advance had already reached my level. Out of the corner of my eye I saw a heavily built Tyzaran deliberately toss something across the decking towards the outer skin of the space dock I was standing on.

I shot him, but I was too late. He disintegrated as the hand-held device detonated.

I leapt the railing in one bound and let myself fall. It seemed like the only way to stay alive. Not a good way, just the only way.

I dropped like a stone. Ironically, I was facing upwards, so I could see a cloud of shards of metal deck plating falling with me. I had time to do a mental check on Galileo's theory. They were neither catching up with me, nor lagging behind. We were all falling through the air at the same rate. I felt some long-forgotten physics teacher would have congratulated me on my experiment.

Then I realized that I was crazy. Who in their right mind would be doing physics experiments as they plummeted to their death? Who cared? Except Galileo Galilei, of course.

I didn't feel anything else. I didn't feel sorry for myself. I felt dissociated, strange, detached from reality.

Then everything changed. There was a sharp crack above me. My body jerked. Air was suddenly gushing past me, ripping up towards the platform. For a split second I felt almost weightless as the forces of artificial gravity pulling me down battled with the outburst of air. The explosion must have caused a massive breech in the hull.

Then there was a sudden jolt as something wrapped around my legs.

I wanted to see what had touched me, but at that very moment gravity won over the escaping air and I resumed my freefall towards the decking far below. Well, not so far now. I was accelerating fast towards it.

Suddenly my legs were wrenched back and upwards. My body seemed to stretch and elongate as the rest of me was decelerated at a ridiculous rate. It felt as though my spine were snapping. What little breath I had left was forced out of me in an involuntary gasp.

I was immobile for what felt like minutes, but must have been one or two heartbeats. Then my whole body seemed to spring back and I was rising again in a recoil, the tension on my feet gone. The pressure in my head built up and up and up. Why, I had no idea. My eyes spiked at my face in pain, crawling to get out of my head. Then the pull upwards reappeared, now more bearable.

I blacked out.

I opened my eyes. I could see nothing. I was invaded by sudden terror at the darkness. For some reason I was blind.

I was upside down.

I felt around me. There was nothing.

I reached up along my body. There was stickiness on my clothes in several places. It could be blood from the slivers of metal.

I shook my head and blinked several times. I still couldn't see anything. I felt further up my leg. I was hanging from something. It seemed important to find out what.

"Do not move." The voice was calm. Impassionate. Distant.

"What happened?" The air was thin. My voice was weak and tinny. It was also anything but calm. I could hear the near lapse into terror. I hoped nobody else could.

"I saved your life." The voice, still distant, appeared faintly amused. "Please make no sudden movements. I am attempting to reach safety. We have very little time."

My sight was coming back. It felt as though I were peering through enlarged blood vessels, but I risked looking upwards.

My heart stuttered and nearly failed. I was hanging underneath some sort of small cargo shifter, being supported only by the loops of a thoria around my ankles and shins. I tracked the thoria upwards. Some five meters above, its upper end had been twisted several times around a stanchion.

I closed my eyes again. In any case, the liquid in them was beginning to evaporate from the now near-vacuum inside the hanger. Cold was also freezing me in place. I began to shiver. From the cold, I told myself, though it might have been from sheer terror.

I flicked open my eyes again, but wished that I hadn't. Apart from it being more difficult to shut them again against the bubbling ocular fluid, the scene around me was ghastly. People still far below me were grabbing at their throats. Some were already down, wriggling feebly as the cold of outer space and lack of breathable air pinned them down in death. Others were stilled, already vanquished by the lethal combination. There was nothing good to see. At least I was still moving, being slowly transported across the huge bay.

I tried to take a breath, but had to abort that brilliant idea. There was no air left to breathe. I clamped my jaws and my eyelids shut and began to send a mental goodbye to Sibby. My sister was the person who came to me at that moment. I wished I had told her how much I cared. I hadn't always been a good brother.

The links around my shin gave a little and I slipped slightly. The thoria was starting to unravel. I froze in place, not breathing, not moving, not even thinking. Now it was definitely sheer terror that held me in place. I dared not even twitch.

I hung, waiting for the end.

There was a long silence. I held on to the sparse air in my lungs, though it was screaming to get out. It was burning into me and I knew that I would last only a few seconds more.

There was another sound, this time a sharp click. Wind rushed past me, now head on, and I risked a gulp of air. It was thin, but better than nothing. I panted, trying desperately to force enough oxygen inside my lungs to survive.

Then there was another click and the air suddenly became thicker. The wind stopped. My head spun, but I was able to get oxygen into my body now.

I felt nimble hands on my legs, then the thoria linking me to the cargo platform parted. I tumbled to the deck. It was only a few feet. Even so, it hurt.

The cargo shifter slipped overhead and settled onto the decking some meters away. A slim Spacelander figure jumped down from the heavy machine, accompanied by a much taller Tyzaran woman.

The Spacelander held out a friendly hand to me. "Hi. I am Neema. Neema Agazed Rubin. I am a friend of Sammy's. My parents mine Agazed alongside his." She indicated the Tyzaran woman standing beside her. "This is Anzany. She is the one who saved your life."

Anzany's crest lowered. "I simply did as you asked, Neema."

"You did it pretty well, though. That use of the thoria was inspired."

Anzany's skin was taut, so she must be a fully mature female. That would put her at around a hundred years old. Old enough not to blush as she was doing at the compliment. I stared between the two of them. I was picking up a certain closeness that was surprising. Perhaps I was imagining it. Any sort of inter-species fraternization would be anathema to most Tyzarans.

Neema was looking at me quizzically. I got the impression she knew what I was thinking and didn't mind. I raised an eyebrow at her and was pleased to see that she inclined her head. So! Interesting.

My lungs allowed me finally to speak. "My friends. Outside. In a PSA. Please help!"

Neema narrowed her eyes. She leapt back onto the cargo shifter and grabbed a communication device. I saw her speaking frantically into it. She listened, but I couldn't quite make out what the muffled reply was telling her.

She was shaking her head as she came back to me. "It is complete chaos out there. All communications are cut. We will just have to hope somebody gets to them in time."

I sank down to the deck, aware of blackness seeping up into my brain. I was done. Somehow, I had survived.

But had the others?

9

I was first aware of a buzzing sound. Pain, all along my shoulders. Then some sort of consciousness crept in and I remembered the PSA. I remembered the explosion.

I sat up suddenly, a movement that caused my head to spin. "The others! Wha ... What happened?"

A cool cloth was pressed to my forehead and one hand pushed my head back down. I was lying on some kind of stretcher. Neema's voice sounded, close to my ear. "It's all right, Mr. Mallivan. Your friends were rescued. They are safely aboard a Tyzaran warship. They were picked up only five minutes after the launch. And they escaped the worst of the shrapnel coming out of the blast zone. They have only minor cuts and bruises."

A feeling of warmth began to spread through me. I breathed a heavy sigh of relief. All the same, I knew many, many inhabitants of Tyzar had died in the last few minutes. There was nothing to celebrate here. Nothing at all. And I was still worried about the Tyzaran captain. Denaraz's leg had looked to be in a bad way.

I grabbed Neema's arm and squeezed it hard. "I have to get to them. Please!"

My hand was gently but firmly removed. "We are aware, Mr. Mallivan. Now, please lie back. You are currently waiting for triage by the station trauma doctors."

I knew there would be many with far worse injuries than mine. I gave a feeble struggle against the hand still pushing my head back. The pressure increased.

"Please stay still." The voice was not Neema's. I squeezed my eyes under their lids to try to make my reluctant brain recall everything that had just happened. Finally it came up with a name to match the voice. The Tyzaran woman. Anzany. That was it. "You are damaged. You require medical attention."

"It was all because of us." The weight of so many deaths dragged my mind back to it.

Anzany gave a long sigh. "You were only the catalysts. The danger has been here for a long time. Our government hoped that it would simply go away, but in fact the lack of control over the main instigators has simply allowed them to indoctrinate others. It may have happened today because you were here. It would have happened sooner or later if you hadn't been."

Her words did help. Not a lot. But she was right. The Enclave had been a powder keg just waiting to explode.

"What will the Supreme Council do now?"

Anzany's crest drooped. "I do not know. I am not important enough to be privy to decisions like that. I hope my government will act decisively against the Enclave. I feel even they cannot sweep destruction like this under the carpet, as you Spacelanders say."

"Under the deck plating," I corrected automatically.

"As you say." The hand on my head attempted to smooth out my wrinkles of worry. It was not an unpleasant sensation. Neema whispered something in a fierce undertone and the hand stilled. I managed to open my eyes. The two women were staring at each other.

A large figure in a doctor's uniform bustled over. He bent over me and cut the back of my space fatigues off. I felt strong fingers kneading the area of skin without abrasions. They were competent, if impersonal.

One of the hands hovered over my skull and beckoned to a nursing assistant. He gave fluid instruction in a tight voice before departing to check on another patient.

The assistant came over to me and busied himself at my back. I was aware of tingling and some sharp pain.

Neema peered behind me. "They are using a portable triage unit. You have torn ligaments in your back and damage to your upper arm. This will help."

"Thank you. Both of you. You saved my life."

Neema reddened but Anzany simply nodded. "We did."

"Why me?"

"We were on the watch for your group," Neema explained. "Sammy had contacted me and explained some of what was going on. I had come to the bay hoping to get a chance to speak to him, and when the insurgents attacked we knew that your group would be the target. After the first explosive device, we suspected it would only be a matter of time before they targeted the outer skin of the space station."

Anzany picked up the story. "We grabbed a cargo shifter that was lying around and headed upwards. We thought we might be in time to evacuate all of you. At least, at first we did."

"Then the second explosion came and we knew we were too late. Neema had already turned away from the superior levels and towards the exit airlocks at one end of the bay when we saw you throw yourself off the platform."

"You fell like a stone. Then the final detonation went off, and it was so big that it punched a hole the size of a shuttle through the outer skins."

"You were in front of us, and you seemed to hang in space, just for a few moments."

"So Neema was really quick. She brought us almost alongside and I managed to get a thoria around your legs." Anzany gave a faintly disbelieving shake of her head. "I just had time to belay one end around a stanchion when you dropped past us again." Her eyes stared into the distance, seeing the past again. "And the thoria held!"

"I'm amazed you were able to get out. Hadn't safety doors come down?"

Neema inclined her head. "Sure. But it turns out that there is a separate cargo passageway that has safety airlocks. They are automatically keyed to the cargo shifters. We were let through without having to do more than point the bows of the thing at the exit."

"Well, thank you. Will you come with me to find the rest of my group?"

The two women hesitated.

"Please?"

"All right." Anzany managed a faint smile. "I guess we won't be missed for a while longer. The whole of the station will be in complete chaos."

"Appreciate it."

Neema managed a grin. "It will be nice to say hi to Sammy again."

"He has a girlfriend now."

Her eyes opened wide. "No! Little Sammy? No way!" Her eyes danced. "His father will go spare!" She leaned in towards me. "Tell me more!"

Unfortunately we were interrupted in our gossip by a Tyzaran spokesdesignate who had been dispatched to find me and take me to a new hanger for transport up to the ship which had found my crewmates. Neema gave me a signal which clearly stated that she would demand full discovery at a later date, and then stood respectfully to one side.

"I am to accompany you to Ty Denaraz," the newcomer told me with a stiff face. He did not appear happy to be sent on a mission of shepherding visitors around when he could be helping the casualties. He looked over at the two women dismissively. "You may go," he told them, making little shooing movements with his hands.

I moved to protest, then gave a grunt. It hurt to move. I gasped in more air. "They are to come with me."

His eyes flashed. "Why? Who says so?"

"I say so. These two ladies have just saved my life. They are to accompany me."

Both of his crests twitched. "I know nothing of this."

"If I go, they go."

He frowned and considered. He must have decided that it wasn't his problem, for he gave a brusque nod and turned to lead the way. I thanked the doctor's assistant who had just completed his ministrations, then the two girls helped me to my feet. I was glad of their support. My head spun as I stood up. We hobbled without much dignity behind our guide. Our conversation ground to a halt, in my case because it took all my energy to force air into lungs which protested at every step.

We were escorted out of the service passageway and into a second large hanger. This one was still intact, which allowed me to see just how impressive the Tyzaran space station really was.

Unfortunately the decks were covered with prone bodies and even more people milling around. It looked as if, although many had been killed, many more had managed to escape the worst effects of the terrorist attack. That was a relief.

Our guide picked his way through the bodies, many of whom were groaning and appealing to us for help. I lowered my head; guilt about being the partial cause of all this carnage overwhelmed me for a moment. I wished I could help.

We were taken up the stairs, rather than via the bank of lifts. It took all of the stamina I had left to get my body up the steep steps. I felt as though my legs were matchsticks and my body a bloated bag. The muscles above my knees groaned at the task of staggering towards the platform. I really thought I wasn't going to make it, but then Neema and Anzany each shoved a shoulder firmly under one of my arms and I was quickly womanhandled upwards with no more fuss. It was painful and more than a little embarrassing.

Security at the platform had been intensified. I was reminded of ancient sayings about closing stable doors and bolted horses. Still, it did indicate that we would be far more secure now than we had been before. That had to be a good development.

We were held back at the airlock as news of our arrival was communicated to the Flight Deck. We stood silently. I tried to be discreet about dragging air into my overworked lungs and propped myself up against the railings to dissimulate the rubbery leg syndrome that was threatening to drop me to the decking.

There was a flash of movement and the guards brought their weapons up as something shot past them.

I felt two sharp pushes against my chest and was bowled over, tumbling to the silvery plating with something light on top of me. What little breath was inside me expelled with a whoosh.

"You are alive!"

I disentangled Zenzie with my one good arm, holding her off me so that Neema and Anzany could pull her away. "I was until you knocked me over!"

"We were sure you were dead!" she wailed. "I failed the Savior Protocols!"

"I was the one who tossed you in the PSA. It was hardly your choice!"

"Yes, but I should have known you would do that!"

I grinned. "Slowing down, Zenzara?"

"Certainly not!" Her wrinkles sagged. "You tricked me!"

I was rather proud of the fact. "I did, didn't I?"

"Well you won't do it again!"

I nodded to Neema to set the young Tyzaran girl carefully back onto her feet, and waved to the guards to indicate they could stand down. "You are now one of the most important Tyzarans there are. Of course I will try to make sure you are safe."

Her crest drooped. "But it is my job to look after you. Because of the Savior Protocols." She stamped one foot. "You know it is!"

"Mmmm." I can't say I had much sympathy for her problem. The idea of an eight year old Tyzaran protecting a thirty year old Spacelander was ridiculous. "I'm glad you all made it too, Zenzie."

"We nearly didn't. The PSA was caught by a large piece of shrapnel and holed. Some of us had the onset of space-swell when we were picked up. Denaraz has had to have a small part of one of his crests amputated."

I knew that was a terrible thing for a Tyzaran. "Are the rest of you ok?"

She nodded. "Sammy's leg is playing up, but apart from that we all made it through, though Seyal is in the medical bay under observation to make sure that her baby suffered no harm."

"What about Denaraz's leg?"

"It was not as bad as it looked. He was put in a Zeroth chamber but is already out and about. He refused to stay there for three days, which is what they recommended. He said the triage chambers would be needed for people much worse off than him."

A clatter of shoes announced the arrival of several newcomers. Mel and Sammy appeared, together with the two Enif. Even Didjal looked pleased to see me.

Sammy was the least effusive. "What's up, Rye?" He spotted Neema. "Yo, Neems, nice to see you again. How are the family?"

Neema was eyeballing Mel with more than a casual interest, having noticed that Sammy's hand had been touching Mel's fingers. Her eyes slid to me and I gave a small nod. Her own eyes glinted. "Sammy! Everyone is fine. Who is this?"

Sammy introduced Mel, who hung back in an embarrassed kind of way. I bent to give her a peck on the cheek. "You ok?"

"Fine, Rye. You?"

"Thanks to these two. They saved my life."

Mel shook hands with the two girls and Zenzara also turned to nod in their direction. I presented them to the Enif. Anzany held out one hand to Eshaan and then froze as she realized the Enif might not have hands to give back. She looked like a hunted animal caught in headlights. I couldn't help laughing.

Eshaan examined the hand held out towards it, giving a slight shiver of distaste. The Enif use their long digits to transmit conversation through their very sensitive forearm skin and are protective of them.

In addition, Eshaan's fingers were the tools he used for painting. That made them even more special. Anzany's action would be invasive to it. The Enif considered for a quick second, and then bent to Anzany, inclining itself from the middle section of its abdomen.

Anzany withdrew her hand as if the air in front of her burned and bowed back, her face wrinkling in embarrassment, crest drooping in mortification. "Pleased to meet you."

"As are we."

"So what happens now?" I asked Denaraz, who had limped up behind them.

The spokesdesignate looked uncomfortable. "I am awaiting instructions. Due to the ... situation on the space station, it is unlikely that Ty Zenzara can be properly protected here."

We agreed on something then. I stared at him. "And ...?"

"I am afraid I do not know. I am not in contact with ... my superiors."

I bet it cost him something to admit that. His crests deflated. I stared at them. There was a bite-sized chunk missing from the back of the one on the left, though it still moved in tandem with the first one. The wound had been cauterized, and was edged with black skin.

I nodded towards the young Tyzaran girl. "Zenzara can't remain here on the station. She is in even more danger here than she would be with me."

"I do not think the Supreme Council will listen ..."

A small figure pushed me to one side and faced off with Denaraz. "You can't stop me from staying with Mallivan Bell!" Zenzie's crest was vertical and her wrinkles so deep they hung off her small face. "I *won't* go with you!"

I glared at her back. She had nearly pushed me over again. Luckily, Neema had grabbed out at my shoulder to steady me. "Thanks, Zenzie," I muttered darkly.

"I am not going to stay on Tyzar!" She stepped back and regarded us both. "I will throw myself out of an airlock first, and then where will your precious Chyzar be?"

"You cannot do that!" Denaraz went two shades paler. "How can you even say such a thing?"

Zenzie put both hands on her hips. "Either the Savior Protocols are prime mandates or they are not. You can't switch things around just because it suits you. Can he, Mallivan Bell?" She looked at me.

I saw Mel give me a challenging look. Sammy and the Enif were also expectant. I sighed. "I guess not. But we have no ship any more. Where are we supposed to go?"

Zenzie considered, her crest doubling over momentarily. Then she brightened and turned to Denaraz. "You can give us one!"

Denaraz almost choked. "What!"

"It's the perfect solution. Give us one with the new ZEPH drive so we can outrun any problems we may have."

"G-G-Give you one ... one ..." Denaraz's crests hit their maximum height and his whole face became smooth with shock. "That ... that is impossible!"

"I don't see why." Zenzara was skipping from one foot to another. "I'm important now. Aren't I, Mallivan?"

She was. I just wasn't sure she was *that* important. "Sure, Zenzara. You are the next Chyzar. They won't want you traveling in a tin bucket."

She gave Denaraz a triumphant look. "See?"

"We are hardly going to give one of our new ZEPH drives to a bunch of ... of ... of ..."

He was struggling, poor thing. I decided to take pity on him. "... allied colleagues?"

He was tempted to answer quickly, then closed his mouth with a sharp click. "Yes. Yes, I suppose you are all allies now. Now that the Terran forces are attacking everything and stealing technology." His voice was grudging. "I suppose there is an argument for ... I suppose I could propose ..." He became lost in his own thoughts.

Zenzie opened her own mouth but I pushed her behind me. She grumbled as Seyal took one arm and stepped backwards with her. I could hear Seyal gently trying to explain that she should leave things as they were. The seed had been planted. Sometimes it took time for things to grow. The Avarak woman continually surprised me. There was so much more to her than the self-effacing nonentity she had seemed at first. Her face was still featureless; her inner self was far from it. The individual we were now getting to know was wise and thoughtful. A very far cry from the warmongering Avarak males. I was amazed at the difference between the sexes. Life back on Rhyveka must have been so hard for her. For any of the female Avaraks, I guessed. I was pretty glad I hadn't been born female in the Veka star system.

Denaraz's glance encompassed us all. "Please wait here. As soon as the recovery teams report back I shall arrange for a meeting with a Supreme."

Anzany gave a small squeak of surprise. Supremes were important, then. Good.

I bowed slightly. "That will be most acceptable. Thank you." There was no point in alienating Denaraz further.

The spokesdesignate peered past me towards Zenzara. "I ... am sorry. The Enclave have been more successful in winning minds than was estimated. You should know that, even so, they are a tiny minority."

I heard Zenzie mumble something. Whatever it was, it served to appease Denaraz. He hobbled slowly off, looking as though the cares of the world were weighing on his shoulders.

It took them three full hours to organize a manhunt to find those responsible for the attack on the space station. They didn't succeed. Several ships had taken off shortly after the event, and investigations led the authorities to realize that these ships had been carrying those ultimately responsible. The smaller fry had been killed while carrying out the attack. It had always been a suicide mission for those members of the Enclave who actually carried it out. The rest ... the heads of the organization ... had disappeared, together with three Tyzaran navy vessels. Denaraz became progressively more depressed.

"The Enclave has become well-rooted in our culture," he told me in confidence. "Our leaders were blind to the attraction of such ill-founded doctrine. Even so, I think they would not have succeeded had it not been for this war that the Terrans have instigated. This war has given us all an excuse to hate. And when we hate, we become protectionist."

"A Chyzar bound to an alien through the Savior Protocols is too much for many Tyzarans to swallow?"

He nodded. "I'm afraid it is." He looked again at the floor. "It is silly, but many of my people have been seduced by the rhetoric. I am sorry."

I grinned. "That's all right, Spokesdesignate. I can hardly claim any better for humans, whether we are Spacelanders or Flatlanders. The Terrans are a case in point."

"You are generous."

Not really. I was getting tiring of Tyzar. I wanted to get away, to find out exactly what was going on in the world, who was beating who in this crazy dispute, what my fellow Spacelanders were doing. Had we armed to defend against the Terrans? Had war officially been declared? Who were the allies? Who formed the axis?

I came to my senses sharply as Denaraz's words filtered through my thoughts. "...So the Supreme will visit this afternoon."

At last! "Will he be able to take a decision on the matter?"

"She. Yes. She has full authority over this."

"How many Supremes are there on Tyzar?"

Denaraz considered. "Around thirty. In total we have fifty. The rest are with our fleet in various parts of the Shells."

"And they all have the power to decide?"

He hesitated, perhaps unwilling to give me any further information. "They do, yes."

Zenzie was staring at him too. She had picked up on his slight pause. She raised one eyebrow, which made the skin above her eye heap up in large craters. I found myself fascinated by the sight, wondering just what she would look like when she had grown enough to fill out all of that loose skin.

"What?" She had caught me gawping.

"Nothing." I held up a disclaiming hand. "Just thinking."

That caused the other eyebrow to raise. Her forehead was so furrowed that her eyes were almost invisible. I grinned, which only made her more exasperated. She tilted her head to one side and narrowed her eyes at me to reiterate her question.

I grinned again. "No, really. I *was* just thinking."

Her eyes by now were mere slits. "I hope you aren't insulting me."

"Me? I wouldn't do that, *Ty* Zylarian. I have far too much respect for you."

"Hmm. I should hope so."

I turned back to Denaraz. "So they have some sort of implanted ansible communication between them?"

His crests told me my guess was correct. They stood straight out from his scalp and went grey. His voice was several pitches higher. "NO!"

"I see." I did. He was hardly about to confirm something like that to someone like me. He had a problem.

But it was interesting. The Supremes could communicate with each other instantaneously. Without needy the bulky ansible machines we all knew about? How? And how had they managed to keep it secret? It must be something known only to a few.

Denaraz was now shaking. The fact that his physical tells might have confirmed my suspicions was clearly anathema to him. He looked horrified. I even felt sorry for the Tyzaran man, who had lost all semblance of serenity.

Zenzie was mirroring his distress, her gaze darting around to identify the source of his fear. She was still just a little too young to have picked up on the subtext. I touched her shoulders. "Don't worry. There is nothing wrong."

"There is! I can feel it!"

"No. Calm down. Everything is all right!"

She shook herself. "Don't tell me to calm down! I am not a human! And if I were I wouldn't let you tell me to calm down!" Her muscles tensed, to ready her for flight or fight.

"Nothing is going to hurt you Zenzara. Now, stop all this nonsense!"

She appeared to be deciding whether to attack me or not. I was careful not to move. Eventually, the tension began to drain out of her. We all began to breathe more collectedly. It amazes me that the Tyzarans can still function with such strong reactions to fear. They have been able to overcome it to become arguably the second most advanced civilization of the eight Shell races. Even my own acute stress response in the prehistoric part of my brain had been triggered by their distress.

I had what I wanted. It was time to move on. "What are your instructions to us until the Supreme arrives on board? How may we help the rescue operation?"

Denaraz relaxed at last. "There is little you can do. I dare not place you back on the space station at this stage. The risk to you is too great. It may also create some distress amongst those affected. I would ask you all to stay here."

I nodded. It galled not to be able to do anything to help all the casualties, but I would probably have done the same if I had been in his position. If we wanted to change anything we would have to go over his head.

We were escorted through the ship, which looked to be newly commissioned, to a large lounge area with several small sleeping compartments leading off it. There was also a well-equipped long galley kitchen with trays offering refreshments already laid out.

We sat down after taking a few things to eat and drink. None of us was really hungry. Too much had happened in too short a space of time. My adrenalin was still spiked, leaving me unable to settle. I found myself squirming on the seat, finally having to get up and walk around. The others, apart from Seyal, seemed to be much the same.

I asked the two Enif about their reactions to fear and stress. Did they have a similar flight-or-fight response ingrained genetically?

There was a short exchange between them before Eshaan replied.

"Not really," it told me. "We have a different response to danger. Our equivalent to your adrenalin is a boost of processing power in our brains. It allows us to calculate the odds of survival very quickly, facilitating a decision that may save us from whatever is threatening us."

Why didn't humans have that? It sounded like a really useful way to react to danger. Sometimes my adrenalin rush actually prevented me from thinking clearly. All it seemed to do was urge me irresistibly into action of some kind. Hmm. Good to know. That, of course, explained why the two Enif had been so useful on the Vaer ship and on other occasions we had been threatened.

I asked Seyal the same question. She laughed. "Female Avaraks have learned not to react very much to danger. We experience it from the moment we are born until the moment we die, which is almost always before the age of twenty."

My eyebrows must have shot up, because she elaborated. "We are completely subservient to the males of our species. Even our voices are altered to their requirements."

I stared at her.

She gave a faint smile. "We are submitted to the treatment at 8 years old. They give us an injection which blocks signals from the nerves to the muscles of the throat. This forces our vocal chords to atrophy. It delivers, on puberty, a small hoarse breathy voice that the male Avaraks find irresistible. Then we await a visit from the seekers."

We were all looking at her now. She looked away for a second or two, reliving some of her own past. "Every noble house of Avarak will have at least three seekers. Their job ... their only job ... is to travel Rhyveka and search out females. They look for the females with the most breathy voices. They find the sweetest voiced females for the males of their own houses. Avaraks can have up to thirty wives at one time, because so many of us die either before or during childbirth. The difference in size makes carrying a male child extremely dangerous."

"Not carrying a female child?"

"No, not females." Seyal looked at the floor. "But we ... aren't allowed to carry females. Not those of us who are chosen. Females are born through insemination. Those who are not chosen on search provide them."

Both Zenzara and Mel were looking thundery. I signaled them to be quiet. I was pretty sure Seyal needed to tell us about this. "Go on," I urged.

"If we are found to be carrying females the pregnancy is terminated." Mel gasped in affront.

"They breed from us until we are twenty-one. Those that survive until then ... about four percent ... become midwives and advisors and are freed from their marital responsibilities."

"Only four percent survive until twenty-one?" Zenzie's face was a study.

"The eldest female Avaraks are in their thirties. We do not live long. Only about one in a thousand reach their thirtieth birthday. I know of none who reached thirty-five."

"But male Avaraks live for a long time, don't they?"

She nodded. "Until they are eighty or ninety. That is why they need so many wives. When a male Avarak dies, his remaining wives are auctioned off to the highest bidder."

Sammy stirred. He wasn't liking this any more than I was. "You mean that females belong to the males?"

Seyal looked gratefully at him. "Exactly! We have no rights of our own. We have no reactions when in danger. Why would we? Our males act for us. No action is required of females."

Mel had been considering Seyal's words. "Then you are at risk with this pregnancy. You are carrying a male child?"

"I am. However, I have a thirty-five percent chance of survival."

Mel gave a nervous laugh. "Thirty-five percent? How can you live with that?"

Seyal treated her to a calm smile. "Precisely because I have no fear response. We must accept what is predestined."

Zenzie was fairly bouncing on her seat. "But you shouldn't ..."

"Thank you for sharing, Seyal," I interrupted, gaining myself a furious look from our burgeoning Chyzar. "That must have been difficult."

"No. Why?"

"When is the baby due? Do you know?"

She cradled her stomach. "Soon. I think maybe two weeks."

Sammy and I exchanged glances. "Then you will need a doctor."

"Why?"

I was thinking that you could take this fatalistic approach too far. "We will make sure there is a Tyzaran doctor available. I am sure they will have better technology than your people do."

"Our doctors only treat male Avaraks."

Now why did that not surprise me? This whole conversation was making me feel even more twitchy than I had been. The Spacelander method of creating a new generation was hardly the most desirable, but it was streets ahead of this. I felt very sorry for Seyal.

"Well, Seyal, *you* will have a doctor attending when you go into labor. I will make sure of it."

Her eyes opened very wide. "Thank you Mallivan Bell. I ... I would appreciate that. My son is going to be most important to the Avaraks."

"And *you* are important to us!" Zenzara could hold her opinion to herself no longer. It came out in a burst of angry air.

Seyal seemed confused. "I am? Really?"

Zenzie huffed. "Yes. Really!"

Mel nodded. The Enif inclined their heads. Even I muttered something.

Seyal's face suddenly became shiny and red. She didn't know where to look. I guess nobody had ever said anything like that to her before.

Neema took Anzany's hand and squeezed it. Sammy noticed and raised one eyebrow. He looked to me and raised the other. I replied in the same way. He lifted his head, silently acknowledging it.

But Seyal's comments meant that we would have to remain here at least until her son was born. That was not good news. I had been hoping to convince the Tyzarans to give us some sort of transport to enable us to make our way back to the Spacelander fleet. I might still be unsure who was fighting who in this ridiculous war, but what I did know is that I would be expected to make my way to the Landau Rift. Even after everything that had happened to us.

Several hours later the doors to the lounge swished open. I was impressed by the tall figure that stepped through them.

She was taut-faced, which made her a very old lady, in Tyzaran terms. All of the wrinkles and folds of her face had been taken up. The skin was stretched tight across her skull.

She held herself regally. There was a presence about her that was impossible to ignore.

She wore a long swirling robe, and I counted three pairs of nivala fastened to the front. That made my eyes track to her neck. There were no fewer than four thoria wrapped around it. This was a woman who could react, and I got the impression she would react very quickly indeed.

Zenzara's crest had spiked, but the new arrival's had not. She appeared utterly composed and confident.

"I am Supreme Oznard. I have been briefed by Spokesdesignate Denaraz." She glided forwards, her gaze fixed on Zenzara. "And you must be our new Chyzar."

Zenzara seemed tongue-tied for once in her life. Good. I stepped to greet the woman, holding out my hand. "Ryler Mallivan Bell. How do you do?"

She slid past me, seeming not to notice my hand. I retracted it. She stopped in front of Zenzara, examining her intently.

"Yes. You are the one who let our ZEPH drive be taken." The only way I knew she was speaking to me was from the slightest twist of her head.

That comment irked. I wasn't even Tyzaran! "Not exactly, Supreme Oznard. I believe it was one of your own traitors who did that."

Her eyes flashed. She wasn't used to being spoken to like that. Too bad. There was no way she was going to shunt responsibility for her own fiasco onto me. I had already lost enough control.

Her lips thinned. "We cannot allow you to take our Chyzar away from us!"

"Excuse me, but it is your own stupid Savior Law that gave her to me in the first place." I was hyperventilating, and I didn't need the kick Mel gave me to realize I was far too aggressive. I bowed, trying to correct the way this was going. "I mean, I am merely obeying your own legislation."

She waved an airy hand. "No need any more. We will pass an amendment to the Savior Protocol, annulling it. She can stay here, with us."

An extremely stubborn look had landed on Zenzie's face. Her eyes flashed. "I will not!"

Oznard examined her dispassionately. "You are unwell, my child. The process of becoming a Chyzar has affected your judgement. I will forgive your speaking to a Supreme like that." Her attitude clearly added *for the time being*.

Zenzie stamped her foot. "It has not!"

Oznard rolled her eyes a little. "Quite a normal effect, I assure you."

I bit my lip. This wasn't a good start.

However, I had not counted on Neema. Both she and Anzany stepped forwards to confront Oznard, though it was Anzany who spoke.

"Supreme. I am Anzany Enordizan, from the Sezzerezz region. May

I address you?"

Oznard's expression was anything but welcoming. She paused, but finally gave her consent. "Go ahead."

"Thank you, Supreme." Anzany steadied herself for a couple of seconds, before going on. "I have been assigned to the Sezzerezz think tank for the last two years. We were required by the justice department of the main Supreme to investigate the legal boundaries of the Savior Protocols."

"Yes. And?"

"There are none."

Oznard's eyes snapped together. "What do you mean, there are none?"

"There are no boundaries. The Savior protocols do not allow for any changes to be made, nor are legal interpretations possible."

"According to the Sezzerezz think tank, I believe you mean." Oznard's tone made it fairly clear what she thought of the Sezzerezz think tank.

"No, Supreme. According to law."

"And just what are you doing here, if one may ask?"

Anzany's chin came up. "I was asked to attend by Mr. Mallivan. I am the appointed legal advisor to the new Chyzar."

This was news to me. And to the new Chyzar. Zenzara turned to the Tyzaran girl in some surprise.

"Your own ... client ... appears to be unaware of this."

Anzany smiled slowly. "As you yourself, said, Supreme, the process of becoming a Chyzar can be confusing."

We all gasped at that, I think. But it was a master stroke. It left Oznard's mouth flapping in the breeze. I stepped forwards. "Our legal advisor has made it clear to us that even the Supreme Council may not alter the terms of the Savior Protocol. Most unfortunate, but don't you feel that it would be wise to make the best of a bad situation?"

"I fail to understand you."

"Oh, I think you understand me all right, Supreme Oznard. I am hoping we can come to some sort of agreement between all parties, here. I quite understand the importance of a new Chyzar to the Tyzaran people, but it seems that Zenzara's obligations under the Savior Protocols must take precedence. Are you certain that you and the rest of the Supreme Council wish to alienate her even further?"

Oznard's face took on a vacant expression. I felt sure that she was communicating with the rest of the Supreme Council. I wished I knew how they were doing *that*.

Then her face snapped back to its previous tautness. "We will discuss this amongst members of the Supreme Council. Please wait here."

"I would like to ask that Anzany Enordizan be attached to us for the duration of our stay. And that Neema Agazed – the liaison between our people here on Tyzar – also be allowed to remain with us."

She breathed in and then out through her nose, considering. "Very well."

Her garments rustled as she strode back through the doors. They closed after her with a slight noise of relief. At least, that is what it seemed like to me.

I smiled at Anzany. "Thank you. That was very helpful."

To my surprise, Anzany blushed. "That's all right. I wanted to help. Neema has told me all about you, you see."

"I hope you don't mind my asking for you to stay here with us. We need all the help we can get."

"I don't mind." She looked shyly over her shoulder and extended one hand to take Neema's. "*We* don't mind."

It was clearly a declaration; Neema's expression told us that much. We applauded and they looked even more bashful. I wondered if it was the very first time that they had admitted to having a relationship. If so, it said a great deal for the repressive atmosphere in Tyzar. Not the great liberals I had taken them for, then. I was learning quite a lot this trip.

Sammy was pumping Neema's hand and making rude comments in the way good friends always have and always will. Mel was shaking her head and rolling her eyes at Sammy's comments in the way other good friends always have and always will.

I left them to it. I needed to think. It was my responsibility to get my group safely off the planet, safely out of the Bifold Shell. It wasn't going to be easy. We were still being bandied from one side to another like a football, according to the whims of each race. I had to find a way to get us out of play long enough for a strategic retreat.

10

The next morning found us still waiting. Tensions inside the room had been rising and we were irritable, to say the least. We had only had a couple of hours sleep each. I had been in a portable Zeroth tank overnight because of my arm injury. We had been kept incommunicado from everybody else, so none of us had any way of knowing what had been going on with the rescue attempt. It was an unpleasant, dragging time. The two Enif were the only ones able to confront the situation with some equanimity. Didjal had dismounted a large table top from its supports and Eshaan had settled in front of it and begun to create art on the surface.

Seyal finally came over to me. She was uncomfortable; her hands were gently massaging her baby bump.

I tried to smile. "Are you all right, Seyal?"

Her features seemed to blur more. "I am within acceptable limits, thank you, Mallivan Bell. But I wish to say something."

"I am listening."

"You must leave me here." She went red-faced at her own temerity, but still held up a hand to stop me speaking. I closed my mouth again. This must be most important to her.

She closed her eyes for a moment. "I wish not to be the reason for any trouble. Please leave me here. My son will be born and then I can find you."

"You might want to stay on Tyzar."

She frowned. "Why? What is there for us on Tyzar?"

"What is there for you with us?"

Seyal went even redder, her features almost disappearing into the smoothness of the rest of her face. "You do not wish me to join you?"

"No! I mean, of course we do! I was simply saying that things might be safer for you and your son here."

She looked doubtful, and I had to agree with her. The Tyzarans hadn't shown themselves in a great light. Blowing up your own space station was hardly an endearing trait.

I felt myself getting nervous again. I hadn't asked for all this responsibility! Now it seemed I had a whole group dependent on me!

I glared at her. Not that it was her fault, but I wasn't entirely rational. "You can't expect me to keep you safe!"

She took a small step back, intimidated by my tone. "I wish only to stay with the rest."

Mel stepped in, putting a comforting arm around her. "Rye, you have to stop snapping at people when you get stressed."

"Me? I don't!"

"Says the guy who threatened to shoot me."

I shuffled a little. "I expect you deserved it."

"I know it is a lot to take on, but you did step up. You can't reject us all now. You know you can't."

"I don't want to!"

"Then stop trying to wriggle out of it all!"

"Stop telling me what to do!"

"See? Your hands are shaking again. Just like in all the fights. You become a ... a different person when you are fighting."

"It is just an adrenaline spike. Everybody gets them."

"Not everybody gets so crotchety."

I made a low noise in my throat and turned away. Nobody likes being criticized. Though it is true that I do get very angry when I am stressed. I guess. Don't know what she expects me to do about it though. It's not as if I can choose how my body reacts.

Mel hadn't finished. "We are not leaving Seyal on Tyzar!"

I spun around. "I am the one in charge here!"

Her lip curled. "Then act like it!"

I felt like putting my hands around her neck and throttling her. Didn't she realize that I had been trying to act like it all this time?

She pulled Seyal another step back. She must have read my mind. "See?" she said. "You are doing it again. You get scary when you look like that."

Seyal did seem terrified.

I sighed. "I am sorry. You ... you may be right. I ... I will try to be better. And I *will* try not to snap at people."

Sammy gave a snort, as if to say 'good luck with that'. I couldn't help glaring at him, which for some reason made them all laugh.

I held up my hands. "Stop it! All of you! I am only doing the best I can!"

Mel pursed her lips. "We know that, Rye. And we trust you. You have kept us all alive so far. Even that is a miracle, considering everything. Just ... just try to relax a bit, will you? You are wound up so tight ... I am scared you will burst."

"I'll try."

Her gaze softened. "It is hard for you, I know. You weren't expecting to have any of this thrust on you. But you have it now, and that isn't going to change. You have to stop feeling cross about it."

I did feel cross. She was right. I was furious at just about every stupid government in the Major Shells. You would think that the politicians could organize things better. That, after all, is what they are paid to do. Look at how many had died, just because of some idiot's expansionist tendencies. It did make me angry. Of course it did. Lives cut short, others completely changed, just for more galactic real estate. It sucked.

At that moment the door slid open and Oznard came back in, accompanied by three other Tyzarans. Denaraz was not with them; he had been ordered by the Supreme to spend at least one night in the Zeroth chamber. He had sent a message that he would join us shortly.

We all stiffened. I stepped forward.

I was still feeling annoyed. My chin came up. "Well, Supreme?"

She looked far haughtier than me. "We have examined the original protocols. They do seem inflexible on some points."

"You mean that they cannot be broken?"

"It is debatable whether or not they can."

"Then Zenzara Zylarian can stay with me?"

"Yes. However ..."

Why did I know that was coming?

".. You will be required to provide for her in a way which is suitable for a future Chyzar."

"Which is ...?"

"Any ship she travels in must be equipped with only the best technology. The Chyzar must be protected."

"And how am I supposed to afford this?" It seemed to me that they were taking my largesse a bit too far. I had lost my only ship, and although I had been very fond of it, it could hardly have been called cutting edge in the first place.

Her head ratcheted back one notch. I wondered whether it hurt her neck. "You will be supplied with a ZEPH prototype."

"Excuse me?" That was about the last thing I had expected to hear. When Zenzara had suggested it I had taken the whole idea as a joke.

"The Tyzar government will loan you a small Myndraka-class patrol ship equipped with ZEPH drive - for your use. We will provide the crew of twelve."

"You will not."

It was her turn to look taken aback. I felt a certain amount of satisfaction to see I could shake her that much.

I went on, "I will not have my life dictated to by Tyzar. If you want to settle a ship on us, or loan one to us, fine. But there are enough of us to crew it ourselves. I will not have any further Tyzaran presence. We already have bridge and engineering crew. New personnel would be unnecessary."

"Unacceptable!"

"Non-negotiable!"

That had gone well. She was staring at me as if I had just grown a pair of antennae. I was just plain angry. I had decided that I was just about as fed up as I could be of us all being mere pawns in somebody else's chess game.

Oznard seemed unaware of my new determination. "The Chyzar cannot be left unattended. She must have Tyzarans with her."

I glanced at Zenzie. Her crest was vertical and she was giving me don't-agree-to-that signals with her eyes.

"She can have one other Tyzaran aboard," I conceded, earning myself a flash of disapproval from Zenzie herself. I held up my hand, so that the girl wouldn't interrupt. From the corner of my eye I saw Mel bend down and whisper something to her.

"... But that person must be acceptable to the rest of the crew," I finished.

Oznard didn't like it. Well, neither did I. But I could see I was going to have to cede in some way in this negotiation. I wasn't exactly negotiating from a position of strength here. They could simply throw all of us in prison and leave us there. I didn't want to tempt them.

Oznard considered. "And acceptable to me," she said finally. "With that proviso, I will agree. It will also be necessary for you to bring the ship to Tyzar itself once a year for a service. If you and the Chyzar agree to come too, we can have an agreement drawn up."

"For how long? The yearly service?" I didn't need Zenzara's start of disagreement to tell me how unwelcome that was.

"Hmm. Let's say ... three of your standard weeks?"

"Three space weeks? Each year? Very well."

"During which time the Chyzar will submit to our medical staff to ensure her continued health?"

I swear Zenzara hissed at Oznard. The Supreme looked shocked. Mel took hold of Zenzie's thin arm, to prevent her from moving forward.

"I won't!" the girl railed, trying to break free from the grasp.

"The Supreme is merely trying to ensure your continued health." I tried to keep my tone even, though she wasn't helping things.

Zenzie's eyes narrowed as she turned on me. "Who got us out of the Avarak ship?"

"You did."

"Then why are you negotiating on my behalf now? It is *my* life."

I nodded. "Then negotiate."

Zenzara gave a bit of a gulp, then settled herself. She stepped forward and met Oznard's gaze. "I will come. I will let your doctors check me over. But I want final approval on any test or procedure or medicine I am given."

"In writing," I said hastily.

Zenzie first glared at me and then tipped her head to one side. "In writing," she repeated.

The Supreme looked away for a few moments, presumably discussing mentally with her fellow members of the Supreme Council. "Very well. You will have to stay here for several weeks longer until we can organize a suitable vessel and get it fully equipped."

"The need for Miss Zylarian's permission for all and any medical process to begin straight away." I suggested.

"Immediately." Zenzara's tone was flat, brooking no opposition.

Oznard's nostrils dilated as she breathed in then out. "Acceptable," she said, with some reluctance.

Zenzara danced on the spot. "Great!" Then she hugged first Mel, and then me. "Freedom!"

Mel looked across at me. It would be freedom of a sort, certainly. But a very different life for all of us than the one we had planned.

I checked around the room. Only Seyal seemed unequivocal about the decision. She was chittering to herself, clearly well-pleased. The rest of us were quiet. We knew we had committed to something none of us had ever considered. It felt very strange. None of us had taken a decision to go in this direction; it had simply been thrust upon us.

I sighed. There was no going back now. The Avarak attack on

Commorancy had put paid to the safe timeline we had been living before. There was no way backward. We had to keep on walking. One step in front of the other.

Sammy was the one to put it into words. "What shall we be?" he asked, staring around at us one by one. "What is our purpose?"

Good question. One I could see mirrored in every single face staring back at him. Who were we going to be, and what were we going to do?

The ever practical Didjal was the one to break the spell. "It is unclear what the future holds for us," it said firmly. "But we *can* help those injured by the explosions here."

Oznard opened her mouth to tell us it would be too dangerous.

Zenzara stepped in front of the rest of us. "I am the Chyzar. At least, I will be soon. We will not sit back while others die. That explosion was meant for me … for us. We must help. We cannot sit penned in here for the next few weeks. Impossible!"

The nostrils flared again. "Very well. You may help in the rescue work. But I will assign Tyzaran Supreme guards around you. I will not risk a similar attack on any of you."

Zenzie looked at me. I gave the smallest of nods. She turned back to the Supreme. "That will be acceptable. Thank you."

Oznard gave a thin smile. "In that case, my work is done. You will see me again when the ship is transferred to you. Please be extremely circumspect as you move through the space station. Emotions are high, and we would wish to avoid any further problems."

We all nodded at that.

Oznard swept away. There was a murmur of sound as soon as she had left. Our future was decided. Now we could go and help some of the people affected by the explosion. There was a rush for the door.

Yesterday's carnage lingered in the docking ring area of the space station. I was horrified to see just how many innocent people had been culled by the explosion.

Even though the explosion had happened the day before, there was still plenty we could do to help. Not all of the bodies had been removed. The Tyzaran authorities were taking their time, it seemed. I was surprised. For such an advanced member of the Major Shells, they were unwieldy. I had assumed, wrongly, that they would be far quicker in their rescue attempts. I was glad to belong to the Spacelander community. We trained exhaustively to combat emergency situations.

The worst area affected was the *Aurynth* dock. And it was not only the space station. Because the *Aurynth* had still been alongside the space station, the force of the explosion had torn into the ship's flank too. Large holes peppered the side of the ship facing the station. I could see several bodies trapped within the debris. Many of her crew members must have died. Decompression would have torn through the ship, and most of those inside would not have been protected by EVA suits. The ship wouldn't be going anywhere anytime soon.

I looked around at what seemed to have become my little group. They were staring expectantly at me. Waiting for instructions. Even Mel, usually fear-stricken into immobility, was eager to help. I gave them a nod. "Let's clear a path through to *Aurynth*. There may still be something we can do to save lives on board. We owe them our support, I believe."

The two Enif led the way. It was the first time I had seen them heading together into physical work. Eshaan was behind Didjal, true, but its arms were just as committed as it began to work its way through bent metal spars and other debris that was blocking the docking ring.

Mel and Sammy were close behind, followed by Anzany and Neema. Zenzara marched in the rear and I was trying to make sure she was safe. She could still be in danger, though most of the people in the area did appear to be concentrating on rescue rather than attack. Seyal had fallen in behind us, but I had shaken my head at her.

"Stay here, Seyal. You are about to give birth. This is not something you need to do."

She had hesitated. Then her small padded hands had gone to her stomach in a protective manner. She knew that I was right. In the end she had simply nodded and stepped aside. She was far too close to going into labor to risk her whole pregnancy again. She had been very lucky so far that all the events we had lived through had not provoked damage to her son. At least, I hoped that they hadn't.

Even so, her face had shown regret as she was left behind. She felt she was letting us down.

Behind me, a rather poker-faced Denaraz had appeared. Whether he had been assigned to watch over us or not was unclear. Perhaps he was there voluntarily. I had no idea. I was finding him a difficult man to read.

The buckled and twisted metal made our progress slow. If it hadn't been for the two Enif, I doubt we could have cleared a passageway to the *Aurynth*. With them, we moved steadily towards the broken hatches.

I stared down at the patch of charred deck plating where the attacker had stood. I could see him if I closed my eyes. His image had been burned into my retina. I don't think I could ever forget it. That split second when I fired, knowing it was too late to change anything.

"You couldn't have stopped them." Denaraz had come up silently and was staring, grim-faced, at the same spot. His leg looked much stronger; he was hardly limping. "There were more than one. This was simply the first assassin. Bombs were detonated there ..." he pointed, "... and there." He pointed again.

"Were they? I was too busy trying to save myself." I could hear the shame in my voice.

"You saved your crew. You were entitled to save yourself. You did well. You saved me." His own voice hardened. "Yet I was not able to save my own crew."

"Do you know how many casualties there were on *Aurynth*?"

He shook his head. "I have been isolated from my ship until now."

I could tell that the uncertainty was eating away at his spirit. "All right." I touched his arm briefly. "Then let's find out."

The pain was written across his face. "Yes."

We began to move more and more of the debris out of the way. I tried not to look at the bodies floating so close on the other side of the airlock. You could not have recognized them, in any case. The prolonged exposure to the vacuum had caused space-swell to bloat their remains into grotesque balloon figures. It was easier not to look.

At last we made it to the airlock. Denaraz shouted over to some of the Tyzarans who were working nearby. They nodded. A portable airlock, roomy enough to accommodate a couple of men in EVA suits, was manhandled across to us, together with a couple of the EVA suits themselves.

He and I struggled inside the suits and then shuffled into the portalock. These are contraptions that clamp up against standard airlocks and can be used once to decompress and once to compress. They must then be discarded. However, they work well to override the failsafes of traditional airlocks, and permit a limited form of transit through to vacuum environments.

Just before the portalock was decompressed a figure pushed its way into the portalock with us. It was Didjal.

"You might be needing a good engineer," it told me with some severity. "I am an extremely good engineer."

Denaraz was staring.

"It's all right," I reassured him. "The Enif can take full decompression for much longer than we can. Didjal will be fine, at least for a few hours. Right, Didjal?"

The Enif gave its equivalent of a grin. "Sure."

Denaraz rolled his eyes, an unspoken comment on the sanity of the newcomer. I nodded. He wasn't wrong.

Didjal squeaked as the air disappeared from around us, but that was the only sound it made. When the air had finally disappeared from the portalock, it grabbed at the safety-overridden hatch and helped us tug the emergency T bar out of its housing.

It took all three of us to force the bar ninety degrees around so that the mechanisms on the other side of the hatch would disengage. I realized just how much force the Enif can put into their forearms. They might seem slim when you first look at them, but they are extremely strong.

Finally there was a quiet snick of metal retracting and the hatch opened for us. We propelled ourselves out into the vacuum to the opposing hatch on the *Aurynth*. It must have been around fifteen meters away.

Since the hatch was now standing as a lonely sentinel between two decompressed atmospheres, the safety was not engaged. It was a simple matter to open the hatch and pass into the ship's airlock.

That too, was standing open.

I checked Didjal, but the Enif was still showing no signs of distress of any type. Some advantage, in a spacefaring race! My own EVA suit was as heavy as hell, making it quite hard to make progress along the corridor.

We worked for six hours, before we had everything tidied up enough to be able to seal the breaches and compress the whole area once more. Didjal had returned to the space station after the first hour, and spent the time getting a replacement docking tube. The two Enif set it up so that once we compressed again there could be free transit between the ship and the station.

We had come across twenty bodies. We knew that more had floated away from the station overnight. The shrapnel expelled was enough to put an outwards velocity on the cadavers. The final total, Denaraz thought, would be closer to thirty. And that was only from his ship. The total casualties were thought to be in the region of 200 dead and 550 injured. It was a devastating blow to the space station.

Denaraz worked ceaselessly for all those hours. I came to respect him. If we were forced to accept a spokesdesignate on whatever ship we were given, then he might not be a bad choice. I could see how affected he was by the loss of so many of his crew. That may not make him a good person, but it did show that he cared for those who worked under him. Most of the Tyzarans I had met seemed to be very cold. I couldn't see Supreme Oznard giving a fig for the people she worked with. She had far too inflated an opinion of herself.

At last we were done. The link to the space station was up and running and fully compressed. The air was breathable.

Just in case, we tested it by removing the EVA helmets. The air was tainted, but acceptable.

I ran a hand through my hair, which was flattened from the EVA helmet. I caught Denaraz doing the same with his crests. We grinned at each other. Such a small thing, but it did bring us closer.

We walked up to the airlock that had automatically sealed the rest of the ship. Denaraz rapped sharply on the bulkhead to one side. We waited to hear corresponding raps back.

He looked at me and then pressed the automatic reset on the safety valve override, inputting a long password when prompted.

There was a click, and then the hatch rolled quickly to one side. We found ourselves staring into the gazes of the remaining crew. Their expressions of wariness quickly became relief as they spotted their commander.

I was glad to get the man back to his ship. Even so, the Tyzaran spokesdesignate appeared shell-shocked. His previous certainty had morphed into hesitancy. He was not the same leader he had been the day before. He had been diminished in some way by the attack.

"I never thought I would live to see Tyzaran attacking Tyzaran," he had said to me in a small voice as his eyes sadly took in the gouged metal which marked the explosions in the skin of the space station. "We always thought we were superior."

I shrugged. "You were. Technologically, at least. None of the other races would have got far in space without Tyzaran artificial gravity plating, after all."

He pulled what few wrinkles were left on his face together. "But not socially, it seems."

I couldn't deny that. What had happened here was barbaric.

He was still bemused. "Why would the Enclave do this? What did they hope to gain by eliminating the new Chyzar?"

"I don't imagine they wanted to gain anything. They simply wanted to destroy something they can't understand."

"But we are Tyzarans!" His voice had gone up in pitch. "Not Nepheals, to be scared of gathering predators!"

I thought that was a little unfair to the Nepheals. I liked the tall beings as a race. It was hardly their fault that the ancestors to the Vaers had come close to exterminating them.

Now his eyes became glazed as he examined inwards instead of outwards. "I shall have to resign my commission," he said firmly. "I have caused too many of the men under me to die."

"You were not to blame for the actions of the Enclave."

"I should have foreseen more trouble. I had warning, after all." His face was stony. He waved his fingers in my direction. "Even you told me to wait!"

"You were under orders."

"I should have exercised discretion. I am responsible for many deaths."

I grabbed up at his shoulder and gave him a fierce shake. "You are not responsible for any of it. Now, stop it! You were under orders and you could not have known what was planned. Stop beating yourself up!"

His eyes came into focus on my face. He made a clear effort to pull himself together. "You are right, of course. I am sorry."

I peered at him. "You are not really going to resign?"

He lifted his shoulders. "How can I remain?"

I pressed my lips together. "Look, will you wait for a week? Please? I have an idea, and it won't work if you have resigned your commission."

He seemed more confused than ever. I squeezed his shoulder some more. He frowned as my fingers bit into his muscles, unused to such informality. "Oh, very well! I suppose I can wait a week."

"Thank you."

It was a good reunion with the rest of the crew, but I saw the emptiness in Denaraz's eyes. He would not forget any of this in a hurry. He waved a hand in agreement as I made signs I was leaving.

I could feel his eyes boring into my back as I walked away. But he would be a good choice. At least he had doubts, was prepared to examine his conscience. I would far rather have him than any of the other spokesdesignates. And I really didn't think the Supreme Council would allow us to fly away with only Anzany to represent Tyzar. This could be a good compromise. If he accepted, that is. He might. It could help to damp down the crippling guilt he was feeling for all the deaths on board the *Aurynth*.

As I walked through the docking tube back to the mangled space station, I saw Mel racing along the platform to meet me.

"Come quick!" she gasped, almost falling in her haste to get to me. "It's Seyal! It's time!"

Well, of course it was.

11

We stared at the ship. It was two weeks later, and none of us could find any words.

She was beautiful. A brand new, shiny, beautiful Myndraka-class patrol ship. She glittered under the artificial lighting in the enormous hold. She was somewhere between a burnished gold and a shiny copper.

We were on a secret base, somewhere behind the second-largest Tyzar moon. We had been spirited off Tyzar as soon as the main space station had been cleared for normal trading. The Supreme Council were taking no further risks with their future Chyzar.

Seyal and her new baby were standing to one side. The baby was making chortling noises as it played with its mother's hands.

"What are you going to call it?" asked Oznard, who seemed to be in a reasonably affable mood for the occasion. She was referring to the ship, not the baby.

I looked the ship over again. She had two normal-height decks on top and a deeper deck below for cargo and shuttles. She was around sixty meters overall, with a beam of about twenty and a similar height. She wasn't sufficiently reinforced or rugged to be a cruiser. But I liked her. She was smooth and sleek, shaped like a rounded chrysalis or lozenge with two slim E.P. receptor rods spiking out some ten feet in front of her. That made her a space-faring patrol ship, not meant to touch planet-side ever. She looked harmless, but I had been told that she was well-equipped with state-of-the-art ABlaser canons and defense rail guns.

There was an organic look about her. Sitting glittering in the hold, she reminded me of something.

"The ship looks just like one of those brooches you wear," I said to Zenzara. "The ones that look beautiful but can be deadly."

Zenzara ran her eyes over the elegant ship. She nodded. "The *Nivala*." Her head tilted to one side. "That would be a good name."

"*Nivala* it is," I told Supreme Oznard. "And it's a her; she's a her." I frowned, trying to figure out which of those two options was right. I find pronouns confusing sometimes.

Oznard inclined her head. "Very nice," she said. "*Nivala*, then." She looked along the ragged line of crew members who were about to take off in the new ship, her gaze stopping at Denaraz. Her pleased expression vanished. "Spokesdesignate."

"Supreme." Denaraz came to full attention. So did his crests. I saw that the site of amputation had healed well. The scar was hardly noticeable now. His leg had recovered well, too.

"I hope you realize the importance of your mission."

"Certainly, Supreme. To take care of the Chyzar."

"At all costs."

"At all costs, Supreme."

The Supreme turned her eyes to me. "Exactly," she murmured. "At all costs."

I shivered. I didn't like the tone she had used. I hoped that I hadn't made a mistake in suggesting Denaraz for the job of liaison between Tyzar and ourselves.

Zenzie was practically jumping up and down on the spot. "Can we see her? Can we? Can we?"

Oznard pasted a smile back on her face. She made it look difficult. "You may, Ty Zylarian. But please return here when you have finished your inspection. I would like to ... err ... ask something of your ... err ... group. Since you will be needing a maiden voyage to shake out any shipyard faults, that is."

I wasn't sure I liked the sound of that. But it would do us no harm to listen. Would it?

Zenzie ran ahead of us onto the *Nivala* and up the gangplank. She touched the shining side of the ship as she raced inside. It was nice to see her laugh again. There hadn't been much of that recently.

In fact there was an air of celebration about all of us. It felt so good to have the prospect of somewhere we could adopt as our own. Like flotsam being finally swept into a safe harbor.

The two Enif bounded along the gangplank after Zenzara. They seemed pleased at the height of the corridor beyond. They disappeared, examining their surroundings curiously.

Sammy stomped along in their wake, still limping slightly. I saw him turn back and grin at Mel. He held out his hand. She hesitated, then her face cleared as she slid her own fingers into his. He squeezed the hand, silently trying to help her over her claustronetia. She smiled back, straightened her shoulders and walked on, head up. I was glad for her that this new support seemed to be helping.

Then our new adepts walked inside. First Denaraz, newly promoted to the prestigious role of Guardian of the Chyzar. He strode on. He seemed glad to be treading new ground, even though he knew that the promotion actually hid a diminution of his responsibilities. Whatever the Tyzarans had claimed about the *Aurynth*, I was convinced that she had never been a research vessel. He was no longer captain of a fighting ship, no longer even figured on the ship's organigram. From now on, he would only be required to monitor and attend the new Chyzar. Yet he was now on an intermediate level between the spokesdesignates and the Supreme Council. His official title was now Adjunct, but he had already told me to address him simply as Denaraz.

It had taken him some days to accept the position. It had been a straight choice between resignation from all his duties or acceptance of this quite undefined new role. He told me that, in the end, consideration for his family had persuaded him. He had twelve siblings. He thought that the loss of face if he had resigned would have damaged their futures. Another reason to doubt that Tyzar was quite as advanced socially as I had previously thought.

I was glad he had decided to accept. I trusted him. Little by little, I had begun to see him as his own person. Our original antipathy had evaporated. Perhaps we could even become friends. One day. I was still watching him like a hawk.

Anzany and Neema I found easier. It could be because I owed them my life. That did help to make them more agreeable, right from the start.

Which left our Avarak lady and her newly-born son. Seyal was looking at me, rather than the new ship. Then she looked down at the bundle in her arms.

"His future," she told me. "He has no other."

I felt a shock of realization run through me. It was true. Seyal could not go back to the Avaraks. Her son Segaton would be rejected too. They really did have no future apart from us.

I swallowed. So much change in so little time.

She patted me on the upper arm. "Do not worry. We will be assets. You will be glad we are with you."

"I ... I already am."

She seemed to shrink in size. "No. You are not. Not yet. But you will be."

She touched me again on the shoulder and then lifted her son up. "See? Your new home. Shiny. Perfect."

Segaton managed a gurgle, which she took to be consent, for she made her way on board with slow, measured steps.

I saw that only the Supreme was left. I tried to beat a hasty retreat, but she was quicker than I was.

"Do you not wish to hear of your destination? For your maiden voyage?"

I gave a faint nod. It seemed only polite.

"Since you will be traveling with a group of our engineers in any case, I thought I would come with you. I have some business with the

Macers."

Now that *did* surprise me. The Macers are a semi-aquatic race of small but agile mammals. They live on the marine planet of Ulon Prime, in orbit around Ulon in the Great Shell. They eat only kelp which they dry on floating rafts on the interminable ocean.

Ulon Prime is a strange planet. Its ocean is of an almost uniform depth of between six to twelve meters. The Macers are air breathers but possess sacks which inflate around their necks to enable them to stay submerged for up to an hour. They have six almost identically long limbs, tipped with skeletal webbed fingers opposed by long thumbs. Underwater, they move on all six limbs at once and their tails help with propulsion. They would be unable to stand on their back two limbs, which are far too long and thin for that.

To our eyes they appear emaciated and ill. So I had been told. I had never seen one in the flesh. They are extremely delicate and find it hard to survive outside their salt water "cushion". They never travel into space. However, in their own habitat I believe they can survive for over a hundred years.

Moving rapidly on their spidery limbs, Macers are extremely bright and inquisitive. They have small intelligent heads with large curious eyes and a tiny nose. They have newt-like tails and the webbing between their digits enables them to move rapidly along the bottom of the seabed.

Their own name for themselves in unpronounceable, but the first visitors who came to Ulon Prime saw them macerating the seaweed on their floating rafts and immediately christened them the Macers.

Originally, the Macers felt very threatened by the alien species, though they tend to accept the Nepheals and the Tyzarans more than the others, as being more inherently pacific races.

I stared. "You have a meeting with the Legacy?"

She inclined her head, as she might have to a monkey who had just solved a particularly easy puzzle. "I have."

The Legacy is the Macer equivalent of government. Macers are loyal to a fault. There are no 'bad' Macers. They sacrifice themselves willingly for the greater good and perceive their own lives as merely being part of a chain of ancestors, linking to a social network. No Macer would dream of "shaming the Chain", which is their biggest possible insult. The Chain is the personal link, vertical, from the past to the future, whereas the Legacy is the way all chains interweave horizontally into a civilization – each individual's place in their current civilization.

Macers are isolationist by nature, but have come to realize that the Macer Legacy must participate in the politics of the Shells in order to have a voice and avoid future danger. They do so most unwillingly but with stubbornness. It is almost impossible to change a Macer's core values of fairness and decency, and they are valued for their ability to examine all options, from all sides.

For this reason they are held in high esteem in the Major Shells as great moderators. I wondered just what it was that the Supreme needed to discuss with them. Interesting.

"Well?" Oznard's foot was almost tapping.

We had to go somewhere on this shakedown voyage. Why not Ulon Prime? I had always wanted to meet the Macers. "Sure." I gave a half bow to usher her before me. "After you."

She sniffed. I followed her on board with a grin. I wasn't so keen to have the Supreme on board, but at least it wouldn't be for long. Ulon Prime is around 500 light years away from Tyzar. If I had still been captaining *Faraday*, it would have taken over six months to get there. With the new ZEPH drive, which I had been told could cruise at around 8 light years per hour, it would take less than three days.

It was exciting. It changed everything.

We disengaged from the space station with great care. It would not do to ding the fuselage before we even had a maiden voyage in *Nivala*. Mel took her out, and she did it with milimetric precision, though her brow was all creased up with worry. Sammy had been coaching her in bridge navigation and was sitting beside her, looking proud. He winked at me, then put one hand over hers. She immediately looked five years younger.

I was staring out of the forward viewport when something cannoned into me. I staggered and nearly fell, only managing to grab out at the pilot's chair at the last minute.

"Hey! What the fitz...?"

"How could you!" Small hands began to pummel me. I found myself taking hold of Zenzie's irate forearms to try to stop her attack. "You let that awful person come with us!"

"Did I forget to tell you? Sorry. It must have slipped my mind."

She was now kicking at my legs, crest vertical, wrinkles flapping. "I hate you!"

"It is only for the maiden voyage! Ow! Stop it, Zenzara, you are hurting me!"

"You should have asked me first!"

I gave her a bit of a shake. "Enough! Why should I ask you? Who is the captain of this ship?"

Her eyes flashed. "Who is the Chyzar?"

I chortled. It hadn't taken her long to take advantage of her new status. "Typical female!"

She kicked me even harder. I was forced to let go of her arms, and she resumed my battering.

"I ... am ... the ... Chyzar," she puffed.

"You ... are ... just ... a little .... girl," I responded, trying to avoid her flailing hands without damaging her. I couldn't help teasing her, just a little bit.

"Oh!" She actually managed to connect with my chin, which made me see stars for a moment. I started to laugh, which incensed her even further.

"Stop laughing at me!"

"Well, then, stop making a fool of yourself."

She fell back, eyes wide. "I'm not!"

"Yes you are. In the first place, you are not the Chyzar yet, as far as I know. You can't communicate properly with the Chakrans. Secondly, even if you could, it wouldn't make you the captain of this ship, so you still wouldn't get to take the decisions. Thirdly, you are a pain in the butt."

She gasped. "I am not!"

"Yes you are. Come back when you are old enough to make reasonable choices."

Her eyes now glittered. "I saved all of us on *Raktor*."

"You have been useful up to now. You didn't throw tantrums before. Perhaps all this Chyzar business has gone to your head?"

She went silent. Then, in a small voice, "I am sorry."

"So you should be." I decided to take pity on her. "Look, Zenzie, I know that your life has changed. It must be very confusing. But it is true for the rest of us as well. None of us can go back to the lives we used to live, to the people we used to know. It is hard for all of us to adapt."

She blinked. She was still too young to put herself in the position of others. I could tell that she had not really considered this. "Oh."

"We are all stuck with each other because some cosmic joke threw us all together. We have to get along. And that means that we won't always be doing what you want us to do. It is impossible. We don't live in a bubble. We interact with other people. The Supreme Council has allowed us to take this ship as our own. I can't refuse a small favor."

She hung her head. "I guess."

"Right."

She looked at my chin. "I'm sorry if I hurt you."

"Think nothing of it. But you could do with some combat practice. You are much better with your nivala and thoria."

"I know. Tyzaran children are taught how to use the nivala and the thoria from a very young age."

"Why?"

She sighed. "Two hundred years ago the Avaraks invaded Tyzar. Hundreds of Tyzaran children were slaughtered because they had no way to defend themselves. Since then, all Tyzarans over the age of four are taught the art of the nivala and the thoria. From eight we are equipped with a small-bore ZR maser, known as a giantkiller."

"Did they win?"

"Did who win?"

"The Avaraks."

"Oh. No. They were defeated by the Supreme Council. That was when the first Raksora Accords were signed. Up until now, the Accords have never been broken again."

"Why didn't they attack the adults too? Or did they?"

She pulled a face. "They did, but the children were targeted because they are the future of the race."

"Interesting. But the Avaraks and the Tyzarans are on the same side now. Aren't they?"

She shrugged. "Who knows? It is your stupid Omnistate that started all this mess."

I held up both hands. "Hardly mine. They are Flatlanders. I'm a Spacelander."

"You are all of human origin. Aren't you?"

"Well, yes, I suppose we are. But you can't compare!"

"You all look the same to me."

I couldn't argue with that. To be fair, we did all look alike. I had never thought of it from the alien point of view. "I suppose we do."

Denaraz stepped forward. "The Raksora Accords are broken, even though the Avaraks have not attacked us directly. There is a paragraph where they undertake not to bear arms against any of the Major Shell races."

"They were attacked first, I believe."

"Irrelevant. The letter of the Accords is broken."

That was just a smidge unfair. The Terrans had started all this by attempting to annex the whole of the Local Shell. But it was true that the Avaraks had been the first to take up arms. Against poor old *Commorancy*. It seemed a shame to burn two hundred years of peace because of Omnistate greed. I realized that I had been viewing all this with tunnel vision, too. It was not merely our own lives that had been affected. The Major Shells would probably never be the same again. It was a chilling realization. You always assume that the status quo will last, until it doesn't. Then it is too late to change anything.

I turned to Denaraz. "Does that mean that there will be war between the Avaraks and the Tyzarans?"

"Not if I can help it." We both swiveled round. Oznard had come onto the bridge. She came to a stop behind us. "Ty Zylarian, please refrain from behaving like a Vaer. You are old enough to know better! And please at least *try* to control that crest of yours a little more."

Zenzie shuffled quickly to the bridge bulkhead and attempted to make herself smaller. She and the Supreme were not exactly soul mates. The Tyzaran girl shot me an accusing look, which I ignored.

I met Oznard's gaze. "You are attempting to prevent a war between the Avaraks and the Tyzarans?"

"Of course."

"You are not worried about the Terran Omnistate? They were the cause of all this."

"The Omnistate live in a different Shell. The Avaraks and the Tyzarans share the Bifold Shell. Rhyveka and Tyzar are only a hundred light years apart. Our first priority must be the situation between the Avaraks and ourselves. The rapid expansion of the dissident Enclave on Tyzar itself comes second. The Omnistate is isolating itself. It can be dealt with later."

"Even if it develops ZEPH drive?"

"Local perturbations must take precedence over interstellar ones."

"I see. Does our journey have something to do with that?"

She nodded. "It might."

I couldn't see what good the planet-bound Macers could do, but it looked as if this side journey was going to be more interesting than it had seemed. I brightened. Taking a new ship into the Great Shell, where Ulon was situated, was anything but boring. The Vaers inhabited the Great Shell too, so we would have to keep our eyes peeled for any of the Nova Vaers. I had already lost *Faraday* to them. I wasn't about to lose *Nivala*.

We dropped into a geostationary orbit around Ulon Prime three days and five hours later. There had been one or two teething problems with the new ZEPH drives, but the Tyzaran engineers had been able to correct them easily. Sammy had been monitoring their work, as had Didjal. Didjal had told me that it felt reasonably competent to take over the maintenance and upkeep of the drives. The Enif seemed to be a fan of the new system.

"It is simple but elegant. Although some intense fluctuations in the local zero point energy seems inevitable. We have no idea how that may affect surrounding spacetime." Didjal's antennae rippled, making it look even more concerned.

Sammy shook his head. "Dunno. Can't see it would make much difference to anything, really."

The Enif clicked in a disapproving sort of way. "It could. I can't find any signs that the Tyzarans have tried to evaluate the effect of such fluctuations on the environment. On Enifa, that would have been a prerequisite."

"And you feel there may be severe contamination?" I asked.

"Not at the moment. The Tyzarans do seem to have kept such effects to a minimum, by fitting inhibitors to all exhaust systems. However, I am doubtful that the Terrans would do the same. I have looked into their history, and they do not have a happy background as far as pollution is concerned."

That was true. "Can you do anything further to the *Nivala* to improve that problem?"

The Enif stopped to think. "I could probably try to add an inverter which would take at least part of that additional zero point energy and convert it back down into something less toxic."

"Why don't you try that, then, Didjal? Anything we can do to keep emissions down has to be good, right?"

"I will start work on it straight away. However, you should know that it is a large project."

"How is Eshaan getting on?"

"My *faliif* is adapting to the *Nivala*. Even so, the loss of our life's work has been very hard to take. Eshaan is still struggling."

"I saw a new painting, though. That will be saved?"

"It was forwarded to Enifa, yes. It is a small beginning. To replace the lost is impossible. We can only hope to produce exceptional quality in the small quantity that will be possible in our allotted time."

"Yet the art is not destroyed. In some place, maybe on Vaer Nova, it still exists."

Didjal curved inwards on itself. "They have the patterns. And the Vaers are not spiritual creatures. Art on their walls is a travesty. Their eyes dishonor the work, detract from it. I would rather it be burnt and turned to ashes. If it were found again, that would be its fate."

I raised my eyebrows. "Even if you got it back it would still be destroyed? I hadn't realized that."

"We believe that all art gives but also takes from the observer. Who sees it becomes a part of its story. That is why we choose very carefully who may own such a picture, and for how long. Cruel eyes alter art, distort its perspectives, warp its message. Such art cannot be allowed to carry the name of its creators; it has been defiled."

I bent my head. "I hadn't realized that the theft of your life's work was so definitive. Forgive me."

"Although our work will now be small in volume, it is possible that being surrounded by such unusual events will heighten our perception. Eshaan is working hard to live up to such friends."

"You think we are special? Why?"

"The future of this whole group is fluid. Most lives are set in the cement of their society. This group is different. It is adaptive and inclusive. That is a fertile environment for art."

"Then you are happy to stay?"

Didjal tapped one foot. It sounded metallic against the deck plating. "We are excited to stay here. We have had little choice in anything since the Avaraks chose to attack *Commorancy*, but this decision was our own. We are pleased to connect with this small group. We are not uncomfortable with you."

"Good. I am glad to hear that."

"I will begin my work on that inverter." The Enif gave a small bow and withdrew. The Supreme instructed the Tyzaran mechanics to remain on the *Nivala*, telling them to use the time to run all necessary calibrations after the maiden voyage.

The rest of us, Eshaan included, piled into the *Nivala's* main shuttle and made our way planetside.

The oceans of Ulon Prime were impressive. The lack of depth meant that the oceans were criss-crossed with white caustics which shimmered against the sandy bottom of the seas. The water itself was a stunning color, one that defied description. It contained blue and green, but it was a tone that you could hardly tear your eyes away from. We stared and stared as the shuttle gently came down to settle in around eight meters of water. Only the top part of the shuttle protruded from the water.

We assembled at the forward hatch and input the clearance codes. The airlock deactivated and the whole door swung outwards.

The reflection of the sun across the water was dazzling. We hastily reached for the sun lenses that had been issued to us. They helped. After a few seconds my eyes adapted. I could see a series of rafts approaching the hatch. There seemed to be no form of propulsion, but they were moving steadily toward us all the same.

Zenzara pushed at me. "Let me see!"

I let her slip through to stand in front of me. She gave a small gasp of pleasure as her eyes adjusted. "It is beautiful!"

The rafts were nearly at the shuttle. We could make out small shapes on top of each of them. I screwed up my eyes, trying to make the most of my first glimpse of the Macers.

They were completely bald, as far as I could tell. Their skin was dark and cracked, so that it had split into tiny raised islands alternating with troughs all over them. Their eyes were enormous and a strange orange-yellow color. Their pupils in the strong sunlight were vertical slits. I had read somewhere that animals that needed to adjust to severe changes in light needed vertical pupils in order to adapt more quickly. Unlike my own rounded ones, they would cut off virtually all light very fast. And no wonder. The light reflecting off the surface of Ulon Prime was dazzling in contrast to the dimmer light under the kelp banks.

Their torsos were small and thin, but their limbs were quite different. Their arms and legs of the same length made them appear rather spider-like. They looked to be all legs. They bustled about on top of the rafts of kelp. I could see, as the raft came closer, that more of the Macers were pushing and pulling at the matted kelp to maneuver it in our direction.

Eventually it was docked safely underneath our shuttle hatchway.

Supreme Oznard pushed through the rest of us to take in the scene below her. She had straightened up to her full height and was looking most imposing. She lifted one foot to take the first step down.

Unfortunately, Zenzie beat her to it. She ducked swiftly through Oznard's legs and threw herself with glee onto the soft kelp platform.

"Wheee!" she cried in a happy voice. "This is great!" She bounced once or twice and then jumped to her feet and began to shake hands with each and every one of the Macers, who were staring at her with their huge nonplussed, passive eyes. I don't think they had ever seen anything like the young Tyzaran before. They extended their long front arms, however, and imitated her with some care. She giggled and pumped at their hands. One or two of them seemed to wince, but most simply resigned themselves to her enthusiasm.

Oznard finished descending to the planet and stood rigid, waiting for appropriate attention to be paid to her. The rest of us clambered down the welded ladder without much ceremony.

Zenzie finally ran out of exuberance and looked back at us, to see what we were all doing. Her crest fell as she saw the expression on Oznard's face. "Have I done something wrong, Supreme?"

Oznard managed a tight smile. "Not at all Ty Zylarian. I am sure our hosts are impressed by your ... eagerness. Although it would now be more appropriate of you to step back."

Zenzie did so immediately, but half tripped over some of the mounded kelp, ending up unceremoniously on her backside. We grinned, though Oznard only seemed irritated. Zenzara backed away, stuttering an apology.

Two of the largest Macers came forward and executed welcoming bows. Oznard unbent a little. "Thank you. It is most pleasant to be here. Where would you like to have these discussions?"

Two of the Macers exchanged rapid-fire signs on their long fingers. The largest one turned to Oznard. "Here is appropriate," it said. The slow speech was at complete odds with the lightning way the Macers moved and exchanged signs with each other. I saw that they were using artificial voice boxes which they pressed against large air sacs that each possessed around their necks. The spoken language was consequently slow and tone limited, dissimulating their natural character.

Oznard didn't like that. She eyed the rest of us up. I realized she was unwilling to talk with us all there.

"This meeting is secret?" questioned the Macer. "You do not wish the Avaraks or the Spacelanders or the Enif to know about what we speak?" It extended a long leg and pointed at a representative of each as it talked.

The Supreme flushed. She didn't, of course. But she couldn't quite see how to say so. "I represent the Supreme Council of Tyzar," she began.

The Macer nodded. "You wish to form an Interstellar Alliance," it said in its measured tones. "Then it is good to have other races present. Is it not?"

Not, if we were to believe Oznard's body language. We shuffled our feet, uncertain what to do.

Zenzara smiled widely. "An Interstellar Alliance? I like that! I am happy to be here!" She sat down on the rush-like matting and settled herself, clearly prepared to be entertained.

The Macers exchanged more flashing finger talk, and then sat down next to her. The leader signaled to the rest of us to form part of the circle. We all obeyed, except Oznard. The Supreme was left standing as we all hunkered down.

I could have sworn that she rolled her eyes, but in the end she sat down too. Denaraz, behind me, folded himself down into a cross-legged position as soon as she did. He was the only one of us who had waited for her. It didn't seem to make her any happier.

"Please ... to speak?" The Macer invited her with an expansive movement of his hand.

She pursed her lips for a moment, before deciding to go ahead. She summarized recent events quickly, telling of the ZEPH drive, its expropriation, and the resulting conflicts. She most definitely said nothing about the attack on the space station at Tyzar by the Enclave.

The two Macers spoke at length to each other, their brown hands flashing in the Ulon sunlight. "We do not travel to the stars. Why do you seek us out in this?"

"Because you are key to the Major Shells. There are only seven races in the Shells, if we count both Spacelanders and Flatlanders as one race."

What? I shook my head. That wasn't right. I opened my mouth to speak. "You can't—"

"Can't what? Call a human a human? You are the cause of all this unrest."

I scrambled to my feet. So did Sammy and Mel. The raft rocked slightly. "We will not sit here if you are to speak of the Terran Omnistate and the Space Trust in the same breath! There are eight members of the Major Shells! Eight, not seven!"

Chatter broke out. Everyone seemed to have an opinion on the subject. Finally the Macer held up a large hand to silence us all. "Nothing can be discussed further until this point is clarified," it said calmly. "Advance is impossible if the boundaries of the groups are unclear. We will meet again tomorrow. We should all reflect on this matter. Please return to your spacecraft until the morning."

We made our way back up the ladder and inside the shuttle. Oznard was furious with me. "How dare you think you can speak at such a time! You have no place at these discussions!"

I glared back at her. "It seems I do. Or did you think you could disrespect the Spacelanders like that? Our home is in the Landau Rift, which forms one of the Major Shells. Or did you forget that?"

Her eyes slid to the two Enif present. "The Landau Rift is home to the Enif. They are autochthonous. You are not."

"I ... I ..." I swallowed, unable to get the words out.

Didjal and Eshaan chattered together, their fingers drumming against the other's arm. They did not tell us what their conclusion was.

"I am going for a swim." Zenzara was still looking happily out of the hatch. "We have time, don't we?"

"We do not." Oznard's tone was icy. "I am not staying overnight in this small shuttle. None of us would sleep! We shall return to the *Nivala*."

"No swim?" Zenzie sounded disappointed.

"Certainly not. Out of the question."

One small crest drooped.

"You can have a quick dip," I told her, prepared to do battle with the Supreme over this. "Just in and out. Tomorrow you can do more."

"Thank you, Mallivan!" She tore off most of her clothes and let herself down hand over hand down the ladder. A couple of seconds later she was swimming in the stunningly-colored water, laughing and diving and dipping and splashing.

"You are not the leading rank on this ship," the Supreme told me icily. "That would be me."

I shrugged. "You gave us the *Nivala*, and this shuttle is part of her. I make the decisions on board. You make the decisions outside."

Her crest was super spiky. Even being a Supreme didn't make you immune to anger, then.

Denaraz stepped in front of me, throwing me a warning look as he did so. "Supreme, may I escort you to your seat? I am sure this delay will be ... minimal, won't it, err ... Captain Mallivan?"

Used to hearing everyone call me Ryler or Rye, the honorific caused me to blink. Captain. Even on the *Faraday* I had never thought of myself as a captain. It sounded so strange to my ears.

Denaraz was still looking fixedly at me. Telling me to pick my battles. And he was right. Of course he was. It wasn't my job to be deciding whether the Spacelanders were considered an independent race or not. That was for people way, way above my pay grade.

I nodded. "Of course. If you would all take your seats, I will effect the necessary checks before takeoff. By the time I have done that all the crew members will be on board." I hoped. Zenzie was still splashing around in seventh heaven down there.

Seyal ushered me towards the bows. "They will be, Captain."

I gave her a smile and went forwards to take my place in the pilot's seat. Time to mend bridges then. Only, I didn't feel at all like mending anything. I felt like tearing the Supreme into little pieces and feeding her to the Vaers. Perhaps I needed the evening to cool down. I was pretty sure Captains weren't supposed to do that sort of thing.

There was a studious effort on behalf of all those on board not to discuss the topic any further. We more or less ignored each other all that evening. I retrenched to my cabin and refused to join the others. It was a cowardly way out of the discomfort, but I guess I wasn't the first captain to take that way out. I pleaded paperwork and disappeared.

"What are you going to say tomorrow?"

I almost jumped out of my skin. "Shells, Zenzie! When did you sneak in?"

She looked pleased with herself. "You were concentrating on that schematic."

"Please knock first!"

"I did. You didn't answer, and I was worried about you."

I thought that was unlikely. Still, I did know that when Zenzara wanted something she would chip away at it until she got it. It would be easier to give in.

"How can I help you?"

She gave me a broad smile and sat down on my bunk bed, on the other side of the cabin. "What are you going to say tomorrow?" she repeated.

"How should I know? It isn't really my business, is it?"

She made a disapproving face. "Of course it is. How could it not be?"

"I'm not a politician."

"Thank fitz! I don't like politicians."

"Well, then. What do you expect me to do?"

"I expect you to fight for your people. You can't let the rest of the Spacelanders down."

"Better people than me will deal with this."

She shook her head. "No they won't, because this will all be decided tomorrow and by the time the high-ups in the Space Trust get to hear about it, it will be too late to change anything. You have to argue the Spacelander case tomorrow."

"Me? Why me?" I thought for a moment, picking and discarding possibilities. "Mel knows more about the law. She would be the better person to do it."

She gave me a pitying look. "You can't foist this one onto Mel."

"I don't foist things on people."

"Yes, you do. But you mustn't, not this time."

"How come you know so much better than me?"

"Because I have been thinking about things while you have been staring blankly at stupid schematics, that's why."

"You are a rude little brat, you know that?"

She giggled. "I know. But, Mallivan, will you take my advice about this?"

"Oh, all right. I suppose I can get Sammy and Mel in here. And, yes, I will try to put a case tomorrow. Now, do you mind leaving me in peace?"

She skipped out of the door. "Of course. Thank you, Captain!"

I growled as the door shut behind her. I had no idea what case I could put the following day. This was going to mean a sleepless night. I bet our future Chyzar would curl up and sleep like a log. I'm pretty sure I growled again.

I hadn't been wrong. It had indeed taken three-quarters of the night to find an argument that might win this debate. Mel, Sammy and I had called in Neema, who had insisted in dragging Anzany into the whole question. Between Mel, Neema and Anzany we had quite a good picture of the history of the Spacelanders. Even so, it took us six hours to wheedle it all down into something even half-way convincing. That left us with two hours of sleep each.

I can truthfully say that I was not at my best when Zenzie sprang into my cabin the following morning, carrying some juice for me. Her bright and cheery face was extremely irritating. I glowered at it.

"This is all your fault," I told her.

"Thank you!" She beamed at me. "I do my best." She did a small twirl on the spot. "Of course, you are getting on a bit. I expect you get tired easily."

"What? I am not old. I'm only twenty-eight!"

She nodded. "I know. I'm eight."

There was a long silence as I tried to think of a comeback and couldn't. So I drank the juice and expelled her from the cabin. I needed to shave and get dressed. The morning was not set to be easy.

The first cloud on the horizon was Supreme Oznard, with a depressed Denaraz trailing after her. He raised his eyes at me, something she luckily couldn't see.

I read the warning in his gesture. I bowed. "Supreme. I hope you rested well?"

"Why should you care how I rested?"

It was my turn to raise my eyebrows. "Do you require anything, Supreme? Can I get you something to eat or to drink?"

"You cannot. I am perfectly well, thank you. I have decided that you and all your group will stay on board *Nivala* today."

"I am sure you have." She looked at me sharply, causing me to rectify. "That is, I am sure you would prefer to go down to the surface alone. Unfortunately I cannot allow it. It would put you in danger."

"Danger!" she scoffed. "What possible danger could I be in from the Macers? They are the most honorable and most pacific race in the Great Shells!"

I made my expression bland. "Even so, it would not be protocol to send you down alone."

"I am a member of the Supreme Council. I make my own protocol."

"I am sure, on Tyzar, you do. Unfortunately I am not Tyzaran, so it is not *my* Supreme Council. On this ship you cannot give the orders."

"I provided you with this ship!" Her crest was standing on end, despite her efforts to control it. "You will do as I say!"

"I'm afraid I won't. I remain the captain of *Nivala*, and I give the orders."

Her face smoothed out completely. It was one of the most menacing things I have ever seen. "You will do as I say!" The last word was hissed through her teeth.

"My whole group will accompany down to the surface of the planet, or no-one will go. Is that clear enough for you?"

Denaraz winced and took two steps back.

Oznard's face went taut then slack then taut again. "I see. You intend to take no notice of Tyzar."

I shook my head. "On the contrary. I intend to take very careful note of Tyzar, and of all the Supreme Council says or does. However, I will not sit back while you eliminate the Spacelanders from an interstellar alliance. I would be a poor sort of patriot if I did."

She considered that, though her crest didn't soften. She was wondering if she and Denaraz could win in an all-out physical altercation against the rest of us. I knew the answer to that one. They couldn't.

She eventually came to the same conclusion. "I will allow you to attend today's meeting."

I bowed again, lower this time. "Thank you for your understanding."

"Yes. Hmm. Don't test me again. You may not like the outcome."

Denaraz was wiping a few beads of sweat off his forehead. I grinned at him and he shook his head slightly at me. I couldn't blame him. I was sweating too.

"Shall we go then?" I invited the Supreme to pass in front of me and make her way into the shuttle. "If you are ready?"

"And tell Ty Zylarian to behave herself," she instructed as she swept past me. "We are not going to an adventure playground. She should remember that she is the future Chyzar."

I looked back to see where Zenzie was, and caught her with her tongue sticking rudely out at Oznard's back. I frowned heavily at her and she giggled. I could see that today was going to be fun.

We landed in the same spot as we had the day before. Again, several small rafts were immediately brought alongside the part of the shuttle that remained unsubmerged.

This time I had taken the precaution of stepping back to Zenzara's side and clamping one of my hands on one of her arms. She was therefore unable to race first to the hatch.

She shot me a look full of reproach. "I wasn't going to!"

"I am sure you weren't."

"Then let go of me!"

"I will, as soon as the others are down on the surface."

She wriggled, and nearly got free. "You don't trust me!"

"Of course I do. I wanted to talk to you about something."

Her wrinkles moved across her forehead. "I don't believe you."

"No? You don't trust me?"

There was a pause. She had walked right into that one. I tried not to look smug.

She bit her lip. "What did you want to talk about?"

"I wanted to make sure you knew that I am the one who takes the decisions on board Nivala and this shuttle. As a Tyzaran, you will also be expected to obey your Supreme. However she is a guest on this ship and if instructions conflict, you should follow mine."

She flushed a pleased pink. "Really? I don't have to listen to her?"

"I hope you will show due respect for a member of the ruling Supreme Council of your planet, but no, you don't have to listen to her."

She skipped on the spot. "Thank you." She stopped suddenly. "Oh! Now I shall never know if you held me back on purpose!"

"Just giving you the good news." I gave her my best crocodile smile, then let her loose. The others were already down on the planet. We hurried to join them.

The same two Macers were facing us. The elder of them surveyed us calmly with his small black eyes. "Have you solved the disagreement?"

Both the Supreme and I said yes at the same time.

Oznard glowered at me. "There is no need to include the Spacelanders, I find."

"On the contrary, it is imperative that the Spacelanders be included in any alliance." My sentence caused Oznard to snap her eyebrows together in anger. She had not expected me to speak.

The taller of the dark-eyed Macers nodded to me to go on. "Explain, please."

I handed out a pamphlet the girls had produced overnight. "As you can see from this original Charter of the foundation of the Spacelanders, six centuries ago, they were granted ... *with the full approval of the Enif race* ... complete authority and permanent abode in the Landau Rift, on all systems south east of the hypothetical line drawn between the Slingshot Binary to the west and Pyrrhus to the east."

"We know all this," snapped Oznard.

"The wording of the charter is important," I said in as mild a tone as I could muster. "That is, and I quote: *'Spacelanders shall exist from the signing of this charter as a new and independent race. All ties with the human Omnistate shall be considered irrevocably broken. At no time may Spacelanders refer to themselves as Terran. All Spacelanders shall forever be treated as a separate species.'*

"Irrelevant. You are all still human. That is one race."

The Macer elder held up one of his long arms. "A moment. I wish to examine this document." The Macers perused the pamphlet carefully. They then addressed Eshaan and Didjal.

"Are you aware of this charter? Did your ancestors accept that part of the Landau Rift, the Shell in which Enifa is situated, would be granted in perpetuity to these people?"

There was some discussion between the two Enif. Then Eshaan stepped forward. It seemed a little nervous, but spoke out strongly.

"We are taught that the Spacelanders agreed to protect Enifa from any outside attacks. For this reason they were granted sovereignty over a large part of the Landau Rift. Enifa had been under attack from the Vaers at that time, and it was thought that to populate a good part of the space between the Landau Rift and the Great Shell would be extremely beneficial to Enifa. At that time in history, the Nepheals had suffered greatly from Vaer incursions."

"And the Spacelanders are considered an independent race on Enifa?"

"They are. The Terrans are disliked by the Enif, but the Spacelanders are highly respected."

Oznard's face was sour. "Just because the Enif say their Landau Rift humans are independent doesn't mean that they really are. We must look at the definition of the word 'race'."

I inclined my neck. "I agree with the Supreme. For that reason we have spent several hours examining the different definitions of 'race'. If you turn the pamphlet over you will find several of the definitions. After all, if we are considering an interstellar alliance, we should consider all existing definitions, should we not? Not only the Tyzarans?"

The Macers nodded. Oznard didn't.

I went on. "As you can see, Terrans define race as 'Any of the traditional *divisions* of humankind.' We would therefore qualify, since we are a division clearly so stipulated by charter.

"I have spoken to Seyal, our resident Avarak, and she says that her people only recognize one race: Male Avaraks. This is regarded as superior to all other living beings. Anyone who does not belong to the Male Avarak race is inferior and unworthy. In their eyes, neither Terrans, nor Tyzarans, nor females of their own species, nor Spacelanders are races.

"Tyzarans define race as 'A group of Aliens, all of whom have similar physical and mental characteristics.' We would qualify, for although we have similar physical characteristics to the Terrans, our mental mindset is completely different."

Oznard gave something rather like a snort. I ignored it, turning instead to the Macers. "How would you define race?"

"We do not have the concept, as we have no names. We even have no name for our race or group. You call us Macers because the first visitors who came saw us bestowed on us that name. Macers neither name nor categorize themselves, or others. We have only vague feelings of similarity and familiarity. Any Macer or Alien who triggers those feelings will be accepted as like beings. Any who trigger feelings of distaste or repulsion will not be accepted and so will become unlike beings. In this case we cannot be of use. This proposed alliance already requires us to accept unlike beings such as the Terrans and the Vaers as like. It is of great difficulty to us."

That wasn't helpful. Or was it? "Then you might call one human a like being and another an unlike being?"

"Of course. We react to the interior of souls, not the exterior. In any case, we are being expected to accept both like and unlike beings into this association, so we have no opinion about this definition of race, which to us appears arbitrary."

"But you would not exclude any group?"

"We would not. By definition, the alliance is necessary to allow like and unlike beings to grow accustomed to each other, and to protect life as we know it. Exclusion is not compatible with those aims."

Thank you! I stepped back. I didn't think I could improve on that.

The Supreme had her eyes almost turned back in her head. She was communicating with the rest of the Supreme Council. Finally she closed her eyes and let her head drop back into its usual position. "I have discussed this with the Supreme Council, and they are willing to accept the proposition of eight Major Shell races, rather than seven."

The Macers exchanged tight glances. They seemed uncomfortable with the Supreme. I wonder whether she was classed as 'like' or 'unlike'. Then I looked at both their tails, tautly wound up into tight concentric rings. Unlike, I decided. That cheered me up.

The spokesperson of the Macers uncurled its long limbs to stand up. "Then we have a basis for continuation. The Alliance will consist of up to eight species, those currently considered sentient in the Major Shells. Only those who join willingly will be a part of it. For the purpose of this Alliance Avarak females will be considered part of the Avarak race. Is this agreed?"

Seyal's eyes opened wide. "The males will not like that!"

The Macer turned his wizened face to her. "Whatever the definition of race, it must include both parties necessary for perpetuation. That, at the least, would appear to be clear to us."

I stepped forward again. "Who can join this alliance on behalf of their people?"

Oznard lifted her head. "The legal government of each people, clearly. We can hardly have people like you signing, without any consultation."

The Macers both nodded. "A consensus which is legal on each planet must decide. Meanwhile, we will endeavor to produce a list of joint aims and regulations. We shall need an independent body of enforcers to police the Alliance."

And there, suddenly, was what all this had been for. Nothing could have been clearer to me. I stepped forwards. "That will be us. The *Nivala*."

Several mouths dropped open. Oznard's not the least. She regarded each of us in turn, and then gave a slow nod. "That is not unacceptable. At least your group consists of several different races. It is a start."

"And we can accept other races within our crew. I don't know if there are any Macers who would like to join us ...?"

Both Macers shivered in distaste. "I do not think so," said the elder. "Macers require water to survive. Though we will make enquiries."

"There is a pool on *Nivala*. Though it may not be big enough."

Oznard huffed. "My understanding of the Macers is that they dislike space."

"We will ask if there are any volunteers. It is most unlikely. We are too fragile for space travel."

Oznard's lips curved down. "Very well." She pressed her lips together thoughtfully. "Neither the Vaer nor the Terran Omnistate will join at this time, I think. We can only hope to convince six of the eight races. The Tyzarans will join."

"So will the Spacelanders," I said quickly.

"I believe the Enif will want to form part of the alliance," said Eshaan after a quick consultation with Didjal.

Seyal was shaking her head. "The Avaraks will not join. Not if females are to be regarded as equal to males." She thought for a few moments. "But I shall be very happy to come with you. I believe the future must be outwards, and that we should stop looking inwards. We should aim further and further out from our routine lives. We should become part of something bigger." Then her face fell. "Unfortunately, I am only a female. And I am only one."

"All things start small, Seyal. Who knows where this will end?" I was counting on my fingers. "That gives four probables and one unlikely. Leaving only the Nepheals." I thought for a second. "I don't think we could make the *Nivala* comfortable for a Nepheal. They are too large, aren't they?"

Oznard gave a shrug. "I expect they could live in the hold, if it were adapted for them. At least for a short time. They would not be able to fit comfortably onto the bridge, certainly."

The Macers began to signal the others in the water. Our two interlocutors themselves slipped back into the wonderfully colored water. "Then we all have work to do," the Elder said. "We will welcome *Nivala* back when all has been decided and a treaty has been prepared for signature. That must take place here. We will await your news."

"Perfect. Please draw up the accords with care. They must be flexible, yet fair, if all races are to agree to them." Oznard gave a small bow and then began to climb the ladder back up to the shuttle hatch.

The elder paused for a moment. He looked at Zenzara. "Would you care to see how we work underwater?"

She nodded excitedly. "Please!"

"We sense something immense inside you. You are not part of your collective."

"She is the next Chyzar!" Denaraz stepped towards the Macers. "She has been chosen by the Chakrans!"

The elder blinked. "Yes. That would explain the difference we can sense in her. She is not yet ready to see her path. But we can help her with that. Come, swim with us."

Zenzie had already pulled off most of her clothes, leaving only a small swimsuit. She dove neatly off the raft and disappeared under the water. Moments later, she came back up and waved a hand at me. "I won't be long!"

Denaraz had stripped down to his undergarments, most unwillingly. He slipped into the water after her. "I will watch over her," he told me.

I grinned. I wasn't sure who would be watching over who. I wasn't worried about Zenzara's safety. With Macers to watch over her, she would be safer than on Tyzar itself. I turned away, to help the others climb back up the ladder to the shuttle hatch. It had been an interesting morning.

12

We dropped Oznard back on Tyzar. She told us that she would send emissaries to visit Enifa, Nephealis and the Space Trust. They would move ahead with the alliance if they could get five of the eight races to sign the accords. Once that had been accomplished they hoped gradually to entice the Terrans, Vaers and Avaraks to subscribe to it. It would be difficult. Like and unlike do not mix well. And we were in the middle of a war. Not the best time to push for unity, perhaps.

We decided to take *Nivala* directly to Talscharin, the headquarters of the Space Trust. I wanted to get back to Spacelander territory, and I thought I should update my government on the events of the past weeks.

We waited only for two days, to restock. Once the few repairs that had come up during the maiden voyage had been dealt with, we left – this time without the extra Tyzaran crew members.

Talscharin is around two hundred and fifty light years north of Tyzar, in the Landau Rift. It was a journey that would take us a couple of days if we kept our cruising speed down to a moderate six light years per hour. It still felt pretty fast, if you compared it to old *Commorancy*. It would have taken that old ship three full days to cover one light year. The speed of *Nivala* was heady. I was feeling much happier. I even contacted Sibby to bring my pet Geiga, Scout, over to Talscharin. There was certainly room for one small Geiga on *Nivala*. Scout would be in his element. He would be good company for our budding Chyzar, too. Zenzie was still having trouble adapting to her new role as interpreter for the Chakrans. I didn't think she was very happy.

It would be great to see Sibby again. I hadn't spent time with my sister for over six months. We were long overdue a catch-up.

I should have known better than to think everything was going well for once. That would have been far too easy. Far too easy.

All went well until we were approaching Aldhiba, still in the Bifold Shell, some twenty six hours later. I was trying to get some exercise in – jogging up and down the main passageway with an annoying Zenzie and a less annoying Denaraz vying to jog in front. We all jumped when the most infernal caterwauling of an alarm started and red arrows began to chivvy us towards the nearest arms cache points.

My own scalp prickled, so I sympathized with the two Tyzarans. Their crests were vertical. We raced back to the bridge, running against the insistent red arrows. Hmm. I would have to try to change that.

I arrived out of breath on the bridge. "What's up?"

Sammy blew out air. "What isn't up? We seem to be surrounded by Avarak vessels."

"Have you told them we aren't Tyzaran? That this ship was ceded to us by the Supreme Council on Tyzar?"

"I have." Sammy sounded noncommittal. "Trouble is, they still seem to think we are not their allies. They have switched to red alert and are targeting us."

"What!" I leapt for the communication console to connect with the Avarak fleet. "Stand down! We are Spacelanders! We are non-combatant! Don't fire!"

I looked quickly behind me to Denaraz. "What weapons have we got at our disposal? Can you get on it, please?"

Denaraz gave a curt nod. He threw himself through the service hatch into the crawl tubing. The weapons bridge was one floor down, directly under the main bridge emplacement and this was not a time to use the lifts. Within seconds I toggled to see him on screen there. He was behind the weapons console and his fingers were flying across the screens. He saw that I was following his progress and pursed his lips. "I will need some moments to get everything online. This ship is well-defended. We should be able to hold our own against one Avarak ship. Unfortunately I am seeing twelve."

"Right. I will try to keep them occupied. Zenzara!"

"I am here, Mallivan. What do you need?"

"Get on the tight-beam and convince these Avaraks that we are not a threat to them. And do it fast! Seyal!"

"Also here, Ryler."

"You help Zenzie. After all, these are your people, aren't they?"

Seyal seemed doubtful. "They were," she admitted. "I don't know as they would say they were now."

"Just speak Avarak to them. I need more time. Denaraz needs more time."

"I understand."

The two women began to spout Avarak at the communications station. There was a long pause, until a tinny voice began gruffly to interrogate them. Zenzie took the time to turn around and look at me, giving me a nod of her head to show me that they were obeying my orders.

I ran over to Sammy. "What about shields, Sam? How long will they hold?"

He screwed up his face. "Even though we have the most modern type of Tyzaran shields, if that battleship starts taking potshots at us, we will be in trouble. Not that I want to be the bearer of bad news, mind!"

"Yeah. Thanks a lot. Not to worry, we have Zenzie and Seyal. They will sort it all out if anybody can."

Mel rolled her eyes. "And I was thinking we were about to become law enforcers for the new Alliance!"

"We all were. And are!" I realized that we could use the alliance to barter our way out. "Seyal! Tell them about the Alliance! Tell them they need to sign. Tell them it is in their best interests!"

Seyal shook her head. "They won't listen to me. I am a female of their own species, and I am now unlanded. I will do more harm than good."

"Zenzie then. Get that convincing patter of yours together, girl!"

She rolled her eyes. "No pressure!" But she began to speak with great emphasis.

At first they seemed very disinclined to listen. Then there was a more receptive silence on the other side of the channel. Finally, they agreed to connect by vid-screen, so that we could see each other.

I put Zenzie in front of me, and pasted a welcoming false smile on my face. Seeing this, the others immediately followed suit.

I was seeing more teeth than I had in a long time. It was extremely disconcerting. I moderated the amount of tooth on display.

The heavy Avarak on screen glared at us. He addressed us in Universal, much to my relief. "My name is Celodon. What is all this about an Alliance?"

"Zenzara Zylarian. Good morning! If the Avaraks joined the Alliance, and the Terrans did not, you would immediately find yourselves allied with the rest of the Major Shells." She frowned, realizing that was not completely true. "Except the Vaers, who we do not expect to join. At least, not in the first phase."

"And why would the Avaraks want to join?"

Zenzie gave a charming little girl smile. If it had been directed at me I would have been extremely worried. "Because," she said in her sweet voice, "if you do then you would immediately obtain the latest technology from the Tyzarans, would you not?"

Celodon's enormous jowls quivered. "We would?"

"Well, I should think that you would. If I were you, I would demand it as a condition. I mean, you could point out to the Tyzarans that joining an alliance where others would have the latest technology but you wouldn't would be very difficult. Especially since this whole war against the Terrans started because of the ZEPH drive technology." She looked down at her hands and took the time to examine her nails.

"It doesn't seem in the least fair. And, of course, by joining you would also ensure that the Raksora Accords be honored. That would be a great importance to my people. You know that we feel very strongly about those accords. The war of succession two hundred years ago is still considered barbaric by my people. Your joining a new alliance would be a way to ensure peace between the Tyzarans and the Avaraks." She looked up again, her eyes sharp. "After all, your people must be feeling very isolated now that they have irritated both the Tyzarans and the Spacelanders. I am sure that your government would like to hear of this offer."

Celodon harrumphed. "It is conceivable that they might. Very well. You will come with us. We will escort you and your ship to Rhyveka. You can tell your tale to the Avarak Grand Council."

I hurried forward. "You know, although we appreciate your kind offer of escort, we really should be getting on with—"

"It is not optional. *Avarak Karax!*"

The Avarak ships penned us neatly in their midst. There was no way we would be able to escape from this show of space might. We were going to Rhyveka. I closed my eyes. At least they hadn't opened fire. Yet.

After the vid-screen went grey again Zenzie did a small dance. "See how good I am?" she told us. "I have saved you all again!"

"Yeah. Terrific. Thank you so much."

Her face fell. "What? You do not think I did a good job?"

Mel took pity on her. "You were great, Zenzie! You saved all our lives. It is just that we don't quite know what will happen to us when we reach Rhyveka."

I noticed that Seyal was looking quite unwell. "What is it, Seyal?"

She swallowed. "They might ... Solutor's family might think they have a right to Segaton. If they find out he is on board, I believe they will remove him from me. I have no rights on Rhyveka, remember."

"I do remember," I said grimly. "Look, we can outrun the whole of this fleet any time. The only danger is the period before we escape their weapons range. We need a diversion. Seyal, we won't let the Avaraks take Segaton. Really. We won't."

Seyal nodded, but I could tell how worried she was. I couldn't blame her. "All we can do at the moment is wait. We will use that time to get ourselves into some semblance of order for any future emergencies. We need some drilling to get a quick response to attack. We will use this time for that."

And we did. We crawled along in the midst of the Avarak fleet, limited to their old-fashioned drives. We drilled and drilled and practiced and practiced. Using the simulator we discovered that both Anzany and Sammy were great at the weapons console. That became their station, under the supervision of Denaraz. He delegated Sammy to the rail guns and Anzany, who seemed almost telepathic about where and when shots would be fired, to the ABlasers. So we put Mel and Neema on pilotage. The two girls got on together really well, and both were becoming excellent pilots. Neema, perhaps had the edge on Mel, but only because of Mel's inconvenient claustronetia. It dogged her footsteps wherever she went in space. I honestly didn't know how she could still function as well as she did. I don't think I could have. She was gaining my admiration more and more. Sammy couldn't hide his pride in her progress. Even if she was sweating with terror, she performed better and better.

Didjal of course took the engines. He was the only one of us who could. Eshaan, although technically not a member of crew because of his status as an artist, offered to shadow Didjal. Engineers usually had whole crews down on the lower deck. Another pair of hands would be essential for him.

Zenzie was too young to fight. It was possible that Celodon would ask after his fluent young Tyzaran interlocutor, but I doubted it. Avaraks didn't take much notice of females. If he did remark on her absence, I could always get somebody to fetch her. She would be safer well out of the way. Her job would be to find Segaton and protect him. They were both to go to the very centre of the ship – the safest place.

I spent nearly a day exploring the crawl tubing of *Nivala*, trying to find where that place would be. Even though she was a small ship at only around sixty meters overall length and three decks, there were still many, many meters of crawl tubing under each deck. There had to be. On a spaceship you could not assume that lifts would always function. The first place that came to mind as a possible safe space was the swimming pool, on the middle deck.

Perhaps swimming pool is a bit of a misnomer. It is in fact a storage facility for the water that is needed both for propulsion and for personal use. The ZEPH drive uses Zero Point energy to split water into its components. The recombination is what drives the ships. So much is needed that the Tyzarans had decided to store it in a pool that could then be used for exercising. One of the great problems of prolonged space travel is the muscle deterioration suffered by space travelers. Swimming is extremely good at combating such side effects, while not putting too much stress on the bones themselves, which are also at risk. There was also a gymnasium, on the upper deck. Health is taken very seriously in space. It has to be.

Although the crawl tubes were perhaps safer if we were boarded, I thought that the water itself would form more of a protection if we should be attacked. Then I realized that it wasn't very practical. On attack, automatic steel covers would deploy over the pool so that the water was kept retained in the event of acute maneuvers. The thought of the two youngest members of our crew being swilled around inside a watertight steel box was not a pleasant one. I discussed it with Zenzie, and didn't need to look at her rigid crest to know how she felt about that. However, we still stowed an EVA spacesuit for Zenzie herself and a child's portable safety airbag in one of the lockers in the pool area. As a last resort it might be a viable option. Water was a great insulator. I showed her how to manually open the access hatch on the retractable cover, and told her that she and Segaton were to get into the pool and submerge if missiles were about to connect with the ship. I agreed a series of code words that would keep her up to date with the threats. She nodded. She would take her job seriously, I knew. She and Segaton got on very well. She absolutely adored the Avarak baby, playing with him whenever she got a chance.

We finally decided that she would take the baby into the crawl space which led under the swimming pool. The entry hatch was close to the pool, which would give them the capability of redeploying to the pool if the situation deteriorated.

I led her to the intersection of the front to aft tube with the starboard to port tube. There was two meters of water above us and nine meters of cargo hold below. It was in the dead center of the ship. It was about as good as we could manage.

We dragged some bedding down into the space, together with nappies and food, both for the baby and for Zenzie. It was hard to stow them in the small space, which was only one meter high by fifty centimeters wide. Finally we were able to lodge most of it under the removable slats that made up the walkway.

It was a good hiding place. I wasn't too worried about sound. The crawl spaces were lined with a plastic derivative which dampened our voices considerably. I was pretty sure even a baby's crying wouldn't be heard.

Finally we made our way back to the bridge. I told Seyal of our exploration. The Avarak's face lightened. "Segaton should be hidden in this place when we reach Rhyveka," she said immediately. "They will not find him there."

I wrinkled up my nose. I wasn't too sure of that. "They will undoubtedly search the ship."

She nodded. "Yes. But the male Avaraks cannot fit in the crawl spaces. They will send females. I will leave a sign with Zenzara to show the females. I do not think that they will betray me. Not when I explain to them. They are like me. They know what life is like for us on Rhyveka. If they can, they will protect me."

She was the one who should know about that. It sounded sketchy to me. However, Zenzie seemed convinced, so I let them organize the signs and take them into the crawl space below the middle deck. After that Seyal seemed calmer. She knew that, in any exchange with the Avaraks, she would have to stay on the bridge with me. I would need her translation. My Avarak had improved over recent weeks, though not nearly as much as Seyal's Universal. I wasn't up to negotiating with irate male Avaraks.

Since she would have to be on the bridge with me, she offered to undertake the job of interpreter. I agreed instantly. Not just for the Avaraks. She told me that she would start to study the other five languages of the Major Shells.

She certainly had a gift for languages. She had become fluent in Universal in the short time she had been with us. I wondered if all of the female Avaraks had been so severely underestimated. I had no doubt she could be chattering away in Nepheal or Vaer in a few months.

She was ridiculously pleased to have found another way to be useful. The factions of her face seemed more angular now. She was less diminished. I was pleased for her. She was becoming an essential part of the crew, quite apart from her nursing training. She was already our first aid specialist, now she would be our translator. And it was not likely to stop there. She told me that she would need to investigate the history of each race in order to conform to social protocols. When Seyal decided to do something, she did it really, really well. I personally thought that the males of her species had been extremely short-sighted.

She had told me all about life as a female on Rhyveka. Whilst most female Avaraks are submitted to injections which block signals from the nerves to the muscles of the throat, Seyal had not suffered this indignity. Her father, Hegaton, had belonged to a small group of Avarak males who thought that females should not be altered in this fashion.

Females are considered of importance only for breeding. No females are taught universal. No females are allowed to do any job considered to require decision making. Most are conjoined to a male by fifteen years old and pregnant by sixteen. As many as sixty-five percent of females die in childbirth, so it is most unusual to meet one who is older than twenty. By then they will have given birth three times, which means that they have only around a four percent chance of reaching twenty-one.

Female Avaraks have no vote on anything in their world and do not enjoy emancipation. They belong to their husbands, who are free to mistreat, sell, exchange and even kill them. Even though this, nowadays, is frowned upon, it still occurs in some mountainous districts of Rhyveka.

A female death is not acknowledged by Avarak society, whereas a male death requires a long ceremony, attended by all his offspring. This goes on for three days by law, and any female wives surviving him are ceremoniously auctioned off to the highest bidders. The resultant moneys are used to erect huge mausoleums to his achievements, so most Avaraks make sure they have at least ten wives at all times. They will search far and wide for the females with the most breathy voices, to ensure, if the worst should come to pass, that their resting places should be worthy of them. The most important Avaraks can have up to thirty wives at any one time.

Since she had not had the injection, Seyal's own voice was not particularly breathy. I asked about this. She reddened. "My father was obliged to ... pay ... my husband."

"A dowry?"

She didn't know the word. "Money to make up for my harsh voice." She lowered her head and blinked rather rapidly. "My father gave him many monies."

"Your voice is very soft."

She blushed again. "It is kind of you to say so, but you will see that it is not so. My voice grates on most males. At least, the ones of my own species."

I grinned. "Well, I am very grateful to your father. If he had altered your voice, I am sure it would have been much harder for you to master Universal. You could not have been our interpreter."

Her head came up at that. "It is true, what you say. Many females would not be able to pronounce your words correctly. I had not thought of it like that."

"We need you, Seyal. Just as you are."

Her eyes opened wide. "I agree, logically, but it is hard for me to feel needed on an emotional level. That is a new experience for me."

"A good one, I hope?"

"A very good one!"

We watched carefully as we were escorted towards Rhyveka. Aldhiba had been left far behind. We had entered the Adhara Corridor, about eighty light years north of Veka. We didn't want to miss any chance of escape. Unfortunately, none presented. We were watched and hemmed in by the Avarak ships, and at any one time at least three of them were in range and had their weapons trained upon us.

The wait was taking its toll. I was ramped up ready to go and it was sapping my energy levels. If something didn't happen soon I honestly thought I would snap. Waiting had never been one of my strong points. If I have strong points. Anyway, waiting is for sure not one of them.

I shook my head at Denaraz and Neema, the only two people with me on the bridge. "I'm going into the gym for a while. See if I can work off some of this stress. I'm only next door. Shout if you need me."

Neema nodded. "Sure, Rye. Take some time. We can cope here."

The gym was situated exactly on top of the swimming pool, only one deck up. It was a large rectangular space right in the middle of the ship, flanked forward by the bridge, aft by the crew's cabins and to port and starboard by the mess hall and kitchen and the saloon and arms cache, respectively.

I slammed one of the mountain routes on the enveloping vid-screen and clambered onto the synchronized bike. That should pound the flutters out of me. Within minutes I was lost on a four percent incline over six kilometers. Enough for me. Enough for many cyclists, I guess. The confines of the ship had extended out to old Earth. I was struggling up one of the blue-grade trails in a place called Italy. It was beautiful. And I was out of practice. I had already had to change gears three times. I only had two changes left. I stood up on the bike. I might not be able to do this.

A klaxon burst into my peaceful little private hell. Again. A loud klaxon.

I tumbled off the bike, almost falling off when the clip shoes didn't disengage. I tore at them and flung them away, racing back to the bridge barefoot.

Already Seyal and Mel were running onto the bridge. I saw Denaraz's back as he hastily let himself through the service hatch into the crawl tube. He would be needed one deck down on the weapons bridge, together with Anzany and Sammy.

"Report!"

"We are under attack. But not by the Avaraks. A Terran fleet has appeared suddenly from the North. They are bigger and much faster than the Avaraks."

I pushed my feet into my shoes, and pushed the comlink. "Zenzie. Code white." That would put her and baby Segaton safely cocooned in their crawl space. Well, more safely, at least.

"Do we run or do we fight?" asked Mel. "And if it's the second, who do we fight?"

A good point. If we ran we would be shot out of the sky. If we stayed we could be shot out of the sky. We were being detained by the Avaraks and fired on by the Terrans. I thought about it.

Mel was shaking. "What do I do?" she shouted. "Rye! What are your orders?"

"Calm down, Melody. I'm thinking."

"Think faster!"

"I might, if you shut up for a moment." She sounded just like my mother, making it harder to concentrate. Not that there was a solution. There wasn't.

Seyal started as a heavy Avarak voice broke into the relative silence. She listened attentively and then took her finger off the com link. "They say we are to throttle back and wait for a shuttle to dock with us. Our ship is to be taken over and flown to an undisclosed nearby space station."

"They think we are too valuable for them to lose. I don't see how they are going to get us out of here. Those Terran ships are all equipped with ZEPH drives, aren't they?"

Mel nodded. "All seem to have new EP receptors on their hulls, yes."

"All right. Tell the Avaraks we will permit landing. There should be room for an Avarak shuttle in the cargo hold. Tell them to use the front cargo bay door though. Our own shuttle is aft, right?"

Mel gave me a withering look. "Yes. Don't you know things like that?"

"I'm not an encyclopedia! I have you for that."

She didn't know what to say, after that. At least it shut her up for a while.

It was hardly a solution. Mel wasn't the only one who felt uncomfortable with my leadership abilities. I felt I should have been able to sweep in with some wonderful answer. But I truly couldn't see a way out of this without *Nivala* being blown up by one or other, or both sides. Whereas before we would have stood a chance of outrunning the Avarak fleet, we certainly couldn't outrun a Terran fleet equipped with ZEPH engines. If the Avaraks thought they could get us out of this situation, we would have to listen to them.

I used the com channel again to pass on this news to Zenzara. "Code Red." At least both she and little Segaton would be out of immediate harm's way. Unfortunately, *Nivala* might still be blown up in the next five minutes, as far as I could see, so their safety was merely relative.

Mel looked terrified and I couldn't blame her. I wasn't too happy either. We slowed down to accommodate the incoming Avarak shuttle. I went down to the cargo bay and walked inside as soon as the green light indicated equivalent air pressure on both sides. Seyal came with me, looking scared.

The Avaraks had already disembarked by the time we reached them. There were seven large males and four females. That shuttle must have been crammed. My eyes widened. The males were led by a huge figure who introduced himself as Akhetor.

"Why is this female speaking for you?" he demanded, as soon as he caught sight of Seyal.

"I speak no Avarak. She is a necessary translator."

"That is not acceptable."

"Then we will not understand each other. Unless you speak Universal?"

"I do, if I so choose." Clearly he did so choose, for I understood what he went on to say. "Your presence here will cause the loss of our fleet against the enemy. *Avarak Karax!*"

"What do you mean?"

"This ship has the velocity to escape the Terran forces, does it not?"

"Perhaps. I don't know. If they are right behind us, maybe not."

"They will not be." Akhetor turned stiffly to the four female Avaraks, giving them fluent instructions in Avarak. Seyal whispered the translation to me. "He is telling them to search all of the ship. One armed male is to accompany each female. All of the present crew members are to be brought to the bridge."

An arm whipped out, knocking Seyal flat to the floor.

"Did I give you permission to speak, female?" Akhetor roared.

I began to shake. I knew I couldn't hit him, even if I tried. He was twice my size and wrapped in extensive armor. But how I wanted to! My adrenaline levels went through the roof.

I told myself that I would make him regret that gratuitous violence. I didn't know when, but I sure as krikk wasn't let another ship get taken away from me. I would wait, but there was some sort of reckoning in our joint future. I promised myself there would be.

I stepped in front of Seyal, who was dragging herself to her feet. I couldn't stop what had already happened, but I could try to stop it happening again. I hoped. At least she seemed to be able to stand. The force of the blow could well have broken her jaw. I raised my eyebrows at her to ask her how she was. She gave me the tiniest of nods, much to my relief.

"Who is this female?" Akhetor asked curtly.

I explained and the large Avarak's face darkened more and more. "Why was this female not auctioned off after Solutor's death?" he asked. "How is that not possible?"

One of the two remaining Avarak males approached Akhetor and seemed to be explaining something to him.

"Oh. *That* female! I see. Get her out of my presence. She is unlanded and should already have been put to death."

"If you touch her I will blow up this ship and you with it."

He glared at me, but that did make him pause for a moment. He considered his options. "If she dares to venture into the same space as mine again I shall see that she is culled."

Culled! How could he even use that word for one of his own species? However, my priority had to be to keep her alive. "Where am I to put her?"

Female Avaraks obviously posed no threat to him. "I care not." He waved an arm. Get her out of my sight."

I nodded. "Go to sick bay, Seyal. Do not move from there."

She assented. She knew that the sick bay was one of the nearest rooms to the crawl space under the swimming pool. In fact she could access the crawl tube network from sick bay. Should she want to, of course.

She walked backward to the cargo corridor. Perhaps females were not allowed to turn their backs on the males? I wouldn't put that past these misogynists. Then she slipped out of sight.

I breathed a sigh of relief. Apart from Seyal being knocked down, that probably had gone as well as it might. Now we just had to hope that we were worth more to the Avaraks alive than dead. I wasn't sure that they would think so.

Two hours went past before the rest of us were all reunited on the bridge. I was greatly relieved when the female Avarak searchers came back in without Zenzie or Segaton. Whoever had found them must have been convinced by Seyal's letter. Or perhaps by Seyal herself. For the time being, the youngest members of our crew remained undiscovered.

Those of us who belonged on *Nivala* were herded together into the mess hall. One of the Avarak males was stationed outside, with the door open. However, we were allowed access to the adjoining kitchen. At least we would not starve to death. Small comfort. This was reminding me most uncomfortably of the Vaers.

I still had no idea what plans Akhetor had. Even if they wanted to get us away from the Avarak fleet, the Terrans were almost on top of us. I couldn't see that they would let any ship away, even if it was Tyzaran.

I mulled over the possibilities, and still could see none.

Until the attack started.

Then I realized all at once what they were going to do. I hadn't happened on the plan because it simply hadn't occurred to me that the whole fleet would sacrifice itself merely to save one ship.

Silly of me. I already knew just how far they would go for their *Avarak Karax*.

We had already seen that with the *Raktor*.

13

The Avarak fleet stopped, turned, and spread out. It disgorged all its ancillary craft, and these spread even further apart, laying some kind of fluid trace behind them.

I was peering out of the mess hall viewport, having switched the lighting off. *Nivala* has viewports in all of the common areas. They are slightly convex constructs, built that way because of the increased strength of the rounded edges. The viewport in the eating area measures around two meters long by one high, which gave us a pretty good panorama. Since the mess hall is wedged into one of the wing fins, there are two viewports, one facing forward and one aft. We clustered around both of them and relayed to each other what we could see.

Denaraz was frowning. "That fluid must be some sort of fuel. I don't see how it could be anything else."

Mel was at the front port, with Sammy. "Oh no! They are going to set it alight!"

I peered out into the darkness. "That would be suicide!" Images of the last minute of the *Raktor* came into my mind. "...Oh!"

We stared at each other. Neema and Anzany reached out to touch hands. Sammy and Mel did the same. Didjal and Eshaan chattered silently to each other on each other's arms.

Denaraz met my gaze. "They will ignite the whole cloud, and fight to the death, hoping we can escape in the confusion."

I blew out air. "You have to admit, the Avaraks know how to immolate themselves."

A large figure filled the doorway. Akhetor loomed over us. He looked sick and horribly angry. "You!" he pointed at Didjal. "And you!" he singled out Neema. "You will come with me!"

They both turned to me for direction. I nodded. "Do exactly as they say, please. It is in all of our interests to get out of here, however little we like the means."

Akhetor rumbled. Literally. He made a sound like an approaching cargo hauler might make. I gathered that he also was unhappy with his lot. I guess, as a good Avarak, he would have preferred to be out there dying in glory. Tyranny and death. An inspiring combination. Personally, I struggled to see the attraction.

Didjal and Neema disappeared, presumably to oversee the escape, one from the engine room and one from the pilot's station. The rest of us waited.

It seemed interminable. The shuttles outside buzzed around, in what looked like random patterns. The larger ships turned their armament to face the incoming Terran vessels. Then they waited, I supposed, for the Flatlanders to get into range. The Terrans were still a long way off. I doubted very much that they could have resolved the movements of the shuttles.

A large piece of the sky was now dotted with the small craft. Certainly our escape along the same vector as the Terrans were using would be covered. For how long, I couldn't tell. I wondered if the Avaraks had devised other actions to take the Flatlander focus away from us.

They had. Just as the Terran fleet hove into range, one of the leading Flatlander ships exploded. The rest faltered and fell back.

And that was what the Avarak fleet had been waiting for. They poured missile upon missile bank into the midst of the Terran ships. The Terrans were still wavering. It must have taken them ten long seconds to get themselves into line once more and reply with their own missile fire.

There was a strident flash of light so strong that we all cried out and covered our eyes. Then *Nivala* sheered away from the Avarak fleet like a nervous Nepheal faced with a Vaer hunting party. The ship flipped up and over effortlessly, narrowly escaping a Terran ultrapulse as she did so.

Denaraz and both raced to the other viewport. The fight we had left behind was warming up. The Avarak fleet had taken advantage of the huge fire flash and its subsequent disruption to scatter towards the Terrans. The Flatlanders were now opening fire with some of the shorter-range Ultrapulses that their ships were equipped with, and the Avaraks were returning heavy torpedo fire, their own specialty.

One thing about torpedoes; you have to focus in order to avoid them. Several of the Terran captains didn't. I saw three of the Omnistate ships hit while we were still in range. That was what was so clever about the Avarak strategy, I realized. They used physical weapons, ones that might still take you out even if you eliminated their ship. Slower-than-light armament could hit you long after an ultrapulse had evaporated the attacking ship. They weren't stupid. They died knowing exactly what they were doing. They were giving one ship time to escape.

I couldn't like these authoritarian male Avaraks, but this was the second time scores of them had died in order to save us. It was humbling and very, very uncomfortable.

We were only able to see the scene behind us for some long seconds. Soon it was all behind us. As we raced away from the battle, I tasted bile in my mouth. I did not feel proud of myself.

Denaraz and I sank onto chairs. Nobody felt like eating. Or talking. We had survived, but the cost was hard to stomach.

About an hour later Akhetor's figure filled the doorway again. "It is done," he said heavily. "We are no longer in range of the Terran instruments."

I scrambled to my feet. "How far is it to this space station you are taking us to?"

He dragged his gaze away from the now empty viewport, where only a few dim stars vied with the blackness. "At this speed, one day." He turned on his heel. "In one hour please have replacements ready for pilotage and engineering. I require two of you to be available on a six hour rotation."

I nodded. "Certainly."

"My commander thought that your news of a possible alliance was important enough to sacrifice himself and over a hundred crew. And that was just one of the ships that died. I hope that he was right."

"The Alliance is very important. We now know that the Terran Omnistate has already equipped its ships with ZEPH drive. That means you can't win this war. Not on your own."

He glowered at this patent truth. "They have no integrity. They are mere thieves!"

"Maybe. But they will still win this war unless you get the same technology they have."

His face contorted with rage. "Why do you think you are still alive, Human?"

"Spacelander," I corrected him. "Spacelander. The Spacelanders will sign for membership of the Alliance. They would be your allies."

He looked as if the very thought of that made him sick. The rumbling started up again. I found myself taking a small step back. He was very intimidating when angry. Then I tried to put myself in his place. He had just lost his whole unit.

"Your friends were very brave. They knew there was no hope. I, too, hope that their sacrifice was not in vain."

He gave a sort of strangled groan. Then he stumped up to me and put his face almost into mine. It was all I could do not to jump backwards. I tried to remember I was supposed to be captain of this ship, not a scared schoolgirl. I straightened my shoulders and met his small furious eyes with what I hoped was fearlessness.

"You speak well," he said finally. "They were brave. I honor them for their sacrifice. *Avarak Karax!*"

The words meant nothing to me, but they did to him. I stood to attention to honor the selflessness of his fellow Avaraks. "*Avarak Karax!*"

He sighed. "You will explain to those in charge of the space station. They must understand. They need to see that this war will be lost without the help of some of the other Shell races."

I inclined my head. It had not been our mandate, but I knew that it would be the right thing to do. "I will do my best."

"Then all will have been worthwhile. My Avarak friends will be avenged." He gave a curt nod back to me and stepped away and back out of the doorway. We settled in for the long wait. Crammed as we were into the mess hall, with no place to sleep comfortably, it was going to seem a very long wait. Still, I suspected that Zenzara would be having an even more difficult time with Segaton. I just hoped that Seyal had been overlooked by the Avaraks, and had been able to help her.

I lay down on the decking. It was not conducent to sleep. Still, I would need to be up shortly for my stint in the bridge.

A day later we came upon the very edges of the Peliss system, still in the Bifold Shell. The space station was perched in space on the spaceward side of the heliopause. The Peliss K star at the centre of the system was visible only as a slightly larger dot of white against the background stars.

It was my turn on the pilot station. I brought *Nivala* gently into the docking area indicated. There were various metallic sounds which reverberated through the hull as the docking clamps extended. I flipped on the comlink. "Docked on the Avarak space station near Peliss, red continues."

"Stop talking!" Akhetor snapped. "I did not instruct you to do that!"

I held up my hands in innocence. "Sorry. Force of habit." I just wanted Zenzie to know where we were and to keep going for a little while longer. I was pretty sure that a baby male would get snapped up pretty fast if they got to hear of it. I was still amazed that none of the females had given the game away. It was clear that the Avarak females were very loyal to whoever they considered to be one of them. Interesting.

Akhetor took Denaraz and me to meet the station head. We were walked smartly along the corridors of the space station, but that didn't stop us taking in quite a lot of detail. I knew that Denaraz was thinking about the Tyzar Intelligence Bureau. I had something similar in mind. The Space Trust would like very much to know about this secret Avarak base. We tried to appear uninterested as we were marched along, but that was very far from the case. I was memorizing as much as I possibly could of the layout.

We were taken along interminable corridors only just wide enough to admit an Avarak. That meant that Denaraz and I could very comfortably walk side by side.

In comparison to the Tyzaran space station, this looked like a child's building block monstrosity. It consisted of large modules, shaped like food containers. Each module had been manhandled into place and welded tight. There was little order and no aesthetic.

But it was functional. However, getting from A to B took an eternity. Our legs, somewhat shorter than the Avaraks', were struggling. Akhetor laughed at our pathetic attempts to keep up. He thought both Denaraz and I were weaklings. I clamped my jaw shut to avoid panting and tried to look as tough as I could.

In fact, there was little to see on our way to this meeting. As far as I could make out, the bulk of the space station was laid out to living quarters. We only caught sight of two technologically advanced computer stations, and neither had any particularly high standard of security. It left me to conclude that the Avaraks were still very much miners, more given to shove than strategy.

Eventually we were shown into a large container given over only to plush seating and a large oval table. We were shown to seats well down one side; the Avarak leaders sat at the other end.

"You will now tell Grand Leader Kelkator about this new alliance."

I bowed. "Certainly." For fifteen minutes I described the basic tenets that had been discussed on Ulon Prime. I made sure I did not mention that equality of the sexes was an integral part of the deal. I was pretty sure the Avaraks would reject such a thing out of hand. And I liked the idea of setting female Avaraks on a level with the males. I thought they deserved it. Seyal certainly did. It was time that the hidebound and rigidly prejudiced society changed. More than time, in fact. But they could find out that small detail if and when they signed. That would be fun. I would love to be a fly on the wall for that news.

"So, the idea is an alliance where decisions are taken mutually and a common policy is decided on disputes."

Kelkator lifted his enormous head. "All would fight together?"

"On the same side. Exactly."

"Against the Terrans?"

"That would have to be decided, but I do not anticipate the Tyzarans fighting on the same side as the Terran Omnistate. After all, the Terrans have just stolen their ZEPH drive technology."

"And there would be provision to share such technology?"

"I think there would have to be."

Kelkator's eyes looked into the distance, unfocussed. "Why are the monkeys so important?"

"The monkeys? Oh, you mean the Macers." The only real resemblance to monkeys was their long tail. If I were a Macer I would have been extremely offended. However, it was not my place to comment. "They are not ..." I bit my lip. "Sorry. The Macers are known for their inability to lie or deceive. They may be trusted where other races could be seeking self advancement. It is a way to promote trust between all the participants."

"And the Vaers?"

"Will not be invited to join. At least, not in phase one of the Interstellar Alliance. It is possible that they could become members in the future. Members will have to adhere to certain standards of integrity which the Vaers may not currently reach."

Kelkator's belly quivered with laughter. "You understate it. They are like savages. The Vaers want only money and more money." His tone became scornful. "They will not change. They are without integrity, for sure."

I couldn't help looking sideways at him. His own idea of integrity was not mine. Though he was an ancient specimen, as indicated by his name. Seyal had explained to me that one generation had the suffix *ton* while the next had the suffix *tor*. Then back to *ton* again. And so on.

That was why Seyal's father had been Hegaton, her husband Solutor and her son Segaton. If this venerable male was called Kelkator, he must be of the generation of Seyal's grandfather. Which would probably make him in his eighties or nineties. He had lived a very long time for an Avarak. Perhaps that made him more tolerant. Perhaps less.

"Are you interested in joining?"

"We might be."

I turned to Denaraz. He would be the one to contact the Tyzaran fleet and tell them the good news. At least, I hoped that they would consider it good news.

"Do you wish me to contact the Supreme Council?" he asked Kelkator in a quiet voice.

"I must meet with the Grand Senate to debate this further," the old male told us in his deep voice. "I will have an answer for you within the day. Please to return to your ship."

We withdrew. There was no chance for any further exploration. We were marched straight back to *Nivala*. There we were left, with our Avarak friends still on board. I sighed. I had been hoping to see Zenzara. I was beginning to get really worried about her. Knowing her, she was probably worrying about me, too. Her need to fulfil the Savior Protocols was very strong.

Mel and the others clustered around as we filled them in on the information.

"Will they let us go?" asked Sammy.

"I think so. It would hardly be a nice way to present your integrity if you annexed the ship that brought you the good news. It all depends if they decide to join or not, I believe."

Denaraz was pleased. "The Supreme Council will be most surprised."

"Another promotion?"

His face froze. "Certainly not. I hadn't even thought of it!"

I continued to stare at him until he dropped his eyes. "I suppose it is possible," he admitted.

I gave him a thump to his upper arm. "And I hope they do, Denaraz. You deserve to be part of the Supreme Council."

He reddened. "I am not sure that I want to be."

"Come on! If I know our Supreme Oznard, she already gave you embedded ansible communication to the Supreme Council. After all, you are their one link to the prospective Chyzar."

He went white. "How did you ...? No. No! Of course she didn't!" His crest wobbled and then stood out.

I laughed and punched him again. "Whatever. You know, we really don't care. That is up to you. But if she did, now is probably a good time to get in touch with them. Once the Avaraks decide, you will be expected to tell them if their membership is likely to be accepted. And, Denaraz...?"

"What?"

"Don't tell them females are equal. It might put them off."

He grinned. "I won't. I will leave that to the Supremes ... once they have signed."

"Good man!"

"You can call me by my first name," he told me, much to my surprise.

"I didn't know you had one."

"We all have one. We just don't let many people use them."

"Then I am flattered to be counted amongst them. What is it?"

"Izan."

"Nice name. Shorter than Denaraz!"

He smiled. "Much."

I thrust forward my hand. "Nice to meet you, Izan!"

He shook mine. "What should I call you?"

I shrugged. "Take your pick. Ryler, Rye, Mallivan, Mall ... I answer to all and any of them."

"I shall rotate them. It sounds more interesting."

"You do that. I hope we will be friends."

"So do I. I have never had an alien friend before."

"Yes. Our governments should have been doing more of this. We Spacelanders really only mix with the Enif." As soon as I said it, I realized that it wasn't true, either. We worked with them. We didn't mix with them. At least we hadn't, until now.

The second time we met Kelkator he seemed more friendly. He was not the sort to beat about the bush.

"The Avarak Grand Senate has decided to apply for membership of this Alliance you speak about, providing there is a free exchange of technology," he told us.

Izan stepped to the fore. "My government is happy to share the new ZEPH drive technology with you."

"When?"

It was a little direct for my liking, but he did have troops that were being decimated every day by the Terrans. I could sympathize with the need for speed.

"I have been authorized to take four Avarak ships to a location near Tyzar. They can be fitted with the ZEPH drive while you and their captains sign the Alliance deeds of constitution. It has been decided that five beings from each shell race shall sign. One, at least, must represent the ruling body of the moment."

"Only four ZEPH drives?"

"You may bring ten engineers on those ships, and these ten engineers will be given details on the function and maintenance of the new drives. They will then be able to install any further drives your government may wish to buy."

"Buy?"

"You cannot expect us to provide them free, surely? Such drives are most costly to make."

Kelkator looked underwhelmed. He had expected something for nothing. At least, that is the way it looked like to me. He wasn't going to admit it, however. "We Avaraks pay our way!" he proclaimed. "We are not like the Terrans, sneaking about stealing technology!"

Izan Denaraz managed not to smile. "Quite."

"Those terms are acceptable. We shall leave tomorrow. I shall travel in your ship."

It was my turn. "I regret, that will be impossible. Our governments will be most upset that our ship has been taken over by Avarak troops. I'm sure they will expect you to stand down, now that agreement has been reached."

The large Avarak shuffled his feet. "It was necessary," he blustered.

"If so, it is no longer necessary."

There was no denying that. He had to back down. "I suppose you are right."

"I am glad you see our point of view."

Izan cleared his throat. "I am also instructed to tell you that this technology is subject to a legal signing of the accords."

"And you will all fight with the Avaraks?"

"Signatories may decide to fight and may decide to remain on the sidelines. However, no Signatory may fight with another signatory. There is to be a new policing service to ensure compliance of all the accords."

"Who may that be?"

"To begin with, it will be *Nivala* and her crew."

The heavy jowls shook from side to side as he digested this. "Well," he said in his deep rumble. "At least your crew is multistellar. That is sensible."

I wanted to point out that we even had a resident Avarak. It didn't seem like the right time to do that, though. It might remind someone that she hadn't been seen for some time.

"Oznard is on board with all this?" I whispered to Denaraz. "She doesn't mind giving them the tech?"

He shook his head. "The Supreme Council was going to do that anyway. But she and the others are pleased. This way Tyzar will get something in return. The Avaraks broke the Raksora Accords. They will find it harder to break the Alliance statutes. Each signatory will have to undertake to uphold all statutes at all times. It is part of the conditions of membership."

"Where are we to take them?"

"To the Kallima Space Station. It is about a hundred light years north of Tyzar, and forms an equilateral triangle with Rhyveka. I guess it must be around thirty light years from here."

I whistled. "How long will it take us to get there?"

He pulled a face. "We will have to go at their speed. With the current Avarak drives, around two weeks."

"At least we seem to have got *Nivala* back!"

"Yes. I wonder how Zenzara has been getting on with the baby!"

We soon found out. As the Avarak shuttle left, a very disheveled Zenzie emerged from the crawl space. She wasn't happy.

"Do you know how long I have been down there?" she demanded.

"We know exactly how long you have been down there. I'm sorry, Zenzara, but there was absolutely nothing we could do about it. Well done! You have saved little Segaton."

"That baby is not so little. You should try holding him in your arms all day! He weighs a ton!"

"Avarak males are densely packed."

"And he cries all the time. I thought I was going to go crazy!"

"Never mind, it is over now. You can have two weeks of complete rest."

She thrust a damp and bawling bundle into my arms. "I shall be in the Spa," she snapped, sounding a lot older than her eight years. "I need a sauna, a shower and two hours under the sun lamp. Please don't speak to me again until I have done that!" She stalked off. Her crest had little indignant kinks all along it.

I held Segaton gingerly. He smelt terrible. "Mel!" I looked all around. "Mel!"

Anzany came up behind me and started to laugh. "Can't find anybody to fob him off on, Mallivan?"

I straightened. "Certainly not. I ... I just know that he would be ... happier in a female's arms. Babies are, aren't they?"

She gave me a wicked grin. "Are they? I wouldn't know."

I held the baby out towards her. "I don't suppose you ...?"

"Nope." She grinned again. "Perhaps you should practice those skills, Mallivan? In case you ever become a father."

"I already am a father! I have six children! Like Neema! Like all of us!"

Then I saw the look on her face and wished I had kept my tongue. Damn it!

"You didn't know Neema had children?"

She shook her head. "I didn't, no."

"Look, we all have to donate gametes when we are eighteen. It's not as if she actually carried any of the children. We go to the Genetic Institute on Zenubi. It has been like that for generations. They make sure that a suitable match is made, one that will avoid any genetic similarities. Six children are born to each of us. Three are eventually returned to the father's family shipstation and three to the mother's. It is possible that Neema has never even met her children. The Prime of the family shipstation has the responsibility for their upbringing."

Anzany shook her head, as if to clear it. "You are telling me that Neema has six children, and she forgot to tell me about them?"

I put the baby on the deck for a moment and tried to give Anzany a hug. She held up her hands as if I was going to attack her.

I stepped back pretty smartly. "I should not have said anything. I am truly sorry."

"No! No, you were right. It is something I should know about. Of course I should. Six children. Six children!" She wandered off rather aimlessly. I thought I could hear her repeating those two words as she vanished.

The baby shuffled at my feet and began to cry. I picked him up again. "Mel! Seyal! Anyone!"

"What?" Mel appeared from the kitchen, looking anything but willing. "What is it now?"

I put on a hurt expression, but she was having none of it.

"Forget it, Rye. You can look after Segaton yourself. It won't kill you. I need to give Sammy his massage. That leg of his still gives him trouble."

"But the baby!"

"He won't eat you. Just change his nappy and find him some food."

I looked at the damp bundle. I would rather have faced Supreme Oznard and Kelkator at the same time. He was still crying.

There was nothing for it; I would have to find Seyal. She would know what to do. I expect she was longing to be reunited with her son. The more I thought about it, the more it seemed the right thing to do.

14

The Kallima Space Station hove into view only ten days later. It seemed that the Avaraks had greatly increased their cruising speed recently by somehow boosting their standard drives. We had been joined by other Avarak cruisers on the way. We ushered their four ships into the correct docking facilities and then clamped up ourselves.

Kelkator was thumping at the airlock before we had even thought about disembarking. I rolled my eyes and signaled to Zenzie and Seyal to stay behind. Zenzara would join us for the talks; I just didn't particularly want the Avaraks to realize that she had been on board the *Nivala* all the time. As far as they were concerned, she would be a new addition to the crew, someone from Kallima.

We escorted the Avaraks to one of the conference rooms on the space station. They stumped stiffly behind us, grumbling in their low voices about the tight dimensions. They seemed to feel that it was beneath their dignity to have to bend to get through the hatchways. I couldn't help reflecting on the future of the burgeoning Interstellar Alliance if such things were of prime importance. I was grateful it would not be my job to sit in agonizingly long meetings discussing details like that. I was definitely not a diplomat and had no wish to become one.

However, once we reached the conference room we found that five plus sized chairs, almost resembling thrones, had been carefully placed around the head of the oval table. The Avaraks looked mollified, and went unhesitatingly to these seats.

Spokesdesignate Xynia was there, much to my unease. I still wasn't convinced of her loyalty to the Tyzaran people. So was Supreme Oznard, looking as chilly as usual. At the last minute, Zenzara slipped in through the door and took her place behind Didjal and Eshaan.

I won't go into the detail of the four-day discussions. To my mind, they went on forever. I found myself falling into a sort of reverie that lasted hours. I simply tuned out all of the droning demands of the Avaraks and Oznard's patient responses. Why had I agreed to sit in on this?

Almost all of the demands of the Avaraks were slowly but firmly denied, one by one, with mind-numbingly long explanations as to why they could not be incorporated. It was clear from the beginning where this was going. The Avaraks would have to sign with only minimal concessions by the other races.

I really couldn't see why our presence was necessary, but Oznard would not release us to work on *Nivala*. Her bargaining chip was Zenzara. She agreed to let the time spent now over the Alliance signing count against this year's obligatory stay on Tyzar. She claimed that the interstellar nature of *Nivala's* crew gave her credibility. Even though Zenzie had begged me to agree, her own crest drooped more and more as the week drew on.

I can't blame her; I even caught Denaraz sleeping at one point. Luckily, Tyzarans don't snore. Strangely, he didn't appear grateful when I kindly woke him up by applying most of my weight to one of his feet. I discovered that Tyzaran feet are surprisingly tender.

Once the bare bones of some sort of agreement had been reached, we were all shepherded aboard a large Tyzaran cruiser and escorted at top speed to Ulon Prime. By that time, other signatories had arrived representing most of the other Shell Races. Only the Vaers and the Terrans had rejected the idea out of hand.

It was good to be back on Ulon Prime. As our shuttle came down, we saw that many rafts of kelp had been brought together for the signing ceremony. There were shuttles from Enifa, from the Space Trust and from Nephealis.

I had never met Nepheals before. They were large creatures, which made space travel uncomfortable for them. Their shuttle was much bigger than anybody else's.

Zenzie was alongside me at the viewport, hoping to catch a first glimpse of the race renowned for its intelligence and reasoning. She gasped as their size became apparent. They must have been over twice the height of an elder Avarak. Twice the height but half the bulk. They were tall, elegant creatures that walked elegantly on their back two legs, although they could also drop to all fours if speed were required. The upper part of their bodies reared up from the forelegs and culminated in a long, curved neck which transitioned seamlessly into a head. The head was slim and their eyes wise.

I stared past Zenzie's ear at them. They were quite unlike any species I had ever seen before. "What do you know about them?" I asked.

It was Seyal who answered. She had asked to accompany us in the shuttle, though of course, she would not be descending onto Ulon Prime. She was, it seemed, taking her duties as an interpreter very seriously.

"They are fiercely protective of all environmental issues," she told us. "They dislike political scheming."

I was warming to them even more. "Go on. Tell us about them."

"They developed like that because Nephealis is a rocky medium-gravity world with abrupt terrain. This means that very little food can grow on it. The one plant that adapted to it was the phyonwe tree."

I started. "Phyonwe? The fruit? The fruit I feed my Geiga?"

"Indeed. It is now exported all over the Major Shells. Phyonwe trees are very tall and grow in extremely rocky terrain, which is why the Nepheals have developed as they are. They are as tall and thin but have long goat-like heads and large soft eyes. They possess an extraordinary intellect. They have immensely strong digits, which on their home planet enable them to anchor themselves to rocks."

The three of us stretched our own necks to get a better view of this amazing race. Seyal pointed out a small group of Nepheals on one of the rafts. "Their civilization developed quickly after a blight killed almost all of the phyonwe trees. The Northern Nepheals were drawn together and they were able to fashion tools out of the pliable bark. Many seeds were saved, and from that point on they began to cultivate the lower, flatter lands. Modern day Nepheals are believed to be only two thirds the size of their ancestors, and have shorter necks.

"Nepheals were hunted almost to extinction by avian ancestors of the Vaers. They still detest modern Vaers. One of their greatest insults is 'You could have feathers' or 'He speaks through a beak.'"

"I'm inclined to agree with them."

"Yes. They developed space travel a thousand years ago, but they are a fundamentally passive race. They prefer the beauty of nature, and their own planet. Exploring is hard for them. Their spaceships have to be very large to accommodate them. Still, they *do* export the excess of their phyonwe fruit production. The fruit is highly prized across all the Major Shells, being full of vitamins and considered to prevent many ailments, especially of bones and cartilage. They keep a circular space station – of huge dimensions – in orbit above Nephealis. This is used as a staging post for the export of the fruit. Nowadays, the Nepheal space presence is almost entirely limited to that space station. Few Nepheals feel the need to leave their own planet. They maintain a small fleet of light cruisers with pulser cannon capacity as a front defense but these generally can be found docked at the Nepheal Gyre, as their space station is called."

Seyal stopped for a moment as the shuttle finally settled on the sea bed. We watched in silence as the rafts were brought over and bundled together. The shuttle engines switched off, leaving a sudden silence. Seyal smiled to herself.

"What?" I asked.

"Do you know about their *Phaala?*"

"Never heard of it."

"Mothers-to-be retire to the wilderness in the mountains where large retreats have been built in recent times. They voluntarily separate from their community and from their partners since in ancestral times the newly born attracted the interest of the predators and thus brought danger to the community.

"The newly born are tended to in a mountain retreat by their mothers until the can run almost as fast as the pack, which is around one year old.

"During this time, both parents separately dedicate their spare time to illumination as a symbol of their mutual love and dedication. Each tries to write a thesis that will enhance the knowledge of the species. A meaningful thesis is considered to be a testament to the profundity of their love. This is one of the reasons that the Nepheals have developed so far and so quickly. They are bright and have the best grasp of quantum mechanics in all the Major Shells.

"A great celebration is held when a mother brings her offspring back to the fold. It is known as the *Phaala*. *Phaala* is when the theses are read to a peer council, when the young are welcomed into city life, when the Nepheal celebrate the successful raising of another of their race. Each of the young are inscribed in the state register and their lineage back to the olden times is immortalized for their future progeny to study. The two theses welcoming them are also incorporated into the inscription. To date, no foreigners have ever been invited to a *Phaala*."

"You make them sound very erudite," commented Zenzie. She seemed a little disappointed.

Seyal nodded. "They are great orators. There is something called the *Dialectis*, which is a weekly competition of logical argumentation where major philosophical or scientific themes are debated and discussed."

Zenzara wrinkled her nose up.

Seyal saw this and tried to convince. "No, really! The most successful orators are idolized by the Nepheals. They command huge sums to give an address."

You could tell that this wasn't exactly selling it to our future Chyzar.

Seyal was frustrated that she hadn't been able to bring enthusiasm to Zenzara's small face. "They appreciate music and art. They especially value Enif art, having an affinity for the Enif way of life. Deference and form are important to them. It is considered rude to break into somebody's speech."

Seyal petered out, looking to me. Her face was sad. She wanted us to admire the Nepheals, wanted us to empathize with them. I thanked her. "You are doing a great job, Seyal. Tell me, what is the correct etiquette when introduced to one of them?"

Her eyes sparked again. "You must lower your head to the floor."

"That's all right if you are a giraffe," snapped Zenzie. "How are *we* supposed to do that?"

"Oh. I don't know. I'm sorry." Seyal reddened and I glared at Zenzara.

Supreme Oznard pushed past us from behind, on her way to the shuttle hatch. "You incline from your waist and attempt to touch your toes or the floor," she said curtly. "These little gestures are things that you are going to need if you are hoping to represent the Alliance."

Seyal deflated visibly even further. She bowed and almost disappeared into the wall.

Zenzie was practicing the Nepheal salute. I did too. I couldn't touch either my toes or the floor. She could touch both. Now I was feeling inferior, too.

"Didj?"

"Yes, Mallivan?"

"Is there a special way to greet Enif?"

It chittered. "Of course!"

"What must we do?"

"That would depend on who it is. We have a pyramidal democracy. Ordinary Enif would exchange a small bow ...," it demonstrated, "... like this. If you are meeting a *Ziifaan*, you would bend one knee ...," again a demonstration, "... so. If you are introduced to a *Belofiin*, you would bend both knees. To a *Sandiif*, you would kneel on your right knee. To a *Mendiliif* you would kneel on your left knee. To the *Aliifat*, you would kneel on both knees."

I turned to the self-effaced Seyal. She shrugged. She hadn't got to the Enif yet in her studies.

"Err ... how do I know which is which?"

Didjal and Eshaan shook with the Enif equivalent of laughter. "You look at their tattoos, of course!" It took pity on me. "*Ziifaan* have a tattoo of our sun, Enifa, on their left neck. *Belofiin* have tattoos of the sun on both sides of the neck. *Sandiif* have tattoos of the sun on the left of the face in addition, *Mendiliif* have tattoos on both the left and right of the face, as well as the two on their necks, of course. The *Aliifat* has a further tattoo in the centre of its forehead, plus all the others, of course."

Mmm, that sounded easy but it wasn't. I might have a problem there. Enif are tall thin black and more than slightly insecty. Aliens with high-gloss reflective body parts don't show up their tattoos very well. Certainly not from a distance.

"What about the ones we are about to meet?"

Didjal peered out of the viewport. "One *Mendiliif* and two *Sandiif*," it told us. "You kneel with both legs, as if you were meeting the *Aliifat* itself."

"Thank you." I guess we were going to have to take some lessons in Alien protocols, but that would have to go on the back burner for a while. I hated to think how many times we had omitted the bare essentials of civility.

There were some very tricky moments with Kelkator over the equality clauses in the final document. The Tyzarans had skated over this issue in the original talks, so the clause on equality came as a nasty shock to the Avarak delegation. Not surprisingly, the Avarak leader was outraged by the idea that females could ever have rights. I gather that they were within an inch of not signing. I had been back on board

Nivala at the time.

Izan, who had been present, told me how they had managed to persuade the Avarak delegation. Apparently, Hekkaan, the Nepheal chief signatory, had regarded Kelkator with some amusement.

"You are worried that the females will rise up against you?"

Kelkator snorted. "Of course not!"

"Do they even speak Universal?"

Another snort of derision. "Of course not!"

"Do they even know about this document?"

"They do not!" The female Avaraks had been left on board one of the Avarak ships, back on the Kallima space station. I think he had completely forgotten about Seyal. In any case, she was unlanded. They thought that meant that she had ceased to be Avarak.

Hekkaan had smiled broadly. In his soft, mellow voice he had sounded triumphant and persuasive. "Then there is no problem, I think? They cannot claim that which is unknown. It seems to me a very small sacrifice on your part for the very great advantages which this document will bring to the Avaraks as a whole." He had ticked them off on his fingers. "Immediate use of the ZEPH drive, preferential fitting of all new technology, powerful allies against the Terrans, access to the Tyzaran shipyards and to our own advances."

Kelkator had licked his lips. It was, after all, a very tempting package. "Very well," he had finally said. "We will sign. But only one copy shall be taken to Rhyveka, and it shall be stored far away from prying eyes."

Seyal would soon circumvent that attempt at burying this treaty. She was buzzing with excitement about the position that fate had put her in. She had every intention of slowly working to bring the female population of Rhyveka into a modern, independent era. She planned to get copies of the new treaty to wives who might still talk to her. She thought that it would take some time, but that female Avaraks would gradually become aware of their rights and even – in the far future – demand some of them. Her eyes grew starry when she thought of this.

"We are usually dead by the time we are seventeen," she said, jaw working with emotion. "And our vocal chords are mutilated just to be more attractive to the male population! It has to change! I want to make them change!"

"Well, *you* certainly have changed," I said. "I don't think your husband or your father would recognize you now."

She nodded. "They wouldn't. I am my own person now. I don't belong to anybody."

"People shouldn't belong to other people."

"No," her eyes looked far into the distance and I thought she was seeing her own past history. "No, they shouldn't. A lot of things are going to have to change."

"Change takes time." I realized how much of a platitude it was as soon as the words were out of my mouth.

Zenzara gave me a thump on my arm. "No it doesn't. You only have to look how fast everything changed for us."

"True. Perhaps it doesn't. Only, I have the feeling that the male Avaraks aren't going to adapt to strong females very readily. The females may have quite a fight on their hands."

Seyal grinned. "Not really. There is now a signed treaty to protect us. We can appeal to the Interstellar Alliance. They are honor bound to protect us."

Zenzie jumped up and down in glee. "Yes! And the really great thing is that the males themselves signed it! It is one of those things. You know, one of those classical things that creep up on you when you are bad."

"Retribution?"

"Yes! A reckoning!"

Seyal illuminated as if she were a Christmas tree. "The Reckoning," she repeated. "That is what we will seek! The Reckoning of the Females!"

I huffed. "That sounds like the title of a bad film."

"Maybe it does, but it is going to happen, just the same!" Zenzie and Seyal did some sort of dance of victory which involved linking elbows and circling while jumping up and down.

"You both look very silly."

Zenzie laughed. "Kelkator is the one who is going to look silly, you mark my words!"

I wasn't about to object to that. He was one Avarak who could certainly do with a change.

So the formal documents were signed and the Interstellar Alliance came into being. The founder members were the Enif, the Spacelanders, the Tyzarans, the Macers, the Nepheals and the Avaraks. Six of the eight races of the Major Shells. I wondered if it would ever admit the other two. The Terrans, with their expansionist plans, and the Vaers with their factions and a total disregard for property ... when it belonged to other people.

I knew that Vaers guarded their own assets very carefully. They like to hoard their money. Control of finance and profit on Vaer Prime is mandatory and enforced with an iron fist.

Many Vaers who found Prime too rule bound and restrictive moved to the new colony of Vaer Nova. Such individuals tend to have fewer principles and are motivated by money more than anything else. Many of them consider killing to get what they want an acceptable option. More and more of Nova's inhabitants have situated themselves well outside what would be considered decent by Major Shell terms. Nova is the place to go to buy arms and weaponry in general. Many of the Nova Vaers dabble in the receipt of stolen goods, and their sale. This encourages pirates of any origin to gravitate to that area. Nova is generally considered to be the best place in the Shells for an unscrupulous individual.

Over the years, Vaer Prime lost its influence over the Novans. Now, there is great mistrust between the two planets. They have become enemies.

There didn't seem to be that much trust amongst the members of the new Alliance, either. After the signing there was a celebratory party with refreshments and drinks. It was not the great success which Oznard had probably envisioned. The delegates stuck together in their own small groups and only the Macers and one or two Tyzarans made the effort to be really sociable. The Avaraks folded their heavy arms across their chests and regarded the whole thing with solid distrust.

Oznard also made a long speech about common aims and goals. This, too, was received with bored faces and a clear desire to leave. Even the Enif delegates were seen to be chattering silently together during her talk.

The Nepheals kept themselves to themselves during the whole meeting. Their long faces were worried. I remember wondering if they were really sure that they wanted to be a part of this whole thing.

However, the refreshments were very good. *Nivala's* crew set to and demolished as much as we could. It was not our fault if the others appeared to find the food unappetizing. We certainly didn't. I saw Zenzie taking three slices of chocolate cake. Chocolate was something she had only recently discovered. I got the impression it was going to be a lasting partnership.

Once most of the shuttles had left, our group was invited out onto the kelp raft. The Macers wanted to discuss something with us.

We clambered down the ladder and stepped happily back onto the soft floating platform.

There was another document. We stared at it.

"When we last spoke to Supreme Oznard, you agreed to undertake the policing of the Interstellar Alliance." It was the same Macer we had met before.

I nodded. "Not the whole of it, though. I don't think one ship can do very much over what ...? Eighty-seven million cubic light years?"

The Macer spread his long hands in an unexpectedly universal gesture. "It is a start," he said. "Everything must have a start, and you are the beginnings of the Interstellar Enforcement Agency."

Sammy stuck his chin out. "Do we get paid?"

The Macer nodded. "Indeed you do. Each race is paying a certain quantity of credits into a common fund to finance the needs of the Alliance. You will receive a sensible amount from that each month."

Seyal, Didjal and Eshaan looked confused. They were unfamiliar with the concept of payment. Zenzara skipped and nearly tripped over a loop of kelp that had become loosened from the rest of the raft. Anzany looked at Neema and smiled. It would give them the independence they craved.

Sammy strode up to the document. "Is the amount in there?"

The Macer nodded.

Sammy ran a finger along the lines until he located the place. "Rye, you get more as Captain, but ..." he whistled. "That is a substantial amount. I'm in!"

I walked up to join him. He was right. That was good money. Two million universal credits annually per ordinary crew member, three million for all officers and four million for the Captain. That would give us all money to spend.

It was such a change. I had never really had any money ever to spend. All Spacelanders worked for their shipstation. We had accounts, and could use those to buy whatever we needed, but it wasn't actually *our* money; it belonged to the family. Individual wealth had been redundant for centuries for Spacelanders. It was a new concept for us.

This was going to be extremely strange. As far as I knew, only Terrans still used the concept of salaries. So it would be ground-breaking for the rest of the Major Shells. I wasn't even sure what you could actually do with money any more. Well, I knew you could buy hotel rooms, and restaurant services, but those were usually on expense accounts and so didn't count. And where would an individual buy food? There were no markets or shops any more. It was just so ... weird.

Which made me wonder what was happening back home. Did I still have a home? What would happen if I stepped onto *Bellaris* again? Would my mother have relented? Would I be welcomed or derided? I wasn't sure I wanted to find out.

"There are two things you should know."

I shook my head slightly. The Macer was still talking. I should be concentrating on what he had to say, not wool-gathering. I made an effort to look intelligent. "Yes?"

"The Terrans have developed a new weapon."

I heard several gasps beside me. My own jaw dropped. "What?"

The Macer's small face screwed up in worry. "Indeed. The evidence is overwhelming. I'm afraid there can be no mistake."

"What is it?"

"The Omnistate refers to it as the RAMP missile. They developed it as a deterrent, but it has already been used in this new war with the Avaraks. One was dropped on one of the Gienak moons, three days ago."

I wondered how they knew what had happened so far away so fast. Gienak was a good two hundred light years away. It is one of the systems in the Local Shell that the Avaraks had taken over for their mining colonies. It provides a high percentage of the Shells' platinum and rhodium.

"What happened?"

"The effect was even more devastating than the Omnistate had predicted. The moon is no longer there. However, things are much more serious than the total destruction of one moon. This new RAMP weapon somehow attacks the very fabric of spacetime itself. Have you ever heard of the ultra-dense phase of the vacuum energy?"

"No."

The Macer shook his head in a mournful sort of way, sad at my lack of knowledge. "Then I can hardly explain to you the danger." He looked around, clearly trying to dumb down the explanation to my level. I could feel my imaginary hackles rising. Zenzara was laughing at me.

She would be. Tyzaran children were started on quantum physics at age six. She probably knew all about this sort of thing. I glared at her, but that only made her smile more.

The Macer pointed to the sea. "Imagine that this sea is the space-time continuum. It is liquid, yes? Fluid?"

"It is." I may have been a bit curt. I was still smarting at being found wanting.

"Imagine then, that I have an additive that makes it solid. Not only that, but that my additive propagates, so that even if I only pour one small drop into it, the whole of this ocean will suddenly turn solid, killing every single living organism inside it."

I frowned. "Are you saying that one RAMP missile could congeal all spacetime? You can't be right, surely?"

The Macer bowed his head. "It is indeed what I am saying, although I do not believe that it is what the Terran Omnistate set out to do. Their level of technology is inferior to that of the Nepheals or the Tyzarans. However, it is what very nearly happened on the Gienak moon. This weapon is terrifying. It must be stopped. Immediately. The Terrans have no idea what it is they have unleashed. Each and every time it is used, there is a chance of total annihilation of our entire universe."

His dark eyes seemed to pierce our souls. "The Nepheal have brought this to my attention. They have apparently been aware that such technology might be produced. As you know, they are the foremost scholars of the quantum world. Several recent *Phaala* theses have postulated the development of such a weapon, and they have expressed their concerns to us. The signature at Gienak is unmistakable. We have been given access to their theoretical work and are satisfied that there are no false assumptions."

Suddenly the four million credits a year were looking mean. I gawked at him. "You expect us to waltz calmly up to the Terrans and remove their new secret weapon? To ensure it will never be used again?"

He seemed pleased. "Exactly!"

"How?"

"Excuse me?"

"How are we supposed to do that?"

The Macer shut his eyes and opened them again, several times in quick succession. "We do not know. It is indeed a challenging problem. We were unable to find any viable solutions in our conversations."

"Great!" I turned to Zenzie. "Any ideas?"

She shook her head. Her eyes were very wide.

I looked at all the others. "Anybody?"

They were all in the same state of shock as me. Nobody had anything to say.

"Do you know how many of these weapons there are? Where they are being held? Are they on planet or on board ships? Where are they being produced?"

"It is believed that five prototypes were constructed ... all of them at the Jupiter Military Base. Of those five, two were deployed at Gienak. One may not have been detonated; we are not sure at the moment. The other three are thought to be distributed on three different ships. All are in convoy with the Eighth Omnistate Fleet, and are currently believed to be traveling from the Local Shell into the Bifold Shell."

"Do you know their destination?"

"Given the hostilities, it seems likely that they will head to one of the Avarak outposts, possibly even Rhyveka itself."

"How many ships form the fleet?"

"Thirty in total: Four battleships, ten light cruisers and sixteen destroyers."

I blanched. One small patrol craft against thirty military-grade ships. Even the destroyers would be larger than *Nivala*.

The Macer was going on. "We know that the battleships are the *Nanhai*, the *Chibuzo*, the *Telzaria* and the *Sanun*. Three of those are believed to have one of the RAMP missiles on board. All must be stopped."

"There is a difference between a policing unit and a full military presence," I told him. This was getting more and more surreal.

"We are aware. However, at this moment in time, the *Nivala* and her crew are the only instruments we have that are authorized legally to act on behalf of the Interstellar Alliance. Your role was specifically agreed with all signatories."

"Thank you so much."

"You're welcome." His tone was so polite that I wondered if sarcasm existed amongst the Macers.

"We should proceed to sign these documents. After that, the Interstellar Enforcement Agency will have come into being and you can accept your first task. I myself am the authorized signatory on behalf of the Alliance."

I found myself meeting Denaraz's stare. He mirrored my own feelings. Total shock at the sheer size of the task ahead. He spoke. "How many of those who were at the previous meeting know about this new weapon?"

"At the current time, only the Nepheals. However, the destruction of the Gienak moon will be common knowledge very shortly. It cannot be hidden much longer."

"I'm sure it can't. You do realize that we may never come back from this mission?"

The Macer seemed to shrink in on himself. His limbs actually contracted in what I took to be pain. "It is a most unfortunate possibility. Yes, we are aware."

I signed the document. "So we answer only to you? Not to Oznard?"

"Only to me. The Tyzarans will be compensated for their ship. The *Nivala* is no longer the property of the Tyzar Government."

Zenzie wrinkles lightened. "So I don't have to go back to be studied?" she asked.

The Macer appeared unaware of any such agreement. "The *Nivala* is now available for your use without any caveats," he said. "However, all crew should sign the original document to witness it, together with the second document to regularize their position as crew members."

I wondered if that would give Izan a problem, but he stepped over to the table and signed both documents with the rest of the crew members. Seyal paused before signing. "What about my son?"

The Macer took her quite seriously. "Your son is not old enough to be a crew member. However, all crew are entitled to accommodation and board for dependent family members. He may stay with you."

Seyal's face radiated pleasure. "Then we have our place in the Shells. Thank you."

"You may not have it for long, Seyal," I told her. "We are about to go up against a fleet of hostile military ships with universe-splitting bombs on board."

She tskked. "We can solve that. We will make them stop, and then we will put an end to this silly war. I am not letting some expansionist bigheads ruin what we have just gained. I want my son to grow up in freedom."

Anzany moved over to the Avarak woman and gave her a cuddle. "You are right. If anybody can do, Rye can."

There was a general murmur of agreement. It was nice to be appreciated, but I couldn't for the life of me see what hope we had of stopping a Terran strike force as big as this fleet was.

I gave them a shrug. "I guess we will never know if we don't try. Let's get back up to the *Nivala* and try to find these Terran forces. Mel and Anzany, can you dig up as much as possible about those ships and the others that constitute the Omnistate Eighth Fleet?"

They nodded.

"Zenzie, can you start to study the physics behind the RAMP missiles? See if there is anything we can do to neutralize them? Izan, perhaps you could help her with that?"

Denaraz inclined his head, as did Zenzara.

"Seyal, we need you to find out anything you can about the lead up to this weapon. What they wanted to do, who designed it, where we can find them, and the recent history of the Omnistate so we know exactly what they are laying claim to?"

She flushed with pride. "Of course I will."

"That leaves Sammy, Neema and I to run the ship, with Didjal in the Engine Room."

Eshaan seemed dejected. "There is nothing for me?"

"The walls of the *Nivala* are pretty empty, Eshaan. We need some inspiring artwork, don't you think?"

Its face cleared. "Definitely. These are important times. I shall document the history of the ship in paint."

"I know they cannot stay with the ship forever, but it would be wonderful to be surrounded by your swirling colors wherever we go. Your paintings make me feel more alive. They really are inspiring. And I think we are going to need some inspiration."

Eshaan stood a little taller. "It will be an honor."

15

The *Nivala* dropped into orbit around one of the uninhabited planetoids inside The Lakshmi Disc, on the border between the Bifold and the Local Shells.

The Lakshmi Disc is a cloud of ejected material surrounding an ancient blue hypergiant called Zuben. Zuben is a dangerous part of the Shells to be in, because it is due to go supernova any time in the next million years. OK, I know that means that the odds are against it being today, but it could come to pass. Zuben is one of the most brilliant stars in the Major Shells, and its bright blue shroud of ejected material is shaped like four arms, which is probably where the name came from.

Because Zuben is such an oversized star, it has any number of large planetoids still in orbit around it, now shrouded by the ejected nebula. That makes detection unlikely. It is a good place to hide a ship and it is also close to the main shipping lanes connecting Gienak and Raksora with the Avarak star Veka and its chief planet Rhyveka.

We got *Nivala* as safely tucked up as possible and then all met in the mess hall.

I couldn't help giving a gasp as I walked through the door. The wing part of the room had been left bare, with just the viewports. However, all of the other walls were now covered with a huge mural.

It started on the right wall, passed behind me to the door and then continued on along the left wall, until the viewports designated the start of the wing section.

It was the scene of the Avaraks saving *Nivala* from the Terran attack, back in the Adhara Corridor. It felt just like stepping back in time. The scene was so true to my memory, so fluid, so vivid and so impacting that I almost flinched at the explosions taking place amongst the Avarak Fleet.

The others were gazing at it too. There must have been around a full minute of silence, before we all burst into spontaneous applause. It was one of the most magnificent paintings I had ever seen. The colors! The depth! The movement! It was spectacular.

Eshaan edged backwards, embarrassed by the fuss. It tried to disappear into the corridor, but Didjal blocked its passage and pushed it firmly back into the room. There, it had to endure our attempts to shake its hand, slap it on the back and generally importune it.

Finally the noise subsided. We all moved to the large table and took our places.

I invited all the participants to speak up and tell us of their findings, but truth be known, we had little more than we had started with six days before. We knew that the developer of the new missiles was a Terran scientist called Chandrayanan. We knew that he was based on the secret science lab on the Sivetas space station. Sivetas is a system between Sol and Tyzar, in the Local Shell. It was way too far away from our current position even to contemplate a visit. We knew that the technology involved manipulating zero point space at a quantum level.

Luckily, Zenzara and Denaraz had worked well together, and had come up with what they considered a weak point.

Denaraz explained. "They were in such a hurry to build five of these things that they had to take shortcuts on the electromagnetic shielding. There is no way that current state-of-the-art Omnistate missile housing would provide a sufficient shield. Not for this device. They should have waited and designed something bespoke that would truly isolate the missile from EM pulses. This technology is more susceptible to such things. We don't think they did that. While nothing can stop the chain reaction which changes the state to ultra-dense, it ought to be possible *theoretically* to block the chain reaction from ever taking place. *If* we can find something to give us a sufficiently strong EM pulse."

That was great news. Denaraz held up his hand. "Note that it only *might* work, and it definitely *won't* work on newer models if they design a better housing – which they will. It is only a short-term answer, at best."

"I'll take it." It was the first good news I had heard for a long time.

That took care of Seyal, Zenzara and Denaraz's research. We all turned to Mel and Anzany.

Mel handed around a list. "These are the ships in the Eighth Fleet. You will see that Admiral Ellison is listed as Fleet Admiral."

Ellison! The Admiral from the light cruiser that had tracked us down when we had taken refuge with the *Rastin* on that small uninhabited planet. The Admiral who had been tasked with finding Cunningham and the secrets of the ZEPH drive. Would Bull Cunningham still be with her, on board one of those ships? It seemed unlikely, but I found myself hoping he was. My teeth grated together at the thought of coming across him again.

Mel was still explaining. "We have found nothing much more of interest. The rest of the fleet is equipped with normal Terran ultrapulse cannons. All of the destroyers are two-battery, the light cruisers four-battery, and the battleships eight-battery. The battleships and the lights are also equipped with standard rail guns and torpedo emplacements."

"All right. That means that the Terrans will protect the ships carrying RAMP missiles at all costs. In a fight they will be prepared to sacrifice the light cruisers rather than risk any one of the three ships carrying the new weapon. That leaves them only one deployable battleship."

Denaraz looked diverted. I raised an eyebrow.

"Sorry," he said. "Just … '*only* one battleship'. You do realize that one battleship is about twenty times larger than *Nivala*, don't you?"

"And what do you think I can do about that?" I wished people would stop saying obvious things. "Do you want to stay here and do nothing?"

Denaraz shook his head. "We can't. The Terrans are apparently unaware of the side effect of that weapon they are carrying. They need to be told. Somebody has to stop them, and I can't see anybody else even trying."

"Yeah. I guess it is up to us."

He nodded. "I guess it is."

"So, how are we going to go about this?"

Zenzara ticked off the steps on her fingers. "First, we pop out in front of the fleet. Second, we board the flagship and speak to Admiral Ellison. Third, they agree never to use the RAMP technology ever again and to bury the research. Fourth, we stop the war. Fifth, we fly away and have some fun somewhere. This is all getting stressful."

"There you go. That's our plan." I stood up. "Any objections?"

Mouths in front of me opened and closed, but nobody said anything. What was there to say? We all knew that we would most likely be blown out of existence as soon as we 'popped out' in front of the fleet.

It occurred to me that we could leave a shuttle in hiding in the nebula. At least some of our group might survive. Zenzara, certainly, should not be risked.

"Seyal, you are to take Segaton and Zenzara to the main shuttle. You will remain here. I expect Anzany and Denaraz will stay with you."

Seyal stood very tall. "I am a member of this crew. Even for my son, I will not abandon my post. And where I go, he goes. *Avarak Karax!*"

As she pronounced the mantra she seemed to grow in size and her face radiated a determination I had never seen before.

Zenzara bunched her fingers into fists. "*I* cannot leave you. Have you forgotten the Savior Protocols? If you go into danger, I will go with you. I cannot do anything else. Please stop trying to protect me. That is my job!" She stamped one small foot on the decking. It hardly made any noise at all.

Denaraz gave me an apologetic shrug. "Where she goes, I go."

Anzany was clear on the matter too. "Where Neema is, so am I."

I sighed. This was hardly what I had wanted for our first assignment as the official Interstellar Enforcement Agency. "All right. Let's make sure everything is in working order. We may not get a chance to use our own ABlaser cannons or rail guns, but I want to know that something would happen if we push the button."

Seyal remained on watch for the arrival of the Eighth Fleet, while the rest of us scattered to check and recheck equipment. I don't know about the others, but I felt a skitter of unease in my stomach – an awareness that reality was about to flip over again. It seemed that every time one thing was overcome, another leapt into the gap. *Commorancy* and a simpler life seemed a long, long time ago.

The strange thing was that I felt more alive than I ever had before. Now that we were walking such a knife edge, it was impossible not to. I had captained the *Faraday* for years, with no real commitment, except perhaps to my sister, to my family. Now I was committed to *Nivala*. To all of them. I would fight for them. I might even die for them. I might die for them *today*.

Zenzie found me on the weapons bridge on the middle deck. "Mallivan Bell, do not worry. I will save you. It is a sacred promise."

I looked the eight-year old up and down. She stopped somewhere around my waist height. "Thank you Zenzara."

"Don't patronize me!" Her crest raised and she practically spit the words out.

I raised my arms. "Perish the thought!"

"You think I am too young to do anything!"

That was patently untrue. "Who threw the nivala and took down several of the Enclave?" I pointed out. "Who convinced the Avaraks to save us?"

Actually I still thought she was too small a thing to physically stand in harm's way, but I wasn't about to tell her that.

"You looked at me as if I were a little girl!" she snapped.

She was.

"Like that! See! Just like that! You don't take me seriously."

I blew out air. "What do you want, Zenzara?"

"Nothing!" She seemed very upset, though I couldn't for the life of me see why. "Nothing at all!"

"Then why do you keep stamping your foot?"

"I don't"

She did.

"Ouch! I don't know why you are so cross with me."

"I told you! I want to be taken seriously."

"I do take you seriously."

"You don't understand. I *have* to go with you to the flagship. I have to be there."

"I can't let you do that. You know I can't."

Her eyes took on a hint of desperation. "I am not permitted to let you go alone into danger. It would break my vow."

"And I can't take an eight-year-old Tyzaran Chyzar into battle."

Her face became very taut. The wrinkles deepened into ridges. "If you do not," she said, speaking very slowly and punctuating each word with a pause, "then we could all die."

"All right. I will look into it. I will ask Mel to check up on the Savior Protocols."

Her face cleared miraculously. "Thanks!" And she skipped off without saying any more, having got part of what she wanted.

I went to find Mel. A promise was a promise. She would know what to do.

I didn't like the reply. Turns out, the Savior Protocol is very clear. She was going to come with me. Mel told me that the rules were explicit. Zenzara's life was considered merely on loan to her. It was actually at my disposition. They thought of it rather as a spare body, one that was currently occupied but reassigned to me. This body was to go with me into any danger I faced. It was there to die for me.

As simple as that.

It gave me an uncomfortable shiver. How could I let an eight-year-old take the bullet meant for me?

Apparently, if I didn't, Zenzara would be forever scorned. First by her fellow Tyzarans, and then by *Zeuma*, their equivalent of God.

I went to speak with Denaraz about it. He was firm. "You cannot break the Protocols."

I thought that was unfair. "Oznard was keen enough to break them!"

"Of course. They put the next Chyzar in permanent danger."

"These rules are ridiculous! She is only eight! How can I take her into danger with me?"

"How can you not? If you refuse her this chance of sacrifice she would be breaking an unbreakable vow. Where do you think that would leave her?"

"I cannot believe that people as sophisticated as the Tyzarans still have archaic customs such as this."

He nodded. "I can understand your dismay. It is inappropriate for the times we live in, certainly. However, you are already bound by the Protocols. You agreed to it!"

"To help Zenzara! I didn't realize what I was agreeing to!"

"Lack of knowledge does not exempt you from obligation."

"I realize that, Denaraz. But this is a child's life we are talking about."

He frowned. "No. It is your life. Her life has been forfeit since you saved her on *Commorancy*. Surely you can accept that?"

"No. I can't. I find the whole process barbaric."

"Then you should have refused the Protocols."

"What would have happened if I had?"

"She would have been provided with the means to kill herself."

"What!!"

"I am afraid so. Her life became yours when you saved it. Her body no longer belongs to her. Her future is your future. If you reject her, she is obligated to terminate the existence of that body."

"I am horrified by what you say."

"Yes. I can understand that."

"Then how could Oznard charge you with her safety? It is impossible!"

"I am charged with the safety of the Chyzar. Zenzara and the Chyzar are two separate considerations. I may not save Zenzara. I am obligated to save the Chyzar."

"And just how are you supposed to do that?"

He managed a smile. "Look at it this way. If you are attacked, I may not prevent Zenzara from throwing herself in front of you. If the Chyzar is attacked I must protect her with my life."

"No wonder you look stressed most of the time."

"I was not given this posting as a sinecure."

"So I must take Zenzara into any danger."

"You must." He paused. "And I must go with her."

"Great! I have to take the two of you along for the rest of my days. Perfect!"

"I do not anticipate that any of us will live past this week, in any case. Why should this small point grate on you?"

I could feel my shoulders locking into rigid tension. But he was right. None of us were likely to survive. And who had the moral high ground? Were my social conventions better than the Tyzarans? Was I qualified to judge? I decided that I wasn't. Both Denaraz and Mel assured me that I was legally obligated to take Zenzara with me. Take her I would. I could not insult the beliefs of an alien race as ancient as the Tyzarans. I would simply have to adapt my own convictions. And do my very best not to put any of our bodies in more danger than they already faced.

No pressure, then.

The Eighth Fleet came into screen range some twenty hours later. The small wait had given us time to finish our preparations and to get some much-needed rest.

I was jogging around the lower level with Izan when the comlink sparked into life. "Captain to the bridge."

I sprinted along the corridor, Denaraz at my heels, hoping we had judged things correctly. Sure enough, the Eighth Fleet had just come into view on the outskirts of the system.

"Get Didjal to prep the small shuttle," I said, in what I hoped was a calm voice. "Call Zenzara to the bridge."

Zenzie arrived, crest suitably rigid.

I grabbed an M596 each for Denaraz and myself and then hesitated. Zenzie seemed too diminutive to wield even the much smaller M487XRS, though I suspected she could give a good account of herself.

She grinned at me and pulled out a Tyzaran ZR ABlaser. "Don't worry about me. I am very accurate with it."

"Fine." I hoped we wouldn't need them. They would hardly do much against battleships. At least they made us look more professional. I hoped.

"We will try to put ourselves directly in the path of the fleet. Neema and Sammy, bring *Nivala* into place behind us, but out of range at least of their rail guns. Sammy, you are in charge."

Sammy's eyes grew rounded. He had not expected that. Neema nodded her understanding.

"Don't open fire on them," I went on, "Our only hope of stopping them if diplomacy doesn't work is to somehow block their RAMP missiles. To do that we have to stay alive. *Nivala* has to be in a condition to catch up with them. Do *not* risk the ship. If the worst comes to the worst, you will have to do it without us."

Zenzara looked at me.

Her gaze reiterated her determination to die than allow me to be killed.

Well, I wasn't about to let that happen.

I nodded, and led the two Tyzarans down the corridor to the lifts. It was time to set this in motion. Time to convince the Terran forces to stand down on the use of the RAMP missiles. Time to become the Interstellar Enforcement Agency.

My sister Sibby flashed into my thoughts. I had managed to get word to her on Talscharin, but not before making her spend a fruitless week waiting in vain for me to turn up. She had already gone back to the family shipstation, *Bellaris*. I wished I had been able to tell her how much I missed her. When I thought of *Faraday* and my past life at home, she and Scout were the only parts I wanted back.

Now *that* was a real surprise.

16

The Eighth Fleet seemed doubtful about stopping. It raced down on our position, and for quite a while I thought that it would simply trample us as it swept on towards the Avarak homeworld.

I had already explained who we were, but that had not impressed them. A cool voice had told us curtly that the Alliance was not recognized by the Terran Omnistate.

They were waiting to see who would blink first.

I had my eyes firmly shut.

Then they stopped.

The whole fleet hung in space, the lead ship perhaps only one kilometer away.

Our vidscreen flared into life. The face of Admiral Ellison appeared. She did not look best pleased. "What?"

"Admiral Ellison. We need to talk to you. It is extremely urgent."

"Well, I don't need to talk to you. I am under orders, and your attempt at delay is laughable!"

"You are wrong. This is nothing to do with the Avaraks. You are in extreme danger."

"And what makes you think I am going to listen to a couple of Tyzarans and a Spacelander?" Her voice was clear.

"We represent the Interstellar Enforcement Agency. I would like to come aboard your flagship and show you the documents we have that authorize us on behalf of six of the eight Shell races."

She thought about it. "Very well. I will give you half an hour. No more. I will not be delayed on my journey to Rhyveka. The Avaraks will learn not to take arms against the Terran forces!"

For a moment I thought she was going to shout the Terran equivalent of *Avarak Karax!* Zenzie giggled, so she must have done too.

"Don't delay. You have permission to come aboard *Chibuzo*."

"Is Bull Cunningham on board?"

Her expression crimped. "No. Why should he be? He is a civilian."

"Just wondered. I thought you might have kept him close."

"Like a lap dog. No, thanks!"

"I hope he got his due reward?"

She stiffened. "He is a patriot. He needed no reward!"

"Hmm." I wasn't convinced. Bull didn't strike me as the selflessly loyal citizen she portrayed. I wondered for a moment if we were discussing the same man. Then she explained. "Though I believe he is to be honored for his contribution to the war effort. His whole family is to be granted Omnial status."

Yep. That would do it. Omnial status meant full rights to a lifetime of comfort with individual isolated housing, real animals and parkland. Omnial status was only granted to those who were considered to have provided great service to the Omnistate, and politicians were only taken from the Omnial classes. It meant that Bull Cunningham had his foot firmly on the ladder to a future political career.

I may have ground my teeth together. I did feel a nasty twinge through my left back tooth.

The Admiral was still staring at me. I woke up. "Thank you for seeing us, Admiral Ellison. We will join you immediately."

She didn't seem particularly pleased at the prospect. "I will be waiting."

Two hours later I sat back in my seat at the conference table on *Chibuzo*. The Admiral was still regarding me with something like amazement.

"You expect me to believe what you say? That for some reason the new RAMP missiles could somehow tear apart the very fabric of spacetime? And you are conveniently telling me this just before the aforesaid weapons are due to be used against our enemy?"

"I *do* expect you to believe what I say. Quantum tunneling cannot be predicted – it is a random event. And although there has always been a tiny chance of a random Higgs particle tunneling from the metastable vacuum point to the true one, the probability is considered infinitely small. At least, it was. Unfortunately your new technology is likely to create a cavity field within the receptors. That, in its turn can cause the particles themselves to coalesce with a photon and form a new transient particle which could easily tunnel through the barrier before regressing to its original form. The chances of these new particles tunneling into the ultra-dense state is now calculated at fifty percent. *Fifty percent ...!*" I tried not to shout, but my voice was going up of its own accord. "EVERY TIME you launch one of those missiles, you are risking the COMPLETE annihilation of the universe. It would only take one ... ONE ... particle to transition for the rest of the entire Higgs field to collapse into the ultra-dense state, exploding outwards at the speed of light. Surely I don't have to tell you what that would do to the Shells, to the Galaxy ... to the Universe?"

Her nose twitched. "An outrageous claim," she said. "You are using false information to stop our engagement with the Avaraks. I will not be swayed by this pseudoscience you are spouting at me." She looked up at her second in command and beckoned. "Take these intruders to the brig. I am done with them."

I gasped. "You can't do that!"

Ellison looked pleased with herself. "Actually, I can. I hardly think your two tame Tyzarans are going to stop me. Not so long ago, you were begging me to take you with me."

My face grew grim. "Times change."

"They do, don't they? Don't worry. I will tell your crew you might be a little late for lunch."

"We are on official business on behalf of the Interstellar Alliance."

"Yes. I know. You already told me. Thing is, I can't see any of their ships here right now. So I guess the Omnistate is the governing body in this area. Under Omnistate rules, any foreigners who do not declare *for* us, are *against* us."

"You are *way* outside the Omnistate jurisdiction."

She shrugged. "Pity, that. Points of view, I suppose. Well, never mind. I expect your ship will limp back to your little ... what was it ...? Ah yes, Alliance."

Zenzie gave a sort of growl deep in her throat. If she hadn't been restrained, I think she would have leapt at the Admiral. Denaraz was standing stock still, his hands in fists, having decided that it would be useless to struggle at this point. Our guns had been taken from us when we boarded *Chibuzo*, and we were surrounded by Omnistate marines. They, on the other hand, were armed to the teeth. Like it or not, we would be staying on the battleship for longer than we planned.

Once we were locked securely in a holding cell, I deliberately stumbled against Denaraz, so I could whisper to him. "Can you contact the Supreme Council?"

He didn't even seem surprised. He nodded.

So his ansible connection *was* some sort of implant. Good to know. "Tell them to inform *Nivala* of our situation. They are to fall back to five light years and trail this fleet at that distance. There is nothing they can do now. Their job will be to develop the electromagnetic blocking device. It will be up to *us* to try to stop the Flatlander fleet getting as far as Veka."

He nodded again, and his eyes got that unfocussed look that I had noticed before.

I turned to Zenzara, who had slumped down on one of the cots, looking dejected. My eyes went to her neck. She was still wearing her nivala.

She followed my glance and gently touched one of the brooches, to show that she understood. Although we had been searched, the hands that had patted us down had been cursory. These Terrans clearly had no idea that Tyzarans habitually used weaponry as adornments. One up to us.

I started to check the cell carefully. First, we would have to get out of the place. Second, we would need a plan B.

Pity I didn't have one.

Zenzie began to shake around three hours later. I could tell that we were underway by the dull hum of the decking under our feet. I had got nowhere in my search for a way out of the brig. I suspect many prisoners before me had done exactly the same thing, with the same result.

I ran over to her cot and gently tried to lift her head. She was in some sort of a convulsion. Her eyes showed white and her tongue was slightly hanging out of one side of her mouth.

Denaraz slid to the other side of the cot and raised her legs a little. We exchanged worried looks.

"Has she been taking those injections?" I asked him.

He shrugged. He didn't know. I was infuriated that I didn't either. I did know that she had asked Seyal to administer the medicine while she was on *Nivala*, but perhaps she had missed an injection here on *Chibuzo*? Could that matter? Surely not? Yet she was as stiff as a board and her whole small body was shuddering.

What was I thinking? I should have remembered that. She should have brought the medicine with her. I should have insisted. And I couldn't tell the Terrans about the problems she had been having. If they knew that she was linked in some way to the Chakrans she would become an Omnistate asset.

"Hey!" I shouted. "Get a doctor!"

Our guard was at first suspicious. It took him five minutes to accept that it was no trick to dupe him into lowering the force field that was retaining us. Once Zenzara's face had turned blue, he accepted the very real desperation on our faces and called for backup. If I could have, I would have killed him for those long minutes when the Tyzaran girl nearly died. I have never felt so impotent in all my life. By then I was shaking almost as much as she was.

A medical team finally bustled into the holding bay. The doctor took one look and signaled to the guard to let them into the cell. Denaraz and I were held back by small ultrapulse hand weapons while Zenzie was evacuated.

I was horrified. For her to die like this, after all we had been through! Surely the universe could not be that cruel? But I knew it could. Fairness still could not be depended upon in this new world I inhabited.

Denaraz was as frozen as I was. We simply stared at each other as the medical team withdrew and the gurney they had placed her on floated out of the bay. The last we saw of her was as the doors closed and silence came back to the cell area.

We slumped down on our respective cots. Time began to drag. There was nothing we could do but wait.

I hated every second of it.

Two days passed and they still told us nothing. We demanded, pleaded, begged and tried to convince our guards to tell us how Zenzara was. We still had no idea whether she had lived or had died. Yet still they told us nothing.

Finally, one of the guards spoke to us. He was bringing us one of the monotonous meals that they provided us with. A bowl of what I can only describe as gruel, some macerated fruit and some water. It was barely edible, but enough to sustain us. We had taken care to eat all we were given. It was hard, because I seemed to have a lump inside my chest that impeded swallowing. Still, we had to. It was important to stay as fit as we possibly could, despite the gnawing feeling of doom that had hung over us since Zenzie had been taken away.

"Now you will see what the Omnistate can do," he taunted us.

"What do you mean?"

"Wait and see."

"Have we reached Veka? Surely not?"

He laughed. "They came out to play."

Ah. The Avaraks had brought their own fleets out to intercept the Terrans. Against impossible odds. The Terrans had ten times the speed, ultrapulse weapons that rang rings around the Avaraks, and now the RAMP missiles for good measure.

But the Avaraks were nothing if not determined. They would die, and die gladly, for their world. I could almost hear their cohorts chanting '*Avarak Karax!*' from here.

Not that it would do them much good. They would be wiped out within a few hours.

At least the Terrans would not use the RAMPs against ships. They only had three of them, and the missiles were so devastating that they would be held back for use against the planet itself. Unfortunately I was pretty sure Admiral Ellison planned to lob a couple of them at Rhyveka shortly after vanquishing the Avarak Fleet. She was nothing if not thorough.

I squirmed with frustration. It was so important to get out there, to try to alter the course of history today, yet we were unwilling watchers of a process we had no say in. Back to being mere flotsam. It was almost unbearable. The combination of worry over Zenzara and impotence against what was coming was very, very hard to take.

I wondered if Denaraz had updated the Supreme Council. From his hangdog expression, I rather thought that he hadn't. He felt he had not done his job. I didn't think he would be particularly eager to admit his failings to the governing body back on Tyzar. I wouldn't have.

Then the thumping started. The Omnistate fleet was putting up some sort of barrage to block physical missiles. We could sense the kickback as each battery flung its charges out into space. The deck began to rattle under our feet; it became hard to stand.

We sat and clung to the edges of our cots. Waiting. Wondering.

After about an hour, Avarak fire broke through the barrage. I could tell that we were still firing back, but not what weapons *Chibuzo* was firing.

A shattering explosion sounded, just above us. Cracks appeared in the ceiling above our heads, and small pieces of the wall showered down on us.

"Let us out of here!" I shouted. "This place is disintegrating!"

It was an exaggeration, but it might work, I thought. Our guard was himself looking up at the ceiling with some fear.

"Come on, let us out! What would the Admiral do? She wants us alive, you know." At least, I hoped she did.

He turned towards me and I felt the hatred in his gaze. He thought we were the enemy. He wasn't going to let us go. It was written in the dark eyes and the even darker stare. My shoulders dropped.

"As far as I am concerned," the guard snarled, "you can die in your own excrement. It is as much as you deserve. I wouldn't let you out if that whole cell exploded. You and your kind are traitors to the Omnistate."

That is what happens when you only teach your own side of history in the schools. People grow into bigots. Pity. I mean, they used to be just like us. Surely we didn't act like that? At least, I hoped we didn't.

A siren began to sound. I wondered if it were telling the crew to abandon ship. I hoped so.

The guard read my thoughts. "No," he spat with some enjoyment. "That merely tells us to prepare for incoming fire. You don't have to worry. None of the Avarak torpedoes can penetrate our armor. You two cowards can cower safely in your cell."

I felt a sensation of pure glee as another explosion battered the *Chibuzo*. He was clearly wrong. He staggered and nearly fell. I wished that he had.

"What about our friend?" I shouted as he struggled to right himself.

"What about her?" he sneered. "Missing your little bed warmer, are you?"

"You shouldn't say things like that," I warned.

"Why not?"

"I have seen her attack a grown man for the same implications."

"Yeah?" He held his hands up in the air and waved them about. "Ooohhh! See how scared I am?"

There was a flash at the side of my vision. I turned my head, but I was too late to pick up what had caused it.

The guard went suddenly silent. He slid to the floor. The shape withdrew something that appeared to have pierced him through the heart, wiped it clean of blood on her sleeve and replaced it in her vest.

Zenzie grimaced. "These people have very impoverished minds."

"I did tell him not to say things like that." I said mildly. I couldn't help feeling that he deserved his rapid demise.

Her face softened. "I was pleased to hear you recognize my strength. You didn't even know I was listening. Now, what is the plan?"

"We are most happy to see that you are recovered."

"No thanks to them. What I needed was one of those injections I have to take, but they didn't believe me. Their Portable Triage Unit wasn't a Zeroth and it said there was nothing wrong with me. So they tied me to a cot in the sick bay and left me there. I thought I was going to die."

"You forgot to take your injections?" I may have sounded rather accusing. It was hard for me to believe she would forget something so important.

She blushed. "I should have brought a supply with me when we left *Nivala*. I forgot."

"Very helpful!"

Her face got even hotter, but she lowered it, acknowledging her fault. "I'm sorry."

"But you seem all right now? Did they give you something else?"

She shook her head. "That is the good news. I felt worse and worse, and then – all of a sudden – something clicked inside my head and I felt fine again! I think something has happened with the Nexus. It is as if the Chakrans can almost talk to me now."

I frowned. "I hope it is not just a temporary respite."

"I don't think it is. I am feeling much better, though I was a pretty queasy the first time I stood up."

Denaraz stared at her. "You have begun to interact with the Nexus?" He seemed skeptical.

"I think so. It isn't as if they can talk directly to me, but I can feel ... I don't know ... a sort of buzzing in one small area of my brain. They seem to be tugging me in one way or another, and I can feel more than one of them trying to speak to me. I think there are six."

"*Six* strands? That has never happened before. Chy Saphezzaraz only felt one strand."

Zenzie puffed out a little with pride. "Well, I have six."

I could see that Denaraz was about to challenge her on that. This was not the time or the place to provoke her, so I stepped in just as there was another tremendous rattling of the walls and the deck plating shivered. "Right. Can you get us out of here, please?"

Zenzara bent down to retrieve the security card from the dead guard. She swiped it over the sensor and then frowned. "It is asking me for a pass code."

It was frustrating to be that close to freedom and to be baulked. I turned to Denaraz with one eyebrow raised.

He pulled a face. "No idea. I didn't catch it when they brought us here."

Zenzie bent again to the corpse on the floor, extracting his ultrapulse hand gun. "Stand back!"

She aimed at the release mechanism and fired. There was an explosion of sparks and the whole swiper housing fell off the wall. A bundle of wiring bulged out of the wall. The force field still held.

Zenzie tutted. "Not helpful." She pulled the wiring further out of the wall. "Now, I just have to figure out ..."

There was another spark, and then a flash in front of us as the force field failed.

"There!" She pushed the cables back into the hole in the wall.

A siren started to sound in the hold. It was soft for all of three seconds, then it began to get louder and louder. That's what happens when you blow open cell doors on battleships. Apparently.

Zenzie's crest stood up. "Oops!"

Denaraz and I raced out. "Don't worry," I told her breathlessly. "Come on, we don't have much time. Even in these circumstances, when they are at battle stations, someone is going to want to find out why that racket is going on."

We bustled out of the holding area, finding ourselves in a long grey corridor. I looked right and then left. There was no clue to tell us which way to go.

Zenzie tugged at my arm, dragging me slightly to the right. "This way!" she shouted. "I came the other way, and there was a breach. There will be fire teams there."

Denaraz and I pounded down the corridor behind her. I was racking my brains on our destination, when I suddenly remembered *Commorancy*. The crawl tubes! That could keep us out of sight for a small time longer. On a ship this size, it would take them hours and a large number of their crew to search all of the miles of crawl tubing.

I kept my eyes peeled for a hatch, and began to drag it open when I found one. Denaraz's eager hands helping as soon as he realized the intention.

We slid into the tubing with something like relief. It certainly didn't feel safe, but it did give us the illusion of being safer. We began to breathe more easily.

"Where to?" Denaraz asked. The tubing led in three directions.

"What's the plan?" whispered Zenzara fiercely.

An enormous explosion shook the whole ship. We all skidded into the wall of the tube. Denaraz grabbed Zenzie so that she didn't fall.

She shook herself free angrily. "I don't need your help!"

"You're welcome!" Denaraz glared back. Both their stares became challenging.

I coughed lightly. "Err ... if you are ready? Perhaps we could get on?"

Zenzara now glowered at me. "Do you know where we are going?"

"Of course I do!" I felt aggrieved.

Zenzara put both hands on her hips. "Where?"

"What do you mean, where?"

"Are we going to get off this ship, or what? What exactly is your plan?"

There were times that I wished this Tyzaran girl were not so bright. I was under a lot of pressure and I had been hoping for a bit more time to come up with something sensible. It isn't easy for three people to make a difference in the middle of a war. I played for time.

"Well, I can't see any point trying to get away from this ship. We would only be torn up in the fighting going on outside."

She nodded. "So ...?"

I made up my mind. "... So we will make for the missile bay. Our priority is to disarm those RAMP missiles. We can make a start on *Chibuzo*."

Denaraz nodded. "*If* this is one of the ships with a RAMP missile on board," he said quietly. "The flagship could have been left without one. Remember, only three of the battleships are equipped with the RAMPs."

"If we could remove one threat out of the three, it would be worth it. It would bring down the probability of failure considerably."

He nodded. "Yes. Certainly worthwhile. Let's give it a go."

"If we can't disarm the thing we can try to park it somewhere safely."

"Park it?" repeated Zenzie. "Leave it floating around out there for anybody to find and use?"

"No." Sometimes she could be very irritating, I decided. "Leave it securely hidden in a location only we know about. Lay claim to it. Remove it from this environment. Take it out of the equation. At least that is better than doing nothing."

Zenzie wasn't convinced. But I didn't care. There wasn't a lot we could do on a battleship with a crew roster of a thousand or so.

"We need to find the missile bay," I told her.

Denaraz shuffled down the center aisle a few feet and then looked back. "Starboard side, top deck. It's a bit of a trek. We must be on the lowest deck, and well back towards the engines."

I stared at him. He shrugged. "What do you think Military groups do except study their opposites?"

Good enough for me. I motioned Zenzie to crawl after him and I brought up the rear. "Move it, Izan. We need to do something before these idiots decide to deploy that thing!"

Progress was slower than I would have liked. Although we did now know where we were heading, we had to be very quiet. I was certain Ellison would have placed security groups inside the crawl spaces, and there would be engineers scrambling around in here, too. We had to take care not to bump into anybody.

We slid along as quietly but as quickly as we dared. My mind was racing. The missile bay would be heaving with crew members in an active operation. Perhaps that could be our salvation. In the middle of a battle people would be less likely to notice unfamiliar faces. They would be tired, dirty, unable to even think clearly.

I made up my mind. We needed Engineering uniforms, and some dirt. We needed a way to hide the foreignness of the two Tyzarans, camouflage of some sort. We needed to hide in plain view.

Tyzarans are taller and thinner than humans. But the main differences are in their skin and their bone structure. It was nigh on impossible to confuse one with the other. The triangular shape to their heads and faces, the slightly paler tinge to their countenances, the crests, the enormous foreheads. And, of course, the huge wrinkles of their skin. In Zenzie's case, they were the first thing you noticed about her.

No, Zenzie would have to stay back. She was far too slight and short to be taken for a crew member. This would have to be done by Denaraz and me. She could protect our backs. After all, that was what she was always telling me her job was. Time for her to do it. She still had the gun she had taken from the guard. She needed to place herself in a strategic part of the crawl tubing. Somewhere there was a hatch or a grille that would enable her to see us as we worked. Somewhere she could monitor our progress.

That meant two disguises. In my case, there was no problem. A little dirt rubbed across my face would make me practically indistinguishable from the rest of the crew.

Denaraz was more difficult. I pondered as we shimmied along the shiny tubing on our hands and knees. Then I realized that it was easy. Many of the engineers would be in IEVA suits, in case of hull breaches. And I knew from experience just how difficult it can be to identify someone in an IEVA suit. A thin coating of dirt and grime across the bottom of the visor would take care of that.

Suddenly, the whole thing felt possible. My spirits rose. As far as I could see, the most risky part of the business would be sneaking into the bay without the IEVA suits and then putting them on. We would be exposed until we were safely anonymous.

I tapped Zenzie on the feet until she did the same to Denaraz and he stopped. We squatted in an uncomfortable huddle as I explained the idea. They nodded, though Zenzara took a little convincing to stay out of the way. Finally, even she could see that she would stand out like a sore thumb. She was only half the size of any of the *Chibuzo* crew members.

Denaraz thought for a few minutes. "There should be a side alcove with the IEVA suits in it. I suggest that you go first, as you might easily pass for a crew member. Once you are settled, you can position yourself in front of me should anyone come."

It seemed like a sensible plan to me. I agreed immediately. I just wished Zenzie had a weapon that might be more decisive. "Keep your eyes out for an M596 or am M487XRS. I would rather Zenzara had something of a larger bore. She won't have to carry it very far."

Zenzie's eyes widened. Then she looked pleased. I suppose she had been convincing herself that I was sidelining her. Now she took on a solid, purposeful sort of demeanor. She looked a lot older than her eight years.

We continued to scramble through the tubing. It must have taken us over two hours to get to the missile bay. All that time the sounds of battle continued around us. I found myself feeling sorry for the Avaraks. If we were getting a battering on the Terran flagship, I could only imagine what was happening to the Avarak fleets. They would be dying out there in waves. I knew that they had a large military presence, but this was pure suicide. Yet there was something admirable about the way they didn't bend in front of this lethal attack. In the way that they defended their planet to the end. I came to the conclusion that it was possible to dislike and yet secretly admire a species at the same time. It was confusing to me. I suppose we all feel pity for the underdog. And this was a battle that the Terrans' greed had originated. I had no stomach for it. I felt that the Omnistate had betrayed its population. Why would they think they could claim the entire Local Shell for themselves? That was an expanse of space that must be nine million cubic light years in volume. *Nine million! Cubic light years!* Unconscionable. It was quite ridiculous. How could they even *hope* to administer to that vast expanse of space? What grandiose pretensions had fed such mania? In the five hundred years since our common ancestral paths had diverged, what had changed? Where did they get the arrogance to claim that they are the most intelligent species in the Major Shells, something that is patently untrue? I found it all very depressing.

We finally reached the IEVA alcove in the main missile bay. We stared for some moments out of the service hatch. Then I gave a sigh. No point procrastinating any longer. I slid out of the tubing and stretched upwards to my full height.

There was nobody in the alcove, which still boasted around ten full

IEVA suits and – to my amazement – a panel with several M596s in a neat row. And that wasn't the best news. It must have been unlocked when the siren announcing our escape sounded, for the armored glass door to the casing was yawing wide open. I could hardly believe our luck. There were five M596s left in the case. Empty housings showed that a further ten had been removed. I grinned at the grille and quickly passed one of the five down to Zenzara. She seemed inordinately pleased to be able to play with such a large and lethal weapon. I shuddered to think what she could do with it. I passed over an ample supply of ammunition anyway.

It only took me a few minutes to secure myself into an IEVA suit. These suits, whose initials stand for Intra-Extra Vehicular Activity, are designed to be worn during operations deemed unsafe. They protect life for a limited time if you are exposed to outer space or radiation. You can't survive for long – normally the oxygen supply is limited to around fifteen minutes – but they are designed to bridge the gap between onboard apparel and full EVA, to give you enough time to find more permanent protection. You can't work properly inside a ship if you are dressed in full EVA. It is impossible. So, under battle stations, most of the crew would automatically have donned IEVA suits.

I clambered into mine and zipped it right up above my chin. Once I had snapped the slim helmet in place I dirtied the suit up with some of the grease that was ubiquitous in an engine room or a missile bay. I left the air source vent at 'atmosphere' to save the suit's own supply of oxygen. It also meant Denaraz and I would be able to speak to each other. IEVA suits have no comlinks, which means that communication with your team when the source vent is on 'self-feed' is like trying to hear underwater. Then I slung one of the remaining M596s over my shoulder before checking there was still nobody around.

Denaraz popped out as soon as I gave him the signal. We fed him into one of the larger suits as quickly as we good and I clamped the helmet on him.

I was smudging his helmet with grease when I became aware of a shadow behind me.

"What's going on here?" It was an officer, his face tight and suspicious.

I saluted and went rigid, Denaraz following my actions precisely.

"Sa!" I intoned.

"Get on with your jobs! No hiding out of harm's way! Not on my ship!"

"Sa! Yes, Sa!" We saluted and marched ourselves smartly out of his line of vision.

Denaraz managed a faint grin. "I always wanted to be a spy," he confessed.

"I thought you already were one." Then, at his outraged expression, I held up one hand. "Did Zenzie get away?"

His helmet nodded. "She did. She said she would try to make it up there ...." he pointed to the ceiling of the large hold, "... though it may take her some time. She said to wait for her to get into place. I think she thinks we will get ourselves killed without her."

As if we couldn't look after ourselves!

We tried to make our walk nonchalant as we moseyed along the passageways between the huge launching ramps. There were crew everywhere. The noise was deafening. I wished the IEVA suits had been equipped with mufflers. They were designed to transmit sound easily through the helmet- which in fact had the effect of amplifying it all. I had no idea what the decibel level was, but whatever it was, it was too much for me. Much more of this and I would turn into a screaming wreck.

Then I saw one of the workers take off his helmet to screw large earplugs firmly into his ears. I grabbed the back of Denaraz's suit and pulled him to a stop. Once I pointed out the earplugs his countenance lightened. His lips moved. He may have been giving thanks. Tyzarans have even more acute hearing than we do. Not up to Geiga standards, of course, but still better than a Spacelander. Or a Terran, naturally.

We scoured the areas we were walking past. Bench after bench of engineering tools and paraphernalia. Finally we spotted two open tins with some earplugs remaining in them. I palmed both tins and as soon as we could dip into a small storeroom we opened our helmets and fitted them hastily into our ears.

The relief was immediate. The level was still uncomfortable but I didn't feel the need to grab at my head and submerge it in cement.

We passed torpedo after torpedo, missile after missile. The scale of this bay was astonishing. The Terrans must have been preparing for war for a very long time.

At first there was no sign of any special missiles, but, as we penetrated to the back of the hold, we saw something that drew our attention. Right at the back of the hold, carefully cradled above the other missiles, was a huge shining tube. It must have measured at least twelve meters in length.

Denaraz spotted it first. He grabbed my arm and indicated the huge bulk with his helmet.

We made our way down the hold until we were standing right underneath the thing. Sure enough, I could see the identifying numbers and letters emblazoned across the housing. RAMP/01/8995 was stamped across the shell.

Izan's eyes were wide. Not only was the thing the size of a shuttle, it was hanging freely from hawsers, and swaying around with the battering that *Chibuzo* was taking.

I stared up at it. Even reaching the thing looked like an impossible task. My spirits slumped. What had I been thinking of?

Denaraz turned me firmly towards him. He indicated himself, and pointed upward towards what was clearly a missile station situated at the top of a crane to the rear of the missile casing itself. Then he made signs with his hand. He pointed to himself and then upwards. Then there were signs of firing something. Then he pointed to me and made signs of something blowing up.

Plan B it was then. We certainly stood no chance of physically touching this thing without them noticing. He was right; our only chance was to deploy it.

Carefully.

Like that would be easy.

And he was right on the other thing, too. He would need a diversion if he was to get away with launching this. I took a moment to examine the missile. The only tube it could possible fit in was some 100 meters away, right on the other side of the missile bay. They could hardly miss the enormous casing being winched over their heads. The thing was the size of a large whale, after all.

Diversion, then. I nodded and started to move away. I remembered seeing some cleaning solvent stashed under one of the benches. The one thing the military always could be relied upon. Keep it all clean.

Their mistake. When we were younger my sister and I had almost blown up *Faraday* when we decided to help my father clean some grease spillage on one of the lower decks. Sibby had had her eyebrows singed right off in the resulting explosion. My mother nearly had apoplexy.

The reaction of my mother and the subsequent punishment she inflicted on us was indelibly engraved in my memory. Lucky, because one of the other things that had stayed along with the humiliation and pain was the exact mixture we had used. I was pretty sure I had seen just those ingredients as we had walked through the engineering stations. Not all together, of course. No machine shop would store possibly explosive combinations close by each other. Close enough though.

I grabbed the solvent and one of the many heavy duty trolleys that were lying around. It was a moment to pile three large containers of the solvent. I covered them with a loose cloth. No point drawing attention to my load.

I rolled them down the aisle as speedily as I could without running anybody down. No one took any notice of me, much to my relief.

Ten minutes later I had everything I needed. Now I had only to pick the ideal place to carry out my small flagration. At least, I hoped it would be small. My intention was not to blow the whole ship up. I merely wanted twenty or thirty minutes of chaos. I bustled along a side aisle. I wanted to be as far away as possible from the RAMP missile.

I found what I was looking for almost straight away. With all the confusion of action stations, they had not been applying their usual hygiene standards. There was a large drum of grease sitting – almost calling out to me – in the corridor to one side.

I loaded it, with some difficulty, onto a second heavy duty trolley. Then, when I had all of my ingredients, I simply pulled them to one of the alcoves on the starboard side of the bay, tipped everything I had collected into the drum, pushed the trolley as close to the pulley mechanism that fed the torpedoes into a firing position, covered the drum, and walked away as slowly as I could make myself.

I had no idea how long it would take. My memory was somewhat blurred on that aspect of our youthful escapade. I seemed to remember waiting for an inordinately long time, but thought that my younger self might not have had a real idea of time's passage.

I reached the RAMP location and gave Denaraz a thumbs-up. He was hunched close to a nearby ground-level console, plugged into its computer. I saw that he had been working on our exact position. Good. We needed to put this thing in the middle of nowhere, not turn it loose on some unsuspecting population.

As I got back, he must have finished his calculations, for he closed down the console and pulled himself up the tube ladder to the crane platform in one fluid movement.

I found I was holding my fingers crossed inside the tough gloves I was wearing. Then it occurred to me that I wasn't doing much to help by just standing around watching Denaraz work. I should probably start thinking about protecting him. Subconsciously my brain had been on hold, waiting for the explosion. Not the right time to sit back and wait. Denaraz was depending on me.

I looked upwards. The control station for the RAMP was perched on top of a ten-feet-high platform. This could be pivoted on a large swivel to take up the appropriate position during launch. The tube ladder ran down from the platform to the deck.

I scrambled up the ladder. There was a small solid balustrade around the control station itself. The balustrade was made of heavy plating. It would be difficult for marksmen to sight us from an inferior position, and we would be shielded to some extent by the metal casing.

I gave Izan a nod as I reached the control chair. He ignored me. His fingers were flying over the controls. I noticed that the missile lights had come up and there was a vibration through the control panel.

It wouldn't be long now. I unslung the M596 and took up my own station behind Denaraz. To get to him they would have to go through me. I gritted my teeth. I just hoped Zenzie had managed to find a safe place from which to watch this. Something told me we would find it hard to get out of the *Chibuzo* after this. But it would be worth it. If we could get rid of even one of these monstrous missiles, we were on the road to success. I checked the gun for readiness and leant over the side of the crane. I was ready.

The explosion, when it came, was disappointing. The noise level in the machine shop was so loud that I heard no sound. All I saw was a small flash, almost out of the corner of my eye. It seemed nothing. At first.

Then there was a ripping sort of detonation, as the oil took. The drum had been blown over on its side and the burning oil was seeping along the passageway, flames now raging above it.

There were screams of warning from those near it. A stampede of men flowed out from the flames. Others attempted to battle their way inwards against the tide of panic to combat the heat, grabbing the chemical extinguishers that were situated on the bulkhead walls.

Denaraz grinned at me in what seemed a demoniacal way for a split second and then stabbed his finger on a button. The whole crane swiveled. For a moment I nearly fell out of the nest we were in. I lost sight of the fire now spreading out from the drum.

As the crane moved out of the way, the RAMP missile began its journey across the ceiling space of the missile bay. It swung grandly and majestically into action.

To my surprise, the control crane followed it. The whole crane was mounted on a track which suddenly surfaced out of the walkway. We trundled along behind the missile as it inched its way across the bay.

My heart sank. They could hardly miss a gurney trundling past them. Or the siren that had just started to scream at them to move out of the way.

Faces began to stare up at us. I waved them to one side. "Move! Move, you fools!"

One or two hesitated. They knew that the RAMP was not meant to be deployed against a fleet, and they knew that we were far too far from Veka for it to be launched at the Avarak homeworld.

On the other hand, there was a fire in the hold, they were at action stations, the whole ship was shaking, and they were under pressure to keep firing torpedoes. I saw hesitation in their demeanor, then doubt, then acceptance. Most of them simply turned away. One or two squinted up at us, no doubt trying to see exactly who was rolling around in charge of their most dangerous missile. I redoubled my arm waving. "Out! Out of the way!"

The crane trundled inexorably towards these few doubters, eventually forcing them to jump to one side.

We made it almost to the firing tube before the fire was completely put out.

Denaraz was now back at the console, fingers flashing as he opened the firing hatch to allow the missile to load.

And it was over. Our anonymity had lasted as long as it could. As the gurney holding the crane snapped into its final position, as the control station tipped sideways to allow the operator access to the controls on the side of the missile and the firing hatch, I saw that we had been made. There was a large group of armed men running down the passageway towards us, and a heavy-built officer leading them.

I brought the M596 up to my shoulder. It was my turn. I was up. I fired into them. I had no wish to kill any of them, but it was my job to stop them, and stop them I would.

The officer went down with a large hole in his leg. His mouth opened and closed as he screamed instructions to his men. Then I could see him berating them as they carried him swiftly out of my line of fire. He was furious. His hands tried physically to push them back, back towards me.

I brought my attention back to the head of the group. I saw that Zenzara must have entered the fray with her long barrel, for there were two others now rolling around in agony. The rest had paused, unsure whether to drag their colleagues to safety or step over them and continue.

A smart shot right through the hand of the next man decided the matter for them. He slapped back into the following man, who prudently decided to withdraw and regroup. I fired a few shots close by, to reinforce that decision. They ducked into one of the many alcoves made by the huge machines that housed all the armament.

Denaraz slapped me on the back. I turned to see what he wanted. He winked through the helmet at me, then held up his right index finger.

I frowned and shrugged my shoulders at him. As if to say *What?*

He grinned again. Then the index finger plunged downwards to a small button on one side of the console. It connected.

There was a second's pause.

Then the whole station shook as the missile tube just beside us emptied.

We were left staring at each other. The euphoria of successful completion of a goal was definitely mitigated by the acute realization that we had left ourselves with nowhere to go.

"Oh shit!" I muttered, even though I knew Izan couldn't hear me. "Where do we go from here?"

Denaraz's eyes were wide open too. They darted from side to side, but I didn't think he was going to see a way out.

We were surrounded.

I made a grab for the control panel, hoping that I could manipulate

the crane and make it go back along the trackway. Denaraz slapped
my hands away, pointing to himself at the same time, and nodding.
He knew what I wanted.

I stationed myself just at the top of the crane, where the ladder tube
reached the platform. They could only come up one at a time and I was
in a definite position of superiority.

Shots were ricocheting off us from many angles now, but we
hunkered down and let the thick steel protect us. Weapons have
improved in recent years, but there are no hand held guns that can
penetrate six inches of space steel. Not yet, anyway. I breathed a sigh
of relief.

Zenzara was still spraying the area with loose M596 fire, creating
dismay amongst our attackers.

I figured Zenzie could still see both Denaraz and I, so I hoped she
would be able to make out my hand movements. I waved, then pointed
to the two of us, then at her general direction. Then I curved my hands
to make a curved shape in the air. Then I pointed up and out. I hoped
she understood. I certainly had no intention of leaving her behind.

I was pretty sure that we stood no chance of actually launching an
escape pod. They would have blocked that possibility as soon as we
escaped. However, pods can be blocked from the inside. While we
would not be able to escape from them, they would not be able to get
at us. Not at first, anyhow. It would take them time to breach the very
heavy shielding inside one of those pods. They were made to burn
safely through heavy atmospheres and crash land.

I thought I saw a flash of light reflected in return. Maybe off a gun
sight.

There were two banks of escape pods. One was to the rear of the
bay to port and the other to the front of the bay to starboard. We were
heading to the bank of pods at the rear of the bay.

I nudged Denaraz and pointed to the pods. He nodded. The crane
trundled on.

The covering fire had stopped. Zenzara would be making her way across and down to the escape pods. I hoped. I had no backup plan if she hadn't understood my signals.

The Terrans had realized what our plan was. There was a bunch of them against the pods. This was not going to be easy. I could make out several officers now chivvying the men into three-deep barriers in front of all the pods. All were armed, and well armed at that.

I turned to see Denaraz's mouth open. He was shouting to me. I couldn't hear a thing. He was trying to show me something above us.

I peered upwards into the space beyond the lighting. Sure enough, there was a thin walkway set right up at the top of the bay. I squeezed my eyes to try to see better. It didn't really work, but it seemed to me I could make out a platform at the back of the bay and another small ladder leading to a hatch.

Denaraz might be right. If that hatch led to the deck above – and I couldn't think where else it might go – then we would come out right in front of the escape pods on the next deck up. Escape pods that were likely unguarded, or at the very worst, only lightly guarded.

But would Zenzara follow our lead? Was she still trying to follow our movements? I had no idea.

I grinned at Izan, and made the universal signal for going up with my right hand – a circular motion with my forefinger pointing at the ceiling. Denaraz closed his eyes tight shut for a couple of seconds. He looked as if he were begging *Zeuma* to intervene. I wished I believed in some deity. I would be praying too.

Denaraz let the crane rumble onwards. Shortly before we came beneath the high walkway, he pulled off the belt to his suit and tied it firmly around the controls of the crane. Then he gave me a what-are-we-waiting-for tilt of his head.

We both jumped at the same time. The crane slid out from underneath us but by the time it cleared our position we were both lying flat against the meager planks, hoping not to have been spotted.

We gave it a countdown from twenty, which I mouthed out loud so Denaraz would follow the intention. At zero we leapt up in tandem

and sprinted along the narrow walkway, which in essence was little
more than a hanging horizontal ladder with slats laid over it.

There was fire. It took a few seconds for them to pick us out from
the background, and it took a couple more for them to get us in focus.
By that time we had reached the steps up to the hatchway.

Shots rang to the left and right of us as Denaraz grabbed the hatch
door and began to spin the wheel lock. I raced up to put my own
pressure against it too.

The shots were on us now. They had the range and the position. One
thudded into the metal about one inch to the left of my head, then I
was hit.

I felt my body sag as my lungs struggled to pull in air. Denaraz
grabbed at me as he pulled the hatchway open. I don't know how
he managed it, because he was winged himself as he dragged me to
safety, but he got both of us through and the hatch closed again.

I looked around. The first thing I noticed was the relative silence. We
were in a corridor. An empty corridor. But there was a large hatchway
to our right. It led into what looked like a zone of sleeping quarters.

Denaraz helped me towards the hatchway. Sure enough, there was
a row of pods against the back wall of the corridor. He half dragged,
half carried me towards the nearest.

"Stop!"

We both turned. A very junior officer was pointing a pulser at us. He
was ranked by two burly security officers. He narrowed his eyes and
tensed. "Don't try anything. If you do—"

As he collapsed to the floor with a large wound in his shoulder,
Zenzie's voice came from behind us. "You shouldn't talk so much," she
informed the prostrate figure.

She sprayed the corridor in front of the security officers with fire,
forcing them to take cover down one of the residential corridors. Then
she pulled a face.

"Got yourself shot, did you? I knew I should have stayed with you
both. Honestly! Can't you two do the simplest of things without

getting into trouble?"

Denaraz held up his hands. "I did my best!"

I was too out of breath to speak, but I hope my look told her what I was thinking.

It didn't, or if it did, she didn't take any notice. "Now look at you both! I suppose you think *I* am going to attend to those wounds?"

Izan pressed some sort of code into the pod's keypad, and the heavy hatch gave a click.

He grunted. "Here kid, help me with this and stop nagging. The captain won't be able to stand for much longer."

She did, but the glare she treated him to threatened retribution at a later date.

"And stop those men from coming back!" ordered Denaraz in a sharp voice.

She turned and sprayed the area with more fire. The men, who had just about decided to attack, prudently retreated once more.

"There!" The hatch swung open and between the two of them they bundled me inside. Zenzie slipped in after me and Denaraz brought up the rear, pulling the heavy hatch shut after him. He threw himself at the control panel and instigated a lockdown.

After around five minutes, he threw his head back and laughed. "If you had told me we could carry that off I would have thought you were crazy!" He looked up at the ceiling. "Never in a thousand years ...!"

I tried to hold my sides together. It felt as though I was lying on a knife. "W-Where ... did you ... send ... the ... missile?" I struggled to get enough air for each word.

"I programmed it to drop into a low orbit at the same Zuben planetoid we used when we arrived at the Lakshmi Disc. It should remain well-hidden there until we get a chance to recover it or dump it in Zuben's corona."

Zenzie had grabbed the first-aid kit and helped me out of my helmet. She ignored the metallic thumping coming from the other side of the hatch. It was going to take them a very long time to get through that.

"Lie still," she snapped. "This tear in your body is quite severe."

"Yes Granny," I said meekly.

She looked up. "What is a Granny?"

I shook my head. I was too exhausted to explain. I could feel my head swimming through some sort of jelly that was getting thicker and thicker and blacker and blacker.

I passed out.

17

When I came back to my senses, nothing much seemed to have changed. I could hear weak banging against the pod's hatch. We hadn't moved. The only thing that was different was that I had been securely bandaged up and that Denaraz was sporting a huge white plaster over his shoulder.

Zenzara was frowning down at me, her wrinkles sagging. "... shouldn't have been out for so long," I heard her mutter.

I struggled onto one elbow. "I'm all right!"

She started back and hit her head against the console. "Don't do that! You startled me!" She massaged the back of her skull in a ginger sort of way. "I nearly knocked myself out."

"Who needs enemies?" I asked, rolling my eyes.

Izan grinned. "We have quite enough of those, thank you. They have been busily trying to break in."

"How long have we got?"

He pursed his lips. "Maybe a few hours. Ten or twelve, at the very most. And that is only if they want us alive. If they decide we are worthless, they could simply zap the whole pod with an enormous electrical discharge and fry us."

"Oh, nice." I thought for a moment and then clambered up. "Put me through to them, will you?"

He nodded and moved his fingers deftly about the console. The somewhat disheveled face of Admiral Ellison appeared. She was not happy.

"You have made yourself an enemy of the people," she said coldly.

"I was afraid of that. However, if you want your RAMP missile back I suggest you don't try to exterminate us, however much you want to. If we die, the co-ordinates die with us."

She looked cross. "You haven't destroyed it then?"

I shook my head. "It is still in one piece. Retrievable. So kindly give your men orders to treat this pod with great care."

She hesitated, before looking to one side and nodding to somebody out of frame. "It is done."

"Thank you. Then I imagine we will be seeing each other in a few hours."

"Why don't you come out now?"

"We would, except that a lot can happen between now and then. Who knows?"

"Have it your own way, then. It is not a matter of great relevance to me."

She cut off the communication. Zenzie shook her head. "She was lying."

"Of course she was. She is furious. She has lost one of only three RAMP missiles. If she doesn't get it back she won't be fleet admiral for very long."

"She should have listened to us."

"She should, of course, but these Terrans are pretty stubborn."

"What are we going to do? They are still using ABlasers to try to cut a way to us. I can hear them."

I shrugged. "I assume Denaraz tried to get this pod out of here?"

She nodded. "We are locked down."

"Hmm. I wonder what would over-ride a manual lockdown?"

Izan, who had been listening, raised one eyebrow. "Ahh. Yes." His eyes stared into the far distance. "Yes!" He leapt up and went back to the far console. "Of course! We need to make the software think the ship is about to explode. If we can do that, evacuation protocols will automatically be triggered and all the pods will be remotely released, overriding any previous instructions. Yes, that would work!"

"Can you do that? From here?"

"I have no idea. But I can try."

Zenzie scooted over to him. "I will help." They went into a huddle and I was able to lie back against the bulkhead and get my breath back. The pain was still pretty severe. It made me gasp as I spoke. I knew I was losing my ability to think clearly. It was frustrating. I was in need of a triage tank. As soon as possible. The pulse had affected one of my lungs, and it was quite hard to keep the panic at bay. It was frightening not to be able to get enough oxygen. Just keeping upright was a struggle.

Zenzie seemed to know what I was feeling. "A few hours in a Zeroth and you will be like new," she told me, over her shoulder. "It is a very clean wound. It just needs closing up."

"T-Thank you for the bandage."

"I am good at bandaging. I took a course. You are lucky I did. You might not be alive otherwise."

I suspected that Denaraz had also taken a few first-aid courses as part of his training, but said nothing. He looked up and smiled with his eyes. He had. However, he said nothing either.

I let my eyes close, and must have slept for a short while, for the next I knew was a gasp of satisfaction that woke me up with a jerk. "W-What ...?"

They were doing some sort of silly jig, holding each other's hands and jumping around in circles. "What is going on?" I felt a little left out.

Zenzie turned to me and did another small dance on the spot. "We found a way!"

"You're kidding!" I wished then I could get up and join in.

"No. I am brilliant." She looked over her shoulder at Denaraz and rectified, "We are brilliant."

Izan laughed. "It's all right. It was your idea, Zenzara. Own it!"

She did. "I am brilliant. I am brilliant. I am brilliant!"

"You can hack their system?"

"Theirs, and all the other ships in the convoy!"

I think time stopped for a couple of beats. I may have heard trumpets far away with some kind of fanfare. I do know my jaw dropped open. "No!"

She danced some more. "Oh yes!"

"How the fitz did you figure out a way to do that?"

"They are Terrans," she said simply. "They don't think in the same way we Tyzarans do."

"I can see that." I would have kissed them both if I had been able to stand up.

"So?" Denaraz raised his shoulders. "Do we go ahead?"

"Wait!" I half-raised one hand. "You are telling me that if we do this all of the fleet will instigate emergency evacuation protocol?"

"They will."

"The Terran forces will actually abandon ship?"

I thought about it. It was tempting, but I wasn't at all sure that the opposing Avarak forces wouldn't simply blow all of the pods up. The Avaraks had acted with restraint in their dealings with us, so perhaps it wasn't likely, but then this fleet was out to annihilate their race. I didn't want the remorse of being responsible for so many deaths, and I didn't think destruction on such a scale would help with any solution to the crisis.

I couldn't do it. It was too risky. "Can you get in touch with *Nivala*?" I asked. "Can they patch you through or something?"

"Yes, I guess. Though I won't be able to receive an answer."

"We don't need an answer. Send them a short burst in the code that was agreed. Tell them to put themselves between the two fleets and to stop the Avaraks from taking punitive action against the pods. The Avaraks signed the Alliance covenant. They are obliged to comply with our wishes." *I hope.*

"I can do that. What are your thoughts?"

"None of the pods have any weapons, right?"

"No. They may have small arms inside. No more than that."

"Can you program the pods' destination?"

He began to look alarmed. "Not for long. I can interfere with the initial programming, but they will be able to change that as soon as they are free of the ships."

If my plan worked, that wouldn't matter. "Do it. I want them to be programmed to form up in a lamina between the two fleets and then switch off. Just give them all an initial position. We'll see later what they do. *Nivala* can tell the Avaraks to try to ... discourage them from leaving, if they appear to be considering breaking that formation. A few shots across their bows and sterns should just about do that. Make it clear they are to chivvy them, not to eradicate them."

"What about us?"

"We will be trying to get rid of the other two RAMPs that are left. I'm assuming you can't do that through your link with their computer?"

He grinned. "I wish!" Then his face fell a little. "You need some regeneration first, if you are thinking of going yourself."

That was true. "Yes. So do you."

"Mine was nothing more than a scratch." He rotated his arm to prove it. "Not all of the crew members will abandon ship. Some will be suspicious and suspect a trap. Some ships may abort the evacuation protocol in time to stop it completely."

"I know. But our primary goal is to weaken the fleet, disarm the other two RAMPS and, then and only then, escape ourselves. Any confusion will make life an awful lot easier for us. Once we have the whole flotilla of pods partitioning the two fleets it will dissuade any Terran attacks. I think it may give us the time we need." I found myself shrugging. "What else can we do?"

Izan considered. "Maybe," he conceded. "It could work."

"It is our best bet. At the very least, it gives us an advantage. Even though we don't know where it will take us, we do know it will move us forwards. *Nivala* will be monitoring the situation closely. You can be sure that they will act if they see any opportunities. I don't think we have any other options at this time."

"Right. What about our own path? Where do you want us to be, if our pod is released as well?"

"Place us slightly ahead of the rest of the pods. If that happens, tell *Nivala* to send a shuttle to pick us up. Tell them we are in IEVA suits. We can get across if they send somebody with a line. And ... wish them good luck."

Zenzie bounced from one foot to the other. "This is going to be fun!" She had a strange sense of fun.

Even Denaraz was keen. His eyes were bright. He turned to the console and spent a couple of minutes on the outgoing message to *Nivala*. Finally, he turned back to me. "Done."

I took a deep breath and nearly passed out. I had forgotten about the lung injury. When I had managed to push back the darkness I nodded. "Do it!" It came out like a sigh – all I could manage to say with what little air I could suck in.

He invited Zenzie to his side, and the two of them began what appeared to be a very complicated intervention via the main console. It took both of them, and they had to go through very many steps to get through the firewalls and security stops.

For quite a time I doubted they would be able to do it. Their crests were taut and their faces absolutely concentrated. They fed the computer with more and more commands, replying to failsafes and avoiding booby traps. No wonder the Tyzarans were the most technologically advanced of the Major Shell races! They were running rings around *Chibuzo's* cyberspace. But it is not something I could have done. It took all of their knowledge and skill, two sets of hands and around twenty minutes.

Finally there was a sigh of relief. They looked at each other. Denaraz stepped back and gestured to Zenzie to give the final command.

Her eyes slid to me, proud and pleased. Then, still looking at me, she gave a mischievous grin and pressed down on the console. I couldn't blame her for her excitement. What she had just done was a major achievement. More, it made the Terrans very vulnerable. It could change the face of the war they had just started. *If* we ever got out to tell people about it.

Even through the pod walls, we could hear the siren as it began to issue short, regular blasts. After a few moments, there was a scudding of background noise that told of many boots thundering along the corridors. Denaraz put my helmet on, then his own, after helping Zenzara into one of the IEVA suits set into a recess in the pod. The suit drowned her. She could hardly walk for the material that dragged after her. Only her frosty expression daring us to comment kept us from laughing.

We were silent now, straining our hearing, trying to follow what was happening.

Denaraz had explained that, once the emergency protocols were triggered, the mainframe computer ceded control automatically to smaller backup modules that were strategically placed deep inside each ship. These modules were designed to function independently if the mainframe became compromised. Each pod also held an independent CPU, which is why they would quickly recover control. But there are no visors in pods. Their occupants would not be able to see what was going on. Their only input would be from their sensors. And they might just assume that their command had *wanted* them to form a barrier between the two fleets.

That would hopefully lead to a lot of confusion. Any of the Terran combatants who were in pods would be cut off from the rest of the force. They would also be blind, although they would be able to see where the rest of their fleet was through the control plotters. I hoped that it would make them doubt their next actions; make them loath to act rashly.

Even though I could hear the chaos around us, I was still having difficulty believing that Zenzara and Denaraz could possibly have succeeded in triggering a fleet-wide emergency protocol. "Can you follow any of this?" I asked Izan, who was still bent over the control panel, monitoring the situation.

He shook his head. "Machine protocols have already been implemented. Our onboard system has been isolated. We cannot reach through the system to the rest of the fleet. Not anymore."

"Then we can go?"

"I wish. Docking release should have been part of the protocol. However, in our case, it wasn't."

My heart sank. That meant that Admiral Ellison had realized what was happening and stopped our deployment. The scheme ... or at least our part in it ... had failed.

As I realized this, it became clear that none of the pods nearby were launching either.

Denaraz pursed his lips. "Ellison has managed to stop the launches."

At that moment the sirens stopped. The chaos outside turned into silence.

About ten minutes later our screen popped into life, showing Ellison. She looked extremely angry. I cheered up. Some part of the plan had worked, then.

"Your game was not successful," she snapped. "You might as well come out of there. You will be very uncomfortable."

"You managed to stop the evacuation? Well done!" I tried to keep her on line. Denaraz had galvanized into action as soon as he detected the connection. His fingers were literally flying over the console. "I didn't think you would be able to."

Things felt much quieter than they had before. Certainly the two fleets were no longer firing at each other; we would have been able to feel it. *Something* had caused a truce. My heart leaped in hope. "If we come out, will you guarantee us immediate medical treatment?"

A deep frown set on her forehead. "Why should I?"

"You want your RAMP missile back, don't you?"

"Not enough to pander to terrorists."

"You will need us."

"What makes you think that?"

Out of sight of the console, Denaraz looked up at me. He raised one thumb and made a screen-like sign with the other hand. Then he signaled the number 14 with the same hand.

I smiled. Fourteen of her ships had been unable to stop evacuation. At an average of some forty pods each ship, that would mean that there were currently some 600 pods running interference between the two fleets. And there were witnesses present, in the shape of *Nivala*. Hopefully more spaceships had been attracted to the area by now. I didn't think either of the combatants would risk the stigma of firing on escape pods. Especially, in the case of the Terrans, their own.

And Ellison couldn't speak to them to order them back.

A large grin spread across my face. It was good. No, it was better than good. It was wonderful. I tried to get enough breath inside me for a long sentence. "If you guarantee immediate medical treatment we will open the hatch. Otherwise we will stay here."

"There is no point. There is nothing you can do now. I shall be severing all cyber ties to the mainframe when this conversation is over. You will not get a second chance at hacking our systems."

I saw from Izan's face that this was possible, and would severely limit his autonomy. It was time to come in. We had done as much as we could.

"We are open to negotiation with you, but only after medical treatment."

"As prisoners, you will not dictate my policy."

I grinned. "Ah, but that is where you are mistaken, see? We are not coming out as prisoners. We are coming out as negotiators. We are here to negotiate a peace treaty."

She practically levitated with anger. "How dare you try to dictate terms!"

"What are you going to do? At least fourteen of your ships are lying uselessly in space." I made signs to Denaraz, asking him how many of the big ships were in those fourteen. He held up two fingers. That is when I knew we had some bargaining power.

I pressed on. "If you fall back you will be leaving RAMP missiles on board those two abandoned battleships. I can't see you doing that. Not when you have already lost one." I raised an eyebrow inquisitively. "Unless you have decided to come to your senses...?"

She started to splutter. I held up my hand before she could speak. The longer we held out, the more information Izan could garner. On the other hand, we couldn't leave it too long. Ellison would not allow us the time to interfere any further with the computer systems. She could cut the connexion at any moment and she would be organizing her troops to regain control of the abandoned ships, especially the battleships.

"Very well." I appeared to give in. "We are coming out ... if we have your word about the medical attention."

It was in her own interests to delay any negotiation. The situation could still change in her favour. She gave a curt nod. "Agreed."

I smiled as she cut the connexion.

Zenzie bounced over to me. "Why?" she demanded. "We could stay here! They can't do anything to us here!"

Denaraz understood. "We have done what we can," he said to her in a stern voice. "There is no point in our holing up away from the action. It is a dead end. Mallivan is right; we need to get back into the action again. This is the right thing to do." Quite apart from the fact that she might still decide to deep-steam us in our enclosed receptacle.

Zenzie chuntered a little, but stepped back as he went to the hatch. Within minutes it unlocked. Outside efforts to breach had warped the latch and he was unable to open it on his own. It took a concerted effort from various Terran crew members on the exterior before they could drag the heavy hatch open.

We were out.

I was placed, none too gently, on a gurney and wheeled rapidly to a medical station. From there, and with an attendant Zenzara refusing to leave me, I was lowered immediately in a Flatlander triage tank.

Actually, I was very happy to have the Tyzaran girl there to watch my back. It meant I could sink into the silky darkness and let cutting-edge science heal my body. I slowly drifted back under again. This was getting all too familiar.

18

I woke up pain-free. It was a great feeling. I took in a huge breath, to test if I could. Warm, revigorating air rushed into my lungs. It was such a relief. It made me euphoric.

As I sat up, there was a rustle behind me. I jumped and then laughed as I realized it was Zenzie.

"Are you better?" she asked, rather cautiously.

I sat up. The gel drained back into the tank. I moved my arms around and then twisted from side to side. "Never better! How long have I been out?"

"About six hours."

"Shells! Why didn't you wake me up sooner? What has happened? Are we still in stalemate? Get me out of here!"

Her crest tweaked. "The doctor said that you could only be cured with that length in the chamber. Any sooner and the hole would not have sealed. So I couldn't wake you up earlier. Nothing much has happened, as far as I know. The bombardments have not been resumed, which is a pretty good sign. And I don't know any more. I have been sitting here, by your side." She glared at me. "And you can get yourself up!"

I rubbed my hair ruefully. "Sorry. I am just worried."

She put her chin firmly in the air.

"Really, I *am* sorry. Thank you for staying with me. I appreciate it."

Her eyes slid sideways, to see if I meant it. I did. The crest began to smooth down again.

"Where is Denaraz?"

Zenzie pointed upwards. "He was only in a tank for an hour. The shoulder wound was reasonably superficial. He was taken away by an armed guard."

I finally struggled free of the gel. It is not easy to clamber out of one of the chambers. It is a bit like dragging yourself out of a bog. The gel never seems to want to let you go. "Taken away? We'll see about that! HEY!"

Despite the raised voice, nobody came. I shouted again. "HELLOOOO?"

Several pairs of boots stamped down the corridor outside and the hatch to the medical facility was pushed open.

Three crew members armed with M487s covered us. I waved at the guns. "Really? That was not in our agreement!"

"You are to come with us."

"I will come with you only if you are taking us to Admiral Ellison. Otherwise you are going to have to shoot me here."

Zenzara looked sideways at me and then slipped in front of me, crest up.

The soldiers began to laugh. "Is this giblet your protector?"

Zenzie hissed. "Giblet? *Giblet?* Who are you calling a giblet?" She turned to me "What the *fitz* is a giblet, Mallivan Bell?"

"The inside parts of a bird." I smiled at the men, raised my hands and waited for the explosion. "In ancient times, when they ate chickens, they were the bits that were thrown away as inedible and useless." I have always liked fanning fires. I'm afraid it is in my nature.

Zenzie's crest reached full vertical extension. Her claws popped out. So did her teeth. She bunched her muscles and launched herself at the first man, who dropped his M487 hastily and put his hands in front of his face to protect his eyes.

She dropped him like a tiger would. She put a restraining hand on his chest and swung her head to give the next man an assessing look. He hurried to point his gun at her. She gave a derisive hiss. "You have been told not to shoot us."

His lip quivered. "I will, though ... if I have to!" He tried to keep the barrel steady, but it was all over the place.

Zenzie gave him a disgusted look but got back to her feet. "You keep your names to yourselves," she told them.

The look of utter relief on their faces was great to watch. It was a great spectacle. I did hope that Zenzie wouldn't grow up too fast. I couldn't see an adult Tyzaran doing stuff like that. More's the pity.

Which brought me back to the matter in hand. "Take us to the other Tyzaran, and then to Ellison," I told them.

They blustered a bit, but a couple of snarls from Zenzara soon ran their manly determination down. They bunched in a trio on the other side of the corridor, as far away from her as they could.

She gave me a look. "*Giblet!*" She was still outraged. "You shouldn't have let them say things like that about me."

"True," I murmured. "But then, you didn't seem in need of much help."

"No." She looked pleased with herself. "I wasn't. All the same, you could have acted first."

"And miss that? You have got to be kidding!" Her face told me I shouldn't have said that. I added a tone of reproof. "I had only just got out of the triage tank!"

She gave another little hiss before she let it go. But she doesn't scare me. Much.

We walked on, coming after some time to the cells where we had been held before.

A very worried Denaraz sprang to his feet as we walked up to the barrier. "He should not be in here," I told them.

"Admiral's orders."

I tapped one foot. "She doesn't want to speak to us?"

"She told us to keep him out of the way while you were recuperating."

"And you have done that. Now, please let him out. We need to see the Admiral."

The boy Zenzie had attacked edged around her, trying not to get too close. Her crest flared and she hissed a little. He flinched. Denaraz gave me a questioning look. I tried not to see it.

They opened the cell door to let Izan out. Then we were marched along the endless corridors. These battleships are leviathans. It seems to take forever to walk from one end to the other.

Finally we made it to the bridge. We were kept waiting outside while the admiral was advised of our presence. After some minutes, we were ushered in front of her.

She was standing glaring, arms akimbo. "What have you done?"

I looked with some interest at the main visor. It was showing a close-up of the centre of the battle zone. I could see that there were still pods between the two forces. Great. It was taking her valuable time to get this chaos sorted out, then. What I wasn't able to see were any signs of what was happening on the other battleships. Pity.

"We are required by the Interstellar Alliance to requisition all RAMP missiles and to mediate a peaceful solution to your conflict with the Avarak people."

"And I told you before that I do not answer to your Interstellar Alliance."

"I think the situation has changed, though?"

Ellison stiffened. "You deserve to be hung! You have interfered in a military Omnistate operation. You will be held accountable!"

"Feel free." I wasn't particularly worried about possible future accusations. Frankly, I didn't really expect to live beyond the day.

That only stoked her anger. "What you did is treason!"

I was confused. "We did as we were ordered. How can that be treasonous?"

"Treasonous to the Omnistate!"

"Oh. That. Well, I suppose, from your point of view, we were. But then, none of us are Omnistate citizens. We do not have to be loyal to them. In fact, we are paid not to be. There are almost always two points of view."

"How did you manipulate our secure systems like that? I need to know!"

"They were not as secure as you thought. Congratulations on keeping control of *Chibuzo*, by the way. We didn't think you would be able to."

Her teeth ground together. "Why should I not have you executed?"

"If you do you will be declaring war unilaterally on the Alliance. Do you really want to do that? Are you authorized to do that?"

She got a very nasty smile on her face. Something in my stomach suddenly felt hollow.

"You think you have won," she told us. "But you have forgotten one thing – the RAMP missiles on the other battleships."

"You won't use those against ships," I said confidently. "It would make no sense logistically. They are ship-to-planet missiles."

She nodded. "They are. However, if what you say is true, every use of a RAMP missile risks splitting the vacuum field and destroying the universe?"

"You wouldn't do that!" Now I was feeling a wave of ice sweeping up my body from my feet. Zenzara's crest was so vertical it was twice its normal height. Denaraz had gone white.

"Try me!"

"You would risk total annihilation? Why?"

"I thought you might enjoy watching it. If you are lying about the risks, your falsehoods will be revealed."

"And if we are not?" I could hear that my voice was tight.

"I believe you are."

I looked desperately at the others. We had to do something! We couldn't allow this to happen.

Admiral Ellison pressed on the console, talking to one of the battleships. "*Telzaria*, fix target on the centre of the Avarak fleet and initiate RAMP Deployment."

"As ordered, Admiral!"

I stepped forward. "Stop! You cannot do this! You mustn't do this!"

"You should have thought of that before you started to humiliate

Omnistate troops!"

I held my hands wide apart. "Look, we can tell you where we found weaknesses in your systems. Everything is negotiable. Let's sit down and talk about it. Please order your ship to stand down, Admiral."

"I almost believe you. I would, if your whole argument about ultra-dense states and catastrophe weren't so obviously fabricated. It puts you in a difficult position, doesn't it? If you admit you lied, then there is no reason not to use the RAMPs. If you continue with this charade, the Avarak fleet will be destroyed."

"So will your pods."

"That is your responsibility. Not mine. You created this situation. Now, tell your ship and the Avarak fleet to move back to Veka, or I will fire."

I closed my eyes briefly. How had this gone so wrong? I was out of time, and out of leverage. The Omnistate fleet could not be allowed to get any closer to Veka. That would lead to RAMP deployment on Rhyveka. At the very best, the entire Avarak race would be wiped out. At worst, the whole universe would roll up on itself and disappear. Fine choices. What had happened to my life?

"Put me through to my ship," I told her, injecting a defeated tone in my words.

Zenzara and Denaraz looked sharply at me.

Sammy's voice and face came up on the screen. "Yes?"

I spoke as quickly as I could. "RAMPs to be deployed. Do what you must!"

I was cut off half way through the 'must', but I thought that Sammy and the others would have heard what I said. Our only hope was that they had perfected the dampening.

I was manhandled away from the console. One of the soldiers clubbed me with the stock of his M487. My legs crumpled and I found myself on the ground. Zenzie crouched down next to me and attempted to help me up, staunching the blood with part of her tunic

I tried to push her away, not very successfully. "I'm all right. Let me be!"

Her face clouded over. "I was only trying to help," she said crossly. "Fine! Get up by yourself!"

"I will!"

I scrambled to my feet and glowered at Ellison. The Admiral's chin was up and she was reciprocating. "You shouldn't have done that!"

"You shouldn't continue with this. It is madness!"

She pressed the button again. "Countdown from ten, *Telzaria*."

"As ordered, Admiral! Ten ..."

I shook my head. In that moment I think everything that had happened in the last weeks ran through my head. Everything had shifted so far that I could barely remember back to the old status quo. The old days of *Faraday*. The old grievances that seemed so petty now.

"Nine ..."

My eyes were looking around wildly now, trying to fix on a way to stop the unstoppable.

"Eight ..."

A wave of disappointment swept over me. I had failed. And what a failure.

"Seven ..."

Denaraz moved closer to Zenzara. He would try to defend her to his last breath.

"Six ..."

Zenzie's crest broke. It had been vertical. Now it simply folded into absolute acceptance of disaster.

"Five ..."

"Four ..."

"Three ..."

"Two ..."

"One ..."

We waited.

I could hear my own heart thudding.

There was a scratching sound on the tight beam. Then we heard a voice. "Admiral?"

"*Telzaria?*"

"Deployment unsuccessful."

I let out my breath in a long sigh. I hadn't realized I had been holding it in.

"What do you mean, unsuccessful?"

The voice on the other end of the tight beam sounded confused. "I do not know, Admiral. It is almost as if there was some sort of interference between the RAMP missile itself and our orders. It was ... deaf."

She swiveled to me. "What did you do?"

I shrugged. "I did nothing. How could I?"

"You are lying again. Your ship somehow managed to stop the missile launch." Her eyes narrowed. "But we still have one left."

I had been afraid of that. I raised an eyebrow in Denaraz's direction. He had been working on the electromagnetic interference technique. He might know if they could repeat the block.

His face was ashen. I didn't need him to answer my unasked question. It was clear for all to see. He didn't think the second RAMP missile could be stopped.

Zenzie gave something like a moan. She, too, was looking at Denaraz.

I began to shake.

"Please, Admiral. Stop this now. The Omnistate cannot hope to claim the whole local shell. It couldn't even police such a vast expanse of space!"

"I am under orders to ensure the capitulation of the Avaraks," she said in a freezing tone. "And I shall carry out my job. I am an admiral of the Omnistate Fleet, responsible only to the Ethnarch himself!"

My head was spinning, unable to process that all hope was lost. I launched myself at the Admiral in a last ditch attempt to stop her, but was immediately clubbed down again by one of the soldiers. Denaraz tried the same thing, and met with the same fate.

Her finger was back on the console. "*Nanhai*. Arm and prepare the RAMP missile. Target the middle of the Avarak fleet. Advise when ready."

"As ordered, Admiral. *Nanhai* out."

Denaraz and I were dragged to our feet and put under restraint. At least they had left Zenzara free, though they were eyeing her uncertainly.

Now the time dragged. I suppose a few minutes went by. It could have been ten hours. In my world the clock was frozen. Even my own body struggled to keep my heart pumping blood around my body. The sheer horror of what was about to happen was just too much for my mind to take.

And yet, all too soon, the voice came back. "*Nanhai* standing by, Admiral."

"Countdown from ten. Mark!"

"As ordered Admiral. Ten …"

I was inside my own body, wrapped in darkness. I was shrouded and protected from the outside. I was floating.

"Nine …"

"Eight …"

"Seven …"

"Six …"

"Five …"

"Four …"

"Three …"

Then I saw Zenzara clutch at her head. She bent double as some sort of pain overtook her and I distinctly heard a whimper. Denaraz and I tried to throw ourselves towards her, but we were held back by our guards. Her face had gone white and the folds of her skin were deepened by the spasms she was undergoing. Her breathing was shallow.

"Two …"

"One …"

The tight-beam gave another crackle and a clipped voice came through the speaker. "Deployment unsuccessful."

Denaraz's shoulders slumped in relief. I guess mine must have too. The Admiral snarled.

"Admiral?" The voice on the other end of the tight-beam sounded wary.

"What happened?"

"There must have been interference. The firing instruction did not reach the missile, Sir."

Ellison's whole face was rigid. She was furious. She whirled round. "You may think you have won, but you can just think again! I will deploy those missiles! I can unload them manually through the cranes, and they can be encouraged to detonate by firing off a couple of kinetic missiles once they are in place."

I could see from Denaraz's face that such a sequence would be enough to deploy the missiles. I deflated even more. We had done our very best, and luck had been with us, but it still wasn't going to be enough.

I put my head up. I would try again to convince her. One last time.

"Admiral Ellison. You must believe me. What you have been told is true. If you deploy those missiles, you risk annihilating the entire universe. I beg you to reconsider."

She gave me a scathing look. "I shall deploy one immediately. That will clear us a path to Rhyveka, where the other will make a good-sized dent in their civilization." Her body language became crisp. She had made up her mind. I blew out air and shook my head. This was a debacle. Far from stopping the RAMP missiles, we had actually contributed to their immediate deployment.

My eyes went over to Zenzie, still bent double. I wanted to telegraph my apologies to her. She was too young to die. Something inside me broke at the thought of all she would miss. I felt responsible.

Denaraz was looking at her too, but I saw that she was straightening up. Her face was still pinched with pain, but she had a determined look on her face that I knew well.

Her voice cut through the blackness in my mind. "You will not do this!"

Admiral Ellison stared at her. "What do you mean, I will not do this? Do you really think *you* can stop me?"

Zenzie made as if to listen to something inside her. Her head tilted on one side. She met my worried gaze and gave me a tiny smile. And then she began to disintegrate in front of my eyes. The molecules in her body splayed upwards and outwards, making her three times the height and width of her normal self.

I squinted. What was happening to her? I struggled to get to her, but couldn't; my restraints were still holding. It looked to me as if the individual cells within her body were separating, moving further apart from each other. You couldn't actually see through her, but she began to shimmer against the background. Like a heat haze on Mallivan. Her head went back and she suddenly lifted some inches off the ground, her arms and legs bending backwards as she did.

Denaraz gave a strangled cry and threw himself towards her again in an attempt to protect her. He was held back by three guards, but continued to struggle to free himself and go to Zenzara.

Her voice began to echo around us.

"The Chakrans have determined that this weapon may not be used. You are endangering the vacuum energy, their habitat. This will not be permitted. Your actions have become a risk to the entire universe. This will not happen. All RAMP missiles shall be destroyed."

The Admiral, who had been staring open-mouthed at this new apparition, closed her jaw with a distinct click. "Who ... ? What ...?"

Zenzie fragmented even more, until her body occupied the whole space between the decks. Now I could see through her. It was a very strange sensation.

"Both missiles will be directed into the blue hypergiant nearby. I believe it to be known to you as Zuben. The individual molecules of the missiles will burn up there. This is a safe way to eliminate the threat."

"Stop this girl!" snapped the Admiral.

Many guns immediately targeted Zenzie.

A blue pulse propagated outwards, with her as its center, and the guns simply expanded outwards until they disassembled. All the internal parts fell quite uselessly to the floor.

"I am the Chyzar, and I represent the Chakrans. The Chyzar may not be touched. If they so wish they can do the same with all your ships. Do you wish them to open the molecules up to the vacuum outside? To open pores large enough for men to slip through?"

Ellison's eyes now held a tinge of fear. "What are you?"

"This body contains a Chakran Nexus and represents the Chakran entities. It may not be attacked." Zenzara gave a quick outward burst that threatened to reach the surrounding troops. As they stepped hastily back, she deflated slightly again. She stared at the Admiral, unblinking.

Ellison signaled to the men around us. They released Denaraz and I and stepped away from us.

Zenzara inclined her head in recognition of this. "You will meet the Avaraks on board *Nivala*. These representatives of the Alliance will act as negotiators. You will discuss the end of hostilities. You will stop your insane attempt to claim living space as your own. All space is their habitat. One single Chakran may be spread over millions of light years. Your space is their body. You will not dare to claim such as your own. You have seen that they can separate your very molecules.

"Through your abuse of the local environment you have forced them to take notice of you. And they do not appreciate your stupidity. Outside your star's boundaries you will travel with respect for the environment, or your fleets and worlds could be held responsible. Tell that to your superiors in the Omnistate. Keep your technology pure and do not contaminate the vacuum energy. If you do, they will act again. Is that clear?"

Admiral Ellison was hyperventilating. But she managed to nod.

"Very well. They will withdraw, but they may act again at any time they see fit. I am their eyes and their ears. And do not forget ... even the very molecules of your planet may be expanded. They do not wish to interfere, but do not goad them any further."

Zenzara began to come together again, her molecules contracting down to their normal size. As she shrank back to her own volume, men rushed towards her from all directions. Zenzie's body ballooned in size again – a sharp burst outwards which frightened them back to the periphery once more.

"Do not touch the Chyzar!" The voice admonished again. Zenzara hung for a moment at the bloated size, as if to check the resolve of the men around her, then she resumed her shrinkage down to her normal self.

Loose from out restraints, both Denaraz and I leapt forward as we saw her feet touch the deck plating again. I could not believe that anyone could survive what she had just lived through, but she smiled at us, albeit a little tremulously, only stumbling slightly as she regained her usual size.

"Well," she said, checking that her claws were still in the same place, "that was new."

We fussed around her, unable to believe what we had seen. "Are you all right?" "What happened?" "Does it hurt?" "Can you walk?"

She gave Denaraz a kiss on his cheek and touched my arm. "Later." Then she turned quietly to where Admiral Ellison was staring, apparently glued to the deck. "You heard what the Chakrans said."

Ellison's lips had gone pale. "What was that?"

"You have come to the attention of the Chakran race. And they don't like you very much. Your actions will damage their environment. They will no longer allow you to pursue this disastrous path."

"Who are the Chakrans?" she whispered, her hand going to her throat and her eyes searching rather uneasily around the bridge, as if expecting them to pop out at her at any moment.

"You don't know who the Chakrans are?" Zenzie's voice was disbelieving. "How could you not know ...." Then she stopped. "Oh, never mind; I suppose there are a million things you don't know. You are only Terrans, after all."

I gave her a sideways look, but she was unaware of the unspoken rebuke. I guess we do all seem a bit ... basic ... to the Tyzarans. They have had millennia more of development, after all.

As to what the Chakrans must think of us ... the mind boggled. Well, mine did anyway. A being whose 'head' is hundreds of millions of light years away from its 'feet'. Zenzie once told me that a Chakran, if visible, would be comparable to a filament of galaxies, something like the size of the Sloan Great Wall in the large scale structure of the universe. Hundreds of millions of light years across. In fact, it gave me a headache just thinking about it. Of course we would be less significant than grains of sand on a beach. We *would* be grains of sand on a beach seen from the other side of the Milky Way. No, we wouldn't even be discernible.

I shook my head to break the train of thought. It was making me dizzy. I had to grab a hold of Izan to stop myself swaying. He gave me a strange look. I can't blame him. I wasn't the one whose whole body had just been swollen up to epic proportions.

"How did your blood flow?" I blurted out, again speculating about the impossibility of what we had just witnessed.

Zenzara giggled. "How should I know? Maybe it didn't need to."

Then where would it go? Would it coagulate? I really just could not wrap my head around this at all.

And I wasn't the only one. Except Denaraz, all of those present were shell-shocked. I mean, you know that human bodies are mostly air and water, but you really don't expect to have it proved to you quite as explicitly.

Ellison bent down to touch one of the guns on the floor. The Chakran had not put the weaponry back together again. It lay on the decking, stripped down. As her fingers made contact, it crumbled to a dust so fine that it was little more than a cloud.

"Get all these bagged up," she instructed. Then she put her fingers up to her own head and closed her eyes, murmuring to herself, "Get me the Ethnarch. Stat!"

She really was shaken up. She wasn't thinking straight. She had just let us know that the Terrans also possessed implanted ansible communication. I was pretty sure they had stolen that from the Tyzarans, too. I wondered if it was one of the things the Tyzaran traitor had passed along to them. I couldn't help thinking it might be a good thing if they had a miniaturized version. With the Terrans using such instantaneous communication openly, it could only be a matter of time before we all had it. It would stop being a privilege for the few Tyzarans who reached the Supreme Council, and their favored acolytes.

Which reminded me. Denaraz had been able to talk via ansible to the Supreme Council. Had he been keeping them up to date with the situation?

I turned to him and made spinning gestures at the height of my head.

He looked put out. "Mine has been disrupted ever since Ellison overrode the Emergency order on *Chibuzo*. I don't know why."

Ellison's eyes flickered. I thought she might have an inkling.

I nodded. Pity. Still, after Zenzie's little demonstration, things were looking a whole lot better.

I took a deep breath and addressed the Admiral again. "When would be convenient to begin peace negotiations?"

Ellison became aware that we were still there. "Put them in back in the brig," she ordered.

Zenzara's crest flared upwards. "I don't think so. We will go back to *Nivala*. All negotiations must take place on neutral territory. Both you and the Avaraks can join us there when you are ready."

The admiral considered. It took her longer than it should; she was still trying to assimilate what had just happened.

I stepped towards her, shaking the restraints. "Please remove these. If you wish our co-operation and that of the entire Interstellar Alliance, you must release us immediately."

Her gaze flickered over Denaraz and myself. It only focussed on Zenzara, however. She gave a short nod. Our fetters were removed.

I rubbed at my wrists. Denaraz and I positioned ourselves to either side of Zenzie. We were a bit late and she clearly didn't need our protection in the slightest, but it made me feel a little better.

The Admiral came to a decision. "I will agree to attend negotiations on the *Nivala*," she said slowly, "but I will not let you go yet. I must speak directly to my supreme commander, Ethnarch Locke, first. He will need to examine footage of what happened here before any decisions are taken." She bit her lip. "However, after that ... err ... expression by the Chakrans, I do see that it may not be appropriate to place you back in the cells."

She walked up and down for a few moments her hand sweeping along the length of the main console. Then she made up her mind. "You will be given a cabin each. You will be free to visit with each other, but I will not allow you to leave the cabin area. You will be restrained again if you attempt to leave. Is that agreeable?" She tilted her graying hair towards me. I nodded. It was probably the best we could hope to get.

She gave the relevant instructions. We were escorted down several decks and along a long corridor until we reached a side passageway with doors reaching off it. Here, we were each shown into a spacious cabin, with en suite facilities including actual water showers. I could hardly believe my eyes. None of us had had water showers since we had been quartered on *Sentinel*.

Zenzie gave something like a moan and disappeared into her cabin. We heard a lock clicking into place. Denaraz and I exchanged a wry shrug. My clothes were stiff with sweat too. I knew what I wanted to do.

"Meet up later?" he suggested.

"Sure!"

Within seconds I was locked securely inside my cabin, under

a pummelingly hot shower. It was bliss. I put my head back and let the water drum onto my face with its thousands of pinhead drops, washing away the tensions of nearly dying so many times. True, unexpected luxury. Nearly the best thing that had happened all day. Climbing into clean sheets and falling into an instant deep sleep had to be the best. By far.

19

It was ten hours later that I was woken up by a thudding on the door of the cabin. I pulled myself, most reluctantly, out of bed and padded over to open it, only stopping to wrap a towel around my waist.

Zenzie and Denaraz were standing on the other side.

"Ellison wants to see us," Denaraz told me.

I gave a curt nod. "Come in."

They did, and sat on the bed as I dragged my uncooperative clothes back on. They were so grimy that they scratched as I pulled them over my skin. Zenzie looked away in a pointed sort of manner.

I threw some of that wonderful water on my face and then smiled. "Right! I hope today doesn't get as complicated as yesterday."

Zenzie blew out air. "Speak for yourself," she said. "*You* didn't get blown up to the size of a space shuttle."

"True. You certainly stole the show. How are you feeling now?"

She blinked. "I slept like the dead. It was all I could do to finish the shower. Having all your molecules expanded is tiring. I felt like I was dissolving."

"I can imagine." I couldn't.

Denaraz was staring at Zenzara as if she had achieved God status. "Do you know what you did?" he asked, his voice reverent.

"Not really, no."

"No Chyzar has ever been able to allow the Chakrans to manifest directly."

"Don't tell the Supreme. Then they really will insist on having me examined."

He shook his head. "I have to. There were scores of witnesses. The Supreme Council would be bound to find out. It is best that they hear it from me directly. Without spin. Without bias. Don't you think, Mallivan?"

"Possibly. I certainly don't think you will be able to keep this a secret. And, from what the Chakrans said, they will be keeping a close eye on the situation. That sort of thing may happen all the time."

Zenzie gasped and large tears welled up in her eyes. "I don't want to become a ... a ..."

"Deity?" suggested Denaraz.

She sighed. "A specimen. I just want to be me. Normal."

I grinned down at her. "You were never that. It may be a bit more difficult now though."

Her crest drooped. "No kidding." Her voice was small.

I draped an arm around her thin shoulders. "We won't let them take you away, Ty Zylarian. Sorry, *Chy* Zylarian."

She slumped even more. "Shells! I suppose I *am* the Chyzar now."

"Not only are you the Chyzar," said Denaraz in an admiring tone. "You are the only Chyzar to be able to channel directly the Chakrans. They have been able to form a complex Nexus inside you. You are our most important Chyzar ever."

Zenzara put out her tongue. "I'll swap if you will."

He grinned. "I wish. What was it like to have a truly incorporeal being take over your body?"

"They didn't. Take over my body. At least, I suppose they did, but they left me room to be me as well. They were very ... respectful of my sense of self. It was all right." She frowned. "And they aren't really incorporeal either. Their molecules are just spread over aeons of spacetime. And, even though they are so very large, they are terribly fragile too."

"They didn't seem it yesterday."

"No." Her frown deepened. "They didn't want to do what they did yesterday. I could feel their doubt. They thought that it might leave them vulnerable in some way. They just weren't able to see any other options."

"But they spoke through you. How did you know what they wanted you to say?"

"I could sense what they were feeling. It was a bit like cold weather causing you to shiver. I sensed how they felt, and so I put what I was feeling into words."

"What about that expansion thing? Was that your idea, or theirs?"

"Theirs, but it was as if they ran it by me first to see if I was all right with what they were doing. I could sense that they didn't want to hurt me. It was new for them too, and even though they were wary about doing it I could feel their excitement."

"They were excited too?" How strange.

"Yes, because they have been searching for ways to interact directly with non-quantum beings for thousands of years. This is a breakthrough for them, as well."

Denaraz was still staring at her in amazement. "You say 'they'. So you *can* identify more than one in the Nexus inside you?"

Zenzie hesitated. But we were her friends. "I was right. There are Six," she said. "Six different entities present. I am aware of them as different strands, different individuals. However, when they are in the Nexus, I can't really separate them out."

I stared at the small Tyzaran girl. "Do you know how special that makes you?"

"I ... I guess." She shuffled from side to side. "But I am still me, as well."

"I know. We will make sure your compatriots don't slice you open. I promise."

Relief shone over her face. "Thank you!"

"Right. Well. I guess we should be moving. We need to try to stop a war, as instructed by the Macers."

"We do."

We wandered up along the corridor, where we were picked up by what I would like to call a guard of honor, but felt more like a prison detail.

Our destination was one of the smaller shuttle bays. Admiral Ellison was waiting for us there, moving from foot to foot and looking angry to be kept waiting.

"You are to come with me," she snapped, indicating one of the shuttles.

We were shepherded onto the small vehicle. It was soon overflowing with Terrans, all of whom were heavily armed.

"Are you intending to negotiate or is this an all-out attack?" I queried.

"We cannot go to a neutral ship without taking precautions."

"I am just not sure that all these men will fit on *Nivala*."

"Please refrain from speaking."

That put me in my place. There was a stiff silence for the rest of the short journey over to our ship.

The shuttle was waved forwards into *Nivala's* cargo hold. *Nivala* is unusual in that she has forward and aft loading doors, enabling the stern loading door to be used for landing and the bow door for takeoff. This is now known as fly-loading-one-way or FLOW stacking. It is generally thought to be more time and cost effective.

Our small shuttle settled heavily on the main throughway and then was picked up on the deployable continuous tracks and automatically stowed in one of the side holds. These are kept with atmosphere at all times, and separated from the open throughway by thin force fields.

The shuttle door opened.

There were many faces peering in at us. All were armed with Tyzaran ABlasers. Sammy was at the forefront.

He waved his weapon at the Admiral. "We were not expecting so many armed escorts." Then he spotted the three of us and his face lightened. "Rye. Zenzara. Denaraz. Good to see you guys. Welcome back."

"Sammy. Believe me, the feeling is mutual." I felt a rush of affection at the sight of my friend. There had been so many times in the last day that I wouldn't have thought it possible.

The Terran weapons swung to cover us, just in case we had ideas of walking away. Sammy's face changed and *Nivala's* crew raised their ABlasers in return. Their faces were fierce and quite determined. I ran my eyes over them. There was Mel, now holding her weapon with something like eagerness. Anzany had a set face that showed how hard she was concentrating. And at the back I could see Seyal, also holding an ABlaser, also pointing it unwaveringly at the Admiral.

The standoff was unhelpful, however. We needed to get Ellison to the negotiating table. I turned to her.

"I suggest you tell your men to lower their weapons. You will be allowed through with a personal guard of three armed men and two unarmed attaches. The same agreement will be enforced with the Avarak delegation."

Sammy nodded and immediately lowered his weapon. "That seems fair."

Ellison hesitated, then bowed her head. "Very well." She turned to her men, singled three out to accompany her and ordered the others to spread out around the shuttle and protect it. She and her two attaches marched down the ramp. Zenzie and Izan followed, with me bringing up the rear.

Mel sidled up to me. "All right?"

I nodded. "I think so. Here?"

"Yes. A bit hairy for a while there, but things seem to have quietened down recently. I don't know what happened though."

"Zenzie happened."

"Did she?" Mel looked intrigued, but said nothing further, limiting herself to treating Zenzara to an encouraging smile.

We were escorted to the gymnasium, in the centre of the upper deck. I saw that all the gym equipment had been removed and a large table set up in the centre. They had used modules from all over the ship to put together something that was as close as they could get to a round table.

Cleared of its equipment, the gym actually had an impressive aura to it. I would never have thought of using it, but the double height gave an air of solemnity about the occasion. It was very effective. I wondered who had come up with the idea. One of the girls, I suspected. Maybe Neema, who must be in charge up on the bridge?

We were seated around one side of the circular table. Ellison edged her own chair forward and her two attaches edged theirs back. Not that there could have been any doubt about who was in charge.

The Avaraks were escorted in some fifteen minutes later, after coffee and some refreshments had been offered. Ellison and her staff refused food, though they did accept coffees. Zenzie, Izan and I grabbed whatever we could. We hadn't eaten for twenty-four hours. My blood sugar perked up within minutes.

I wasn't best pleased to see who was attending for the Avaraks. I didn't know the leading male, but the one tucked in behind him was unmistakable. Vebor. I heard Sammy suck in his breath too. The Avarak doctor had sabotaged our vessel. He was not our favorite person. And he hated us with a ferocity that bordered on murderous.

Zenzie touched my hand. "If it weren't for him I would never have been found by the Chakrans," she said.

True. And if it weren't for the Chakrans we could never have got Ellison to sit down at this table. We had to move on, not look backwards over our shoulder. "All right, but don't take your eyes off him. I wouldn't put anything past him," I grumbled.

She smiled. "Look around you. Nobody here is going to let him get away with anything."

She was right. *Nivala's* crew had their attention riveted on the large Avarak. He would certainly be hampered in any sabotage attempts on *this* ship.

The Avaraks settled themselves on the other side of the table. Sammy had not been able to find special chairs for them, but had provided reinforced benches that were adequate. At least, I thought they were adequate; the Avaraks were not so sure, from their surly comments.

Vebor spotted Seyal. His scowl deepened and he leant forward to speak to the leading Avarak. This worthy swiveled to examine Seyal.

"A point of order," he said in a heavy, gravelly voice.

"Yes, Admiral Vykron?" Sammy said.

"That female Avarak must be removed. She is unlanded and may not be in our presence. It is an insult to Rhyveka."

This wasn't the time to force anything. Seyal's time would come, but not here and not today.

I met Vykron's stare. "Very well, Admiral. She will withdraw."

Sammy nodded to Seyal who seemed almost to evaporate. She hadn't lost her ability to move almost unnoticed.

"Any further points of order?" I asked, moving to the centre of the table, between the two delegations. I motioned to Zenzara and Denaraz to join me. They did so, Zenzie scooping up the remainder of her breakfast as she did. I heard a faint giggle from *Nivala's* crew, who were now stationed at strategic points around the gym.

Ellison glared at me. "Why should you lead these discussions?"

"Because I am so authorized by the Interstellar Alliance. That guarantees any accords that come out of these discussions. Without us you are merely bilateral. With us, we represent almost all of the Major Shells."

"Very well." She cleared her throat. "I am commanded to offer a ceasefire on very beneficial terms. All the Human Omnistate requires is full withdrawal of all star systems within one hundred light years of Sol."

She lifted her head and stared at us, rather like a small bird might have done when dropping a worm at its children's feet.

The Avarak delegation roared. Both Vebor and Vykron smashed their fists on the table in front of them. The rest of us jumped and the table almost shattered. "You have brought us here under false pretenses!" shouted Vykron. "That is unacceptable. Totally unacceptable! How dare you!"

I stood. It took them some time to quieten down, but eventually they let me speak.

I gave Ellison a flat smile. "Admiral. You have been told that you must withdraw to your own star's boundaries. The Chakrans were not joking."

She blinked. "My ... my superiors were not privy to the demonstration that was given on board *Chibuzo*. They do not think an alien lifeform can dictate their policy. They will be generous, however. They are prepared to forgo their claim to the areas of the Local Shell further out than a hundred light years."

"Impossible!" howled Vykron. "That would include Gienak and Raksora. Berennis! Sivetas, too!"

"It would. However Yenguan would be outside of that radius."

"Yenguan!" scoffed Vykron. "What is there to mine on Yenguan? It is a system of no strategic or geological significance. What good would that do us?"

"It is a concession," said Ellison. "My government is offering a compromise."

Zenzie began to tremble. "No race may claim anything other than its own star system," she said in a shaky voice. "Open space belongs to no-one. It is unclaimable and untameable."

"Who says?" demanded Ellison.

"You were told!" Zenzie's crest was standing out from her scalp and she was looking distinctly fuzzy around the edges. "You do not listen!"

"I am under orders!"

"Then who can decide? Who has the authority? Where are they?"

"My superiors are on Earth," said Admiral Ellison curtly. "Obviously."

"Then talk to them."

"They are too far away."

Zenzie shivered even more. I took her arm but she brushed away my hand. "You cannot touch me at the moment, Mallivan Bell. I am sorry." She fixed Ellison with a long stare. "You have an ansible implant. Call them."

"How do you ... that is ... I can't possibly ..."

A shout went up from the Avarak side of the table. "You have an ansible implant! How is this? We do not have ansible communication."

Well, that cat was well and truly out of the bag.

A pale Admiral Ellison closed her eyes in concentration. The air in front of us, in the middle of the tables, began to shimmer with curving wisps of light. Slowly, these solidified more and more until the familiar face of the Ethnarch of Earth appeared in front of us. They not only had miniaturized ansible communication, they had somehow been able to tie it into a hololink. I didn't think the Tyzarans themselves had been able to do that. From the look of astonishment on Denaraz's face, they hadn't.

We had all gasped, but Ethnarch Locke was horrified. He looked around at his surroundings and glared. "What is this, Admiral? What is happening?"

Ellison leapt to attention and saluted. "Ethnarch Locke! This ... this ... alien ... wishes to speak with you."

The Ethnarch appeared amused. His gaze slid over Zenzie and then away with a disbelieving air. "This young Tyzaran girl? You have broken ansible silence for *this*?"

Zenzie blushed crossly. I took a discreet step backwards. That's what the Ethnarch should have done too, but he was too busy looking down on her. I guess, when you are Ethnarch of the whole of the Sol system, you get to feel pretty important. I could have told him he was making a mistake, but I don't suppose he would have listened to me. In any case, I was beginning to enjoy myself.

Sure enough, Zenzie began to blow up again. Right in front of him.

He smiled with bravado. He thought he was safely back on Terra. He thought that nothing could touch him through an ansible hololink.

He faced up to the oversized Zenzara, his expression one of contempt. She expanded even more, and when her molecules touched those of the hololink, they seemed to pause and then push in on them, exerting some sort of real force.

The Ethnarch gave a strangled sort of yelp and attempted to jump backwards. His legs wavered and then sort of smudged in the light. The top part of his torso began to fall. He was only able to stay upright by flapping his arms around like a child on a tightrope.

He compromised by holding his face as far back as he could. Zenzie's expanding body was almost crossing over his now. His eyes were wide open and the whites showed his panic.

"Stop it!" he shouted. "You will hurt me! I order you to stop!"

Zenzie ignored him. His eyes went even wider and he screeched at the admiral, his voice high and panicky. "Stop this! Fire at this ... this ... abomination!"

The Admiral dropped her hand and the three guards that had been allowed in all raised their weapons, only to have them disappear into dust within seconds.

In fact, all of the weapons in the gym evaporated.

"Please order the RAMP missiles destroyed." said Zenzie in a calm voice.

Locke was terrified, but he blustered anyway. "I don't know why I should have to do that."

"Of course you know. Are you not the Ethnarch of the entire Omnicompetent State, as it was once known?"

His head was now jammed back as far as it could go. His chin was almost facing the ceiling. "The Omnistate, yes. But I do not know everything."

"You know this. I have told you. The Chakrans have told you. I presume you have consulted with your scientists this last night?"

"I ... may have."

"And what did they say about the ultra-dense state?"

"The Omnistate does not take advice from young Tyzaran girls about its policy."

There was a shriek as the figure standing in front of us began to expand, much like Zenzara had done. His molecules separated, his body ballooned outwards. He twisted and turned, but was held tight by something invisible. Much as he struggled, he could not get free.

"Let me go!"

"One moment please. You may experience temporary discomfort. Are there any more of those RAMP missiles?"

"I will tell you nothing!"

Zenzie gave a small giggle. I waited for something more, but she decided not to comment further. Her own body was now mingling freely with that part of the Ethnarch's that was in front of us.

"Chy Zenzara!" said Denaraz, trying to reach upwards to restrain her.

Her voice came now as her own. "It is all right, Denaraz. Nothing will hurt me. I have given them permission to do this. It is the only way to convince this ... stubborn man."

And slowly the two shapes began to mix. As they expanded further and further out their molecules filtered through each other's shapes, like two galaxies colliding.

Nobody said anything. Nobody did anything.

Then there was a slow sigh from the mixed molecules in front of us. Zenzie began to disentangle herself from the atoms of the Ethnarch, who also began to collapse back down to his normal size.

As she returned to her normal self, her face held an intense expression of disgust. "Your thought processes are anathema to a free-thinking person. You believe things that are contrary to the Interstellar Rights. You have carried out atrocities greater than any Vaer. I hope never to be forced close to your mind again. You are a despicable living being."

Locke's eyes flashed. "You had no right to do that!"

She sighed, then looked at me. "There are no more RAMP missiles and his scientists have agreed that it wouldn't be prudent to build any more of them. They are now convinced of the risk they present. They have been working all night to evaluate what we have told them. They now agree that the missiles could precipitate a runaway conversion to the ultra-dense state. Locke was updated on all this earlier today." Her eyes slid back to him in a most accusatory way. "Although he seems to be rather unwilling to accept the results of their investigation."

Zenzie turned back to the Ethnarch. "You know what to do. All existing RAMP missiles must be eliminated." Her whole body flashed with energy, pulsed outwards, and then became a young Tyzaran girl again. She looked him straight in the eye. "Contact your ships and tell them to accept Denaraz's orders on the deployment of the missiles!" Then she turned to Sammy. "Let them deploy this time."

Sammy nodded, looking very serious.

Denaraz gave an eager step forward.

Locke brought his head forwards and closed his eyes. He steepled his fingers in front of his head, reluctant to take the final decision. It clearly felt too much like a capitulation to him.

Zenzie watched for some moments, and then lost patience with him. He began to balloon out again.

The look he treated her to was of intense dislike. "All right! All right!" He turned to a console in front of him and typed some instructions. "You will be given restricted control over the missiles on *Telzaria* and *Nanhai*."

She gave a small curtsey. "Thank you *so* much."

I could feel the sarcasm oozing out of her. How she hated this man! "I believe there is one other RAMP missile? Over that Gienak moon? The one that did not explode."

"If you think that will ... Aaagh!" The cry came when the expanded molecules that now formed his body formed an amorphous cloud and seemed about to filter through the shell of the ship out into space.

Zenzie left him there for several long seconds. Then the Chakrans brought him down to twice his normal size.

He typed hurriedly into his keyboard some more and then nodded to Denaraz. "Send your current console identification here," he put up a ship identification code, "here, and here." Two others followed the first. "Put me back to normal. I have done what you wanted."

He looked hopefully towards Zenzara, but she let him stay expanded while Denaraz and Sammy left the conference table. I handed around beverages and food as we waited to hear whether or not the remaining RAMP missiles were safely on their way into the center of a blue hypergiant.

"Are we sure it is safe to dump them into Zuben?" I asked her.

She nodded. "The outer casing will evaporate and the rest of the components will be vaporized before they can interreact with each other. The Chakrans seem to believe that it is the safest way to dispose of them."

Admiral Ellison was asked for confirmation of each order as it came through. Each time she looked towards the Ethnarch and only replied when she received his nod of assent.

Finally, after about twenty minutes, both Sammy and Denaraz came back into the gymnasium.

Denaraz was smiling. His crests were relaxed. "They are on their way. We need to maintain this meeting for another ..." he checked on his handset, "fifteen minutes. Then the missiles will all be past the no-return stage. I picked up the one we had in orbit around that moon as well, and we sent the Gienak one into the white star, which is hotter than its binary red dwarf."

Zenzie seemed pleased. She allowed Ethnarch Locke to shrink back to something like his normal size. He rubbed his arms and glowered over at her.

She wasn't intimidated. "I have only a small Nexus inside me. Each Chakran's body covers hundreds of billions of light years. Did you really think to evade the consequences? Did you really think you would be allowed to trample over their environment? Your mind is dense and narrow and you have misused your power. You will now sit down and agree a boundary for your star or I shall expand your body until it is the size of the planet you call Earth. It is up to you."

There was a deathly silence in the gymnasium as Locke contemplated what was happening. I suppose his mind was spinning with different options. It took him that long to realize that he no longer had any. I saw the moment when his shoulders slumped as the knowledge of defeat slipped into that stubborn brain.

He bit his lip. "Very well," he said. "We agree to keep to our own borders. Now will you let me go?"

"What border?" I asked quietly.

"Fifty light years around Sol?" he suggested.

I shook my head. "No."

"Ten?"

"No."

He was a broken man. "What then?"

I pulled up a diagram of Sol. Borders had been one of the subjects discussed in those long and dreary Alliance meetings I had so much disliked, so I knew what would be acceptable to the other signatories of the Ulon Alliance Accords. "You can have up to the Sol system Termination Shock. From now on the boundary of all stars will be their own Termination Shocks."

He gave me a pleading look. "At least to the Heliopause. Surely?"

"No. The Heliopause is never symmetrical, due to Interstellar motion. The only quasi-symmetrical boundary to a star is its Termination Shock. That is all you will be allowed."

Zenzie made a movement. "It is all anybody will be allowed," she said carefully, looking at the Avaraks.

Admiral Vykron murmured a little. But the Avaraks have never been expansionist. They do like to use other stars for their mining operations, but they have never claimed sovereignty over them. "We have no objections," he said. "If these Terrans agree, so will we."

Vebor nudged him and whispered in his ear. The huge head bent for a few moments and then turned back to us. "But we want the miniaturized ansible technology."

"Never!" Locke seemed horrified.

"Agreed," I said, which put me squarely back at the centre of attention. "The Terrans stole it from the Tyzarans, in any case. They must have. If the Terrans have the implantable ansible technology, the Tyzarans will surely give it to all their allies?" I raised an eyebrow at Denaraz.

Denaraz gave a sigh. He closed his own eyes to try to contact the Supreme Council. After a couple of minutes he shifted position and opened them again. "They will release the technology." He glared at the Ethnarch. "Though the Terrans will also be required to release the technique of combining it with a hololink."

The Ethnarch ground his teeth together, but did not reply. Finally he gave a brief nod of his head.

The Avaraks were happy. They had evaded confrontation and gained valuable technology. They thought they had won.

They had no idea that their elation would be short lived, if I knew anything about Seyal. The Avaraks might have avoided this war, but the real battle for supremacy was about to start. The one that would start when all the females on Rhyveka claimed equal status. I grinned widely at the Avarak delegation. They would never know what had hit them. They stared back blankly. They had no idea what was going on in my head, thank fitz.

Admiral Ellison was murmuring something under her breath. I had to lean closer to hear what it was.

"Termination shock. Termination shock." She sounded stunned. I suppose I could understand why. In just a day she had gone from being in a position to exterminate an entire race to being shackled to her planet of origin. Termination shock in more ways than one. She wasn't taking it very well.

"Do we have a cease fire agreement then?" I asked both parties. They nodded.

"Fine. Then I will have these accords drawn up and they will be signed by Admirals Ellison and Vykron before being sent to Rhyveka and Terra to be ratified. Until ratification is complete, there will be no bellicosity from either side. Is that understood and agreed?"

Vykron was quick to agree. It took Ellison longer.

I caught her quick glance of appraisal at the Ethnarch. Defeat would not make her popular, however much it really was not her fault. They would have promoted her if she had wiped out the whole Avarak world. She had to be thinking about her own future.

I didn't think she would get reassurance from Locke. It was obvious to me that he was never going to accept responsibility for this. Why would he? It would be too easy to spin it as a major failing of the Eighth Fleet. This fiasco was going to mean the end of her career in the Omnistate.

After some moments she came to the same realization. Her jaw hardened. She was going to do what she perceived as her duty anyway. She nodded. "We agree."

Locke began to fade. The missiles were now past the no-return point. The RAMP menace had been contained. The Chakrans were sending him back to Earth. If he had ever been here in the first place. For all I knew we could have been looking at a mirage. Yet, somehow, I rather thought we hadn't. The impression I had was that the real Ethnarch of Sol had been standing in front of us. It sounded quite impossible. It was a day for impossible things to happen.

The war was over. Our first mission was over – a success. Yet the idea that the Chakrans could inflate the space between the molecules of animate and inanimate things just by thinking about it made me feel somewhat queasy.

All of our lives had just changed. Again.

Admiral Ellison got to her feet. She seemed much older than when she had sat down. I almost even felt sorry for her. Then I remembered that she and her people had been within an hour of mass genocide. The sympathy evaporated. Even so, I offered her my hand as she made to leave.

She ignored it. "What happened here has changed the Major Shells," she said, her voice accusing.

"It has," I replied, trying to keep my tone even. "For the better."

Nobody could have missed the flash of anger in her eyes. "Cunningham should have killed you when he had the chance."

I ignored that. I escorted first the Terrans, and then the Avaraks to their own shuttles. It was a relief to watch both shuttles fly safely out of the bow doors of the cargo bay. The Avaraks turned to starboard, the Terrans to port.

Maybe all career officers were taught that particular tone when they were commissioned, I mused, as I made my way back to *Nivala's* bridge. That wonderful way of blaming everyone except yourself. It had been a particular strength of Captain Tevis's, too.

That led me back to the days on *Commorancy*. They felt such a long way back in my past. They had been hazy days of some sort of innocence. Days of illusion. Days of a status quo that we thought would last eternally. All that was long gone, along with poor old *Commorancy* herself, the first casualty to the war we had just ended.

I wondered where Captain Tevis was now, and whether I would ever run into him again.

I had reached the bridge without realizing it. Zenzie, who had been waiting for me by the hatchway, tugged at my arm. "Why are you looking grim?"

I shook my head. "Sorry. I was just thinking about *Commorancy*."

Her crest drooped. "Yes. Too many people have died."

"They have."

She gave my arm a quick squeeze. "I am glad you found me, back on *Commorancy*."

"You don't regret the Savior Protocols?"

"I do not." She gave a couple of little skips. "We are the Interstellar Enforcement Agency now. We can go wherever we want."

"Wherever we are needed," I corrected.

She waved away my doubts. "*Now* we can begin to have some fun! Where next?" She put her arms out and pirouetted away.

Sammy had somehow procured two bottles of champagne and all

of *Nivala's* crew had congregated around them. He handed me a glass. Everyone was chattering together and laughing as they watched our new Chyzar dancing around and around the bridge in ever larger circles.

I held up my flute of champagne to toast them all.

Where next, indeed?

Next in series:

Interdicted Space
(Interstellar Enforcement Agency, Book 2)